FORGIVING THAYNE

TRUE MATES: BOOK TWO

J.R. LOVELESS

1

———————

NICK

AN OVERWHELMING scent of earth and pine assaulted his senses the moment Nick Cartwright stepped into the Wolf's Den in the small town of Senaka. His eyes scanned the dim, slightly crowded establishment, seeking the source of the smell. Not even the sharp tang of booze dampened the earthy aroma, causing his cock to harden like a brick, and he clenched his jaw, knowing the only reason his body would react that way. His destined mate stood among the dozen or so men and women, several of whom were also wolves, who littered the bar. The only thing saving Nick from facing a room full of angry wolves was his ability to wrap his scent in his power as a true wolf. If they knew Nick's real nature, there'd be no doubt in his mind they'd believe him to be a Created One, much like Kasey Whitedove had believed his best friend Seth Davies to be.

Loud country music played from a jukebox in the far-off corner of a makeshift dance floor. Nick felt all eyes turn his way. He'd been in a few small towns before and knew how it worked. Strangers were noticed, especially ones entering a local tavern. He approached the bar, still searching for his true mate, but more discreetly.

The bartender lifted an inquisitive eyebrow at him, asking him without words what he wanted. "Whiskey, straight up."

The man placed a snifter on the bar in front of Nick and pulled a bottle from behind the counter to fill it with two fingers of Jack Daniel's. Nick tossed a twenty down and picked up the glass. He took a small sip while studying the other patrons in the mirror. A good percentage of the clientele were Native American, with perhaps two or three of Caucasian descent. It reminded him of Kasey Whitedove, Seth's true mate and the local sheriff, and the man's prejudice against white men. Kasey had believed Seth to be a Created One after discovering Seth was a wolf.

At the moment, though, Nick's focus remained on finding out which one of the locals was actually his true mate. Nothing else mattered except claiming him or her.

"What's a gorgeous guy like you doing in a place like this?"

Nick almost sneezed at the strong smell of a flowery perfume that bombarded his senses. Long red fingernails trailed over his arm, and he had to bite back the urge to toss the hand off. He turned on the charm and swiveled on his stool while giving one of his famous "fake" smiles. The woman, though gorgeous, wouldn't be able to hold his attention for long. Short dark hair feathered lightly around her naturally tanned face, accenting the dark eyes devouring his long, lean form.

"Just visiting an old friend in town for a few days. Stopped in for a drink or two."

"Oh? And who might your friend be?" she asked, pressing closer to him.

If it weren't for his wolf traits, he might have leaned far

enough back on the stool to fall off, but he managed to perch on the edge without ending up on his back. "The veterinarian, Seth Davies."

"I haven't had the pleasure of meeting Doc's replacement just yet, but I may have to go on over with my Georgia," she purred, leaning in even closer. "You wouldn't want to buy a thirsty girl a drink, would you, cowboy?"

Before Nick could think of a polite way to refuse her, the scent of his mate washed over him, and he sucked in a breath, knowing beyond a shadow of a doubt the person standing behind him was the one meant to be his. And he was a wolf. The scent of it clung to his skin, deep and primal. He lifted his gaze to the mirror and met a pair of eyes so dark they sucked him in. He couldn't look away, couldn't breathe, couldn't even think. His mate was stunning. Tall, taller than Nick by a good three to four inches, beautifully tanned, and well-defined muscles bulged beneath the gray T-shirt he wore. High, strong cheekbones complemented the firm chin and jawline, one Nick desperately wanted to follow with his lips. He swallowed hard as his gaze slid down the smooth skin of his mate's throat and farther still to the hollow at the base. When he brought his gaze back up to the dark eyes watching him closely, the answering lust caused his cock to jump in excitement. He wanted to dominate the man staring at him, to hold him down and mark him for the entire world to see.

The contrast between them couldn't be more obvious. Nick's own skin was lightly tanned but still pale compared to the other shifter. Blond hair versus raven's wing black hair, and emerald-green eyes snared by pools of dark chocolate stood out starkly against each other in the mirror. While the stranger's face was smooth, unmarred, Nick had a scar over his left eyebrow. Nick's body was more of a toned runner's form than the obvious boxer or weight-lifter size of his mate.

He wildly imagined how their skin would look tangled up on the nearest bed.

"Is there a problem here?" the man rumbled. Nick tensed, wondering if maybe he'd read the man's expression wrong.

"Go away, Thayne," she snapped. "He's not bothering me."

"I wasn't talking to you, Lilianne. I was speaking to him."

Surprise held Nick immobile for a split second before his mate's words sank in, and then he had to choke back a laugh at the woman's expression.

Murder shone in her eyes, and she glared at Thayne. "Don't make me tell your mother how you spoke to me, Thayne."

Thayne snorted at her threat. "Stop bothering the man, Lilianne, and go find some other poor sucker to leech off of."

Huffing in indignation, Lilianne stomped off toward the back of the bar.

Nick chuckled under his breath, hiding his grin behind his glass. He froze when Thayne sat on the stool next to his.

"She's been looking for husband number three for a while now. The men here in town know better than to mess around with her, so she's started in on any of the rare visitors we get. I'm Thayne."

"Nick," he murmured and took another sip of his whiskey. "You live around here?"

Thayne rested one arm on the bar while taking a long draught of his beer before answering. "Most of my life. Only back for a visit, though."

Nick breathed in his mate's scent, dying to ask questions about him, but held his tongue, not wanting to scare Thayne off. "Nice place."

"Not if you've lived here your entire life, it isn't. Everyone knows your name, and there are no secrets." Thayne set his empty beer bottle down on the bar. "I heard you tell Lilianne you're visiting the new Doc. He a relative?"

Nick downed the last of his whiskey, savoring the smooth burn of alcohol as it traveled to his belly. "Near enough. Known him a long time."

"How long you in town for?"

"Not too sure. He's going through some problems right now. I'm just here to help until he's okay." Nick sucked in a telltale breath when Thayne swayed in close to him, the tiny hairs all over his body standing on end at the almost contact.

"How about we get out of here?" Thayne purred right next to his ear. His breath whispered over the sensitive skin of Nick's earlobe, causing Nick to shiver in need.

Without a word, he nodded at Thayne, desire blazing through him. He wanted nothing more than to taste his mate, to feel his hard cock on his tongue as Thayne came down his throat. As he followed Thayne from the bar, he wondered if Thayne would react to his being a wolf the same way Seth's mate had reacted to Seth. Thayne disrupted his line of thought abruptly, shoving him into the darkness along the side of the building and slamming him against the wall. His lips crashed down on Nick's in a harsh kiss like no other he'd ever experienced. His tongue eagerly danced with Thayne's, twisting together in a sensual storm, sweeping away every thought except the desperate need to feel Thayne's cock buried inside him.

Thayne's hands slid down his sides, hips, and straight to his ass, cupping it in a strong grip before squeezing. Thayne growled low in his throat when Nick ground his hard flesh into Thayne's lower belly.

"I want to fuck you," Thayne rasped close to Nick's ear, his slick tongue flicking over the soft skin.

"Fuck, yes," Nick moaned, latching on to Thayne's neck and sucking deeply. His hands slid beneath the hem of his mate's shirt, palms gliding over the smooth skin of Thayne's back. The desire to feel Thayne's heated flesh on his ate at him. He yanked the shirt over Thayne's head, breathing in sharply at the well-defined muscles of his mate's chest.

Thayne reached for the front of Nick's jeans, tugging at the button and sharply parting the zipper. His big hand sank inside and cupped Nick's already-leaking shaft. Nick nearly howled in lust and pleasure, leaning his head back against the wall behind him. Thayne shoved the jeans down to reveal the small black briefs Nick wore, and he made a sound of approval. He dropped to his knees in front of Nick and buried his face in the fabric.

Nick shuddered at the hot breath seeping through the thin cloth. His fingers trembled as they wove through Thayne's dark locks, sinking into the lush strands, gripping tightly as Thayne sucked at him through his briefs. Nothing prepared him for the moment Thayne's tongue circled the tip of his cock, which peeked through the hem, and Nick gasped, panting in desire.

Thayne hooked his thumbs in his briefs and tugged them down, releasing Nick's straining length. It slapped lightly at Thayne's cheek, leaving a smear of precome along the tanned skin.

"Beautiful," Thayne breathed. He wrapped his lips around the tip, teasing Nick with tiny flicks of his tongue along the crown before delving into the small slit to gather the seeping liquid.

Nick swore, clenching his jaw to keep from losing control and jamming his cock down Thayne's throat. "Suck me," he snarled almost angrily when Thayne continued licking slowly.

Thayne hummed and slid to the root in one quick motion. Nick groaned and gave an uncontrollable thrust of his hips forward. Pulling off and chuckling, Thayne spun Nick around, pushed his pants down farther, and gripped his ass cheeks, parting them to bare his tight hole.

Nick jerked at the feel of Thayne's tongue swiping over the puckered flesh before spearing inside him. He clenched his hands into fists against the wall, his nails lengthening and digging into his palms to draw blood.

"Enough, inside, now."

After standing, Thayne quickly unfastened his jeans, allowing his cock free from the confining fabric, and pulled a condom from his back pocket. Nick spun around and snatched the condom from Thayne, ripped it open with his teeth, and quickly rolled it down Thayne's hard shaft. Thayne felt huge and hot in his palm. He squeezed the bulging prick, stroking for a moment. It disappointed him to have the thin latex between them, knowing neither of them could transmit diseases and wanting nothing more than to feel Thayne's flesh sliding over his.

"Turn around," Thayne ordered, his voice gruff and hoarse. Nick faced the side of the building once more and shoved his hips back, thrusting his ass at Thayne, who eagerly stepped forward to slide his cock along the crease. He nudged at the saliva-slickened hole and pushed in, piercing Nick's body, both of them groaning at the sensation. "So fuckin' tight," Thayne moaned in Nick's ear once he was seated deep inside him.

Nick clenched his muscles around Thayne's cock, milking the throbbing shaft. Thayne's fingers dug into the flesh at his hips as he pulled back until the crown caught just at the tight ring of muscle and shoved back in, expertly nailing Nick's prostate. Nick stifled a loud cry, biting down on his arm as Thayne fucked him, slamming into him over and over, rough and hard, just the way he liked it. Their bodies slapped together, the sound echoing in the empty alley. Nick's teeth elongated as he began to near his peak. His cock dripped profusely, drops staining the concrete beneath his feet.

"Harder."

Thayne slammed deeper and more violently, breathing heavily. When Nick tensed up, getting ready to come, Thayne's hips went into overdrive, pile driving deep into his ass. "Oh, yeah, baby. That's it. Come on my cock," Thayne ordered.

Nick splintered. His balls drew tight to his body, his spunk spraying the wall in front of him in thick, creamy spurts. He was dimly aware of Thayne's teeth biting down on his shoulder and the grunts Thayne made as he came inside Nick, filling the condom with his own essence. They slumped into the wall, bodies shuddering in mutual pleasure.

When Thayne finally moved, he carefully gripped the base of the condom and pulled free from Nick's body. He stripped the condom from his cock, tied it off, and tossed it into the nearby dumpster.

"Fuck, that was hot."

Grinning weakly, Nick nodded. He sensed Thayne mentally withdrawing from him now that he'd gotten off. "You're my mate," he blurted out once he'd turned to face Thayne again, his wolf desperate to keep from losing his destined partner.

Thayne stilled, his gaze piercing Nick. "What the fuck are you talking about?"

Nick quickly pulled up his pants, fastened them, and ran a hand through his hair. "Shit. I didn't mean to just come out and say it, but… you're my mate."

"How the fuck do you know about mates?" Thayne demanded.

Nick hesitated, but he couldn't keep the truth from spilling forth. "I'm a wolf."

Thayne's eyes narrowed at him, and he bared his teeth, now elongated slightly. "You're a Created One."

"No!" he protested, holding out his hand toward Thayne, who instantly backed away as if Nick would taint him. Nick's heart broke as he watched the look of satiation turn to one of hatred. "I was born a wolf!"

Before Nick could say anything else, Thayne shifted and launched himself at Nick. Nick felt time stop. He couldn't hurt his mate. He could only watch and wait for the impact. Their bodies collided, and Nick went down, his back slamming into the unforgiving concrete. He grunted, lifting his arm up to shield his face from the snapping teeth. Pain ripped through his forearm and radiated along every inch of his body. Thayne snarled, wrenching his head from side to side in an effort to tear at Nick's flesh. Nick cried out in agony, hot blood soaking his shirt.

Unable to take it anymore, he used every bit of his strength to shove Thayne away from him. Thayne crashed into the nearby dumpster, stunning him long enough for Nick to stand and shift. Thayne struggled to his feet as Nick gave him a sorrow-filled look. Thayne paused, watching him intently for a moment until Nick turned and ran. He darted between cars, keeping to the shadows to prevent anyone from spotting him. His chest hurt. It felt as if a huge gaping hole was left where his heart was meant to be. The accelerated healing ability of being a wolf left little to no mark when he finally shifted back to human a few blocks from Seth's place.

During the walk to Seth's, Nick made plans to leave Senaka the moment Seth's situation was settled. He couldn't bear the idea of remaining in the same town as his mate, not when he'd been rejected with such finality. His wolf cried out with every step, urging him to return to Thayne's side. Nick forced himself to ignore his wolf, to keep moving forward, one foot in front of the other. Each step broke him bit by bit until he felt he was nothing more than an empty, hollow shell. Nick knew he would never forget this night until the day he died.

. . .

Six Months Later

"Hey, Nick, is there anything left to handle with the Synergen project?" His friend and business partner, Ryan Driscoll, interrupted his musings and brought him back to the present. Nick blinked several times to clear his vision and glanced up from his computer monitor. He looked around to remind himself he was at his office in Emerald Lake Hills, California and needed to focus on work rather than the one night of heaven and the six months of hell since meeting Thayne.

Seth had settled well into his role as Kasey's mate and was well protected by his new pack. Nick no longer had to worry for his best friend's safety and found many excuses to steer clear of the small town, especially after finding out Thayne was Kasey's brother. Thayne still refused to accept him despite the discovery Nick wasn't a Created One. Knowing his mate truly didn't want him snapped something inside of Nick. He no longer found his world as colorful as he once had. He had tried unsuccessfully for the past several months to forget Thayne, to immerse himself in the bodies of others, but they couldn't make him forget the smell, the taste, or the feel of Thayne against him. He didn't allow himself much time to dwell on any of it, forcing himself to concentrate on projects and designs until all hours of the night, working himself into exhaustion, but sometimes his mind managed to wander to that time before he could stop it.

"Nick?" Ryan stood before him with an expectant expression as he waited for Nick's response. They'd known each other for eight years, having met during one of Nick's infrequent visits to the pack while helping to protect Seth. They'd even hooked up a handful of times, but it had never gone beyond sex. Mutual pleasure. Ryan was a dangerously attractive man. Two years older than Nick, six foot four, nice body, he kept in shape by swimming—not overly muscular but well defined. Dirty blond hair he kept in a neat fade, and hazel eyes that seemingly changed color with his mood made a gorgeous match.

Nick rubbed his eyes and sat back in his desk chair. Ryan knew something had happened when he'd gone to Senaka, but he wasn't one to pry unless Nick wanted to share, and for that Nick was grateful. Since he'd returned home, he'd worked himself into exhaustion almost every night. He'd even managed to complete two projects in a matter of a couple of weeks that normally would have taken a good two to three months to finish.

"Nope. Everything is ready to go. Kuraski should be quite pleased with the results."

"Great." Ryan hesitated a moment. He walked in and closed the door behind him. "Look, Nick. You know I wouldn't normally ask, but since you've been back, you haven't been yourself. You work until you almost drop, you've lost at least twenty pounds, and I never see you smile anymore. You ended up in the hospital a month ago from exhaustion, and considering you're a wolf, that's a pretty big deal. What happened in Senaka?"

Nick's face instantly became shuttered. "Nothing happened."

"Bullshit. Even Cole's noticed you're not the same person." Cole Ferris was the soon-to-be Alpha. His father, Elijah, would be stepping down in six weeks, handing the reins of the pack over to his son, so he could retire and take the time to see the world. "You know he expects you to become his Beta, but he's not sure if you can handle it right now. If ever, from the way you're heading. What's going on?"

Sighing, Nick closed his laptop, reached into his bottom drawer, and took out a bottle of Johnnie Walker Blue and two small glasses. He silently poured two fingers in each and pushed one of the glasses toward his partner. Ryan strode over, picked up the glass, and sank elegantly into one of the chairs in front of Nick's desk. He remained quiet, waiting for Nick to speak.

"I found my mate."

A broad grin broke out over Ryan's face after a moment of silence in which several emotions fluttered across his friend's features, one of which almost seemed like sadness. "That's great! Isn't it?"

Nick snorted and tossed back the entire contents of the glass, trying to gain false courage to put into words what silently tormented him for months. "Is it? He rejected me. Not only did he attack me, believing me to be a Created One, but he didn't want me even after he found out I'm a true wolf."

Shock flitted over Ryan's handsome face. Rejecting your mate isn't something normally done. Not only because of how unlikely you were to find them, but also because of the bond. It began to form the moment you met. Even now Nick could feel the strands of fate tying him to Thayne. Though unseen, they bound two mates as one. The longer you were apart, the more they "vibrated," pushing a wolf to seek physical contact. Nick figured it was the reason most wolves who'd lost their mates allowed themselves to shut down and cease to exist.

"How is that possible?" Ryan demanded.

Shrugging one shoulder, Nick poured another glass. "I don't know, Ry. But I know it fucking hurts. I know every day that goes by and I can't see him is torture. It feels as though a part of me is missing. I've never understood how a wolf could allow themselves to become so depressed they just give up. Now I get it. It's a struggle to get up in the mornings, at least on the nights I can sleep."

"That's why you've been working yourself to the bone." Ryan sighed, rubbing his chin lightly. "Do you know why he rejected you?"

"No. He refuses to even talk to me. Kasey, Seth's mate, says it's because Thayne has been saying almost his entire life that he doesn't want a mate. But I feel as though it's more than that. He wouldn't even let me near him. I finally had to just leave Senaka. I couldn't stand being that close to him and not having him." Nick stared broodingly into his glass. "I've always been told the mating bond is the most amazing gift. It's the foundation I was raised on. Granted, we haven't claimed one another yet, but all of the stories tell of it beginning from the moment you lay eyes on one another. The strings of fate begin to weave the souls of each wolf together. Yet he never even seemed affected by it. I knew it the moment I caught his scent."

Sympathy flashed through Ryan's gaze. "I can't imagine what it must be like for your mate to reject you, but the Nick I know doesn't give up so easily. Find him, Nick. Get the answers. Cole says the first summit is next month, the new moon. It's being held on neutral ground to cut down on the possibility of territorial fights breaking out. Maybe he will be there."

After Kasey's father revealed the existence of other wolves to his pack, they'd reached a truce and would gather once every six months, giving the members of each pack the chance of possibly meeting their destined mate. True mates were rare, since most wolves ended up restricted to their own pack due to proximity and the lack of exposure to others. Until recently, Nick had begun to wonder if he'd ever meet his own. Now he wished he hadn't.

"Not likely. He doesn't want a mate, remember? Why would he go to a summit designed to find one?"

"His father is the current Alpha, isn't he? Perhaps he will command him to attend to show good faith between packs?" Ryan pointed out.

"Doubtful. He's the type who won't be 'commanded.' I'm not certain I can take being around if others do find their mates among Jeremiah's pack. I'm happy they now have a greater chance, but I don't want to be forced to watch. Not when my mate hates my existence."

Nick's phone rang, interrupting any further conversation. "Cartwright."

"Nick!" Seth's voice came over the line.

"Hold on just a second, babe," he said quietly, covering the receiver with one hand before addressing Ryan. "If you want to schedule the wrap-up meeting with Synergen, I'll take care of the final presentation."

"Sure thing, Nick." Ryan stood and moved to the door. With his hand on the knob, he glanced back at Nick. "Don't give up, Nick. Don't let him go."

Nick waved his hand at Ryan and turned his chair around to face his window. He heard the soft snick of the door closing behind him. "How's the easy life in Senaka?"

"Easy life?" Seth snorted indignantly. "Living with the hulk of a sheriff called my mate is not easy. Did you know that Kasey leaves his clothes all over the house? I'm constantly cleaning up after him! I can't believe how much of a pig he turned out to be!"

Laughing, Nick leaned his chair back slightly, putting his feet up on the sill of the large window. Seth had always been a neat freak. After his experience living in filth for several weeks at the hand of a cruel and abusive Created One, his

OCD complex had gotten even worse. Seth even color-coded his socks. "Cut the man some slack, Seth. He's not only the town sheriff and future Alpha of the Senaka pack, but he's also got a Rho for a mate."

Seth was a rare wolf called a Rho. They were only born once every one hundred years and were gifted with an even rarer ability. Seth could heal other creatures, human or animal. It made Rhos one of the most coveted wolves in any pack, which in turn led to Kasey's constant watchful eye on Seth. Especially after the last incident where another wolf terrorized and kidnapped Seth, claiming to be his mate.

A grumble came over the line. "Blah, blah. So what if I'm a Rho? Kasey has every wolf in the pack practically trailing me wherever I go! It's getting a tad annoying."

"He's just worried, babe," Nick soothed gently. "He almost lost you. Give him some time. I'm sure it will get better after a while."

"How've you been, Nick?" Seth asked quietly, changing the subject.

Nick knew his friend worried about him after the rejection of his mate. He couldn't lie to Seth, not anymore. When Seth found out Nick knew about his past and how Nick had been sent to watch over him, he'd almost cut Nick out of his life. He couldn't take the chance of hurting Seth again and possibly losing the one person who meant almost as much to him as Thayne.

"It's been hard."

A sympathetic noise issued from Seth. "You sound tired. I hope you aren't working yourself to death."

It always surprised him whenever Seth saw straight to his heart. They knew each other way too well. Seth didn't know about his recent trip to the emergency room when he'd all but collapsed in exhaustion. He didn't volunteer the information. He didn't want to worry Seth further.

"I'm fine, Seth. I don't have any other choice than to be fine. It's not like Th… he is giving me any other option."

Nick could practically see Seth scowl over the phone as he responded. "I could kick Thayne in his balls for hurting you. Kasey still doesn't understand why his brother is so adamant about not having a mate. The bastard left town almost as soon as you did. He didn't even tell anyone, except his mom."

The sound of Thayne's name caused his stomach to clench, and he winced, rubbing at the offending area. "Can we talk about something else, Seth?"

"Of course." Seth launched into a detailed story of the Senaka pack's preparation for the upcoming summit. Both packs would be meeting in Kamas, Utah, at Bear River Lodge. The cabins bordered the Wasatch National Forest and provided the needed area for shifting, hunting, and running.

Zoning out, Nick flicked the touchpad on his laptop and studied the newest website he'd designed for Synergen, a company based in Los Angeles that custom built computers. The name flashed across the screen before giving the option of watching the slideshow on the prebuilt models or clicking a link to skip the slides, taking the viewer straight into the site.

"Nick! Are you listening to me?" Seth asked, irritation evident in his voice.

"Yeah, I'm listening," Nick lied. He didn't really care about the summit. At the moment, he found it hard to care about much of anything. "Seth, I have to go. I've got a big presentation to prepare for. I'll call you later this week, okay?"

Seth didn't reply for a moment before saying, "You know if you need to talk, I'm here for you, Nick."

"I know, babe. I promise I'll call you if I need you."

Nick hung up after saying good-bye and opened the e-mail from Ryan. He had an appointment Friday with the bigwigs at Synergen. His assistant, Annie, had already booked him a flight Thursday night and set him up in the Wilshire Grand Hotel, a few blocks from the Synergen building. He set the flight time in his BlackBerry. He'd stayed in the Wilshire several times and knew the exact location. At least there were night clubs in LA. Maybe he could find a warm body to fill his bed and make him forget, even if only for an hour.

It had been a week since he'd shifted, and his wolf prowled restlessly beneath his skin, causing him to feel on edge. Sighing, he stood and started packing up some items to work from home, including his laptop.

He hit the intercom button. "Annie?"

"Yes, Nick?"

"I'm going to head home and work from there. If anything urgent comes up, give me a call on my cell."

"Sure thing, Nick," Annie replied. She was a blessing in disguise for Nick. She kept him organized and neat to a fault. Also a wolf, she remained unmated because she believed she would find her mate. It had slipped out one night when they'd all gone out for drinks and Ryan left Nick and Annie alone at the table. He'd always hoped she would find her true mate, but now he wasn't so sure it would be the best thing for her. He knew lumping everyone into the same category as Thayne didn't exactly ring fair, but he couldn't stop the bitterness rising inside of him. It only grew stronger with each passing day.

Nick packed his laptop into his black satchel and slipped it over his head. After grabbing his keys, he left his office and took the elevator to the first floor. The front desk receptionist smiled at him as he walked past, and he managed a half-assed smile back. He exited the building and crossed the parking lot to the second love of his life: a black, fully restored 1967 Chevy Impala.

The car had belonged to his grandfather while Nick was growing up. He could still remember the joy he felt riding in it and had even told his grandfather that one day he'd have one just like it. His grandfather passed away while Nick was in college, leaving him the car. Nick had kept it in storage until he'd returned to Emerald Lake Hills to open his business with Ryan. Its gleaming black paint job and polished silver fenders were well maintained, and Nick made damn sure it stayed that way. His grandfather never would have forgiven him if he'd let it deteriorate after all the work they'd put into it together during Nick's childhood.

He opened the door, climbed in, and set his laptop bag on the passenger seat. The car started with a loud rumble, and he pulled out of the parking lot, heading for home. On the way, he tried to distract himself from the itch beneath his skin by thinking about his home and his pack.

Emerald Lake Hills had a small population compared to some of the cities in California. Just under five thousand people lived there, and a good hundred or so were pack members. The sleepy little burg had been named for the two beautiful lakes inside the city limits. The pack Alpha owned one of the large private homes on the Upper Emerald Lake shore. Due to the seclusion of the property, the pack meetings were normally held there before everyone headed to the park for the full moon run.

His own home—a single-story, two-bedroom house—sat on the border of Edgewood County Park, which ran along the edge of Pulgas Ridge Open Space Preserve. The park and preserve gave him and others in the pack miles of land to roam as wolves. They still ran the risk of humans spotting them, especially since wolves in California were rare even in the densely wooded areas, but it provided a modicum of coverage for their monthly pack runs. On occasion, like now, Nick felt the restless urge to run as his wolf, to let go and allow his animal instincts to overcome him. Sometimes he wondered what it would be like to remain a wolf forever, to let his humanity go. Those thoughts only increased after Thayne's rejection. Seth had given him a reason not to give in to his desire, but Seth no longer needed him. He had Kasey now.

The drive home seemed interminable, longer than ever. His wolf scratched at the surface, causing him to fidget in his seat multiple times. A sigh of relief slipped free when he finally pulled into his driveway and turned off the engine. He rushed inside, dropped his laptop bag and keys near the front door, and headed toward the back of the house. He barely managed to make it into the trees before he shifted, running the instant his paws met the earth. A long, lonely howl ripped free from him, echoing through the woods. In his true form, he felt the rejection more keenly than ever, his heart aching with need for its mate.

Nothing soothed him. He ran until his legs gave out. He collapsed beneath a tree, panting heavily and dropping his head to his paws. A light wind ruffled his fur, sending a shiver through the long length of his body. The same question he'd asked himself more than once over the past six months rolled around in his mind. Would the pain ever fade?

2

THAYNE

MUSIC THUMPED at a deafening volume through the club as the dancers on the floor rubbed and gyrated against each other. Thayne sat in a booth in the corner of the establishment, broodingly sipping at a drink. In an attempt to forget the encounter with Nick, he'd spent the first two months afterward fucking as many men as he could, trying to ignore the deep sense of unease in the pit of his stomach. He fought it, raged at it, tried to drown it out. Nothing made the feeling dim. The burn of the alcohol sliding down his throat felt like a tickle in comparison. Yet for the last month, he no longer achieved the temporary relief he felt when rutting in the back room of some club or pounding a random twink into the mattress of whatever seedy motel room he was renting.

"Want to dance, gorgeous?" a husky voice murmured near his ear, interrupting his thoughts.

Thayne turned his head to see a beautiful, muscular, blond surfer standing near his chair. Six months ago, Thayne would have had the man beneath him in less than an hour, thrusting his cock as deep into him as he could get, but now all he could do was admire the man's physique and reply with a shake of his head, "No, thanks."

The guy shrugged. "Your loss."

I know, he thought bitterly, watching the tight ass as the blond walked back into the crush of dancers. He'd never imagined going home for a couple of weeks would be the lead-in to meeting his mate. He'd needed a place to rest for a while, to process what he'd done. How could he have been so stupid to let it happen? And now the knowledge that his true mate was out there added to his stress. He couldn't run away forever. Some day he'd have to find a solution, a way to clean up the fucking mess he'd made, and a way to forget his mate existed.

Shoving away from the table, he stood and then pushed his way through the crowd to the exit. He'd had enough of the cloying scent of sweat, alcohol, and sex. The evening was still relatively early, only ten o'clock, but instead of bar-hopping like he'd have done before, he started toward his motel. A chill dominated the air, yet because of his wolf counterpart, he didn't feel it. His blood ran hot in his veins, keeping him warm and warding off the cold.

A bone-deep weariness set in as he walked. Knowing he couldn't change what he'd done didn't make it any easier. In twenty-seven years he'd never been so careless before. The only thing he could do for now was to keep moving. If he didn't, his mistake would catch up to him. Tomorrow he would leave, hop in his truck, and drive. Find the next temporary place to set up in for a few days before moving on. Odd jobs kept him with enough funds for gas, food, and booze.

Thayne's lip curled into a snarl as the look in Nick's eyes that night at the bar in Senaka flashed through his mind once again. Shock, betrayal, and pain. Anger had blinded him at first. As much as he didn't want a mate, he didn't want a

Created One for a mate even more. He'd begun to process everything after their initial encounter when Thayne found himself face-to-face with Nick during a dinner to introduce Seth to his and Kasey's parents. Including the other wolf's emotions and his lack of fight. He'd roughly shoved the remorse so far down inside it left a ball of acid in his belly. If he'd been human, it would have most likely caused an ulcer, but with his advanced healing as a wolf, it couldn't form fast enough to cause any real damage.

Every couple of weeks he called to speak to his mother and father. His mother constantly berated him to come home, to stop running around the country and take roots in Senaka like Kasey did. She also told him to stop being such a selfish bastard and claim Nick, although not in those exact words. Thayne just interpreted them in his own way. He never offered any excuses for not claiming Nick or allowing Nick to claim him. He couldn't disappoint his mother by telling her the truth. By the time the call ended, it took another week to drown out the memories of Nick's firm body, the heat of his hands on him, or the feel of Nick's tight hole wrapped around his cock.

Thankfully he hadn't broken the skin during their frantic fuck in the alley. Just a single drop of his mate's blood as they had reached their climax would have sealed the bond. Even now the strings of fate had already begun to tie them together. The moment the recognition of one's mate set in, the strings start to twine as one, even though Thayne had no clue who Nick was when he'd rescued him from Lilianne. He'd found out from Kasey later on that Nick and Seth had learned a way to bury their scent and true nature beneath the power of their wolf, something about protecting themselves. Even now Thayne still didn't understand the whole thing, but he knew with certainty he hadn't been able to detect Nick's shifter side.

Snarling under his breath, Thayne pulled out his wallet to retrieve his keycard. He reached the stairs, took them two at a time, and strode down the second-floor balcony toward his room. He stopped short when he saw the door slightly open. The hairs at the base of his neck stood on end, and he crept forward, barely breathing, to peer in through the crack. His room was a mess. The mattress had been torn apart, his meager clothing strung about the room, the paintings hung haphazardly on the wall, and the television lay broken in pieces.

Thayne carefully stepped in, danced around the shattered furniture, and picked up his clothing. He grabbed his duffel bag and stuffed the clothes not shredded into it. He couldn't stay here. His past had found him sooner than he'd expected. Swearing, he continued to gather his stuff, knowing he needed to get out of there soon or he'd be faced with a piece of his history he didn't want to see. Not before he was prepared for it.

When he'd finished collecting his belongings, Thayne rushed out of the room and back down the stairs to his truck. He tossed his duffel onto the passenger seat and climbed in, glancing around nervously as he did so. The truck started with a low rumble, and he wrenched it into reverse, tires squealing as he peeled out of the parking lot. No matter how fast he ran or how far he went, his past always found him. He clenched his jaw and tightened his hands around the steering wheel. Would he ever find peace?

TWO HOURS later, Thayne pulled into a rest stop to gas up and grab something to eat. He groaned as he stretched the tense muscles in his lower back. He took out his wallet, swiped a credit card, and slid the nozzle into the tank after removing the gas cap. Once the pump clicked off, he finished the transaction, then moved his truck to a parking space, climbed out, and walked into the small convenience store. A white middle-aged guy stood behind the counter, a phone plastered to his ear and a bored look on his face. Thayne snagged a couple of twenty-ounce Cokes, a bag of cheese Doritos, and a Slim Jim. The attendant didn't even look at him as he rang up the purchases, tapping the small register screen to indicate the price. Thayne passed him a twenty while glancing at a magazine on a nearby rack. His breath caught in his throat, and he coughed hard to clear his passageway.

The face of Nick Cartwright stared back at him. He couldn't seem to stop himself from grabbing the magazine and flipping it open to the article on the man who'd haunted him for months now. Twice in one night he was hit square in the solar plexus by his past. His lip curled into a snarl as he shoved the sensation of regret behind the cold steel of his wolf's presence.

"Are you going to buy that?"

Thayne looked up at the attendant. "What?"

"Are you going to buy that? This ain't a library, mister."

Glaring at the attendant, Thayne viciously shoved the magazine back onto the rack and snatched his change along with the bag of snacks from the counter. He slammed open the door and strode toward his truck. Dammit. Why had the bastard come to Senaka? Why hadn't he known what Nick was before fucking him in the alley? How could he have been so blind? His conscience pricked him for the thousandth time as he remembered the blood covering the other wolf after he'd attacked him, but he buried the guilt, refusing to let it fester for more than a split second. Even if he'd known Nick wasn't a Created One at the time, he wouldn't have accepted him anyway. He didn't want or need a mate.

The truck started with a muffled, guttural sound, and the

tires squealed as he roared out of the parking lot, his anger getting the better of him. His wolf prowled restlessly beneath his skin. It had been about a month since he'd last shifted. Being on the move so much and knowing his past was right on his heels, he didn't take time to stop and smell the grass very often. But recent events and the sight of Nick on the cover of the magazine forced him to find a remote place to pull over. Exiting the vehicle, Thayne breathed in the cool evening air and closed his eyes. He felt the change deep inside of himself, and his wolf's joy at finally being able to shift after so long spread through him. The magic of his people slithered over his skin, causing a blinding flash of light to fill the small clearing he'd stopped in. Shifting didn't happen the way the movies showed. Fur didn't erupt along their skin, their bones didn't break and reform, and their clothing didn't tear into shreds. It certainly wasn't a painful or long process to become a wolf as the stories depicted. Whatever earthly magic existed in the soul of every shifter caused them to take on another form with a mere thought, their human side hiding behind their wolf. Shifters found the transformation freeing and beautiful. Something to be cherished and treasured.

The instant his paws hit the ground, he threw his head back and issued a mournful howl. Thayne snarled at his wolf, who snapped back at him. When in his true form, he could sense more keenly than ever his wolf's despair, and it was a constant battle to retain control of his faculties, his wolf pushing at him to let go and let him find Nick, to hunt him down and put his mark on him. Thayne held on to his power over his wolf's instincts by a mere thread whenever he allowed himself the pleasure of shifting. Depression and exhaustion threatened to consume him.

Darting into the dense trees nearby, Thayne ran. His muscles bunched with each shove of his strong paws against the spongy thistle, branches brushing over his fur like a lover's touch. His wolf reveled in the freedom and urged his legs faster, listening to the soft sounds of the night: the hoot of an owl, the whisper of a mouse among the dried leaves, the light rustle of wind through the trees overhead. The moon, half-full, loomed high above in the night sky, illuminating the way through the thick foliage. His keen sense of sight gave him the needed guidance to avoid obstacles and savor the shadowed woods.

Thayne could feel the spirits of his ancestors reaching out to him, sensing his agitation and his ever-increasing hopelessness. How could he have been so stupid? Would he ever be able to atone for the greatest sin he'd ever committed? Even though he'd never been scared of anything in his life, the idea of telling his father, the Alpha of the Senaka pack, and his mother, the sweetest woman he'd ever known, terrified him out of his mind. More than what was coming for him. More than the idea of having a mate. The image of his father's face twisted in anger and disappointment haunted him much like the memory of the agony in Nick's green eyes when he'd rejected him. Would Nick look at him with the same disappointment if he knew the truth?

Shaking his head in agitation, he raced along the edge of a clearing, letting out another low, mournful howl. An answering cry came from a long way off, and Thayne skidded to a halt, his hackles rising. How? It couldn't possibly be.... No. Another bay, closer this time, caused Thayne's heart to beat faster. That first howl had to have been at least a mile off. There was no way it could already be that close. Horror held him locked in place, and before he could gather enough of his wits around him, a large, impossibly huge wolf entered the clearing, crashing through the branches and snapping them like twigs. Thayne's eyes widened in surprise and revulsion. It had grown three times in size since he'd last seen it. How the hell had it gotten so big?

Thayne remained hidden, the darkness of his fur and the shadows surrounding him provided a level of coverage, but the creature knew he was there. It lifted its huge head, scenting the air around it, searching for him. He crouched low, waiting for his chance to run, alert to the muscles rippling along the Created One's form. He tensed further when sharp red eyes narrowed in on his hiding place. The ferocity in that gaze sent a shiver racing down his spine. He'd been so sure he could deal with the creature on his own, but now… he realized he was going to need help. There was no way around telling his parents and Kasey the truth.

The Created One stepped toward him, and Thayne knew if he was going to get away, he had to move. Pulling all of his power around him, Thayne turned and launched himself through the trees, forcing himself to move faster. The creature's breath whispered across the fur on his tail, and Thayne's blood nearly froze in his veins. Suddenly, there was silence behind him as he approached his truck, and he skidded to a halt, gravel pinging against the metal siding. He whipped around and peered into the emptiness surrounding him.

Fucker! It was toying with him. He growled fiercely and shifted. "What are you waiting for, you son of a bitch?" he yelled, his voice echoing along the trunks of the trees. "What are you waiting for, huh? Come and get me, you bastard!"

His challenge was met with no response, not even a shifting of branches or the crackle of leaves beneath the monster's paws. How could it have just disappeared so quietly? The fear of telling his parents began to dim in the face of an unknown enemy. He'd heard the stories of Created Ones, but they'd never mentioned their increased size, strength, or ability to hunt its prey. Shifters were only meant to be born, not made.

The legend of the Senaka wolf pack told of their gods answering the cry of an ancestor to end the suffering of his human true mate. He wanted to ease his mate's pain over never being able to join in on the nights of the full moon or run with him in wolf form. The gods granted him the ability to change her, but warned the shifter that he could lose her to the beast inside. The shifter accepted the risk, and the gods gave him the knowledge he desired. Only by exchanging his blood and the seed from his loins with her during a full moon could she become one of them. He completed the ritual and the first created wolf was born. Their happiness could be felt by all within their pack, but as time passed, the shifter's mate began to show the characteristics of the wolf, becoming pure instinct and cunning. When the animal inside took over completely, the Created One attacked the human mate of another shifter, forcing the pack Alpha to command her destruction. Her mate took his own life out of guilt and despair, knowing it was his fault for ignoring the caution the gods gave him.

The stories never told of anything other than the animal half becoming more dominant, eventually leading to the loss of any human traits the Created One might have had. They could still become human, but typically they chose to remain in their wolf form, believing their human side as weakness. Seeing the sheer size and sensing the power radiating from the beast, Thayne realized the truth of what being a created wolf really meant. What the hell had he done?

Thayne scurried around his truck and wrenched open the door. He slid inside and started the engine. He knew he couldn't outrun it. It found him every time he stopped. Despair threatened to choke him as he put the truck into drive and pulled a U-turn, heading back the way he'd come and onto the main highway. He took the next exit and got back onto the road leading north. The only thing he could do now was put his tail between his legs and go back home, back to his pack, and pray they could stop the biggest mistake of his life.

3

NICK

NICK SHOOK the hand of the CEO of Synergen and bid him good-bye just as his cell phone rang. "Cartwright," he said as he gathered his briefcase and suit jacket.

"Nick." Seth's voice came over the speaker.

He instantly knew something was wrong. "What's the matter?" He rushed out of the boardroom and toward the elevator at a fast clip while waiting for Seth to answer him.

"I need you here, Nick," Seth said flatly.

"Why? What's going on?" Nick slapped the button several times, ignoring the disgruntled look the secretary seated nearby gave him.

"There's a Created One here, Nick. They... they think it's Taggart."

Nick swore as the elevator doors slid open, and he stepped inside and stabbed the button for the garage. "How do they know it's him?"

"He looks like him."

Normally Nick would have forgone the twenty questions and raced to Seth's side, but knowing Kasey and his pack would protect Seth, and that the town brought bad memories for him, Nick tossed out question after question.

The elevator stopped at the parking garage level, and he stepped out just as Seth growled, "Nick!"

Halting by his car, Nick realized he was letting his fear of running into the cause of his heartache stop him from being there for the best friend he'd ever had. "I'll be there as soon as I can," he finally replied, foregoing asking any further questions.

"Thank you," Seth breathed before disconnecting the call.

Nick unlocked and opened the door, tossing his jacket and briefcase in the backseat before climbing in and starting the rental. Thankfully, he'd been ready to leave to go home today, so his bags were in the trunk of the car.

He made a couple of calls on his way to the airport. The first was to his assistant, Annie. "I need you to cancel my flight back to Emerald Lake Hills and book me a flight to Casper, Wyoming, as soon as possible."

Casper was the closest city to Senaka and the only airport he could fly into that wouldn't take hours of drive time to get to Seth. "Sure thing, boss. I'll call you back in a few minutes."

He hit the speed dial on his phone for Ryan and tossed the phone into the cup holder, turning on the Bluetooth capability in the car. The traffic to LAX caused his hands to tighten on the wheel in frustration. Urgency to get to Seth nagged at him while his heart begged him to stay in California, to run in the opposite direction of the airport as fast as possible, and avoid any further heartache waiting for him in Senaka. He ignored his heart. He couldn't let his own pain prevent him from being there for Seth if the Created One did turn out to be Taggart. Seth would need all of the support he could get.

"Hey, Nick. How'd it go?" Ryan answered.

"Great. Synergen is on board and ready to launch. Listen,

Ry. I gotta head out to Senaka for a few days. Something's come up."

"Everything okay, Nick?" Ryan asked curiously.

"Yeah. Seth called. There's a Created One in the area, and they seem to think it's Taggart."

Ryan swore into the phone. He knew the story of Taggart and the months of torture Seth had endured at the hands of the sick, twisted bastard. But he also believed the same as Nick, that Taggart had perished in the warehouse fire. No one could have survived. The roof of the building had collapsed just after Nick pulled Seth out of the window Nick had broken to get in. All of the doors had been barred, locked, and there'd been no way out for the others. Sometimes being pure instinct isn't always a good thing. It overrode common sense and didn't allow for freethinking.

"Are they sure it's him?"

Nick sighed and shrugged, even though he knew Ryan couldn't see it. "After the last wolf terrorizing Seth turned out to be that psycho Drakson, I thought for sure Taggart was dead. I don't know. I won't know for sure until I get there, and I can't leave him to face the son of a bitch alone. Even with Whitedove and his pack there. Seth needs as many of us around him as possible."

"I understand. Keep in touch, Nick, and... be careful. You've already worked yourself into exhaustion over... well, you know who I mean. I need you back here in one piece. You're the brains of the operation, remember?"

Chuckling, Nick replied, "I'll be fine, Ry. He's not even there. I'll be back in Emerald Lake Hills before you know it."

They disconnected the call as Nick pulled into the LAX airport, making his way to the rental area to return the car. Annie texted his flight number and the time of departure to him. He saw he had a couple of hours to waste, and after turning in the rental and grabbing his bags, he headed to the first bar he came across. He sighed as he dropped his carry-on bag and briefcase next to a stool.

The bartender nodded at him. "What can I get ya?"

Barely registering the man in front of him, Nick snorted and said without thinking, "A strong grip on my sanity?"

The bartender laughed, winking at Nick. "I can get a strong grip on something else… if you want, that is."

Nick's eyebrow went up at the implied come-on, surprised he would so blatantly flirt with a customer without knowing if he was into men. He finally concentrated on the guy in front of him more clearly. Not bad looking, the bartender was around his height with a nicely built body, brown eyes that sparkled lustily at him, and gel-slicked hair as dark as a pitch black night in the middle of Wyoming. His nametag read Thomas. Normally Nick would have casually brushed off the guy's come-on, but the frustrations of the last few months and because he reminded him a little bit of Thayne kept him from rejecting the man immediately. Guilt over feeling desire for anyone other than Thayne nipped at his conscience, and he ruthlessly shoved it away. He owed no loyalty to a mate who didn't want him, no matter what his wolf thought. The idea of bending the bartender over and pretending he was pounding away at his wayward other half caused his cock to perk up a bit. He couldn't deny the tiny part of him that wanted to punish Thomas for looking like the one whose very face taunted him every night in his dreams.

Tilting his head slightly, Nick asked, "When do you get off?"

Thomas smirked and leaned in closer, huskily murmuring, "Whenever you want, sexy. My break is in ten minutes."

Nick glanced at his watch. "Meet me in the men's bathroom near gate sixty."

"Is there anything else you'd like in the meantime?"

Thomas offered, leaning back and wiping at the nonexistent water on the counter.

"Jack and Coke."

The bartender pulled a glass out from under the bar, scooped a bit of ice into it, and poured two fingers of Jack Daniel's before filling the rest with soda.

He set it in front of Nick and winked. "It's on the house."

Nick tipped his head in acknowledgement, picked up the glass, and sipped at the liquid. He'd gone to a club the first night he'd been in LA, hoping just for what he was about to do except he'd been unable to go through with it. The smell of human sweat, alcohol, and the crush of bodies had turned him off, made him long for the earthy-pine scent of Thayne's skin and the heat of his body against him. It had been this way for the last couple of months. After he'd left Senaka, he'd been able to lose himself in a random stranger a few times, but then it lost its appeal. The random stranger wasn't Thayne.

He sneered into his drink before tossing the rest back and slamming the glass down on the counter. He stood, pulled out his wallet, and dropped a five on the counter as tip. Thoughts of Thayne wouldn't ruin this for him. He was horny and needed to let off some steam before he ended up back where the outlook of his future had turned bleak. Grabbing his bags, he nodded at the bartender and headed toward the restroom near his gate.

There were a handful of others in the bathroom when he entered, and he chose the stall farthest from the door, entered, and dropped his bags in the corner to wait. It wasn't long before there was a light tap on the door, and he opened it, allowing Thomas to enter. Nick found himself plastered to the wall with the bartender glued to him, the man's mouth covering his in a heated kiss. He gasped as Thomas cupped him through his slacks, squeezing his hard cock in a passionate grip.

"Holy fuck, you're big," Thomas whispered breathily.

The old Nick would have grinned and eaten up the compliment, but the new Nick merely ground into Thomas's palm for a split second before turning the tables, taking over, and dominating the human. He shoved Thomas against the wall, attacking the fastening on the front of his pants and practically ripping the zipper down.

"Greedy boy," Thomas panted, cutting off a groan when Nick's hand wrapped around his leaking prick.

Nick covered Thomas's mouth with his again, wanting to stifle the man from speaking. He didn't want to hear a voice that wasn't Thayne's. He didn't want to taste a kiss that wasn't Thayne's, or smell the scent of alcohol and human musk instead of earth and pine. *Dammit!* He snarled, forgetting they were in a public bathroom—or maybe uncaring, really. Why couldn't the memory of that blasted wolf leave him alone right now? Thrusting his tongue down Thomas's throat, Nick deftly slid Thomas's cock free from his pants, stroking the hot length in a strong grip. He could practically taste the tang of salty fluid dripping from the small slit, and slid his thumb over the head, smearing the sticky substance down the shaft.

The realization that he couldn't go through with fucking Thomas—no matter how badly he wanted to immerse himself in the man's body, even if only to block out the thoughts of Thayne for a few minutes of pleasure—hit him as he moved his mouth down to Thomas's neck, raking his teeth over the skin there. *Son of a bitch*, he snarled mentally before dropping down to perch on the seat of the toilet and yanking Thomas forward by the hips. He swallowed Thomas's cock in a split second, sucking hard and fast, his intention to merely get the man off so he could leave to lick his wounds in private yet again.

He felt Thomas thread his fingers through his hair, urging him to take his prick deeper. A low moan rattled in Thomas's chest when Nick did so, his nose buried in the dark hair at the base. The shape of it was wrong. All wrong. It wasn't Thayne. His wolf raged at him, demanding he stop, that he let the man in front of him go. Nick struggled to ignore him, to shove his wolf's thoughts and emotions down inside him. He could hear Thomas's breathing grow harsher, shallower, his pleasure rushing through him. The sounds signaled the impending explosion, a release Nick would never find with someone who wasn't Thayne. Was this why wolves ended their lives when their mates were lost? This emptiness? This inability to feel anything except pain and regret?

Thomas stiffened, his fingers tightening on Nick's scalp, and Nick could feel the hard shaft in his mouth throbbing, ready to empty the man's essence down his throat. The first blast tasted awful, bitter and foul. Nick pulled off, stemming his gag reflex. Before he could pull Thomas's cock away far enough, some of his come splattered on Nick's cheek. The thought of allowing Thomas to come inside his mouth or to mark his body with his semen disgusted Nick rather than turned him on. Thomas gripped at Nick's shoulder, steadying himself on shaking legs as he shuddered through the last of his orgasm. Once he was replete, he leaned away to look at Nick, questions burning in his sated gaze. Nick knew Thomas sensed something had happened at the end but didn't know what. He didn't intend on informing him either.

Standing, Nick grabbed some toilet paper to wipe his cheek and hand. Thomas stopped him when he reached for the door latch after discarding the tissue in the toilet and flushing.

"You don't want?" he asked quietly, gesturing toward Nick's crotch.

Nick's erection had faded, no longer interested in the brief moments of stolen pleasure. He shook his head, opened the stall door, and walked to the nearby sinks to wash his hands and wet a paper towel to rinse his face. The man's scent clung to his skin, and Nick scowled, hating himself and Thayne at that very moment. How could he possibly feel regret and guilt over a man, a wolf, who didn't want him?

Thomas stopped next to him, setting Nick's bags on the floor. His dark eyes met Nick's in the mirror. He set his hand on Nick's shoulder in sympathy. "Whoever he is... he's one very lucky man."

"Tell him that," Nick snorted derisively, swiping at his cheek again with the wet napkin.

Squeezing Nick's shoulder and then letting go, Thomas replied, "If he doesn't realize what he has, then he doesn't deserve you. I lost someone a long time ago because I was young and stupid. I would go back and fix it in a heartbeat if I could. I hope your man opens his eyes before it's too late."

Nick's throat tightened, and he felt his wolf's reaction to Thomas's words—the pure hope and eagerness to be with his mate. Hope is the cruelest emotion. It can lift you up to the highest peaks and make you so happy, but it can also yank that peak out from under you and send you freefalling into a bleakness so agonizing, being dead can seem a better alternative. A few months without his true mate and the desolation rolling through him was already so intense he wasn't sure if he could spend fifty or sixty years—maybe longer, since wolves lived an exceptionally long life—with this weight pressing down on his chest. It seemed as if his heart would implode on itself.

"Thanks, but I don't think he's going to open his eyes. He

was pretty adamant," he said softly, closing his eyes at the burn behind them.

"Well, you know where I work. Come see me any time you want to try and get over him," Thomas teased gently, rubbing Nick's bicep in a comforting gesture.

Nick gave a husky laugh and opened his eyes, managing a half-assed smile. "Thanks."

"No problem. I'm in customer service. I live to please."

Laughing again, this time with more sincerity, Nick stood straighter and picked up his bags. "Ever thought about trying to repair the damage?" he asked as they walked out of the bathroom together.

Thomas gave a sad smile. "I went to see him once but never spoke to him. He was at his favorite coffee shop, and I saw him with another guy. I knew it was too late. Besides, that was years ago. He's probably even forgotten I exist."

"We never forget those whom we've loved. No matter how things ended."

"Maybe." Thomas glanced at his watch. "I need to get back."

Nick could sense Thomas's discomfort and nodded. "Thanks... for everything."

Thomas chuckled and winked at him. "I think it should be me saying thank you."

They bid each other good-bye, and Nick walked to a chair near his gate, sat, and zoned out. He couldn't wait to take a shower to rinse Thomas's scent off his skin. Humans couldn't smell it, but as a wolf, he knew he reeked of Thomas: come, sweat, and cheap cologne. Seth would know the moment he stepped off the plane.

He spent the rest of the hour until his flight was called trying to steel himself for the disappointment and censure he'd surely see on Seth's face. After Seth had accepted Kasey, Seth finally understood about mates and how important they are. Nick was beginning to wonder if it was true. How could the moments leading up to where he now sat be considered as anything except awful and painful? The deep-seated ache he carried around in his chest didn't feel amazing, and the hollowness in his belly didn't seem beautiful.

It made him long for the days before Seth had moved to Senaka; the footloose and careless existence he lived, going from city to city for his work, the nights or entire weekends with a willing human where it was about nothing but pleasure, and the anticipation of a future with a warm and accepting mate. At least then he had hope. Now that hope had been crushed out like a firefly between someone's palms. Wasn't that the only thing that hadn't escaped Pandora's Box?

"Flight 235 boarding for Casper, Wyoming" came over the loudspeaker above Nick, pulling him out of his musings. He stood, picked up his bags, headed to the agent, and passed her his ticket to scan.

"Have a nice trip, Mr. Cartwright," she said to him as she gave it back.

"Thank you," he replied by rote.

Nick spent the time in flight trying to think of anything other than Thayne or where he was going. His jaw clenched for the hundredth time in an hour, and he closed his eyes, rubbing at them between forefinger and thumb. Pain throbbed at his temples. All he wanted to do was take a shower and wash the scent of Thomas off him and sleep for a day. His wolf prowled restlessly beneath the surface. It hated flying, being locked up in a tin can in midair, but it also knew where they were going and it anticipated a chance… just a chance to find his mate. *Stop it,* he snarled at his counterpart. *He's not there, and even if he was, he doesn't want us. So cut it out.*

His wolf growled back but calmed and faded into his subconscious, waiting. Nick reached overhead to turn on the little fan over his seat, hoping the cool air would help. It wafted over his skin, and he breathed in deep.

"Nervous flyer?"

Turning his head, he saw a younger man, no more than twenty, seated next to him. Blond hair cut into a neat fade with bright blue eyes and firm, full lips normally would have had Nick feeling out the man to see if he was of legal age. His anxiety, agitation, and a throbbing headache brought on by thoughts of Thayne made him short-tempered and not interested in even trying.

"No."

The man smirked as if he assumed Nick was lying. "You seem nervous."

Nick glowered at him. "I'm not nervous. How are you in first class anyway?"

"Touchy, touchy." The blond shrugged. "My dad owns a huge cattle ranch in Wyoming. He wanted to see me."

Grunting, Nick rubbed at his temples, then glanced at his watch. Another forty minutes until they landed.

"I'm Andrew."

Nick didn't supply his own name. He ignored the other male and stared out the small window, watching the clouds streaming past the wings of the plane.

"You know, not returning your name is rude."

"Will you leave me alone if I tell you?" Nick muttered.

"Probably not, but at least I wouldn't be calling you... well, you."

Sighing, Nick gave his name, and for the next forty minutes, Andrew didn't stop talking. He told Nick all about his father and the estrangement they'd been in for the last five years. Turns out Andrew was actually twenty-six, and ever since he'd decided to go to college and major in engineering instead of in agriculture to take over the business, his father had disowned him. Something had apparently changed, which is why Andrew's father had called him. Nick almost wanted to jump out of the plane by the time the fasten seat belt light came on. He'd wanted to spend the entire flight to Casper in quiet, wallowing in the realization he'd come to at the LAX airport, not listening to some human wax on and on about his life. A stranger who didn't know when to stop talking.

"Has anyone ever told you that you talk too much?" Nick finally said.

Andrew laughed, blue eyes twinkling at Nick. "More than once, but I say meeting someone new is like a friend we haven't met yet. How can you become friends with someone if you don't talk?"

Shaking his head in bemusement, Nick wondered how he'd managed to sit next to the one person on the entire plane who didn't believe in sticking to themselves around others. "Should be careful who you make friends with, Andrew. You never know who they may be."

"Maybe, but I have an excellent intuition about people, and I can sense that you're a good person. Something's happened to you recently that's made you look at things differently, though. I see it in your eyes. Ever heard the eyes are the window to the soul? It's kind of true. You can see a person's emotions in them."

Nick's head spun with how quickly the conversation twisted, and a new topic started in seconds. As hard as he'd tried to stop it, the younger man had managed to make him forget about everything for a while, and he could feel his spirits lift a tiny bit.

Smiling finally, he raised an eyebrow in Andrew's direction. "I bet you were a handful for your parents when you were a kid."

"Pfft. I was an angel." Andrew's eyes sparkled mischievously.

"Uh-hmm. Somehow, I find that hard to believe."

The plane thumped to the ground, bouncing a couple of times before settling. "Are you going to be in the Wyoming area for long?" Andrew asked as they stood to grab their bags once the aircraft had stopped moving.

"A friend of mine needs my help. Not sure how long that's going to take. Maybe a couple of days." Nick lifted his carry-on down, slung his laptop bag over his head, and followed Andrew down the aisle to the exit.

"Well, if you ever need a place to stay, let me know. Dad's ranch is called the Rocking M. M stands for Marsden. My last name, by the way. It's about an hour north outside of Casper."

"I'm actually heading east to Senaka. Not sure I'll get up that way, but thanks for the offer." Nick heard his name called and looked away from Andrew to spot Seth standing with Kasey, frantically waving at him and smiling.

"Is that your friends?" Andrew asked, staring at Seth and Kasey speculatively. "They're together, aren't they?"

"Yes and yes." Nick felt his lips twist up in the first real smile in days. He had always felt good around Seth.

Andrew glanced back at Nick, a sad look in his blue eyes. "My father disowned me once for choosing the career path I wanted instead of becoming a rancher like him. I think if he knew I was gay, the reunion we're about to have wouldn't happen. My uncle on my mother's side is gay, and my father never spoke to him after he came out of the closet publicly."

Nick couldn't help but feel sorry for Andrew. He'd never truly understood how anyone could possibly think of disowning their own child for being who they are.

Reaching into his pocket, he pulled out one of his business cards and passed it to Andrew. "If you need to talk, give me a call. I've known a lot of people whose parents weren't exactly accepting of their sexuality either."

Surprise crossed Andrew's face as he took the card from Nick. The sadness in Andrew's eyes disappeared. "Thanks! See? Talking to strangers really can help you make new friends," Andrew replied cheekily, the sparkle once more in the blue orbs staring back at him.

Laughing, Nick shook Andrew's hand, bid him good-bye, and walked toward Seth and Kasey.

Seth lunged at him as he neared, only to draw back, his nose wrinkled. "You smell like sex. Did you...?" His gaze flickered to Andrew's retreating form.

"No. And he's not as young as he looks." Nick didn't offer any further explanation for the scent on his skin.

Kasey held out his hand to shake Nick's. "Good to see you again, Cartwright."

"Whitedove," Nick greeted. "You guys didn't have to drive all the way here to pick me up. I was going to rent a car."

"Seth insisted," Kasey drawled, dropping his arm around Seth's shoulders and pulling him into his side protectively.

Seth gave Kasey an exasperated look but didn't pull away. There were questions Seth was most likely dying to ask, but instead he looked Nick over. "You've lost weight," he said solemnly. "You haven't been taking care of yourself. I talked to Ryan this morning. He said you've been running yourself into the ground."

Nick frowned. "I'm fine, Seth. Working keeps me busy, and Ryan needs to mind his own damned business."

"Nick Cartwright," Seth snapped. "He cares about you, and he's worried. So am I, for that matter."

Kasey held up his hand. "Let's get out of here before you two start arguing. Dad's waiting for us at the house, and I don't want to have to go chasing one or both of you down. You can fight once we're in the car."

Seth tried to argue, but Kasey covered Seth's mouth to

stem the flood of words and tipped his head toward the front of the airport. "The car's this way."

Despite his protests, Kasey grabbed Nick's carry-on from him and started toward the exit. Resigned, Nick hitched his laptop bag higher onto his shoulder as he followed the two of them out of the terminal. Seth elbowed Kasey in the ribs lightly, not enough to hurt him, though. Nick could see the affection and love between them had grown so much deeper in the few months since their mating, and it caused his chest to ache once again. His wolf remained in the back of his mind, almost dead silent in the wake of such strong heartache rolling over him. Nick gritted his teeth and tightened his hold on the strap of his laptop bag, his fingers turning white.

After they were on the road toward Senaka, Seth managed to maneuver himself to look at Nick. Nick could see the concern buried in Seth's blue eyes. "I'm fine, Seth," Nick said gently.

Seth reached out to touch one of the dark circles Nick sported on a regular basis now. "You don't look fine."

Nick gripped Seth's hand and carefully tugged it away from his face. "I'm all right. I survived and will keep on surviving. You don't need to worry so much." He felt Kasey's gaze on him in the rearview mirror and released Seth's hand.

"Tell me how you're so sure this Created One in the area is Taggart." A strange look passed between the two men in the front seat, and Nick knew something was up. Sitting straighter in the seat, he demanded, "What?"

They didn't say anything for several heartbeats.

"Tell me," Nick commanded.

Seth nibbled on his bottom lip, which instantly made Nick even more alert than before.

"Seth...." Nick warned him, eyes narrowing at the corners.

"Just tell him, Seth," Kasey stated flatly.

"I wasn't entirely truthful when I told you it was Taggart." Seth's gaze darted away from Nick. "The Created One isn't Taggart. It's a lot more complicated than that."

He stayed quiet, waiting impatiently for Seth to finish.

"It's about Thayne."

4

THAYNE

THAYNE SHIFTED in the saddle, staring out over a large canyon. His shoulder-length dark hair was tied in a short ponytail, except a few strands had slipped free and drifted around his face in the slight breeze. He wore a bright red T-shirt beneath a worn jean jacket, tight, faded jeans hugged his thighs like a second skin, and his dark brown boots dug into the stirrups. His hands were encased in brown leather gloves that loosely held the reins, resting on the pommel of the saddle. Anyone looking at him from a distance might think he was relaxed, enjoying the cool air and beautiful scenery, but up close, anyone would be hard-pressed to miss the tightness at the edges of his mouth and the slight air of defeat around him. A wary look of dejection remained buried in the depths of his gaze, one he'd seen in the mirror just that morning.

The dark red bay beneath him moved restlessly from hoof to hoof, snorting every once in a while. Though the animal knew his outward appearance was human, it sensed the predator beneath the skin. Most horses would have panicked in the presence of a beast with killer instincts, but the bay Thayne rode had been in their family since he'd been a child. It knew him, and though it was wary of his wolf, it trusted him not to harm it.

Thayne patted the horse's neck lightly. "Calm down, Nahtse."

He thought back over the last few days since his return home. At first he'd procrastinated in telling his parents, but finally a single moment of affection between his father and himself caused him to break down and spill the entire story to his parents and Kasey. What surprised him more than anything was that his father wasn't angry with him or disappointed in him. His mother had merely hugged him and kissed his cheek. Kasey had gripped his shoulder and squeezed it in a comforting gesture. It made him realize how unfounded his fears really were, and if he'd only come forward sooner, maybe the situation wouldn't have led to such a monumental, life-altering choice. Maybe it would have, as he couldn't see any other way out. The one thing he wanted more than anything was to be free of his mistake and to remain unmated. It seemed his only alternatives were to either continue to run from his error in judgment or accept the one thing he never wanted. Neither appealed to him in any way.

His grip on the reins tightened slightly, thighs tensing on the horse's side. One of the decisions he had to make was on his way to Senaka at that very moment: Nick. Unable to bear the tension of waiting, Thayne had saddled Nahtse and ridden into the forest. His father, and Alpha, hadn't given him any leeway, demanding he allow his mate to claim him to break the connection between Thayne and the Created One. Thayne knew the only way to stop the mating from happening was to leave the reservation, but if he left, he couldn't come back, couldn't see his family again unless he destroyed the Created One hunting him. Except... how could he kill the Created One when it was his fault? He'd lost control in a moment of lust, and now that man, that beast, had paid and was still paying the price for it.

And who knew if Nick would even want to help him. Especially after the way he'd rejected him and then attacked him. Thayne's stomach twisted sharply at the memory of the blood on Nick, blood he'd drawn in a moment of anger and fear. The acidic taste of his error had risen in the back of his throat when he'd believed Nick to be a Created One, and it had blinded him to rationality or coherent thought. His emotions got the better of him once more. He'd instantly shifted and assaulted Nick without giving the other wolf a single second to fight back. Only Nick hadn't fought back. He'd allowed Thayne to hurt him. Even when he'd thrown Thayne off him, he hadn't even tossed him as hard as he could have. Then at his parents' house, the sheer anguish in Nick's emerald-green eyes… everything bundled together in the pit of Thayne's belly, burning and roiling.

Nahtse danced to the side, and Thayne came back to the present, realizing his wolf prowled close to the surface, the scent disturbing the horse. "Shh, girl. It's okay," he soothed, patting her neck once more. Her coat still quivered nervously, but she stopped moving. Thayne knew he was only delaying the inevitable by staying out there any longer, and Nahtse couldn't take much more of the restless energy his wolf kept giving off. "Let's head back, girl." He sighed and lightly flicked the reins, turning her around to head home.

The closer he got to the house, the more his anxiety increased and the more anticipation spread through him from his inner beast. His heart beat faster and harder as they rode up to the small barn at the rear of his family's property. The sound of voices talking drifted through the open windows over the kitchen sink, and Thayne knew Nick, his true mate, had arrived. Swinging off the horse, he led her into the barn and tied her lead at a stall to unsaddle and brush her.

Kasey walked in just as Thayne stepped out of her stall, shutting the door behind him. "Nick's here," Kasey said, leaning against a support pillar in the center of the barn.

Thayne picked up Nahtse's saddle and bridle and brought them into the small tack room to put them away. "And?" He'd never admit it, but he'd almost feared Nick wouldn't come.

"He knows what's going on. Seth told him on the way here from the airport."

Thayne stilled his movements. "And he stayed anyway?"

Kasey sighed, pushed away from the pillar, and walked to his side. "I've never understood your aversion to having a mate, Thayne. True mates are precious and rare. I can't see how you can so easily throw yours away." When Thayne didn't offer any words of explanation, Kasey continued. "Yes, he stayed. He wants to talk to you, but he hasn't agreed to fully claim you, and I can't say as I blame him after your actions previously. It can't be easy for Nick, knowing that you're only doing this because you have no other choice."

Sneering, Thayne jammed the reins onto its nail and spun around, glaring at his brother. "My reasons for not wanting a mate are my own, Kasey. Not everyone wants to settle down and breed a few pups while living the perfect life. And no, I wouldn't be doing this if there was any other choice, damn it! I don't want this, and it fucking sucks that I don't seem to have a choice except to let him mount me like a bitch in heat and claim me!"

A noise near the front of the barn brought both his and Kasey's gaze toward the doors to see Seth and Nick standing there. Thayne's breath stuck in his throat at the pure anguish on Nick's face before it was shuttered behind a stony facade. Nick spun on his heel and stalked back into the house, allowing the screen door to slam behind him.

Seth gave Thayne a murderous look. "What the hell is wrong with you? Are you a jerk just because you can be, or were you born that way?" Seth turned and followed quickly after Nick, rushing into the house.

Thayne sank onto a nearby stool and dropped his head into his hands. He heard Kasey move to his side and felt him grip his shoulder.

"There are so many wolves who would give anything to be in your place, brother, but if you really are against allowing Nick to claim you, it isn't fair for you to go into this just to break the connection between you and the Created One. Despite his anger at Seth for duping him into coming here, he wanted to help you."

"He was just doing it because once the claiming is done, he'll have what he wants."

Kasey released Thayne and stepped back. Thayne looked up to find Kasey staring at him in the disappointed manner he'd expected when he'd told his family about his mistake. That look brought guilt rushing in on him, and he closed his eyes, trying to stop it from overwhelming him. Kasey's next statement crashed over him, sending the heat of embarrassment and shame straight through him.

"I may have judged Nick to be a pompous ass when I first met him, but he's a good man, Thayne. He wasn't doing this because he wants to claim you. He's doing it because he wants to help his mate even though his mate doesn't deserve his help. You need to think long and hard before you use him to clean up your mess."

He couldn't reply. His throat had closed over, rendering his vocal cords useless. The situation had gone from bad to worse in seconds, and Nick hadn't even said a single word to him yet. Swallowing hard, he gave Kasey a helpless look and ran a shaking hand over his face.

"Come up to the house when you're ready," Kasey said and walked out of the barn back to the house.

Thayne winced when he heard the screen door slam behind his brother. He really was an ass. His desire to not have a mate wasn't shared by the majority of the shifter community, and Nick had probably been raised in a pack that believed mates were the end-all, be-all of life. If Nick had been anyone else, he would have been trying his best to get him into bed. Again.

The scent of Nick's skin and the heat of his body invaded Thayne's dreams every night, driving him crazy. The only relief he'd been able to grant himself in weeks was by his own hand and memories of the very man sitting in his parents' house. He knew if Nick claimed him, he'd at least be able to taste and feel the real thing again, but to allow something he'd been so vehemently against chafed horribly. And he knew it wouldn't be another one-night stand. If the mating took place, he'd be tied to Nick forever. No more nights with random twinks in a back room, no more careless existence, and definitely no more privacy. Once cemented, a mating connection allowed true mates into each other's thoughts and to feel one another's emotions. Even if they were halfway around the world from each other, neither could hide anything. His bile rose at knowing his entire heart and soul would be laid bare to Nick. The truth behind his disgust for mates would be known, along with the fear that Nick would shatter him.

He knew he couldn't put off facing Nick any further and stood, steeling himself mentally as he approached the house. At the bottom of the porch stairs, he stopped and took a deep breath. Every one of his instincts cried out for him to turn tail and run, but his wolf demanded he enter the house and snatch Nick up, grab him, and never let go. His entire being was in a total, outright war with itself. He didn't know how much longer he could keep fighting. Exhaustion pressed in on him, forcing him to realize he'd been running for so long even he couldn't remember the last time he'd truly been happy.

When he entered the kitchen through the back door, his mom stood at the stove, stirring a large pot of stew. No one else was around. His mom looked at him and sighed. She tapped the large spoon on the side of the pot and set it down on the stove.

Turning toward him, she asked, "Are you over your tantrum?"

Thayne gave her a tired look and leaned into the side of the nearby refrigerator. "I'm not having a tantrum, Mom."

She snorted. "You could have fooled me, baby, because that's exactly what it was. Railing at the world because you have to make a difficult choice is throwing a tantrum. You put yourself in this position." She held up her hand when he went to protest her words. "I'm your mother, Thayne, and I love you and that will never change. I'm not angry with you or disappointed in you, but I do expect you to clean up your mess, and I expect you to stop acting like a child while doing it. You have no idea the difficult position you've put your father in or how much pain you've inflicted on that young man in the other room."

He looked at her in surprise. His dad? "What does this have to do with Dad?"

"You know it's against pack law to make a Created One. Accident or not, you still broke pack law. As Alpha, he has to enforce the law or others will see weakness if he allows you leniency as his son." His mother moved to stand in front of him, looking up at him. "He will have to punish you, Thayne, and the only choices are exile or death."

Thayne's eyes widened in shock and horror. In his desperation he'd forgotten the regulation against creating a wolf, or maybe it was because he'd never thought they would hold the law over him for an accident. His stomach clenched, and he stumbled to a chair and dropped into it like dead weight. Never being able to see his family again? That was assuming his father would choose to exile him. He broke into a cold sweat.

"I…," he choked out. "I didn't think…."

His mother sighed and turned another chair to perch on in front of him. She brushed his hair back from his face, caressing his cheek. "Baby, your father would never choose death as punishment, even for a wolf who wasn't his son. Nick has already spoken with his pack's Alpha, and after the mating, they are willing to accept you into their pack as Nick's mate."

Thayne jerked and swallowed hard, sawdust suddenly coating the inside of his mouth. He knew he'd fucked up and had to be punished, but how could he be forced from the only place he called home?

"Mom," he whispered, anguish in the single syllable.

Her eyes filled with tears, and she leaned forward, resting her forehead against his. She wasn't as calm about it as she seemed. "I wish I could help you, that I could change pack law, but as mate to the Alpha, I can't intervene. I can't change your fate, my son." She sniffled and swiped at one of the tears sliding down her face.

He hadn't wanted to keep running because he didn't want to give up his family, but now he was going to lose them anyway. Pulling away from his mother, he said flatly, "If I'm going to have to leave here anyway, why should I have to go through with Nick claiming me?"

"Thayne Whitedove!" she exclaimed sharply, standing and jamming her hands on her hips. "Did you not listen to a word I just said? Not only will you still be connected to that… that monster if you don't, but at least if Nick's pack takes you in, we will have a chance to be together again at the summit, and we'll be able to visit you in Nick's home, and you'll have a place to call home!" She allowed her hands to fall from her hips and stepped closer to him, tilting his chin to look up at her with a gentle touch. "Please, Thayne. Don't run again. I don't understand what's caused your total disregard and hatred for the mate bond, but never setting down roots and always moving is no way to live. I ask you, as your mother, to allow the mating and break the connection between you and the Created One. Allow Nick to show you the true meaning of being a mate."

Thayne's heart skittered inside his chest at giving up control of his life to Nick, to anyone. He felt cornered. He could run and never be able to stop without looking over his shoulder, or he could stay and bind himself to another wolf forever. Unless he never wanted to see his family again, there was no other option except to go through with bonding himself for all eternity.

"I don't have a choice," he murmured in defeat.

She hugged him tightly. "You'll see what mating is all about once it's over. Now then, why don't you go into the living room and join the others? I want to finish fixing supper."

As a child, he'd been fearless—careless, really—doing things others wouldn't, taking any challenge thrown his way, and just outright daring anyone to take him on. But the last year since the incident, he'd found himself turning tail and running more than once. How ironic. And now he felt more terror than he'd ever known.

He mentally shored himself and stood, dropping a kiss on the top of his mother's head. "I love you, Mom."

"I love you too, baby. Now go." She swatted him on his backside to get him moving.

His palms were sweating, and he rubbed them on his

jeans as he softly trod down the hallway to the living room. He could hear his father and Kasey talking, Seth interjecting a word or two every now and then, but there was no silky tenor added to the mix. Thayne paused just outside the doorway for a moment, his heart in his throat, and closed his eyes, leaning his forehead against the wall. In his entire life, he couldn't ever remember having to do something so difficult before.

"Are you going to come in, Thayne?" he heard his father, Jeremiah, call out.

Grimacing, he pushed away from the wall and stepped into the room, looking anywhere but Nick's direction as he slunk over to a reclining chair and dropped onto it. He could practically feel Nick's gaze burning a hole in him. His fingers tightened on the chair arms when he heard Nick's heartbeat speed up and his own wolf responded to the nearness of his mate.

A slight tang of human sweat stung his nose, but before Thayne could concentrate on the source, his father asked, "Is your mother joining us?"

"No," he muttered. "She's still preparing dinner."

"Then I think we should discuss the matter at hand," Jeremiah said calmly. "Have you made your decision, Thayne?"

Thayne tensed further, and his jaw clenched, increasing the throbbing pain already stabbing at his temples. He sensed Nick's perusal on him again.

Except it was Seth who sat forward and glared at Thayne. "Are you going to do this or not?"

Censure rang clearly in Seth's tone, and Thayne winced. He knew he deserved it after how he'd treated and hurt Nick.

He opened and closed his mouth a couple of times before he managed a strangled, "Yeah."

"Why?" Seth demanded.

Anger bit into Thayne, and he met Seth's harsh look with one of his own. "You know why."

Nick still hadn't said a word. Seth glared at Thayne. "If that's the only reason, why should Nick bother? Why should he put himself out there if you're only going to reject him again when it's over?"

Thayne felt his nails lengthening into claws in his rage at being questioned when they already knew his situation and his desire to remain free from the mating bond. His claws dug into the stuffing of the chair.

It took effort to snarl out his next words. "I never asked for him to come here. It's not as if I have much of a choice in the matter. I either choose to accept Nick's claim or I lose my family and spend the rest of my life alone, packless."

Seth grew angrier, but before he could say anything else, Nick abruptly stood. He gazed at Thayne without emotion. "Enough. I have no illusions of why you're willing to bond with me. I offer my help freely and without strings. Once the mating has been completed, you will be initiated into the Emerald Lake Hills Pack and will be free to come and go as you please." Nick stopped for a second, staring straight into Thayne's eyes, a tiny bit of his emotions shining in the seafoam green orbs. Emotions which set Thayne's inner wolf whining in distress at his mate's pain. "I agreed to this because you are my mate, as unfortunate as that may be for either of us, and my wolf would allow me to do nothing else, but do not think that makes me weak or that I will permit being treated with such blatant disregard. As the wolves of my pack would not understand any separation between true mates, you will be forced to reside with me in my home and, therefore, you will respect me while doing so. If you cannot abide by that, say so now and we will end it before it begins."

Thayne's wolf wanted to roll over and bare his belly in obedience to Nick, while he wanted nothing more than to just get up and run. He managed a brief nod, but it seemed Nick wouldn't settle for a wordless answer.

"Say it," Nick said flatly.

He wasn't sure he could utter it out loud. The instant he did, the shackle would be in place. He had to clear his throat more than once to be able to manage a choked, "I understand."

Nick gave a sharp nod and sat down, crossed one leg over the other, and turned his head to gaze out the window. The dismissive gesture bit deep for some reason. The almost cold shoulder, though deserved, wounded his wolf and his pride. He allowed himself to really look at the man across from him and felt the same tug of pure lust in his lower belly that he'd felt all those months ago in the bar. The severe line of the black slacks Nick wore and the snow-white button-down shirt hugging the lean cut of his body made Thayne's mouth water. His hair had obviously been slicked back before, but now it hung wild and free, tousled as if he'd run his hands through it more than once or he'd just been thoroughly… he inadvertently sucked in a sharp breath at the idea of Nick in bed. He felt his canines lengthen, and it took every ounce of willpower not to launch himself across the room and drag the man to the nearest mattress.

"I think we should leave you two alone to talk," Kasey muttered, eyeing Thayne.

Thayne knew the scent of his arousal had to be strong in the room, and he thanked his ancestors for his tanned complexion, or the heat flooding his cheeks would have embarrassed him even further than he already felt at his obvious reaction to Nick. His father, Kasey, and Seth all stood and left them alone together. Dead silence followed, the only sounds were those of his mother in the kitchen and their combined breathing.

Nick abruptly got up and walked to the window, crossing

his arms over his chest, his back to Thayne. If this was any indication of what living with Nick would be like, Thayne wasn't sure if he could handle it.

The tang of human sweat he'd smelled earlier upon entering the room struck him again, and he wrinkled his nose, sniffing surreptitiously. The stench was faint, but it made his wolf shudder in disgust, and then it hit him. The scent clung to Nick's clothing and skin, wafting his way when Nick had stood up. Soap mingled with the odor, except it couldn't hide the fact that Nick had been with someone else recently and hadn't showered afterward. A low growl reached Thayne's ears, and it wasn't until Nick turned to look at him in surprise that he realized the sound came from him. His wolf snarled and snapped beneath the surface. *Mine,* it howled. Thayne sensed his eyes shifting and closed them, sweat beading on his forehead at how tight a hold he had on himself not to change. His wolf raged and demanded to be released, to find the one who'd touched its mate and rend the flesh from their bones.

"What the hell is wrong with you?" Nick queried angrily.

"W-Who?" Thayne ground out.

"There's no one else in the room is there?" Nick said sarcastically, not understanding Thayne's question.

The rumble intensified, and Thayne opened his eyes. Nick took a slight step back at whatever he saw in Thayne's gaze. "Who did you fuck?" Thayne managed to rasp out.

Shock flashed across Nick's face, quickly chased by guilt and then stoicism. "Not that it's any of your business," Nick replied stiffly, "but I didn't fuck anyone. It was merely a blowjob in a bathroom at the airport."

Thayne's hands balled into fists, claws digging into his palms and drawing blood. His chest heaved with every breath, and he could feel the shift crawling along his skin, screaming for release. He couldn't stop what he did next.

Nothing in the world, save a pack of wolves, could have stopped him. He sprang across the room, straight at Nick, and shoved Nick against the wall with a loud thud. His harder, muscular body pinned Nick in place while he buried his nose alongside Nick's throat, rubbing his scent into Nick's clothing and skin to eliminate the human who'd dared to lay a hand on what belonged to him. He grabbed hold of Nick's hands, forcing them to the wall beside Nick's head, effectively trapping him.

"No one…"—he slid his tongue over the corded muscles at the base of Nick's throat—"touches…"—he tongued higher up to circle the shell of Nick's ear—"what's mine." He bit down on the fleshy earlobe, lightly scraping his teeth over the sensitive skin and relishing the shudder that wracked Nick's body.

"Stop," Nick whispered, turning his head farther away from Thayne. He struggled in Thayne's grip, but Thayne easily held him prisoner, anger and jealousy increasing his strength.

Ignoring Nick's plea, Thayne slipped his thigh between Nick's, pressing firmly but gently against Nick's groin. He could feel the response of Nick's body to him, the hard length digging into his leg. His wolf's rage was quickly turning to lust and passion. A fact Thayne had no desire at that moment to fight.

"Months," Thayne breathed, "*months* I've thought of nothing, no one, but you. Every touch that wasn't yours, the bodies that didn't feel or taste like yours. I could still feel you, smell you, no matter how far I went or who I fucked."

He rocked forward, satisfaction crashing through him at the inadvertent moan Nick let out. He moved his hands up to entwine with Nick's, fingers naturally twisting together as one, as he skimmed the tip of his nose along Nick's cheek in a caressing gesture, seeking the full lips he'd dreamed of more than once over the last few months. Both of them groaned as their mouths met, tongues instantly lashing across one another, dancing together in the long-awaited ballet of flesh. Thayne felt the heat of Nick's body seeping into his, could smell the heightening of his arousal, and growled low in his throat. The deeply buried Alpha in him surged forth, demanding Nick submit, but Nick pushed back, denying his command.

Pain seared through Thayne's senses, and he yanked back from Nick in surprise, stopping a few feet from his mate. Several breaths passed before the fog lifted enough for Thayne to notice blood on Nick's mouth. Thayne realized his lower lip hurt. Touching it, his fingers came away red. Nick had bitten him! The memory of everything that had just occurred rocked him to his core, and he stumbled backward even farther, grabbing hold of the mantel to stop himself.

Nick fairly trembled in abject outrage. His green eyes were like hard emeralds in his pale face. "Don't ever touch me without my permission," Nick said in a voice so cold it sent a chill down Thayne's spine.

"I…." What could he say? His jealousy and his wolf's need to imprint itself on his mate overrode any part of his human side. The ice in Nick's tone made his wolf cower and his stomach clench in outright horror.

Nick straightened his shirt and pushed away from the wall, his back ramrod straight. "You and I… once the mating is complete and you're initiated into the Emerald Lake Hills pack, I will stay at the apartment above my firm's offices. I cannot, will not, subject myself to a mate who is unable to bear the idea of being with me or one who would force their true mate to submit to unwanted touches."

Thayne winced and flicked his tongue over the wound on his bottom lip.

"The claiming is to take place tomorrow evening at Kasey

and Seth's home. They will remain here at your parents' until the following morning. In the afternoon, you'll face trial in front of the Senaka pack. We will leave for Emerald Lake Hills immediately after. Once there, you'll have the freedom you so desperately want. The only request I make is that my pack does not know of our dissention. You'll meet with my Alpha and act as a mate should and participate in the pack run each month without question."

Everything Nick outlined slammed into Thayne's solar plexus. One piece of information after another was a new nail in his coffin, sealing him into an inescapable fate. It almost brought him to his knees. Could he act the loving mate one night a month? He'd never been that great of an actor, and to convince others around them of their supposed mated bliss seemed impossible. Out of everything Nick could have demanded of him for his help, he knew he'd gotten off light compared to what Nick was giving him. Yet… he wondered if the positions were reversed if he would have done the same for Nick. Would he have been able to accept a mate who didn't want him and help him without asking for a lot in return? Would he even have come to Senaka, knowing the reason he was being asked to? Nick's courage and strength made him feel smaller than the tiniest creature on the planet. Here he was, throwing temper tantrums and raging at the world for his own stupid mistakes, and the one man who could have thrown his error in judgment in his face for revenge hadn't. How could he not give Nick what he wanted in return?

Straightening his shoulders, Thayne removed the hand supporting him from the mantel and allowed it to fall to his side. "I understand," he murmured.

Nick gave him a stiff nod in acceptance of his answer and turned to leave.

Thayne stopped him. "Nick?"

Nick halted in the doorway but didn't look at him.

"I'm sorry… for before."

If it hadn't been for the slight twitch of Nick's shoulders, Thayne might have thought Nick hadn't heard him or he was going to ignore him. "Just don't do it again," Nick said quietly and then left him alone.

Thayne stared after him. His shame increased as the knowledge that he'd hurt Nick again, badly, sank in. He touched the tiny wound on his lip and resolved to at least try not to make the situation worse by acting like a child. Besides, he didn't really have much of a choice except to learn to live with the situation at hand.

5

NICK

WHEN SETH had revealed the truth behind his request for Nick to return to Senaka, Nick had been livid and hurt, but he didn't know which of the two deserved his emotions more, Seth or Thayne. Seth had lied to him and deceived him into coming to Senaka. After everything they'd gone through together when Seth had moved to Senaka and the revelation of Seth's past, they had made a pact to always be honest with each other. His best friend had broken that pact by not telling him the truth until he'd already arrived.

He couldn't fault Thayne for the mistake his true mate had made because he'd inadvertently done the same thing years back. A mistake that had led to Seth's capture and torture. No, it wasn't Thayne's accidental turning of a human into a Created One that caused his rage. What made him so angry at Thayne was that the only reason Thayne would accept the mating bond was because he wanted to cut the ties between him and the Created One stalking him. His soul ached at knowing his mate still didn't want him.

He'd been tempted to say "fuck no" and go back home, but his wolf wouldn't hear of him abandoning his mate in a time of need. The hour and a half drive to Senaka after Seth's bombshell had been made in relative silence as Nick mentally fought with himself and his counterpart over what to do. He could walk away and let Thayne deal with his own problems, or he could step up, be the bigger man, and agree to help. His heart leapt at being close to Thayne, being able to claim him and bind them together forever, but his mind knew it would only be a temporary happiness. The moment Thayne had what he wanted, he'd leave and never look back. Could he live with that? Feeling Thayne's emotions halfway across the world? Knowing every time Thayne had sex with another and dying inside just a little bit more?

But could he live with the knowledge that he'd turned Thayne away when he needed him most?

The thoughts went round and round inside his head, almost driving him mad by the time they'd arrived in Senaka. When Kasey pulled the truck up in front of his parents' home, he'd turned it off and the three of them sat quietly for several heartbeats. Seth stared straight ahead, watching a man down the street mowing his lawn while Kasey gazed at Nick through the rearview mirror.

"In the end, it is ultimately your choice to make, Nick," Kasey said. "None of us would judge you or think badly of you if you decided to just turn around and leave."

Nick gave Kasey a weak, half-assed smile. "You'd like that, wouldn't you, Whitedove?"

Kasey snorted. "Who wants to be related to you, even if only by the mating bond, Cartwright?"

A brief, rough chuckle fell from Nick. "Still haven't changed, Sheriff."

"Nope. You're still an irritating pain in the ass."

"And you're still an arrogant son of a bitch," Nick shot back.

Kasey laughed. "I'm going to head in and let them know you're here. Come inside when you're ready." He climbed out of the truck, slamming the door behind him and leaving Nick and Seth alone.

Seth turned in his seat, giving Nick a puppy-dog stare. "Are you still mad at me?"

Nick sighed and looked out the window at the Whitedove home. "You know I can't stay mad at you, Seth, but you should have told me the truth over the phone."

"You wouldn't have come!" Seth protested.

"Of course I wouldn't have come, Seth!" Nick replied heatedly. "You know as well as I do that if it weren't for Th—that man's stupid mistake, I wouldn't be here. How can you ask me to do this, knowing full well what it means?"

Seth's voice cracked as he spoke. "I just wanted to give you the chance you gave me, Nick."

Nick immediately felt like a heel. He moved his gaze back to Seth and reached out to flick at a strand of dark hair grazing Seth's cheek. "Your situation was different, Seth. Kasey is different."

"How?" Seth demanded gently. "I didn't want Kasey when we first met. Even after the mating bond was completed, I still didn't want him. It took me time to come to terms with it. I know Thayne will too. This is your chance to show him what Kasey showed me."

He didn't understand how, even after everything Seth had been through, he could still have so much faith in others. He knew Thayne wouldn't change his mind. The sheer determination in those dark eyes each time he'd encountered Thayne all those months ago had convinced him in no uncertain terms that Thayne would never want him.

"Things were different because deep down you truly wanted a mate, Seth," Nick stated softly. "You always wanted one, which is why Taggart—" He broke off, not wanting to bring up bad memories for Seth. "It just took time for you to trust Kasey. Thayne's rejection is more deeply rooted. I don't know why, maybe I never will, but he sincerely doesn't want anything to do with being mated."

Perhaps Seth saw the truth in his words, or maybe there was something in his face that convinced Seth, but he held out his hand to Nick.

Nick joined their fingers, looking at the slender digits so skilled at repairing the damage to an animal, and wondered how something so fragile could hold so much power.

Nick tilted one corner of his mouth up in a slight smile. "Your mate would kill me if he saw me holding your hand."

Seth rolled his eyes. "Pfft. I have him on a short leash."

"I just bet you do," Nick teased.

"He just doesn't know it." Seth grinned.

Nick couldn't help but laugh. Seth grew serious a few breaths later and squeezed his hand. "If you don't want to do this, tell me now, babe. I'll grab the keys from Kasey and take you right back to the airport. I don't want to cause you any more pain than you've already gone through."

Was Seth right? Would there be a chance if he claimed Thayne, or would he be exposing himself to even more heartache? His wolf kept nipping at him, snarling and urging him to help Thayne. Seth had explained that Thayne had broken pack law and would be exiled from their territory. He could insist Thayne return with him to Emerald Lake Hills by offering acceptance into his own pack after their mating. It would give him something of a chance to convince Thayne being bonded wasn't a bad thing. He knew his Alpha would accept Thayne since they would be a mated pair and their laws were a bit more lenient, in a manner of speaking. After all, if they weren't, Nick wouldn't still be a part of their pack. Could he handle it if Thayne said no or if Thayne left after the bonding, though? From what he knew, Thayne liked his freedom, always moving from place to place and returning home once every couple of months for a visit. Would Thayne choose to continue his roaming existence, or would he decide to stay with him?

Nick knew he couldn't just leave his mate to a fate worse than death. A wolf without a pack wasn't something he would wish on anyone. Thayne might stray freely, but he always returned home. Now he wouldn't have anywhere to return to.

Heaving a sigh of defeat, he swallowed and sighed. "I can't abandon him. Just as Kasey couldn't abandon you when he found out the truth of who you are, I can't let him suffer through exile and dealing with the Created One stalking him alone. He's still my mate. Even if I wish he weren't."

Seth gave him a saddened look. "I'm sorry, Nick."

Nick shrugged one shoulder. "Fate decided to deal me these cards, and I have to play my hand, no matter what it may be. Only I can choose to gamble and pray I don't lose, right? Maybe you're right. I will try to have faith that he will come around like you did with Kasey."

"And if he doesn't, I'll kill him," Seth said while smiling sweetly.

Laughing, Nick squeezed Seth's hand again and let him go. He took a deep breath and gestured for Seth to climb out of the vehicle. "I suppose I should face the music."

Thayne wasn't in the house when they went in. Nick chatted with Thayne's parents and tried to ignore the roiling ball of acid in his belly. Had Thayne run already? Where did he go? They all heard the horse hooves clopping into the yard and the jangle of the buckles on the saddle as Thayne returned to the barn.

Kasey stood and walked past Nick, giving him a light touch on his shoulder in comfort. "I'm going to let him know you're here. If you want, come outside to the barn in a few minutes."

At first he'd debated on waiting inside but figured it would be best to get it over with quickly. Then he wished he hadn't. Thayne's words speared his heart, each one an arrow of distaste and hatred. The second those beautiful dark eyes landed on him and a light of recognition sank in, Nick had to get away, so he'd run. Against his nature and usual instinct, he'd fled back into the house and almost right out the door to the truck. He'd picked up Kasey's keys from the table by the front entrance just as Seth came in, preventing him from leaving.

"Nick, please don't go like this." Seth approached him cautiously, laying his hand on Nick's forearm. "He didn't mean it."

Nick hung his head, his hair falling over his face to hide the anguish he felt inside. "Didn't he? It sounded like he meant every word to me."

Seth leaned into Nick's side. "I saw his face after you left, babe. He regretted it immediately."

He peered at Seth from the corner of his eye. "Really?"

"Honest," Seth replied, hugging Nick's arm reassuringly. "I don't think he's as unaffected as he seems, Nick. Just give him time. Remember? Faith."

He slowly set the keys back down on the small table. Seth tipped his head onto Nick's shoulder briefly in a show of comfort and affection before pulling back and wrinkling his nose up at his friend.

"You seriously need a bath."

Nick had sincerely forgotten about his encounter at the airport and felt heat suffuse his cheeks. God knows what

Thayne's father thought! He reeked of come and human sweat! "Is there a bathroom I can use?" he muttered.

Seth laughed and pointed down a hallway. "That way. Don't worry. Jeremiah is too polite to mention the smell."

Covering his eyes with one hand, Nick groaned. "I can't believe I forgot. If I'd known we were coming straight to their home, I would have washed up at the airport."

"Go on. There's a towel on the rack that you can use. Just lay it over the edge of the tub when you're done so Emily knows it needs to be washed. If you want to take a shower, I don't think they would mind."

Nick uncovered his face and shook his head. "No. I'll just clean up enough to where I don't reek of sex."

Seth patted him on the arm and stepped away. "Come into the living room when you're done."

Nick walked down to the bathroom and entered, closing the door behind him carefully. He caught his reflection in the mirror and sucked in a deep breath. He looked as haunted as he felt. Dark circles ringed his eyes, making the green appear duller than usual, and fine lines of tension and exhaustion creased the edges of his mouth. Maybe Ryan had been right. The almost-gaunt figure in his reflection wasn't him. These last few months since meeting Thayne had taken a larger toll on him than he'd thought.

What was he doing? Could he really go through with this on a single seed of hope that Thayne might eventually accept him? He moved closer to the mirror and stared harder at himself. He'd been through a lot of things in his life that required his strength and cunning ability to think on his feet, and he'd always prided himself on being one of those men who have the courage to stand strong in the face of adversity, no matter what it might be. But now he had to question whether he truly was as tough as he thought. The sheer terror that Thayne could reject him again made him want to run as fast and as far as possible.

Ryan considered him to be the level-headed one, always planning and coming up with solutions. Right then Nick had no idea what to do. Where did he go from here? Not having a true course of action made him feel as though he were a sailboat set free from its mooring. He gripped the counter tightly while trying to figure out how to handle the situation. First, his Alpha, Elijah, would need to know about Thayne and the potential of what might be coming behind them. The Created One. Then he needed to tell Ryan.

After pulling out his cell phone, he spoke to his Alpha first, explaining the situation and that when he returned, he'd be coming back with a new mate with the possibility of a Created One tailing them. Nick had no illusions that the Created One would give up so easily. His experiences with them and the information he knew about them had increased over the last few years. Since they ran on pure instinct and desire rather than the common sense of their human side, the made wolf would most likely still lust for Thayne, believing him to be his mate.

Elijah agreed to accept Thayne into their pack since they would be a mated pair and out of the desire to strengthen the pact between both the Senaka and Emerald Lake Hills packs. He asked a few more questions of Nick before disconnecting the call. Nick knew Elijah would put more of his soldiers on watch for the Created One when they arrived there.

The call to Ryan was harder. "Cartwright and Driscoll," a cheery voice answered.

"Hey, Annie, it's Nick."

"Nick! How was the trip to Senaka? How's Seth and his mate?" Annie asked eagerly. She'd practically hounded him for any information he'd give after he'd completed his trip to Senaka last time. She still believed in happy endings and fairy tales, believed all true mates were destined to be together and would never allow themselves to be apart. If she only knew.

He couldn't stop a small smile, though. Her bubbly personality could certainly be infectious. "Seth and Kasey are fine, Annie. The trip was painless. Listen, is Ryan around?"

"He stepped out a little bit ago. Cole called in about an hour ago, and after a somewhat short conversation, Ryan took off. I don't know what it was about since Ryan wouldn't tell me, but it seemed pretty serious. You could try him on his cell."

"Thanks, Annie. Hey, did Synergen call?"

"They did, and they were raving over the new site. They loved the smooth design and feel, said you did an amazing job. The check's already in the bank."

Nick disconnected the call and hit the speed dial for Ryan's cell. It went straight to voice mail, which surprised and concerned him. "Ry, it's Nick. Is everything okay? Annie said you took off from the office after some mysterious call from Cole. Give me a call back when you get this."

He hung up and stared at his cell for a minute. What would be so important Ryan would take off like that and then turn off his phone? Was Cole in trouble? Or had something else happened? Elijah hadn't seemed upset or agitated on the phone, so it must be something to do with Cole. Not knowing killed him, and he absentmindedly removed his jacket and laid it over the counter with his phone on top in case Ryan called. Cole, Elijah's son and the soon-to-be Alpha, wasn't the type to fly off the handle over just anything. It must have been something major, and the knowledge he couldn't help just made his agitation at being in the dark all the greater.

After rolling up his sleeves, he turned on the water, picked up the small bar of white soap, and lathered up his hands and lower arms. He rinsed, threw some water on his face, and used his fingers to comb his hair into a somewhat cohesive mess. He grabbed a towel hanging on a rack and dried his face and arms. Not all of the scent of Thomas was gone, but it had been dimmed. He could still catch the scent of come mixed in with lavender at the odd turn of his head, but he hoped Jeremiah couldn't pick up the smell anymore. He decided to leave his jacket off and dropped it on a peg near the front door, stuffing his cell phone into his pants pocket just in case Cole or Ryan called.

Seth and Jeremiah were alone in the living room when he entered. Seth gave him an encouraging smile. "Kasey is on his way into the house, and he says Thayne will be in soon."

The mating bond link allowed for wonderful things over time: silent communication, being able to feel each other's moods and hear each other's thoughts. Sometimes more, but it varied per pair. Seth's reminder of that connection brought melancholy down on him again, and he gave a harsh smile as he sat beside his best friend.

"I informed Elijah of what is happening. He is willing to accept Thayne into the Emerald Lake Hills pack once we're mated."

"That's good news to hear," Jeremiah replied, relief evident in his voice. "Emily is glad to hear it as well."

Kasey came in at that moment. "I heard," he said as Seth opened his mouth to repeat what they'd been talking about. Seth rolled his eyes and closed his mouth. "I'm sorry you overheard that outside, Nick."

Nick waved his apology away. "It isn't your fault, and I certainly didn't expect to be welcomed with open arms if the last encounters were any indication. As I told Seth, I'm doing this because he's my mate and my wolf won't allow me not to, despite the fact that Thayne despises me."

"He doesn't despise you." Kasey frowned.

"I'd laugh if the situation weren't so dire," Nick said. "It doesn't matter. What's done is done. Once we are back home, Elijah will set up patrols in case the Created One follows us, as I am sure it will. It won't give up so easily, even with the bond broken."

Another fifteen minutes passed before Thayne joined them, and the air in the room grew tense, uneasy. Nick's wolf howled inside of him when Thayne gave his agreement to the mating. He tried to stop the feeling of joy his wolf flooded him with, but couldn't. It was only the arguing between Seth and Thayne over why the bonding should or shouldn't happen that tempered it, causing his own anxiety and anger to rise to the surface. He exploded, or he felt he did. When he outlined the plan in his head and saw the sheer panic on Thayne's face, he'd demanded Thayne make a choice right then and there. Him and his pack or the Created One and no home. It wasn't entirely fair of him to force Thayne to say it, but he'd had enough of the sheer agony eating away at his belly. Why shouldn't Thayne be forced to suffer as he had for all these months? He viciously denied the guilt at his thoughts, but damn it, he'd grown tired of being the only one in pain.

Of course, none of that prepared him for Thayne's reaction when he'd scented Thomas on him. The pure fury in Thayne's eyes, eyes that shifted between lupine and human, had caused Nick to step back slightly in fear. But what Thayne did next had his wolf demanding he bend over the nearest object and let Thayne take him where he stood. The feel of Thayne's muscular body pressing his into the wall and the rigid thigh rubbing against his aching cock had overwhelmed his senses. The harsh kiss had brought him back to his senses, and he'd felt anger rush in on him. His wolf had whined at injuring Thayne, but he'd bitten down on Thayne's lip, hard.

Thayne's confusion over the pain had cleared when he'd come to his senses. Nick knew the only reason Thayne had kissed him or touched him voluntarily was because of his wolf's intense reaction to someone else, a human, having sexual contact with him. Knowing Thayne never would have kissed him otherwise increased the burning ball of acid in Nick's lower belly. He couldn't take the sight of Thayne's distaste and again found himself running. He'd gone out to the front porch and sank onto the steps to stare blindly. Maybe if he stopped thinking for just a little while, he could escape the clawing agony scraping at his soul.

Jeremiah joined him some time later. Nick had no idea how long he'd been sitting out there, but it had grown dark and there were lights coming on in the houses around them. "My son is stubborn," Jeremiah said in a sympathetic tone.

Nick snorted. There was the understatement of the year. "Is that all?"

A rumble of laughter rattled in Jeremiah's chest. "He's fiery, passionate, reactive instead of proactive, and he has my temper."

Nick lifted an eyebrow at Jeremiah. "You seem pretty easygoing, sir."

"None of this 'sir' stuff," Jeremiah scoffed, waving a hand at Nick. "Either Jeremiah or Dad will do."

Surprise caught the breath in Nick's throat. Did Jeremiah, the Alpha of the Senaka pack, just ask him to call him Dad when his own son wouldn't accept him? Emotion clouded Nick's vision, and he blinked heavily, looking away from the older wolf.

"I was a lot like him as a younger man," Jeremiah continued. "Stubborn as a mule and never thinking before I made a decision. I never told Thayne or Kasey, but that almost cost me their mother."

Nick looked back at Jeremiah, questions racing through his mind.

"The moment I met her, I knew she was the one for me, the mate I was destined to be with. She lit up the room the moment she entered, and her strength shone so brightly amongst it all. I ignored the advice my father gave me on how to woo her and went about it in the same impulsive way as I did everything else in my life. Except Emily wasn't the kind of lady who would put up with a brash, arrogant youth like me."

"What happened?" Nick asked curiously.

"In my blindness, I pushed her away, and it took almost losing her to another man to realize I had to change my ways, to learn how to have patience and earn her trust. Thankfully she gave an old fool like me another chance." Jeremiah chuckled at the memory, an obvious far-off gleam in his eye as he remembered something he shared with his wife. It made Nick envious, and he wondered if he would ever have those memories only he and his mate would hold. Jeremiah patted his knee in comfort. "My boy will wake up, son. Once the mating bond is complete and you are connected, he will see just how precious that union is."

He gave Jeremiah a weak smile. He wasn't so sure he believed the Alpha's words. Thayne's continual rejection made it unlikely he'd suddenly roll over and accept it. "I think you have more faith than I do, si—er, Jeremiah."

"Perhaps. But I know my son, Nick, and though I may not be certain what has caused him to hate the bond between true mates, I am sure he will surprise you one day." Jeremiah sniffed at the air and smiled. "Dinner is ready."

The two of them stood and went back into the house. Seth and Kasey were setting the table as they entered the dining room. Thayne came in behind them carrying a steaming bowl of vegetables that he set down before looking up at him. Nick thought he saw something akin to contrition in the dark eyes, but Thayne looked away too soon for him to tell.

Dinner was a relatively quiet affair, mostly Kasey and Jeremiah discussing pack business and Seth talking about his veterinarian practice. Emily prodded Nick more than once with a question about his own firm, but other than a few sentences, Nick didn't have much to say. Thayne remained silent, picking at his food and grunting here or there whenever his mother asked him anything.

Once the plates had been cleared away and the small clock on the mantel in the living room chimed 8:00 p.m., Seth glanced at his watch. "I think we should get back to the house soon. I have a busy day tomorrow, and Riley Greyfox needs me to stop by at the end of the day to check on his horse. He thinks she is going to drop any day now. Nick, you're staying with us tonight."

Nick felt more than grateful that he wouldn't have to stay under the same roof with Thayne. He didn't even know how they were going to get through the next evening together. A nervous tick flickered along his eyelid, driving him crazy. He rubbed his eye more than once, but the twitch continued.

He gritted his teeth and stood. "Thank you for a lovely meal, Mrs. Whitedove."

"Emily or Mom," she admonished.

He couldn't help but notice when Thayne tensed at her prompting to call her Mom.

Giving a wan smile, Nick nodded in understanding.

"Kasey will bring Thayne by our house tomorrow evening, and then we'll be coming back here," Seth said, smiling at Emily and Jeremiah. "Thank you for dinner, Mom."

"You know you're always welcome."

After an awkward moment of silence, Kasey and Seth

stood, indicating they were ready to leave, and Nick eagerly pushed his chair under the table. There were hugs and good-byes made, and then the three of them were in Kasey's truck on the way back to their home. Nick could feel Seth glancing at him from time to time, but he didn't say anything, just stared out the tiny window at the trees flashing by.

6

THAYNE

THAYNE FOUND it hard to sleep that night and spent most of it tossing and turning before deciding to give up the fight. He rolled out of bed and hit the floor, palms down. The muscles in his arms bulged as he lifted and lowered himself. He pumped out fifty pushups and then rose to take a shower. His mind revolved around thoughts of what was coming. That night would be the end of his freedom. Nick would bind them, and he'd be forever connected to the one man that destiny or perhaps the spirits of his ancestors claimed was meant to be his. A shiver traveled down his spine at the memory of Nick's touch and the heated kisses they'd shared in the alley behind the bar in Senaka. He scowled and entered the bathroom across the hall from his room, carefully closing the door behind him to keep from waking his parents.

Turning on the water, he let it heat up and removed his sweatpants, dropping them in a pile on the floor. Would he be able to enjoy the sex, knowing what it meant? It had been over a month since he'd felt the pleasure of someone else's skin on his, but would his human side be able to forget long enough to lose himself in the primal act of passion? His head throbbed, and he clenched his teeth so hard it would be surprising if they didn't crack. He stepped into the tub and yanked the curtain closed behind him. The hot water slid over his tanned skin, and he thrust his head beneath the spray, drenching his hair and causing it to cascade around his face.

His throat tightened. Despite knowing Nick would allow him his freedom to roam as he always had, it still grated and felt as if a noose were tied around his neck and tightening even more as the hour of his nightmares approached. His entire soul would be laid bare to Nick, his barriers stripped away, leaving nothing hidden. He'd never understood how anyone could want to be with someone they couldn't at least have some privacy from. But keeping secrets wasn't the reason he didn't want a true mate. Having a mate left you vulnerable and weak.

When he and Dakota were twelve, Thayne had been there to witness as Dakota's father fell apart because of his mate bond. Dakota's mother, a human like Thayne's mom, passed away from cancer. Even the link with a shifter mate couldn't cure such a despicable illness. They'd watched Dakota's father waste away right along with her, and the day she died, he took his own life, unable to bear being without her and uncaring that he'd left behind a thirteen-year-old son and an eight-year-old daughter. Thayne and Dakota had discovered him on the living room couch, a gun gripped in his lifeless hand while blood stained the sofa and the wall behind him. The lifeless look in the man's eyes forever haunted both of them. The day of the double funeral, they'd made a pact to never accept their mates, never to allow anyone to make them weak or helpless.

When he'd first professed his disgust of the binding and claimed he would never have a mate, his mother had been horrified and tried to convince him how beautiful being connected with another could be. After a while, she'd given up, frustrated because he stubbornly refused to even consider the idea, but continued to believe he would give in when he'd found his mate. Until she'd discovered how he'd rejected Nick the very night they had met. It was only then that she realized he'd been serious all these years.

He turned off the water and wrung out his hair before grabbing a white terry cloth towel. He made a cursory pass of the towel across his skin while stepping out of the tub. After picking up the sweatpants, he slid them back on, his hair dripping down his bare chest. Instead of returning to his room when he left the bathroom, he headed downstairs to the kitchen, intent on grabbing a beer and sitting on the front porch for a while.

Despite the darkness, Thayne easily made his way down the stairs to the kitchen. His parents had lived in their house since before Kasey had been born. He couldn't ever imagine calling any other place home, and it nearly broke his heart that he wouldn't be able to return there. His mother always kept the wood floors spotless and smelling of pine cleaner, while his father's den had the distinct scent of tobacco from his pipes. He could still hear his mother reprimanding both him and Kasey for running through the house, chasing each other, and the many times she'd shooed them out the back door into the yard, where they would wrestle in the grass like newborn pups. The memories of each and every Christmas spent ripping open presents, family and pack members crowding the house from top to bottom, and the succulent smell of the ham baking in the oven permeating the house bombarded him.

Thayne gripped the edge of the countertop to steady himself. His fingers trembled as he realized what he'd really be losing in two days' time. The sound of feet shuffling behind him brought his hand to his face, swiping at the dampness on his cheeks, and he coughed to hide the tightness in his throat while reaching to open the refrigerator door for a beer.

"You okay, son?" he heard his father ask behind him.

The fridge door shut with a soft *shush* as Thayne coughed again, a beer in his free hand. He turned around to spot his father in the doorway, the stove light casting an eerie shadow across the finely weathered creases of his dad's face.

"I'm fine, Dad. Sorry if I woke you."

His father waved his apology away. "Do you need to talk?"

Thayne snorted and practically ripped the cap off the beer bottle before tossing it into the nearby recycling bin. He took a huge swig and swallowed before asking, "About what?"

His dad moved closer and touched Thayne's shoulder. "A real man knows when to show his emotions, Thayne. I can feel your anger and your sadness."

As Alpha, Jeremiah Whitedove had always been able to tell when one of his pack was hiding something or when strong emotions overwhelmed one of them. Thayne gripped the beer bottle harder, his eyes closed as he fought back what he saw as weakness. The cracking of glass sounded like a rifle in the silence. Liquid seeped from the spider web of lines in the bottle.

"I can't talk about this, Dad."

"Why not?"

"Because I can't show that I'm fragile!" Thayne snarled, wrenching away from his father's touch and smashing the bottle into the sink, listening to the satisfying crash of glass. "I can't let myself be weak!"

"Why do you think it makes you weak to share what's inside your heart?"

Chest heaving in his rage, Thayne slammed his fist onto

the marble countertop, uncaring that his mother was going to be pissed when she saw the damage he'd just done. Slivers of marble tinkled as he lifted his fist away.

"Because letting someone in makes you vulnerable. It strips you of who you are."

"Is that truly what you believe, my son?" his dad asked, a strange note in his tone. "Do you really believe letting someone love you, care for you, takes away your strength?"

"Doesn't it?" Thayne challenged, whipping around to stare at his father. "If something were to happen to Mom, would you be able to keep going? To keep on living? What if one of our enemies were to take her and use her against you? She's your weakness!"

"Your mother *is* my strength, Thayne. She's my everything. The rock I lean on, the ear I bend when I can't find a solution to a pack problem, and more than anything, she gives me the reason for rising to face the sun every single day of our lives. If something were to happen to her, it would tarnish her memory and the foundation of our bond for me to give up, to just lie down and stop living.

"I've always suspected what made you distrust the mating bond so much, son, but I hoped I was mistaken. Watching Lionel Blackfoot waste away alongside his wife and finding him after she passed made you see the connection between mates as a limitation." His father sat in one of the kitchen chairs and ran a tired hand over his face. "Thayne, the bond didn't make Lionel weak. Even as a child, he'd been fragile. He had a long history of depression and attempted suicide more than once before he found Loretta. She kept him tied to this earth longer than any of us thought possible."

Dakota's father had suffered from depression? "That's a lie. Dakota would have told me!"

"Dakota didn't know, son. His father was already mated

to Loretta when they had Dakota. Lionel wouldn't share the information with his son out of shame and embarrassment."

Thayne's entire world shook on its foundation, and he found himself reaching out to the back of a nearby chair for support. "Did… did he find out later?"

His dad frowned. "I'm not entirely sure. I spoke with his grandmother after the funeral, and she said she would eventually tell him the truth when she felt he was old enough to handle it. She died about three years ago, and I never did find out if she explained that side of Lionel to Dakota."

"Jesus," Thayne whispered and managed to move around the chair to sit. A bitter laugh welled up, and he couldn't stop the sharp bark he let forth. He hadn't seen Dakota in almost five years, but would the truth change anything for either of them? They'd made a pact, and yet it seemed the pact's very foundation rested on an omission of the facts—a lie, really. He didn't even know if he wanted to break the oath. Especially after everything he'd done to Nick, he couldn't exactly blame Nick if he told him to get lost. It was all too much to take in, and he could feel his stomach twisting into even bigger knots than before.

"Perhaps these truths will make it easier for you to choose. Being part of a mated pair is a beautiful thing, something which gives you strength, and if you have the courage to release your fears, son, you'll see what the rest of us already know. The real power comes from facing what you're afraid of instead of running away from it. Love does not come instantly, but rather softly, slowly. Even with true mates. I think if you explain what happened to Dakota's parents and why you're so afraid to let him in, it might help Nick to understand why you're against accepting him."

"No!" Thayne denied vehemently. "It's none of his business, and I don't want you to tell him either."

Love… he didn't even know what that was. He knew he

loved his parents and his brother. The type of love his father spoke of was an entirely different emotion from familial feelings. He couldn't deny it existed because of his parents, and he'd seen the way Kasey looked at Seth. But did he, could he, believe his future would hold such a connection? It didn't change how much he would be losing in the coming days. He would effectively be cut off from his family and thrust into a pack that wasn't his. The only lifeline he'd have would be Nick. The idea abraded his need to never be dependent on anyone.

"Even if Lionel Blackfoot did suffer from depression, it still doesn't change the fact that having a mate makes you weak," Thayne stated flatly. "It forces you to rely on others instead of standing on your own."

His dad lifted an eyebrow at him. "So you still feel loving someone and letting them love you is something that makes you vulnerable?"

"Yes," he replied.

Shaking his head, his father gave him a saddened glance. "For the sake of both you and Nick, I hope you change your mind after the binding has been completed. I will accept your wish not to tell him, although once you're bound it may not be so easy to hide the truth from him. It's going to make for a very lonely existence if you continue down this thought path, Thayne. Once your souls are joined, seeking contact from others will become difficult, if possible at all. Your wolf will try to force you to your mate for comfort and sexual release."

Thayne shrugged. "I'm good at ignoring him."

His dad huffed with knowing laughter. "Right now you are. Once you've been claimed, it won't be so easy to ignore him."

"I meant my wolf," Thayne said in exasperation.

"So did I."

Thayne didn't say anything again for several long heartbeats of silence and then quietly added, "I've always respected my wolf as you taught me, Dad, always understood the primal instincts he stirs inside of me, but... I won't let him control me or what I do."

"If the spirit of our ancestors has shown me anything in this life, it's that our wolves are a part of us and they cannot be separated from who we are. Animal nature does not allow room for the insecurity or doubts a human can hold and will break the chains holding them if they feel there is danger or desire for something they need. There will come a time when you can no longer suppress your wolf, and he will gain power over your human until something strong enough stimulates your human side. I'm a bit surprised that he hasn't already."

Thayne's mind flashed back to the moments in the living room with Nick. A red haze had filled him, and only the pain of Nick biting him had brought him to his senses. *A momentary lapse,* he argued with himself.

"But it's dangerous to let it go so long that he is forced to the surface," his dad continued. "You need to understand that, son. There is always a balance, a give and take between us and our wolf spirits."

"I got it," Thayne snapped, irritation building.

"I don't think you do, Thayne. You're still fighting him even now. I can sense the struggle for dominance between you two."

The backrest of the chair slammed into the floor as Thayne stood abruptly, his hands balled into fists. "I got it, Dad! Just stop harping on it, damn it! I don't want to keep hearing it. This is hard enough without you shoving this ancestral-wolf-spirit shit down my throat."

Jeremiah rose from the chair, slow and steady, his gaze pinning Thayne in place. The power of the Alpha wolf shone bright and clear in the dark orbs, causing Thayne's wolf to cower in fear.

Thayne realized he'd gone too far. This was his father, but also his Alpha, and he wouldn't tolerate disrespect. "I'm sorry," he stammered, dropping to one knee in front of his father and baring his throat in submission. "Please forgive me."

"I will allow this trespass once as I know you are reacting out of anger and panic, but do not disrespect me again. I have been lenient over the years and allowed you to do as you please without commanding you to remain in Senaka. Maybe that was my mistake, as you seem to have forgotten the ways of our pack."

Swallowing hard, Thayne held his position, waiting for his father to release him.

"The bonding will take place tonight, and tomorrow you'll be sentenced to exile from Senaka and our people. However, I expect you to uphold the rules of Nicholas Cartwright's pack and to obey his Alpha just as you would me. Understood?"

"Yes, sir."

His father held his hand out to Thayne and waited for him to take it. Thayne carefully placed his palm in Jeremiah's grasp and allowed him to help him to his feet.

His father pulled him into a tight embrace. "Never forget who you are, Thayne."

"I promise," Thayne murmured, fighting back the sting of tears. It had been a long time since he'd cried in front of anyone, and he didn't intend to start now. "I love you, Dad."

"I love you too, son." His father stepped back and gripped the sides of Thayne's neck, urging him to look at him. "You have no idea how it breaks my heart to have to send you away. But you will always be in our hearts, as we will be in yours."

Thayne closed his eyes and leaned his forehead against his father's. His throat clogged over with the unshed tears. Never had he thought his mistake would cause him to lose his family, and now that the reality of it was right around the corner, his heart hurt as if it would explode inside his chest.

"Dad," he choked out.

His dad pressed a kiss to each cheek and released him. "Your mother would like to spend the day together with you until Kasey comes to pick you up, so make sure you stick around the house, okay?"

"Okay," Thayne managed.

His father patted him lightly on the shoulder. "I'm going to go back to bed now. Got a few things to take care of tomorrow, but I'll be home early so we can spend time together as a family. Have a good night, son. See you in the morning."

"Good night, Dad." Thayne watched his father leave the kitchen. He lifted a shaking hand to run across his face in exhaustion. Somehow, he would have to get through the day without having a mental breakdown. He grabbed another couple of beers from the fridge and headed out onto the front porch to sit in the swing. This would be the last time he had the chance to listen to the chains creak or watch the sun come up over the house across from his parents' or smell the clean mountain air of his birthplace. Since he'd begun traveling, he'd never really thought about what he'd do if he couldn't come back here. Now he didn't know how he would be able to leave.

Familiar night sounds came from all around him: the hoot of an owl, the whisper of leaves shifting in the slight breeze, crickets chirping in the early morning hours. He'd never asked about Nick's home and wondered if he lived near a forest or if he lived in a city where there were little to no trees and wildlife. Would a wolf pack actually be in a city?

Where would they shift on the nights of the full moon, then? It wouldn't make sense for them to be in a bustling metropolis, so he figured they most likely lived in a smaller unpopulated area with a preserve or forest nearby. He couldn't remember if the name of Nick's hometown had ever been mentioned before and made a mental note to ask the next chance he had. *If you can remove your head from your ass long enough to think that far,* he silently berated himself.

The fingers of light were just beginning to show when Thayne managed to bring himself out of his thoughts. Both beer bottles were empty, and he was still no closer to having any type of solution that would prevent the mating claim or keep him from being exiled from his home. That coming night would seal the fate he'd fucked himself into, literally, and he couldn't do anything about it.

"Have you been out here all night?"

Thayne blinked and managed to focus enough to see his brother at the bottom of the steps. He wore his sheriff's uniform and looked as if he hadn't slept all night. "Kasey? What time is it?"

Kasey glanced at his watch. "It's almost seven thirty. I just stopped by to talk to Dad for a minute. There was a disturbance in town last night."

"What happened?" Thayne sat straighter on the swing, his muscles tensing. His brother wouldn't look him in the eye, and he knew his biggest fear since returning home had come to life. "Tell me, Kasey!"

"Bryan Crowsfeet was attacked last night. By a Created One."

Ice trickled through his veins. "Is Bryan alive? Do they know what it looked like? Did they kill it?"

"He survived. Barely. He's in intensive care at the hospital in Riverton. Bridget from the diner is the only eyewitness. The only thing she could tell us about it is that it's big—

bigger than any she'd ever seen before. She thinks the Created's fur was mottled, almost brownish-blond, but she couldn't be sure in the dark. If she hadn't called the station, we're pretty sure Bryan would have died. By the time we arrived, it had run off. Probably because of the sirens."

Horror slammed into Thayne, and he stood, knocking the swing into the side of the house with a loud bang. "If Bryan dies, his blood is on my hands."

Kasey walked up the steps and pulled his brother into his arms, hugging him in comfort. "It's not your fault, Thayne. You couldn't have known this would happen."

"But if I hadn't been so irresponsible, Bryan would be okay! I never should have come back here. I brought danger to everyone by returning here!" Thayne cried out, ugly shame threatening to eat him alive.

"You did the right thing by coming home, Thayne," Kasey said. "You shouldn't face this alone. I may not have seen the creature, but if Bridget's terror is any indication, it is nothing like we've encountered before."

"No. I need to leave. I can't bear the idea that he could hurt anyone else in Senaka." Thayne winced when his wolf thrust the image of Nick into his mind. If he bound himself to Nick, it would place him directly in the line of fire. "I need to leave. I need to go somewhere far away where he can't be a danger to anyone else."

Kasey pulled back in order to see Thayne's face. Whatever he saw caused an emotion close to pity to flash through his eyes. "Thayne, you are my brother, and I will not let you deal with this alone. Nick will not allow you to go through this unaided. No matter what's happened between the two of you, he is your mate and would die to protect you."

"That's just it!" Thayne exclaimed wildly. "I don't want anyone to die trying to help me! Especially Nick."

His brother gripped his shoulders and shook him. "Stop.

No one is going to die, Thayne. Our pack and Nick's will bring this to an end. The Created One will be destroyed."

"And another man's blood will be on me," Thayne whispered.

"No. He is no longer a man. It would be an injustice to let him live as the beast he's become. I do not believe he would be okay with knowing he's hurt others and may potentially harm or kill more. Do you? Was he a good person when you met him?"

Thayne thought back to the moment he'd met Matt Anderson at the bar in New Orleans. After a few drinks and an hour of lusty flirting, they had gone back to the seedy motel Thayne had checked in to. They'd spent the entire week there, barely leaving the bed or each other's bodies for longer than it took to eat. They had even showered together every time. Matt, a twenty-four-year-old college student on spring break, had been all smiles and laughter, with frosted brown hair, cerulean-blue eyes, and a well-toned physique Thayne had thoroughly explored with his tongue and hands. The little talking they'd done while eating revealed Matt wanted to be a pediatric thoracic surgeon because of his little brother dying at the age of three due to heart problems.

He was the first hookup Thayne had ever developed strong feelings for, and he'd slipped up one night after several drinks, revealing them to Matt. But Matt needed to go back to college to finish his schooling and it would be another four to five years before he could begin the work he'd set out for. Thayne hadn't wanted to hinder Matt's future and reluctantly bid him good-bye at the end of the week, despite his attempts to get Thayne to return to his home state with him.

"Yes," Thayne murmured sadly. "More than I can say about me."

"Would he be happy knowing what he was doing?" Kasey demanded.

Knowing Matt's desire to help children, Thayne knew Kasey's words made sense, and it made him feel even worse. He'd taken such a beautiful soul and turned it ugly. All because of a broken condom and the sharp cut of Matt's teeth on his neck as they'd fucked. He'd been amused at Matt's love bite at the time, not realizing the implications when he'd pulled out and seen the condom bunched around the base of his cock, his seed well and truly planted in Matt. He'd only come inside Matt the one time, but it had been enough.

"No."

"Then we need to stop him, Thayne."

God, for months he'd been living under the thumb of guilt and shame. He hadn't been able to overpower those feelings, and now he had to make the choice of whether to allow Matt to live or die.

"I can't choose to kill him. Not when it's my fault he's a Created One."

Kasey squeezed his shoulders and stepped back. "The decision has already been made. Whether it is here and our people who destroy him or Nick's pack and their Betas, he will be put down."

Thayne helplessly sank onto the porch swing again, his hands hanging uselessly between his thighs. "I did this, Kase. I did this to a beautiful human who had such a promising and amazing future ahead of him. You can't imagine the burden I carry on my soul for being the cause of it."

His brother sat next to him, staring out across the road to the neighbor's house. "This may bring little comfort, but mistakes happen. We all do things we regret, things we will carry with us throughout our entire lives."

He knew Kasey's thoughts were centered on how he'd

rejected and emotionally hurt Seth when they'd first met. Except Thayne's mistake would cost someone their life.

They didn't speak again until their mother came out to get them for breakfast. Kasey declined and went straight to their father's study to discuss the events of the previous night while Thayne followed his mother to the kitchen. He merely picked at his food while she chattered on about pack news. One of the Redfox twins had a baby girl, and Sharon Deerborn was to wed Jesse Greyfeather in the summer. Both of those events were things Matt would never have. He'd never get married, never have children, never be a doctor. The person to blame sat there in his mother's kitchen, eating breakfast, with a future ahead of him.

Anger brought the fork down on the table with a loud bang. His mother stopped talking and looked at him, sympathy buried in her eyes. She reached out and put her hand on top of his.

"Baby, you have to stop torturing yourself. You can't change what's done. You can only choose to find a solution for the problem."

"That's just it, Mom. The only solution is to destroy him. How is that a choice?"

She gave him a sad smile and patted his hand reassuringly. "Sometimes the choice we must make is one we don't always like. I'm sorry that I am unable to help you with this, my son. If I could take this burden from you, I would, but you will have to find a way to live with it. The mating bond will ease some of the pain inside of you through the connection."

"You mean Nick is going to feel these… emotions?"

"You really don't understand how being mated works, do you? Today I will tell you about the beauty of the connection between mates. Now, finish your food." She released his hands and went back to her own meal.

Thayne couldn't stomach eating and, after a halfhearted attempt, pushed his plate away. The guilt and shame inside of him increased tenfold at the realization that Nick's wolf would not only be able to sense what he felt inside, but would actually take on the burden of those feelings as well. Even though he'd done some stupid things in his life, the chain of events that had begun unfolding that week in New Orleans had to be the biggest of them all. He had not only destroyed his life, but he'd also devastated two others. He should beg his father to put him to death instead of exiling him. Except he knew he was too selfish to give up his life. Being self-centered is what had gotten him into this mess in the first place.

Kasey and their father left to go see Bryan Crowsfeet in the hospital and to begin a game plan to try to locate and trap the Created One. Thayne didn't offer to go with them, unable to face his greatest failure. His mother spent the remainder of the day telling him about the joys of mates, the ups and downs, and most importantly, to her, the benefits of being a mated pair. Thayne only listened with half an ear, silently praying for the clock to stop, but it only seemed to speed up, and before he could make himself mentally ready for it, Kasey returned to the house to bring him to his ranch as the sun hung low in the sky. The ride to his brother and Seth's home seemed to fly by, and his heart stopped in his chest when they pulled up to the front porch and he spied Nick standing by the railing, watching the truck come to a halt.

His brother gave him an encouraging smile while Seth came around to his side of the truck to open the door. "Out," Seth said quietly, waiting for him to exit.

Thayne thought for sure his legs would fail him as he stepped down from the vehicle. His knees felt weak and his hands shook. Gods, he couldn't believe how terrified he was.

He'd always thought of himself as a strong man, but the mere idea of allowing the claiming to continue almost sent him running in the other direction. Nick didn't smile as he approached the white porch steps. A solemn look dominated the gorgeous, sculpted lines of Nick's face. Seth climbed into the truck, and Kasey reversed out of the driveway once Seth had closed the vehicle door. It was all he could do not to turn around and cry out for them to come back.

"Let's get this over with," Nick said flatly, spinning around and walking into the ranch-style house. He allowed the screen door to slam behind him instead of holding it for Thayne.

Wincing, Thayne slowly climbed the stairs, taking them one at a time, reluctantly, as if he were heading for his own execution. He opened the screen door and stepped into the cool interior of his brother's home, letting the wooden frame tap his shoulder as it shut after him. Several lights were already on inside, and Thayne could see there were already changes made in the short time Kasey and Seth had been mated. Pictures of them together lined the stairs leading to the second floor, a colorful area rug dominated the short entryway, and some of the furniture had been rearranged. Had the combining of their lives together been seamless, or did they disagree and squabble like other couples? He couldn't help but wonder if being a mated pair made living together easier or if there were still the usual bumps that came with going from being alone to suddenly sharing everything.

The sound of Nick's heartbeat led him to the living room, and he found Nick standing by the window, his arms folded over his chest as he stared out toward the barn. The sight of Nick dressed in form-fitting blue jeans and a well-tailored emerald-green button-down made his cock sit up and take notice while Thayne's wolf eagerly wagged his tail at being so close to Nick, despite the frosty reception. He berated his wolf and his cock, but both stubbornly ignored him, his inner beast mentally whining and urging him to cross the room and take Nick into his arms. He curled his hands into fists and shoved them into his jean pockets while looking anywhere but at Nick. Neither of them spoke, and it seemed as if they would go on forever just like that until Nick turned toward him. The obvious hostility in Nick's expression made his wolf cringe, and Thayne fought the desire to slink over to Nick in supplication.

"We both know you don't want this," Nick began, "but unfortunately we will need to get through it. Once it's over, you won't ever have to touch me or bear my touch again."

He couldn't quite comprehend why those words hurt so damn much. His and his wolf's emotions were getting harder and harder to separate when it came to Nick. All he could do was give a stilted nod of his head in recognition of Nick's decree, even though his heart ached at doing so.

Nick let his arms drop to his side and started toward Thayne, obvious lack of enthusiasm in his step.

Thayne swallowed hard. He had no clue how he would get through this night.

7

NICK

THE MOMENT Nick had seen Thayne step down from Kasey's truck, his shoulder-length hair loose around his face, tight blue jeans hugging the obvious muscles in his upper thighs, and a dark brown T-shirt almost a size too small for the hard physique, he knew it would be difficult to keep his emotions and lust in check. He'd always been good at hiding his feelings behind a facade because of his time in Seth's life as a secret guardian, yet he'd barely managed to prevent the mask from slipping as Thayne approached the stairs, so evidently dreading what was coming. It broke Nick's heart, and he dug his nails into his palms, pain bringing him partially back to his senses.

Now they stood in the living room, no words spoken, the only sounds their breathing and their heartbeats, which immediately fell into sync with one another. *The perfect half of a whole*, he thought bitterly, his gaze trailing a horse out in one of the paddocks. Unable to take the silence any further, he spun around and said the first thing that came to mind. He almost thought he saw anguish flash through those dark eyes, but it was gone so fast he couldn't be sure he hadn't imagined it. It took all of his willpower to force his body to move toward Thayne. He stopped in front of his mate and lifted a shaking hand to Thayne's chest.

Thayne jerked at the touch, and his gaze swung upward to Nick's, his hands still at his sides. Nick laid his second hand against the other pec. He slid his palms down to the hem of the T-shirt and grasped it, tugging and mutely urging Thayne to raise his arms to help him. He thought Thayne would refuse at first, but seconds later, Thayne gripped the shirt and pulled it off, letting it fall to the floor beside them. Nick hid a shiver at the sight of the expanse of broad, tanned skin. He wanted nothing more than to have the right to touch, lick, and explore every single inch. He knew this was only about claiming Thayne to break the tie between the Created One and him, not about enjoying themselves or being one with each other.

Placing his hands against Thayne's chest once more, Nick heard the almost inaudible sharp intake of breath from Thayne and bit back a smirk. Despite his mate's attempts to remain aloof, Thayne felt desire at his touch. He ran his palms along the warm muscles, over the defined six-pack, and traced the light dusting of fur leading into Thayne's jeans. An obvious bulge protruded along the front, and Nick allowed his lips to quirk up at the corners, uncaring this time of hiding it. He deftly slipped the button free from the loophole and grasped the metal zipper. The backs of his fingers brushed along the ridge of heated flesh as he unzipped the fastening, savoring the way Thayne's cock swelled even further beneath his touch.

Lust took over, and Nick dropped to his knees, pulling the flaps of Thayne's jeans wider, and almost groaned at the sight of dark briefs encasing the throbbing prick he couldn't wait to feel on his tongue. He didn't want to think of anything except this right now. He shut out the thoughts of how destroyed he would be inside when it was over and how this meant nothing to Thayne except a means to an end. No, he wanted to savor every scent, every touch, every slick glide of his tongue over Thayne's body. It would be all he'd have left once they'd returned to his hometown.

He drew the black briefs down and let out a guttural sound as the hard, hot cock gently tapped him on his cheek, leaving a moist smear of passion along his skin. He barely heard the noise Thayne made as he swiped his tongue over the tip, tasting Thayne for the first time. Even in the alley behind the bar, he hadn't had the luxury of sampling Thayne's essence. The flavor exploded on his taste buds, causing his wolf to howl in joy. Closing his eyes, Nick wrapped his lips around the bulbous, perfectly plum-shaped head and sucked, lapping at the slit as more of the delicious liquid spilled free. He felt Thayne's fingers tangle in his hair in pleasure, and swallowed another couple of inches, working the shaft with his tongue along the way.

Several breaths passed as Nick continued his way down the stiff length until he'd reached the base, his nose buried in the coarse dark hair while his throat convulsed and massaged the, surely, seven inches of tasty cock. Thayne's fingers tightened in his hair. Nick bobbed back to the head and dove to the bottom once more. Time became infinite in those moments. He relished the pants and sighs Thayne let forth as Nick continued his oral assault and took great pleasure in the uncontrolled buck of Thayne's hips to attempt to drive his dick deeper into his throat. Thayne's loss of control only served to stir the primal instincts in his wolf spirit. The need to claim and be one with his true mate warred with the desire to drink Thayne's seed, to have the sweet tang to remember on the lonely nights ahead. He maintained his hold on his wolf by a thread. The sooner this was over, the faster he'd have to let go.

He gripped Thayne's thighs, holding his mate steady, sucking harder and more rapidly. He could sense Thayne teetering on the edge of flying, but his stubbornness kept him from letting go. Greedily, Nick slid one hand around to Thayne's balls and fondled them, gently squeezing and caressing the come-filled sac. Thayne suddenly grabbed at Nick's shoulder with one hand, the other tightening even further in Nick's dark mahogany locks. A grunt and the throb of Thayne's cock signaled the first spurt of juice to splatter the back of Nick's throat, and Nick drank quickly, but the volume became too much and some spilled from the corners of his mouth. Salt and fire battered his senses, and Nick almost came with Thayne at the erotic taste of his seed. Thayne continued to grunt with each burst until they had slowed to a mere trickle.

Nick didn't stop even when each brush of his tongue over the sensitive tip caused Thayne to shudder in almost painful pleasure. He didn't want to give Thayne the chance to regret or to run. Not now. His own prick pulsed with need inside of his jeans, straining for release, for Thayne's touch. When he felt certain Thayne would remain hard, he finally slipped off with a wet sucking noise and wiped at his mouth with his hand, bringing it to his lips to lick his fingers clean. A choked sound finally brought him partially to his senses, and he opened his eyes to find Thayne staring at him, animalistic passion and lust shining down from Thayne's dark brown eyes.

He took several seconds to gather his own wits around him before standing. He started undoing the buttons on his shirt, watching Thayne's gaze follow his hands. Though he was nowhere near as muscular as Thayne, he still felt proud of his body, and a warm glow spread through him when he saw Thayne's obvious approval. Nick spent a lot of time outside when he wasn't working or trying to stave off the depression of Thayne's rejection, and his tanned skin clearly showed his love of the sun. Fine lines spliced his stomach into sections, hinting at a barely defined six-pack. A sprinkling of dark hairs followed a tantalizing path to the top of his jeans. He tossed aside his shirt and began to remove his pants, sliding the fastening free first and then pulling the zipper down. The harsh sound of the teeth separating seemed loud in the utter silence surrounding them.

A sharp sense of satisfaction struck him when he saw Thayne swallow hard as he separated the front of his pants, hooked his fingers in the hem, pushed them off his hips, and allowed them to hit the floor. Tight cobalt-blue briefs strained under the desire of his hard cock. He toed off his black loafers and stepped out of his jeans before slipping his thumbs under the band of his briefs, calculating Thayne's expression while taunting him without fully removing the piece of clothing.

"Off," Thayne growled, his jaw clenched.

Holding back a smirk, Nick unhurriedly skimmed the briefs down his legs, exposing his shaft to Thayne's heated gaze and the cool air in the room. A haze seemed to come over Thayne's features, and Nick knew his mate's wolf had taken over as Thayne gripped him by the wrist and yanked him closer. The moment their bodies collided, Nick couldn't quite suppress a gasp, electricity zipping along his nerve endings. His reaction changed in an instant when Thayne tried to kiss him. Ice entered his veins, and he wrenched his head to the side. He would not kiss someone who only wanted him for a means to an end.

"No," Nick snapped.

No reply came from Thayne except that of his mouth latching on to the side of Nick's throat. Nick dug his fingers into the hard muscles of Thayne's upper arms, panting from the hot wetness sliding along his skin. He unconsciously ground his erection against Thayne's thigh, tilting his head back in pleasure. Thayne feasted for long, suckling moments on his neck and then moved to where his shoulder met his collarbone, nipping at the prominent ridge.

Nick shut off his mind and lost himself in the heated touches and hungry lips. His body trembled with need as Thayne made his way down his chest and farther still, his nose brushing along the curls leading into the crisp hairs at the base of his cock. He almost came on the spot when Thayne's breath whispered over his sensitive shaft, suppressing a groan of need. Thayne bypassed the aching length to the heavy orbs beneath, this time ripping the deep moan from Nick's chest. Thayne's tongue swirled around one, weighing it, and then shifted to the other, sucking it into his mouth. Nick's knees almost gave out, forcing him to grip onto Thayne's shoulders to steady himself. *Oh God.*

When Thayne released his balls and at the first swipe of his tongue over the weeping tip, Nick tilted his head back and almost howled at the delicious sensation. The smooth, slick muscle circled around the head and along the twitching length while Thayne drew Nick's cock into his mouth and down his throat. The tight grip of Thayne's mouth and esophagus was almost too much. Nick could feel the urge to come rising and shoved at Thayne's shoulders, pushing him back against the couch and knocking him onto his rear end.

The hurt look in Thayne's passion-glazed gaze almost broke Nick's heart. He dropped to his knees before he realized what he was doing and ran his hands along Thayne's chest. "I didn't want to come too soon," he murmured, reaching behind Thayne and digging under the sofa. He was fairly certain Kasey would keep a tube of lube under the sofa, since Seth and he could barely keep their hands off of one another.

The injured expression faded at his words, and Thayne

leaned forward to kiss at Nick's shoulder and neck, his hands grabbing at Nick's hips to pull him closer. Nick grunted in satisfaction when his fingers brushed over a small tube under a cushion, and he yanked it into the light of the nearby lamp. Dusk had settled over the corner of their world, and the sun had already sunk beneath the horizon. He sat back onto his heels despite Thayne's attempts to hold on to him. He ignored the twinge in his chest at knowing Thayne's wolf was in control of Thayne's faculties. He tapped Thayne's thigh, indicating he should turn around.

At first he thought Thayne would object, but after a slight hesitation, Thayne faced the sofa, his arms braced on the cushion. Nick set the lube on the floor beside him and removed the boots and jeans Thayne still wore, his eyes hungrily exploring Thayne's muscular backside. Thayne's thighs were thick and dusted with very little to no hair. He gathered Native Americans tended to have less body hair than others, as he'd noticed the same with Kasey when he'd accidentally walked in on Seth's mate in the bathroom. The quick glance had shown him nothing but smooth, tanned skin much like the man before him. Nick grinned when he saw a dimple in each cheek and couldn't resist leaning in to lick at one of them. A barely disguised shiver slid through Thayne's hard form at the moist touch.

Nick placed his hands on the back of Thayne's thighs, massaging the firm muscles, slowly moving higher as Thayne relaxed. He knew it would be hard for Thayne, a clearly born top, to submit to him. He'd already figured out he would need to move with care throughout their claiming. Although he'd spent the entire night tossing and turning and wondering if he should just get it over with, quick and fast, uncaring of Thayne's emotions, much like Thayne hadn't cared for his. Except his wolf wouldn't allow him to be so callous of Thayne's feelings, and he'd resigned himself to taking this as measured as he needed.

Thayne grunted when Nick cupped the inviting backend and started squeezing and rubbing, spreading them gradually at the same time and giving him the chance to get used to the feeling. He glimpsed the dark pink rosebud each time, making his cock throb with the need to be buried inside of it, to feel the hot tightness surrounding him. Nick leaned in closer and pressed a kiss to each cheek, then moved up to Thayne's tailbone and carefully down into the crease, urging Thayne to spread his thighs farther apart. He felt Thayne tense when his lips touched the tempting entrance, and with one hand, he reached between Thayne's legs to grip the still-hard shaft, stroking the silken length to distract Thayne from what he was doing behind him.

The tension drifted from Thayne the longer Nick fondled him. Nick resumed his exploration of Thayne's most likely virgin or near-virgin channel. He pressed his tongue against the puckered flesh and tasted Thayne for the first time, groaning at the burst of flavor on his senses. Delving into it, he slowly coaxed the muscle barring his way to relax, allowing him to go deeper. By the time he'd buried his tongue as far as he could go, Thayne's form shook in pure lust, hinting that Nick could continue with the purpose of the evening. Nick resumed tugging on Thayne's weeping prick while picking up the tube of lube. He managed to twist the top off, squeezed a small dollop of lube out onto his fingers, tossed it aside without care, and warmed it up before pulling his tongue free of Thayne's hole. He slid the tip of one finger around the rosebud, dipping in on each full circle, testing the waters. When Thayne thrust his hips back on one of the revolutions, Nick knew his mate was ready for more.

A quick intake of air was the only indication Thayne gave of his surprise when Nick slipped his finger in to the knuckle. He moved it in and out, continuing to edge farther in until he felt confident enough to add another. Thayne shuddered as Nick scissored both digits, stretching him until Nick could easily slide in a third. It was the sharp buck of Thayne's body that told Nick he'd hit that magic button inside. He worked the walnut-shaped bump for a few moments, stoking Thayne's passions higher for what was to come. When precome coated Thayne's cock, making it so slick Nick's hand slid easily along the length, Nick knew it was time.

He drew his fingers free of Thayne's channel, grabbed the tube lying on the floor nearby, and hissed when the cold cream came into contact with his heated shaft. He jerked himself for a moment, lubing his dick liberally, before rising to his knees behind Thayne. The change in position forced him to release Thayne's prick. Nudging the tip of his cock against the loosened entrance, Nick gently pushed in, his eyes never leaving the sight of Thayne's body accepting him. It took all of his strength not to come right then. The tight heat felt incredible, indescribable. Nick tipped his head back in pleasure as soon as he'd seated himself fully inside. Gritting his teeth, he remained still for several breaths, calling on every ounce of self-control inside of him to hold on and give them both a ride they'd never forget.

Finally confident he could move without coming, he slid back until the crown of his cock caught on the ring of muscle and then slid back in deep. He repeated the move, again and again. Each time his thrusts grew harder and faster. Thayne's moans and huffs sang of his enjoyment, the wolf truly having taken over now. Negative thoughts tried to edge in, but Nick forced them away, wanting to savor every moment, every sound, every sensation for it would be his only chance to know what it was like to have Thayne. He dug his fingers into Thayne's hips, plunging faster and farther into him.

Nick could feel the half-moon rising high into the inky-dark sky, feel the power of her light even through the ceiling. She smiled down on their coupling, bringing the joy of their ancestors with her. Another mated pair finding one another, becoming one together as their gods intended. If only this were a real claiming, a claiming to be made with a mate's eternal vow. He leaned in over Thayne, pinning his larger body beneath his, preparing himself to take the final act that would bind them forever as one. An act that was undoable, inescapable. A bond only death itself could break.

He reached beneath Thayne to stroke his cock, to bring him closer to the precipice waiting for both of them. The hard shaft in his fist throbbed as Thayne began to come, pulsing with each spurt of essence from his soul. Nick felt his teeth elongate, readying for the bite, and the moment they were long enough, he sank them deep into his mate's shoulder. Thayne's life blood flooded his mouth, ripping his orgasm from him, and he shuddered through it, his entire being soaring like an eagle. The strings of their mating had already begun to knit together, tightening around Nick's chest with each revolution, each knot connecting them to one another.

Long, silent moments passed as they both came down from the pleasure. Nick could sense the second Thayne's human side started to take over, the emotional withdrawal. Agony sliced through Nick as he slid free of Thayne's body. Nick quietly gathered his clothing and stood on shaky legs, hiding his true emotions behind his practiced stoic facade. He needed to lick his wounds in private, and facing Thayne right then wasn't going to happen. He never stopped, never said a word, as he left the room, heading straight up the stairs and into the guest room he'd been staying in since his arrival.

The snick of the door closing shattered his calm, and he dropped his clothes, sunk down to the floor, and buried his face in his hands. His eyes burned behind his lids, but he found himself unable to shed any tears. His heart ached so fiercely it made him wonder if it would burst from the pain. *Maybe it would be better if it did*, he thought bitterly. There would be no more pain to face or long, lonely years ahead of him without being able to find solace in another. The only consolation, weak as it was, was Thayne wouldn't find any peace either. Yet that thought didn't make him feel any better, but rather worse at how petty and vindictive it made him seem. He'd always thought himself to be a good man. The other warm bodies he'd indulged in over the years had always been a willing partner, someone who knew the score and didn't cling after the night ended. He'd helped other members of his pack in times of need and donated every year to many different charities to help humans. What had he done in his lifetime to deserve the pain he suffered now? Was it from a past life? A life he couldn't remember but his ancestors were still making him pay for his crimes? Nothing could be so bad as to warrant this kind of suffering.

Nick fell onto his rear and leaned against the door, his head thumping lightly on the wood. It would be a long night and an even longer couple of days until they reached his home and parted ways. He knew he wouldn't sleep tonight. He stood, moved to the dresser to pull out a pair of sweats, and put them on. His laptop already sat out on the small desk Seth kept in the spare room for working on his patients' records from home. Nick's own work had been his solace for the last several months, and it would continue to be his crutch to cling to his sanity.

His wolf prowled restlessly beneath his skin, demanding he return to Thayne. Nick ignored him and sat at the desk, slapping the spacebar to deactivate the screensaver.

His desktop background was an image of him with Ryan accepting their first business award from a prestigious organization that recognizes the fast growth and customer service of small companies. They'd received it just over a year after opening their doors. Their design of a Fortune 500 company website had garnered a lot of attention and demand for their business.

Nick logged in to check his e-mail and replied to several. An instant message popped up as he hit send on the last one.

RyanD500: *Hey, Nick. Everything okay out there?*

Nick debated ignoring the message, but he knew Ryan would just call, and he didn't think he could handle speaking aloud about the pure agony spiking through him right then. This way he could hide behind text on a monitor.

NickC: *Everything is fine, Ry. Just going through some emails. I see Kuraski recommended two of his business partners to us.*

RyanD500: *That's good to hear about Kuraski, but don't lie to me, Nick. Elijah filled me in on what's going on out there. I'm sorry I wasn't available yesterday.*

Smiling, Nick shook his head. Ryan knew him too well. He should have known even words on a screen wouldn't deter Ryan.

NickC: *It's okay. What happened that Cole had you rushing off in the middle of the day like that?*

RyanD500: *Nice change of subject, bud. There was word of a Created One being spotted in the area.*

A frown crossed Nick's face. Another one? What was going on out there?

NickC: *Did you find them?*

RyanD500: *No. The trail had grown cold. Cole and Elijah believe it may have just been passing through. We can't be sure, so Elijah has bumped up patrols. Now, back to the real subject. What is going on out there and when are you coming home?*

NickC: *We'll be home tomorrow evening. Late.*

RyanD500: *We?*

NickC: *Yes. We. He'll be returning with me.*

RyanD500: *The same one who rejected and attacked you all those months ago? Did he finally have a change of heart?*

Gnashing his teeth together, Nick quickly reiterated the situation and waited for the blow up. He wasn't disappointed. His cell phone rang. He knew if he didn't pick it up, Ryan would just call again and again until he did. With a sigh, he hit the green accept button.

"What the fuck, Nick! Are you serious?" Ryan shouted over the line.

Nick grimaced and snapped back, "What else am I supposed to have done, Ry?"

"Let the bastard deal with it himself! He made the mess, and he should be the one to clean it up. What the hell were you thinking?"

"He's my mate," Nick murmured low.

Ryan fell silent for a minute and then sighed in defeat. "I just hope you can live with the decision you've made."

Nick snorted. "Not like it's not going to be constant torture for the rest of my life with the binding completed."

"What are you going to do?" Ryan asked sympathetically.

Nick outlined his plans to allow Thayne the house while he moved into the apartment over their offices. They used the apartment for clients visiting their business before making the decision to hire them, but it was few and far between because usually Nick or Ryan went to them. It would give him time to find a new place to live.

Ryan bellowed loudly. "After everything else that fucker has done to you, you're going to let him run you out of your home? You love that house!"

It was true. Nick did love his home. Single story, ranch-style, and with the best bathroom money could buy. The master bath had a huge Jacuzzi tub with pulsating jets that he loved to soak in after a long day, with a snifter of whiskey and soft jazz music playing. He'd spent weeks designing the house and another week just deciding on how to set up the bathroom. Despite traveling a lot, he still considered it his safe haven. Now he'd be losing that too.

"It's just a house, Ry."

"Bullshit," Ryan challenged.

"Just let it go, Ryan. It's done. There's no going back now. I can't live there with him, and I can't leave him without a place to live. His pack is exiling him tomorrow, and no wolf should have to go through that alone."

"No wolf should have to go through being rebuffed by their mate either," Ryan pointed out.

"Ry," Nick warned.

"Okay, okay. Just saying to be careful."

Rubbing at his eyes with thumb and forefinger, Nick murmured, "I don't think he can hurt me any more than he already has, but thanks."

"I'll see you in a couple of days?"

"Yeah. Going to spend some time on the plans for Grayson Technologies. I've got some ideas on a way to incorporate their main product into the site overall."

"Don't work too hard and try to get some rest."

Nick disconnected the call, set his phone down, and opened the project file for Grayson Tech. He'd already built half the demo site, so with another couple of days' production, he could have it ready for their review. Switching off his thoughts of anything other than the task in front of him, he spent the next several hours lost in the comfort he found in focusing on creating something from nothing. It wasn't until his back began to ache and his eyes felt dry and rough that he sat back and rubbed his eyes to clear the fog. Satisfaction filled him at the almost-completed website. Maybe he could finish up the rest on his way back to California tomorrow evening. A deep chill chased away the satisfaction when he remembered he wouldn't be returning alone.

He glanced at the clock and saw it was almost four in the morning. Most likely Thayne was asleep and he could go downstairs and grab a drink without running into him. He needed to swallow some aspirin and grab a couple hours of sleep himself if he intended on being strong enough to handle what the morning light would bring. Seth insisted on returning to the house at sun up to make sure Thayne hadn't injured him in any way, so he wouldn't have to face much alone time with Thayne until they were on the plane and heading to his home in Emerald Lake Hills.

Tilting his head slightly, he listened for any sounds coming from the house, but nothing met his ears, and he stood up to almost tiptoe to the bedroom door. He cracked it open and slipped out, leaving it ajar as he continued his soft tread down the stairs to the front entryway. Thankfully his wolf's sight allowed him to see in the darkness and he didn't have to turn on a light. Once in the kitchen, he grabbed a glass from a cabinet near the sink, wincing when he accidentally let the door slam closed. He filled the cup and hurried out of the kitchen to the stairs.

He breathed a sigh of relief once he found himself in the bedroom with the door shut and locked. It might make him a coward to act like a criminal, but he couldn't bear the idea of facing Thayne just yet. Maybe in the morning. Maybe the light of day will make the upcoming days seem less ominous and disturbing. Somehow... he doubted it.

His cell rang as he resumed his seat at his laptop, and he smiled when he saw the caller. Picking it up, he greeted Cole as warmly as possible considering the fucked-up situation he found himself in.

8

THAYNE

WHEN NICK slid free from his body, picked up his clothing, and left him there without a word, Thayne's chest felt as if it had caved in, hollow and empty. Bereft. Is this what Nick had felt all those months ago? His wolf whined in agony, urging him to go after Nick, to make amends for everything he'd ever done. Yet he couldn't—wouldn't—allow himself to give in or show any weakness in front of Nick.

Nothing prepared him for the monumental change he sensed happening inside. He couldn't separate his own emotions from those of Nick's. Could the emptiness be coming from Nick? Did Nick pick up on Thayne's turbulent thoughts as well? The idea left him terrified and panicked. He'd always been able to hide in his head. What the hell had he been thinking to believe binding himself to Nick was preferable to being on the run from Matt!

Thayne didn't even bother with his clothes. He raced out of the house, shifting midstride and heading straight for the woods. He needed to run, to clear his head, and hopefully be able to separate his own feelings from Nick's. The half-moon had already risen high over the trees, casting thick shadows onto the ground, and small shafts of light dazzled his eyes as he ran. Memories flashed through his mind, but the images were of things and people he'd never seen or met: a dark-haired man laughing and smiling, other wolves shifting and hunting, and another of watching a woman ripped to shreds while helplessness swamped him. Thayne threw his head back and howled. It was a long, forlorn sound that echoed off the bark of the trees around him.

They weren't things he'd experienced in his past, which meant they could only belong to Nick. Not even his parents had warned him of this. Who was that woman? The man? Another image slammed into him of looking up at a smiling, black-haired man wearing a nametag, one that said Thomas. The picture changed, and suddenly the man's face wasn't smiling but twisted in pleasure and lust. Searing rage bit into Thayne, and he skidded to a stop, his claws digging into the ground as he realized what he was actually seeing. His throat rumbled with a furious snarl, and he wanted nothing more than to rip the bastard's throat out for even thinking he could touch Nick.

Plunking down onto his hindquarters, Thayne hung his head. He'd known completing the binding would be difficult, but he'd never anticipated or imagined any of this. No one had told him about the gut-wrenching memories he'd see or the emotions he'd feel upon seeing them. He'd expected at least his own brother to advise him, especially since Kasey knew his aversion to having a mate to begin with. Was Nick experiencing the same thing? Viewing his memories like a movie reel? Oh God! The idea of Nick witnessing the many men he'd slept with over the years sent another long howl ripping through the trees.

What else could he anticipate? Was there more to come? Thayne needed to know. Pushing from the ground, he spun around and started running toward his parents' place. He barely registered the wind ruffling his fur or the sounds of other night creatures skittering around him. Nothing had prepared him for this, and he felt out of control, something he passionately hated more than anything. It took him an hour to reach the reservation, and he halted at the bottom step of the back porch.

Kasey already waited for him. "Hello, little brother."

Thayne shifted, uncaring of his nudity. "Why?" he demanded, stalking up the steps. "Why didn't you warn me of this?"

"Would it have made a difference if I had?"

Thayne paced the small porch restlessly. "At least I would have known to expect it. I see things. Things I don't want to know about him." He ran his hands through his hair, gripping at the strands. "I saw him… with another man, a human," he spat. "I could smell the bastard, taste him. I wanted to rip his head off and break every finger he dared to touch *my* mate with." If he'd been in a rational state of mind, his own words would have given him pause, but right then, his wolf felt more in control, and his wolf was furious.

Kasey chuckled, grabbed a quilt off the nearby porch swing, and tossed it at Thayne. "That's called jealousy, little brother, and it's natural. Nick is your mate. Your wolf will not allow you to deny that, and his feelings matter as much as your own. Besides, forewarning you of it would not have prepared you for the emotions you are feeling or will feel in the future."

"Did you see these things with Seth?" Thayne grunted, snatching the blanket midair and wrapping it around his large form.

"Of course. Not everything at first, and it took a long time before Seth's barriers dropped enough for me to be able to see the torture he'd gone through at the hands of Taggart."

Thayne stopped pacing and looked at his brother. "How were you able to handle it?"

A humorless laugh passed from Kasey's lips. "It brought me to my knees. Thankfully, it was when Seth was at work, and I've never told him about it. You can't mention it to him."

He nodded at Kasey in acknowledgement of the request before asking, "Is there an off switch?"

Kasey grinned. "There is no off switch. You just have to learn to block the memories when they come or stand strong against them. The hardest is when your mate's emotions run high. The memories come faster, relentless."

Despite Nick's apparent cold withdrawal, he still cared! Thayne's wolf leapt for joy, but he was less than overjoyed himself. Thayne mentally snapped at his wolf to calm down and stop acting like a newborn pup in heat. His wolf whined but settled.

"It works both ways, Thayne," Kasey warned gently. "When we are angry, sad, or even happy, the memories and thoughts come. It doesn't happen overnight, but you'll even begin to be able to speak to one another telepathically. No matter where you are in the world. Running will no longer be an option for you."

Thayne snarled and resumed pacing. He felt caged. A wild beast trapped behind bars. Except… his wolf didn't feel that way. His wolf was ecstatic, beyond happy. "I never thought it would turn out like this. I thought if I found my mate, I could just walk away, reject them, and never let them know I knew they were my mate."

Kasey reached up and grabbed Thayne's shoulder, bringing him to a halt. He peered into Thayne's eyes. "Life gives us unexpected events. I never thought my mate would be a white man, but the spirits of our ancestors found the irony too great not to make it so. Maybe it was to teach me a lesson that not all white men are cruel, uncaring bastards.

But I accepted what fate decided to gift me with. Seth is a beautiful soul, and he cares so deeply for everyone and everything around him. My life is so much better, brighter, with him in it." Kasey paused and quirked one corner of his mouth in a half smile. "Give Nick a chance, Thayne. Give the bond you've started to form with him a chance. No wolf is blessed with two mates in a lifetime, and I know you'll regret it more than anything if you let him go. I almost made that mistake myself."

The idea of just accepting what he'd spent years telling himself he didn't want aggravated him. It scraped his nerves raw, and his hands trembled as they gripped the quilt tighter. He would accept his banishment and return with Nick to his home in California, but he couldn't remain there. The only answer was to keep moving.

He shook his head at Kasey. "No. I refuse to believe I have no choice in my future, in what happens to me. I've never wanted a mate."

Kasey gave him a saddened look. "It is ultimately your decision to make, Thayne. Just remember you aren't the only one whose happiness is at stake here."

They stood there in silence for a long time, staring out into the darkness surrounding their parents' home. Finally, Kasey glanced at his watch and asked, "Do you want me to give you a ride back to the house? It's going to be a long day tomorrow, and I think you should at least get some rest."

Hesitating, Thayne wondered if he should go back. Would Nick be asleep? He couldn't imagine facing him right then. Not with how abraded his emotions felt. He'd never entertained the thought of himself as a coward, but more than once in the last few days, he'd found himself turning tail and running.

Taking a silent inward breath, he nodded. "A ride would be great."

Kasey went inside for his keys and his shoes and came right back outside. Thayne climbed into the passenger seat and remained silent on the way back to Kasey and Seth's home. They'd fallen into their mating relationship so flawlessly despite the rocky beginning. Thayne wondered if they would have been so quick to adjust if it hadn't been for the threat against Seth's life. *But Kasey had accepted Seth before he knew of the danger to Seth,* his mind whispered. Thayne slouched farther in his seat and glared out of the passenger window.

The dashboard clock read close to four in the morning when they reached the ranch house, and Thayne remained in the truck with his brother, engine idling, for several minutes. The house was dark except for a small light in one of the second-floor windows. He wondered if Nick was still awake.

"I never wanted this," he murmured to Kasey, his eyes locked on that tiny glow.

Kasey didn't reply. He reached out and patted Thayne on the shoulder in support.

No one in their family had ever understood why Thayne didn't want a mate. They had always told him he would change his mind when he met them, but even then his human side wanted nothing to do with the man in the upstairs bedroom. Sighing, he gave a resigned look at Kasey, opened the door, slid to the ground, and closed it behind him. It was only after Kasey had turned around and headed back to the road that Thayne managed to force himself to move toward the front porch.

Inside the door, he stopped and listened, cocking his head to the side slightly. His wolf whimpered when the sound of a computer mouse and typing indicated Nick hadn't gone to sleep yet. Thayne gritted his teeth and went into the living room to pick up his clothes and get dressed. He'd just sunk into one of the recliners to put his shoes on when he heard the snick of a door opening upstairs. He froze and waited. The padding of bare feet along the hallway and down the stairs made him stiffen further, but Nick didn't stop in the doorway or even glance into the living room—he headed straight to the kitchen. Thayne heard the gentle bang of a cabinet door closing and a glass clinking on the countertop. It was more than obvious Nick didn't want him to know he'd come downstairs. His wolf pleaded with him to go to Nick, but he stubbornly remained where he sat until Nick had practically tiptoed past him and up the stairs.

Thayne wondered if this would be how it was in California. It only strengthened his resolve to not stick around once they'd gotten there. He finished jamming his feet into his boots and laced them, tying them tight. He couldn't remain in the house with nothing to do. He'd end up brooding about the man upstairs. An image flashed through his mind as he stood, and his breath caught in his throat. His hands balled into fists at the sight of another man in Nick's memories. A dark-haired man held Nick, kissing him passionately. The memory was older—the youthful countenance of the man caressing Nick indicated their age to be early twenties perhaps—but the strength of emotion behind their touches and the fondness swamping Thayne indicated it was someone very much in Nick's present.

A low growl rumbled in his throat before he could suppress it, and his nails lengthened, digging deep gouges into his palms. *Stop it*, he demanded of himself. His strong willpower was the only thing keeping him from rushing up the stairs and throwing Nick onto the bed to wipe out all thoughts of another man. Except that could never happen. Not now, not ever. A muscle ticked in his tightly clenched jaw as he stomped from the house. He barely noticed the mist hanging above the dewy grass or the chirping of a Mormon cricket. His focus lay on the barn and losing himself in the mindless task of feeding the horses and mucking out a couple of stalls. He needed something to occupy himself, or he would end up making himself insane between thinking of what the light of day would bring and the images bombarding his mind from Nick.

The warm barn air washed over him, bringing a sense of rightness to his restless soul. Horses he knew. They were beautiful creatures with huge hearts that loved unconditionally. Many people would question why the horses didn't shy away from them, being able to sense the predators inside of them, but they'd always made it a point to acquire their horses as foals. It gave the horses the chance to learn they wouldn't hurt them. Nahtse, his own horse, had been found cuddled next to her dead mother in the forest, a wolf having gotten to her. She'd protected her foal but had been unable to protect herself. It still amazed Thayne that Nahtse had survived several days without becoming prey to a wolf or other animal. His parents had brought her home, and they'd taken to one another immediately.

Kasey owned four horses in all, ranging from a quarter horse to a thoroughbred. He'd gifted Seth with one the night they'd cemented their union in front of the pack with the customary tying of the hands. Grabbing the feed bags, Thayne took them to the tack and storage room at the back of the barn to fill them. The soft swish of grain filtering into the bags calmed him, and he smiled for the first time in days. He breathed in deeply, savoring the scents and allowing them to remind him of other memories of working in the barn with his father and brother. One of the horses snorted and stomped its hooves, urging him to hurry along. Thayne laughed and finished the last one, carrying it to the impatient beast and strapping it onto his muzzle. He patted the horse's neck before picking up the other bags and doing the same for the other three.

The sounds of their teeth crunching the grain echoed quietly in the silent barn while he prepared the necessary hay and rolled a wheelbarrow close to the first stall. He leaned one shoulder on the stall door and waited for Harley to finish his feed. The moment Harley finished, he detached the bag and attached a lead, unlatched the door, and urged the horse out. He tied him to a post and started the laborious process of mucking out the stall. By the time he'd reached the final one, the sun had risen and he could hear the birds waking up outside. Mitsy, Seth's horse, lipped his shoulder as he put the halter on her and led her to the post.

Tires rolling over gravel signaled Kasey and Seth's return to their home. Thayne grimaced but didn't stop his task.

He swiped at his forehead with the back of his hand and grabbed the pitchfork again, scraping more hay and manure from the floor and tossing it into the half-full wheelbarrow. The squeak of the barn door alerted him to the presence of another. He didn't even glance up, continuing to scoop out the stall.

"You cleaned all of the stalls?" Kasey asked behind him.

"Yep."

"And fed them?"

Thayne grunted in reply.

"Thanks, little brother. You didn't have to do that."

Thayne shrugged.

Kasey sighed and moved to Mitsy's side, running his hand along her flank. "Are you doing okay?"

Snorting, Thayne tossed another batch of dirty hay into the barrow. "You really askin' me that, Kase?"

"You always did throw yourself into whatever manual labor you could find whenever you didn't want to think." Kasey patted Mitsy and returned to Thayne, leaning against the outside of the stall door. "Dad said for us to be at the circle by noon today."

Thayne stiffened but didn't break his movements. The circle… the place where all pack ceremonies, judgments, and punishments took place in the Senaka wolf pack. The idea of being put on display in front of the others in his pack made his hands tighten on the handle of the pitchfork. There was no way out of this, no way to fight it. And he didn't even know if he wanted to fight it anymore. Maybe he really should just ask his father to give him the death sentence. It would be so much easier. But that would make him a coward, and he was no coward.

"Fine."

Finished, Thayne set the pitchfork next to the open door and picked up handfuls of fresh hay, tossing it across the floor. Kasey silently helped. They worked in tandem until the floor was adequately covered. Kasey led Mitsy back into the stall and closed the door behind her. Thayne hefted the wheelbarrow by its handles, pushed it outside to the compost heap, and dumped it on the side before bringing it back to the barn. His brother stood there, waiting for him.

"Thayne?"

He stopped, staring straight ahead.

"Everything's going to be all right."

Lips flattening into a thin line, Thayne didn't respond. He returned the barrow to where he found it. He needed to shower. If he had to face the pack, he didn't want to smell of sweat and horse shit, but he didn't have any of his clothing here.

"I need to borrow some clothes," he bit out, his back to Kasey.

"Take anything you want."

Thayne nodded and spun on his heel, brushing past Kasey. This would be the last time he would set foot on the ranch. It would be the last time he ever saw Mitsy or Harley. There would be no coming back after this. He'd die before he'd ever admit it out loud, but his heart ached. It felt as though a fist had clamped tight around it and was squeezing relentlessly. He was practically gasping for air as he rushed into the house and up the stairs, ignoring Seth's call of his name. He raced down the familiar hallway and into the bedroom Kasey shared with Seth. Slamming the door behind him, he slumped against it, sliding down to his knees and burying his face in his hands. His eyes burned behind his lids, threatening to spill forth tears, something he hadn't done in years. The only place he'd ever called home would no longer be his in a matter of hours. He would not even be able to return to his parents' home to pick up his things. He'd be banished from the pack's territory, and if he ever came back, he would be put to death.

A sob caught in his throat, and he choked it back, refusing to let it out. He couldn't give in to it. He wouldn't. Forcing himself to stand on shaking legs, he strode with purpose to the closet and found a white T-shirt and jeans. Taking those into the bathroom, he set them on the counter and toed off his boots, stripping his shirt off at the same time. The bathroom had creamy earth-tone tiles with a large Jacuzzi tub and an ultramodern glass shower stall with three showerheads jutting from the wall. Thayne reached in and wrenched on the water, letting it heat up while removing the remainder of his clothing. He blocked out all thoughts of the upcoming trial, Nick, and how he would soon be homeless.

Steam began to fill the room and fog the mirrors before long. Thayne stepped into the stall, closing the glass door behind him and thrusting his head beneath the spray of scalding-hot water. He stood there, allowing it to wash over him, removing the dirt and muck from his body, the hay in his hair. He braced his hands on the wall in front of him, the muscles in his forearms corded from the tension caused by his situation. Not even the hot water could melt it away.

When he finally found the desire to move, he soaped his hair with shampoo and rinsed it quickly. The scent of fresh ocean breeze stung his nose, and he wrinkled it, knowing he'd smell like salt and seaweed. Seth apparently liked the less masculine shampoos. The soap turned out to be no better. Thayne rolled his eyes in exasperation and hoped the fragrance wouldn't cling to him afterward.

His skin was bright red by the time he finished and shut off the water. Steam had clouded the entire room and shifted in the air as he stepped out of the shower, grabbing a towel off the nearby rack. Briskly, he dried off and pulled on the jeans, snatching up the T-shirt and boots to walk out into the bedroom. Cool air drifted over his heated flesh, and he dropped his shoes near the bed to sit and yank them on without socks. The shirt clung to his still-damp body when he put it on, but he ignored it, figuring it would dry soon enough. He finger-combed his shoulder-length hair and left the bedroom, walking back down the hall to the stairs.

He stopped at the top when he heard voices. Using his wolf's increased ability to hear, he picked up Nick's and Seth's voices. They were talking about him and what had happened the night before. He almost growled when Nick admitted to leaving him right after, but Seth's soft reprimand stopped him. His eyebrows went up at hearing Seth actually on his side. He'd figured Seth hated him after he'd hurt Nick.

"You shouldn't have left him. I know you weren't in the right place, Nick, but that was a bit on the screwed-up side. His wolf must have been devastated."

"I'm sure he didn't even notice," Nick replied bitterly.

Thayne stifled a snort. What did Nick know? They barely knew one another. How could he possibly know what he did or did not notice?

"Perhaps Thayne didn't, but his wolf sure as hell would. Even I didn't do that to Kasey!"

Seth hadn't wanted Kasey as much as Kasey hadn't wanted Seth… in the beginning. When Kasey finally came to his senses and stopped being a racist bigot about Seth being Caucasian, it had taken him some fancy footwork and smooth talking to convince Seth they were worth fighting for. Once Dad had assured the pack of Seth's origins being of a true wolf rather than a Created One, their pack and Seth's had reached an agreement. Many of the wolves from the Senaka pack were overjoyed at the knowledge that there were other true wolves out there and the potential of actually meeting their destined mate. Some were more wary of the pact between the two packs and hesitant on attending the impending summit. Thayne had heard the grumblings among some of the older wolves, the more set-in-their-ways adults. He hoped, for his father's and Kasey's sake, it would go without a problem. Except bringing two packs together—especially since the other pack consisted of a majority of white men who up until then had been believed could not be true wolves—smelled like disaster to him.

"Can't you feel him, Nick? Sense his emotions? Aren't you experiencing the glimpses into his memories?"

Silence met Seth's questions for several minutes. Thayne waited with breath held to hear what Nick had to say.

"No."

The single word speared straight into Thayne's chest, and he sank onto the steps, trying to understand and come to grips with why that simple word could make him feel as though his heart would implode.

"Nothing? That seems impossible. You're bound to one another now. You should have been able to pick up on his emotions immediately."

Frustration echoed in Nick's voice. "I have no idea, Seth. Maybe he's blocking me out! Or maybe I'm blocking him out subconsciously! How the hell should I know? I just know that I can't pick up on anything from him."

"I'm sorry, Nick. I'm surprised, is all. I thought it was something that just happened when mates claimed one another."

Nick grunted in response.

Before they could talk further, the front door opened and Kasey walked in, spotting him on the stairs. Thayne stood again to hide the fact that he'd been listening and casually continued down to the first floor. Kasey gave him a look but didn't say anything. Thayne did not feel guilty at all for eavesdropping. He should be happy Nick couldn't see his memories or pick up on his emotions. It would make it easier to leave after everything was over. Only it didn't make him happy, and it pissed him off even further that Nick didn't.

"Did you eat yet?" Kasey asked.

Thayne shook his head. "Not hungry."

"You really should eat something," Seth said from behind him.

For the first time since Nick left him lying there after claiming him, Thayne turned and locked eyes with Nick. Nick's eyes were flat, devoid of expression, but he could still sense Nick was anything but unaffected. Anger, distrust, and a hint of pain edged in on Thayne's own emotions, magnifying what he already felt a hundredfold. Thayne waited for Nick to say something, anything, but Nick merely looked away in a dismissive manner. Thayne ground his teeth together and spun on his heel, stalking into the kitchen.

Fucking bastard! Thayne thundered under his breath. He opened a kitchen cabinet door and snatched a glass from the shelf, slamming the door afterward. Right then he would have loved to have a huge snifter of whiskey—several of them. Everything seemed to be falling apart, and he had no idea how to stop it. Now he found himself saddled with a mate he didn't want, a connection he loathed, and about to be ejected from the only home he'd ever known. The glass cracked as he banged it on the counter, and he swore, profusely and loudly.

"You should have just thrown it against the wall," Seth said dryly near his shoulder.

Thayne jumped. He hadn't even known Seth had followed him. He glared at Seth. "What do you want?"

Seth's dark brow arched at his words. "This is my kitchen, but I wanted to see if you were all right."

"As if you care," Thayne sniped.

"Of course I care," Seth huffed. "You're my mate's brother and my best friend's mate. Whether you choose to accept him or not, you're still important to both of them."

Thayne studied Seth for a few moments of silence, searching his face for any fallacy. He found no guile in Seth's bright blue gaze and dropped his challenging stance, his shoulders drooping slightly.

"I'm sorry."

Seth touched his forearm with a gentle hand. "It's okay, Thayne. I may be angry, but that doesn't mean I don't care. I know how hard it must be to have to face losing your family and home."

"How can you possibly know how I feel?" Thayne asked flatly.

"My parents were killed in a car crash before I graduated college. They were all I had except for Nick. I don't know what I would have done without him."

Thayne hadn't known that particular detail, and he felt like a real ass. He ran a tired hand across his face and gave Seth an empathetic look. "I'm sorry. Again."

"Don't be. It was a long time ago, and I have come to terms with it. Besides, I have Kasey now, and that's all that matters." Seth picked up the glass Thayne had cracked and walked it over to the garbage can, stepped on the little lever to open the top, and dropped it inside before allowing the lid to close. "I don't remember the pack that Nick and I belong to since my parents took me away as a child. But I know that they are good people, wolves, from everything Nick has told me about them. If they weren't, Nick would never have remained a part of their pack."

Seth grabbed another glass from the same cabinet, opened the fridge, and removed a carafe of orange juice. He set the glass on the counter beside Thayne and poured the drink, then replaced the carafe in the fridge.

"I used to think the same way you do, Thayne," Seth said, smiling a soft little grin. "Then I met your brother, and he was so stubborn I couldn't help but change my mind. He made me realize that if I let him go, it would be the biggest mistake I ever made. I would have regretted it until the day I died. Perhaps longer, if there is such a thing as reincarnation." He walked toward the doorway, stopping just inside and looked over at Thayne. "Don't let fear keep you from allowing yourself the chance to get to know him. I truly know in my heart if you give him a place in yours, you will never regret it."

Thayne watched Seth leave the kitchen. Everyone kept telling him to give Nick a chance, but no one realized that Nick might not want to give him that option. Or how the idea of becoming a hollow shell as his friend's father had been toward the end sent a shiver of terror down his spine. There were so many reasons to just cut and run, yet he couldn't find the strength to walk out the door and never look back.

He chugged the orange juice and saw the clock had somehow edged its way to half-past ten. Another hour and they would have to leave to arrive on time for his banishment. He mindlessly rinsed the glass out and set it in the drain to dry. The sounds of the others talking in the living room were muffled. He supposed he could probably hear them if he really tried, but he just wanted to shut the world out for the next hour. Exiting the house by the back door, he walked over to the fence and spied Harley trotting around one of the corrals. Kasey must have let the horse into the paddock while he was showering.

The bright burnished-red coat gleamed in the sunlight. Harley's tail flicked as he moved, and his mane flounced against his neck and forehead in the soft breeze. Thayne wondered what it would be like to be so free. No cares except when you'd get your next meal or be allowed out of your stall to run. The idea of turning wolf and never shifting back came to his mind again. He'd had the thought more than once over the last few months since he'd discovered just how badly he'd screwed up. If a wolf remained shifted long enough, they could lose their humanity entirely, remaining a wolf for the rest of their life. Only a handful in their pack throughout the last hundred years had ever been lost to the shift, usually because they were mourning the loss of their mate. He hated to think himself capable of such cowardly thoughts: giving in to his tears or giving in to the desire to become wolf and never be human again. Both were actions of a coward. He'd never wanted to believe he could be that gutless except the pain inside of him grew sharper and more intense with each day's passing since he'd turned Matt.

Thayne grabbed hold of the fence and hoisted himself up onto the top railing, straddling it and leaning his back against the post. Harley neighed, rounded the corral to him, and bumped Thayne's thigh with his head.

"Hey, boy." He slid his hand down Harley's muzzle in greeting. Harley snorted and nipped at Thayne's pant leg. Thayne chuckled. "Sorry, boy, not today."

Since Harley's birth ten years ago, whenever Thayne would visit the farm, he would run as a wolf with Harley, playing tag in a manner of speaking. Thayne never understood the horse's lack of fear around him in his true form, but the horse never shied from him or showed any distrust of him. It humbled him.

He patted Harley's neck affectionately. "Go on, Harley. Go run."

The horse gave him a saddened look and snorted again, turning his back to Thayne and prancing to the other side of the paddock, refusing to look at him. *Much like Nick*, he thought bitterly. He immediately rejected those thoughts. He continued to watch Harley and listen to the familiar sounds of the creatures in the trees around Kasey's ranch. Were there katydids in California? What sounds would he hear? What smells would he have to adjust to? He kind of wished he'd taken the time to google information about Emerald Lake Hills, California. At least then he might know what to expect.

Before Thayne realized it, Kasey stood on the front porch calling his name and waving his hand to get his attention. He figured it must be time to go and swung his leg over the fence, hopping down to the ground. Seth appeared near Kasey's shoulder, and Nick followed behind, carrying a couple of bags. Thayne's back stiffened at the blatant hint that they would be going straight to the airport in less than two hours. Nick placed the one suitcase in the back of the ranch SUV, but the laptop bag remained on his shoulder.

"You ready for this?" Kasey asked Thayne.

A bark of laughter croaked from Thayne, and he eyed Kasey dubiously.

"Right…. Dumb question," Kasey replied flatly.

Kasey climbed into the driver's side with Seth riding shotgun. Nick chose to sit behind Seth and left the seat behind Kasey for him. Thayne braced himself for being so close to Nick and opened the door, stepping in and closing it a bit too hard. Seth tossed a look of exasperation at him, and he merely ignored him. The Explorer started with a smooth purr, and they were on the road to the reservation in seconds. The miles disappeared so fast that they were pulling onto the dirt trail leading to the pack circle before Thayne was able to steel himself. His chest grew tight and he barely managed to keep his emotions in check as the circle and the rest of the pack members came into view. Not really a praying man, he found himself begging his ancestors to give him the strength to get through the next hour without resorting to pleading to remain in the pack.

9

NICK

NICK HADN'T been lying to Seth when he'd told him he couldn't sense anything from Thayne. Even then, sitting right next to him in the backseat, he couldn't pick up on any of the emotions going through Thayne. Thayne's face was stoic, impassive, almost as if made of stone. Somehow, Nick sensed that it was only a facade. Thayne hid whatever he felt behind a solid wall. Maybe that wall was what stood between them and why Nick didn't feel the connection Seth said should have been instantaneous.

Kasey steered the black SUV they were in up a dirt path. Nick wondered about this "circle." They'd made it seem so important. He supposed it was a ritual for them, much like his own Alpha's meetings under the new moon each month. The first thing Nick saw as they pulled into a clearing was a crowd of men and women and several vehicles gathered around a large dirt circle outlined with several jagged rocks, another larger and flatter one in the middle. Huge trees surrounded the clearing, towering over the others and making them appear so small in the grand scheme of things. He wondered if they chose this place for that very reason.

Several of the crowd turned their heads to stare as Kasey stopped the truck on the outskirts of the crowd. Nick shivered at the outright animosity in their stares. Both Seth and Kasey exited the vehicle first, closing their doors and walking toward the center of the circle. Thayne didn't move, his hands balled into fists on his thighs. Nick's wolf whimpered, wanting nothing more than to offer Thayne comfort and gather him into his arms, except he knew Thayne wouldn't want him to, wouldn't accept him. He sat there in the silence with Thayne, listening to the other man breathe.

When the stares and silence became too much, Nick finally asked, "Are we going to get out?"

Thayne didn't answer him right away, and Nick thought maybe he would ignore him. After several moments, Thayne answered, "Yeah. Just… not yet."

Nick accepted his answer and relaxed into the seat, watching the others milling around the circle, whispering to one another. God, even in the Senaka pack there were gossipmongers, ones who loved to spread dirt and lies amongst the others. If the situation weren't so serious, he would have casually tossed the bird at them, but he figured right then it would be extremely crude.

"You don't have to remain here with me," Thayne murmured.

Shrugging, Nick replied, "I don't really have anywhere else to be."

Thayne grunted.

Nick wondered if they would ever hold a normal conversation that didn't come down to snarky or sarcastic comments or ignoring one another. His heart ached at how close yet so far Thayne was to him. He couldn't wait to be home. He'd called Annie that morning and already arranged a flight for them in the late afternoon. As soon as this farcical trial ended, they would be on their way to Casper and the airport. Maybe on the flight they could at least discuss the arrangements like civilized beings, come to some sort of agreement that didn't end with them leaping at one another's throats in the end.

"Let's get this over with," Thayne finally muttered and shoved his door open, stepped down, and strode with purpose toward the almost altar-like stone.

Nick wondered idly if they'd ever sacrificed anyone or anything to their gods on the stone as he followed suit, staying on the fringes of the crowd to witness whatever was going to take place.

Jeremiah stepped up to the stone and raised his hands to quiet the few shifters still talking. "You are all aware of why we are here today. The law of our pack is clear. Any pack member found to have bitten and turned a human is under penalty of exile or death. Even the son of the Alpha is not exempt from this law. We are here to pass judgment on Thayne Jeremiah Whitedove's trespass of the pack law. He has broken the most forbidden rule and so must be punished."

"He should be put to death!" a voice cried out from the pack.

Another voice agreed. Nick found himself growling before he could stop himself, his eyes shifting between lupine and human rapidly. Seth moved to him and touched his arm, shaking his head. Nick quieted but did not allow his guard to drop, his eyes scanning the crowd for any who would so challenge Jeremiah in his ruling.

"Perhaps. But as Alpha of this pack, it has been decreed that he shall be exiled from our pack and our lands. If he ever returns to our territory, he will be put to death." Jeremiah's voice boomed over the crowd.

Several cries went up in protest. "He has brought danger to us! He should not be allowed to live!"

"You've only chosen exile because he's your son!"

Jeremiah let forth a roar so fierce, so angry, that the pack members quieted down immediately. Even Nick felt Jeremiah's power roll over his skin, and he shivered, the fine hairs along his skin standing on end. His wolf cowered in fear.

"You challenge your Alpha's ruling? Is there any brave enough to back up that challenge with a fight?" Jeremiah demanded. No one came forth. "I have decreed Thayne Whitedove's punishment as banishment from our pack. He is dead to all of us. No one is to acknowledge his presence or to speak of him from this day forward." Jeremiah turned his gaze on Thayne, who'd stood staring out amongst the pack with an expressionless face. "You have one hour."

Nick had no idea what would happen now, but Seth whispered into his ear. "The keys are in the truck. Go. Take him and go. Leave the keys under the floor mat, and we'll drive in to pick up the car."

Surprise held him immobile for precious seconds, and then Nick hurried to the Explorer. He opened the door and climbed in, starting the engine. Thayne hadn't moved, and Nick stepped back down from the truck and approached his mate carefully.

"Thayne?" he said in a soft voice.

Thayne looked at him then, and Nick sucked in a breath at the powerful punch to his solar plexus when he saw the utter devastation in the dark brown eyes.

Nick reached out and slowly circled Thayne's wrist with his hand. "We have to go," he whispered.

The agony disappeared beneath a cold shutter, and Thayne shook him off, giving a curt nod and brushing past Nick to stride to the SUV. He got into the passenger seat and sat staring straight ahead. Nick ignored the hurt he felt at Thayne's rejection of his comfort, giving Seth a quick glance before returning to the truck and resuming his place behind the wheel. He turned the truck around and retraced their tracks to the road without a word. Thankfully, he'd made the trip back to Casper a couple of times already, or he would have been lost.

No words or sounds came from Thayne as Nick drove. If it weren't for the slow rise and fall of Thayne's chest, Nick might have worried. He glanced over at Thayne more than once on the ride to the airport but didn't speak. When they reached the parking garage, Nick pulled into a space and shut the Explorer off. He kept his hands wrapped around the wheel, looking out the front window at the other cars.

"Our flight is in a couple of hours."

Thayne thrust open the door and exited the vehicle, slamming the door behind him. Nick followed, eyeing Thayne and wondering what he intended on doing. Instead of walking away from the truck, Thayne stopped in front and stood there, head hanging down and his hands balled into fists. Nick remained at the driver's side door, warily waiting. Sounds of other cars entering and exiting the garage, voices of travelers, and airplanes taking off and landing echoed off the cement walls. The noises grated on Nick's nerves, and he was just about to say something when Thayne suddenly turned toward the SUV and slammed his fists down on the hood, snarling low in his throat. Nick winced at the dents, knowing Kasey was going to be pissed. Thayne did it again and again, bending the hood even farther inward.

The muscles in Thayne's arms bulged with each downward swing. Nick ached for Thayne, wanted to help him, but he didn't even begin to know how, especially with it being unwanted. He simply stood there in silence and watched. He prayed no one would come to investigate the noise or walk by before Thayne could get a hold of himself. Thayne lashed out at the headlights, his fist bashing in the plastic and crushing the bulb inside. Sharp edges sliced open Thayne's knuckles, but he didn't stop, and Nick barely kept the instinct to go to him in check.

Thayne's breath wheezed from his lungs by the time he'd stopped, and the truck looked like it had been hit by a wrecking ball. Nick ran a shaking hand through his hair. He'd send Kasey a check for the damage. When it looked as if Thayne's anger had been exhausted, Nick opened the driver's side and yanked the keys from the ignition, lifted the floor mat, and tossed them under it. He went around to the back, opened the trunk to remove his carry-on, and shut the door again. After retrieving his laptop bag from the backseat, where he'd left it when they'd arrived at the Senaka ceremonial circle, he slapped the auto lock and closed the driver's door.

Dropping his bags next to the truck, Nick crouched down and unzipped his overnight case to pull out a T-shirt. He acted quickly and tore off a strip for Thayne's hand. He didn't speak as he stood again, moved to Thayne's side, and carefully gripped Thayne's wrist. At first Thayne attempted to resist, but it was halfhearted and held no real desire to break free. He settled down and allowed Nick to tend to the cuts on his fist.

"Thankfully we heal fast," Nick muttered. "Not sure how I'd explain this to TSA." Nick released Thayne and stepped away to pick up his bags. "We need to get moving. Still have to get through security, and I need a drink."

"A-fucking-men," Thayne muttered, following Nick through the garage toward the terminals.

If the situation hadn't been so sad, Nick might have laughed, but he just couldn't find the energy or heart to. Thayne didn't speak again until they'd made it through TSA, having discarded the bloodied strip of fabric in a trash can moments before. Light pink scars were the only thing remaining on Thayne's fist by the time they got in line for security.

Nick spotted a bar not far from their gate and gestured to it. "Thank God."

They chose to sit at the counter. Nick ordered his usual whiskey while Thayne went with a shot of bourbon and a couple of beers. If anyone looked at them, they'd think the two of them were a couple of friends waiting on a flight and enjoying a drink together beforehand. He looked morosely down into the dark liquid, swishing it around. Would they ever be those friends? Would he be able to handle being just friends? What if Thayne… no, he couldn't allow his thoughts to go in the direction of his mate with another man. His wolf snarled at the idea, and Nick knew the only chance of them both getting out of this unscathed was to separate themselves from one another. His only other option was to leave his home once Thayne settled in, and considering his entire life, friends, and business were there, it wasn't even a remote possibility.

God, his life had gone from amazing to utter shit in less than six months. What had he done wrong that karma would turn around and bite him in the ass so painfully? Maybe his lies to Seth for so many years had finally caught up to him, maybe it was the dozen or so broken hearts he'd left in his wake throughout his travels, or maybe it was Taggart. Whatever he'd done couldn't have been bad enough to deserve this —a mate who wanted nothing to do with him but needed his help to right a mistake he'd made with another man. He couldn't even be sure how he'd react if he ever did come face-to-face with the Created One in question. His wolf wanted nothing more than to rip it apart. Had Thayne cared for the man who'd become the monster? Seth hadn't been able to give him any details or tell him exactly how Thayne had come to make such an error in judgment. Even Kasey didn't have the story. All they would tell him was that Thayne had bitten the man in the heat of the moment and the condom he'd been wearing had broken. Even hearing those minor facts had brought a red haze to his vision. He'd stopped asking after that and kept his thoughts to himself.

"They called our flight." Thayne's voice interrupted his intense stare into his drink.

Nick looked up at Thayne. "What?"

"They said our flight is boarding."

He'd been so lost in thought, the forty minutes until they could board had passed quickly. Picking up his glass, he tossed back the contents, fished out some cash from his wallet, and dropped it on the counter. He stood, picked up his bags, then walked out of the bar and toward their gate. The sound of Thayne's boots behind him reassured him Thayne followed. They stopped at the gate and gave their tickets to the lady along with their IDs. She scanned their tickets and handed them back, motioning them through the tunnel. He nodded at her in thanks, and they headed down the long walkway.

They entered the plane, and Nick immediately hung a left, moving into first class. Thayne hesitated at the door. Nick glanced back and said, "Our seats are this way."

Thayne seemed tentative in following, but the flight attendant urged him down the aisle to where Nick already had stowed his carry-on overhead and sat in the seat near the window, his laptop bag under the seat in front of him. Nick felt Thayne's heat as Thayne sank into his own seat.

"Never flown first class before?" he asked.

"No. Never had the dough."

Nick shrugged. "I fly too often not to enjoy the comforts of first class."

"Why?"

"Sorry?" Nick queried.

"Why do you fly so much?"

"Work. I have to meet with clients."

Thayne gave a small grunt. Nick wondered if Thayne always did that or if it was only when it came to him. Their conversations were stunted enough. Adding a single sound as a reply didn't help the matter. He didn't elaborate, figuring if Thayne really wanted to know, he could ask.

The flight attendant began her usual demonstration, and Nick turned to look out the window as they pulled away from the terminal and moved into position for their turn to take off.

"What do you do?"

It surprised Nick that Thayne had actually asked. He hadn't expected it. "I design and build websites."

"Like on a computer?"

"No. Pen and paper," Nick replied dryly.

Thayne grunted again, adding a word this time. "Sorry."

"It's fine."

His response killed the stilted conversation, and Thayne stopped asking questions. Once they were in the air, Nick pulled out his laptop to do some work during the short flight. He lost himself in the usual hustle of going over his notes and project specs for his next assignment. Ryan had booked an electronics company looking for a more cutting-edge website. The company had expanded quite a bit in the last year, and their site needed a huge upgrade to continue their growth and momentum. Nick had some pretty good ideas for the site already and had drawn up some basic designs for the owners to review. The mock-ups were almost ready to be sent over for initial approval. Nick added some color on one of the menus and made a few notes in the file to look at later. It wouldn't take long to build once the CEOs gave their approval.

The fasten seat belt light dinging caught Nick's attention, and he realized they were close to landing. He efficiently packed up his laptop, slid it back under the seat, and settled into his seat to enjoy the descent. He'd nearly forgotten Thayne sat next to him—if it weren't for the tantalizing earthy scent assaulting his nose, that is. The captain gave the usual speech of reaching their destination, and the flight attendants made a final check of the cabin for any trash or anyone not belted in properly.

Nick glanced to his right and saw Thayne had polished off three bottles of beer and several packages of peanuts during their flight. "You could have asked for something else to eat if you were hungry."

Thayne shrugged. "Don't have a whole lot of money in the bank and I don't mooch. As it is, I still have to come up with the money to pay you back for the ticket."

Nick waved his hand carelessly. "It's a business expense. Tax write-off. Don't worry about it."

"I'll pay you back."

Thayne's tone clearly showed the man's pride, and Nick bit his tongue. He didn't want to start an argument. Not this early on, anyway. There would be plenty of other things to argue over later most likely. Nick let it go and turned his head to stare out of the window as they descended into John Wayne Airport. They would have to drive the rest of the way to Emerald Lake Hills, but he'd left his car at the airport when he'd flown out to LA so they wouldn't have to rent or wait for a car. The plane bumped lightly and then settled to the ground, taxied through the airport, and stopped at their gate. It took several minutes before they gave the go-ahead to disembark, and Thayne stood immediately, almost pushing to get to the door. Nick sighed, grabbed his laptop and overnight case, and followed at a slower pace.

Thayne made it to the exit way ahead of him, and Nick

wondered if he intended to stop for him to catch up. Maybe now would be when Thayne would bolt. He had no doubt in his mind that Thayne didn't plan to stick around for long. The connection to the Created One had been severed, and the beast could no longer track him. After all, isn't that what he'd wanted in the first place? To be free of the Created One? And now he had what he'd wanted all along.

Thayne did halt just outside the gate, looking around the small airport. Nick reached him and pointed in the direction of the exit to the parking garage. "I left my car here as I didn't expect to be long."

A grunt was his only reply. Nick strode toward the end of the airport, leading the way. He dug his keys out of his laptop bag as he walked. One of the security guards waved at him in greeting, and he smiled, tossing a wave back. A lot of the employees knew him well because he traveled so much and spent a lot of time there waiting for flights. When he brought his hand down, an intense blast of anger rolled over him, and Nick frowned. He glanced at Thayne, but Thayne's face was unreadable. Had that anger been his own, or had he finally picked up something off of Thayne? Why would Thayne be mad? Then again, why would he himself be angry? Deciding to ignore it, he pushed open the glass door to the garage and moved to the stairwell. He hated elevators and avoided them as much as possible.

No words passed between them throughout the entire time it took to reach his black '67 Chevy Impala. Then Thayne asked, "This is yours?"

Nick opened the trunk, tossed his bag in the back along with his laptop, and slammed the trunk. "Yeah."

"Nice."

Pride at Thayne's approval struck him, and he couldn't quite keep the smile off his face. He unlocked the door and climbed in, leaning over to open the passenger side. The car really was his most prized possession.

"It was my grandfather's. We restored it together, and when he passed away, he left it to me in his will."

Thayne ran a strong hand along the dashboard, and Nick followed the movement unconsciously with his eyes, envying his car the almost erotic touch. He gave a wry twist of his lips at his absurd reaction and put the key in the ignition. The car started with a loud roar, and he reversed from the space. He put the car in drive and took the ramp down to the first floor. He winced at the total for the week-long parking, but gave over his credit card to the attendant. Minutes later they were on the highway, heading toward Emerald Lake Hills and his home. Nick suddenly felt exhausted. Not only had he not slept for two days, but the flight, the tension between him and Thayne, and the claiming had drained him. He hoped he could stay awake for the drive.

"Do you mind if I put on some music?" Nick asked.

"Not my car."

Nick gritted his teeth. The situation already sucked, and Thayne's short, antagonistic answers were not helping. Fine. He didn't care if Nick played music, then so be it. He jabbed the power button and chose the second CD in the changer. AC/DC blared from the speakers, and Nick got a certain satisfaction from the tiny wince Thayne gave at his choice. Even though he'd kept most of the car in the original condition and with the original look, his music was the only thing he wouldn't settle. He'd installed a six CD changer with a GPS and built-in Bluetooth almost from the day he'd inherited the car.

"Not your kind of music?" Nick asked.

"Not really."

"What do you like?"

It almost seemed as if Thayne didn't want to answer at first, or maybe he just didn't want to share anything personal between them.

Thayne finally seemed to give in and replied, "CCR, The Doors, John Mellencamp, shit like that."

Nick lifted a brow at him. "Doesn't seem like your style."

Snorting, Thayne challenged, "You don't seem the type to drive a classic car or listen to this crap either."

"Oh? What do I seem like? Speaking of cars and music, that is," Nick said curiously.

"Jazz. Easy listening maybe. BMW or some sporty two-seater."

Nick cackled with laughter, his whole body shaking.

"It's not that funny," Thayne muttered darkly.

When he could finally respond, Nick said, "That's really what you thought? Why?"

"The clothes, the fancy job, flying first class. It reeks of money and high class."

"The night we met, I was wearing jeans and a T-shirt," he pointed out.

Thayne shrugged. "I haven't seen you in anything except slacks and dress shirts this time."

"I was on a business trip!" Nick protested. "I didn't exactly expect to get called to Senaka." He didn't quite know why he felt offended that Thayne believed him to be such a materialistic person, but it stung. "My partner and I built our business from the ground up. It took a lot of work, late nights, and no personal life. Neither of us had rich families growing up, and we sure as hell didn't choose to spend our lives with no responsibility and rolling in the sheets with any warm body that was willing."

"What the fuck is that supposed to mean?" Thayne snarled.

"I just don't think you have any right to judge me," Nick stated in a flat tone, hiding the hurt beneath an emotionless front.

"But you have the right to judge me?"

"That's not what…." Nick abruptly stopped speaking. Maybe he had been… a little. "You're right. I'm sorry." Thayne didn't reply. Nick glanced at him and saw Thayne studying him intently. "What?" he asked, trying not to squirm under the dark brown gaze.

"Nothing." Thayne turned back to looking out the windshield.

The remainder of the drive was made in relative silence, AC/DC filling the void. Nick's tension grew the closer they got to Emerald Lake Hills, and the moment the town limits sign came into view, his hands clenched on the steering wheel. His life was irrevocably changing. His home would no longer be his. He drove through the familiar streets instinctively, making the correct turns and stops without thought. Before he felt ready, his house appeared in the windshield. His heart tripped a beat as he pulled the Impala into the driveway and turned off the car. They both sat there in the quiet. Nick gazed at the one place he'd called home for the last few years but now would, in essence, belong to Thayne, as he wouldn't be staying there.

"This is yours?" Thayne finally broke the silence.

"Yes."

"Nice."

"Thank you."

The exchanged pleasantries seemed odd in light of their situation. Nick pushed himself to get out of the car, and he took the key from the ignition, opened the door, got out, and slammed it behind him. He didn't bother getting his bags from the trunk since he didn't intend to stay long. Thayne followed him up the walk to the front where Nick found a Post-it note from Annie on the door. *"Mail is on the front table, newspapers in the bin by the back door, and I left dinner in the fridge. Heat it at 360 degrees for an hour."* Nick grinned for the first time in a while and unlocked the door, entering it and just assuming Thayne would follow.

Nick snatched up the mail and thumbed through it, striving to ignore the large warm body that brushed past him. He watched Thayne out of the corner of his eye as Thayne looked around his home, taking in the black leather sofa and love seat, beige carpeting, and huge fireplace. The walls were a sterile white broken up by colorful paintings of forests and sunsets. His dining room had a large round cherrywood table with matching chairs and a beautiful chandelier over the center. Even though he lived alone, he'd wanted the room for pack members to visit, and from time to time, Ryan and Cole would come by to play poker with a couple of the others.

He found himself holding his breath, wondering what Thayne thought of his place. Did Thayne think it too sterile? Too neat? Nick wasn't home much to make a mess, and he had a cleaning crew that would come in a couple times a month to clean and dust. The mail dangled in his hands, forgotten as he waited.

An expression flitted over Thayne's face and was gone before Nick could figure it out. "It's nice."

The bland word almost made him wince and convinced him Thayne didn't care for it. Nick tried to act nonchalant, dropping the mail back onto the table. He'd grab it on the way out.

"I'm not here much really. I spend a lot of time either traveling or at the office. Make yourself at home. I'll be out of your hair soon."

"What?" Thayne asked in surprise, turning to finally look at him fully since they'd arrived.

"I'll be staying in the apartment over the office."

"You're not going to be here?"

Nick cocked his head at what sounded like dismay in Thayne's voice. "I thought you'd be happy. You'll have the house to yourself. You don't have to worry about us living together or being around a mate you don't want."

Thayne gave him a dark look. "I'm not going to kick you out of your own place!"

Shrugging, Nick replied, "It's not a big deal. I am barely here as it is. You're free to use whatever you'd like. As I requested back in Senaka, we will keep our arrangements a secret from my pack. Every month, our pack meets to run on the night of the full moon. There's an extra set of keys by the door for the pickup in the garage. It's yours to use."

Thayne held up his hands. "Stop. Just stop. I don't want any of this."

Nick tried to hold on to his patience. He knew Thayne had to be feeling overwhelmed and out of his element. Except he also didn't want any of this. He wanted a loving mate who desired him, who'd searched for their own true mate just as he'd hoped to find his. Anger bit deep, and Nick clenched his hands into fists.

"You made your bed, Thayne. You chose to accept my help, and in doing so, chose to accept what I required from you. I will not attempt to hold you here against your will or try to stop you from leaving, but you owe me at least the courtesy of not insulting me in my own home."

"Wai—"

Nick growled fiercely, his vision vaulting between lupine and human, swift and effortless. "Enough! It is all I can do to hold on to my wolf. I've done all I can to help you, and yet you continue to reject what I offer, to reject me. You may not have wanted a mate, but I did! I have to live with knowing the one true wolf the ancestors have designated as mine doesn't want me in return. A mate who downright despises my existence! But it doesn't give you the right to continue to heap your emotional garbage on me and treat me without respect."

"I wasn't—"

A bark of laughter, sharp and lethal, leapt from Nick's throat. "You've done nothing except that since the moment we got on the plane. Hell, even before that, from the second you found out who I am and every time after."

Thayne's teeth clacked together as he shut his mouth. Thayne didn't even try to say anything further. A car driving by sounded loud in the dead silence. Nick hadn't been lying when he'd said he barely had control of his wolf. Breathing deeply, Nick closed his eyes for several beats of his heart, reining in his fury and pain to a tolerable level.

"Once you've met my Alpha, you are free to leave. I don't care. But know that if you choose to remain here in my home and with my pack, you are agreeing to abide by the one thing I ask of you. We do not even need to speak unless absolutely necessary, but you will act the part on the nights of the full moon and whenever we are called for pack business. I am going to go and put together some things now. I'd prefer nothing more was said."

Nick opened his eyes to find Thayne staring at the floor, his dark hair hiding his expression. He moved around Thayne and walked down the hallway to his room. The beige carpet in the bedroom matched the one in the living room. A large king-size bed with twelve-hundred thread count black sheets dominated most of one side and jutted out into the center of the room. A dark mahogany headboard broke up the monotony of the white wall. Two matching nightstands were placed on either side of the bed, a clock and lamp on one, and a book on the other. None of it really registered. Maybe because he'd seen it every day for the last few years or most likely because of Thayne in the other room.

He went to his closet, grabbed a second dark blue overnight suitcase he had, and set it on the bed, unzipped it, and flipped the top open. He blindly shoved clothing into the case, socks and underwear on top. If he needed anything, he could come back. There were also some things at the apartment for whenever they had a guest stay. Once he'd stuffed the case, he closed the top and crammed it down, struggling to close the zipper. The last thing he grabbed was the book off the nightstand, putting it in the side pocket. He'd been wanting to finish it for a while now. Perhaps he could use it to at least forget about Thayne for a little while.

He lifted the bag off the bed and returned to the living room. Thayne hadn't moved. Nick ignored the twinge of pain in his gut and set the suitcase by the front door. "There's food in the fridge. I had Annie stock everything she could think of, and the extra set of keys is on the peg by the door. If you need me for anything, the number to the office and my cell are on my desk in my office. You can choose whichever room you'd like to sleep in. I don't really care. I'll come by tomorrow and see how you're doing. If anyone shows up from the pack, just tell them I'm at work and to call my cell."

Why did it almost feel like they were divorcing and he was moving out? Nick grumbled internally and shook off the melancholy feeling crowding in on him. He picked up the suitcase and turned to open the door.

He paused with his hand on the knob. "Will you be okay?"

Thayne finally spoke. "I'll be fine."

Nick gave a brisk nod and wrenched open the door, stepped out, and closed it behind him. The latch clicking into place sounded so final, and the noise made his wolf howl mournfully. Nick chastised himself and his inner beast. They knew the score. Thayne didn't want them. Nick walked to the Impala, opened the trunk, and tossed the bag on top of the other, then slammed the lid shut. He glanced at the house once more before sliding into the driver's seat, starting the car, and backing out of the driveway. He needed a good, stiff drink. Now.

10

THAYNE

THAYNE STOOD in the silence after Nick left and wondered what the hell he was doing. He should run. Now. He couldn't stay here. It even felt wrong to be there in Nick's house. His mere presence had caused Nick to up and leave his own damned home. The thoughts and emotions racing through him twisted his gut, fierce and harsh. Remorse and guilt warred with anger and another emotion he found himself unable to identify. Gratitude? Could he possibly be thankful to Nick? But why shouldn't he be? After all, Nick had turned his own life upside down for him. The idea of being beholden to anyone left an acrid taste in his mouth either way. He'd never liked owing anyone anything. And if he remained here after meeting the Alpha, he'd owe even more to Nick.

He thought back to the moment his father announced to their pack that he was exiled and that the pack was to treat him as dead. It had taken the very last ounce of strength he had inside him to remain standing. He'd known it would hurt being banished from his home, but to actually hear it cracked something inside of him. He could no longer get into his truck and drive to see his parents on the spur of the moment. There would be no more impromptu visits to Kasey's ranch. When his brother became Alpha, he wouldn't be there to witness it. If Seth and Kasey ever decided to have kids, he couldn't spoil them rotten. Riding Nahtse through the forest was gone.

Reality finally crashed in around him, and Thayne sucked in a deep breath as if he'd been punched in the stomach. He dropped to his knees, his arms slack at his side. His chest burned, and his lungs ached. It seemed like invisible hands were wrapped around his throat, choking him. His airway closed off, and he swallowed hard, again and again, to work at forcing himself to calm down. The last time he'd felt such crushing panic he'd very nearly passed out. His vision dimmed at the edges. Black spots danced across his eyes, and Thayne closed them, breathing as steadily as possible. He'd blocked out the truth this whole time. Maybe he'd hoped and prayed his father wouldn't actually carry through on the law. Or maybe he'd just thought it a nightmare and he'd wake up any minute. Only… it wasn't a nightmare, and his father had done it. He had no one now. Even Nick didn't want to be around him, and who the hell could blame Nick.

Part of him demanded he run and keep running. The other part of him, the one that carried the last tiny flame of hope he had, urged him to stay, to give in to his wolf. *Claim Nick. Don't run. If you run, you'll be alone forever.* But how could he ever repair the damage he'd done? Did he even want to? When he'd made his vow of never having a mate all those years ago, he'd never realized just how much of a tailspin it would send him on. Mentally and emotionally. He'd always heard about how strong the bond was between mates and how one couldn't deny their mate. He'd always laughed it off and rolled his eyes or stubbornly argued how stupid that sounded. Everyone was in control of their own destiny.

Nothing chose someone for you or the paths your life took. You made the decision on who you wanted in your life. Now Thayne wondered if maybe he'd been wrong.

Since meeting Nick, Thayne had spent more time obsessing over him than he cared to admit. Even in the weeks after, when he'd tried to pound some twink into the ground trying to ignore it, he'd found his mind constantly straying to Nick. It took him time to realize it, but every anonymous hookup had somehow reminded him of Nick: the tall, lean, and muscular body or the neatly cut dirty blond hair or even the deep green eyes that shimmered like emeralds when emotion got the better of him. The moment Thayne saw what he had been doing, he'd been in the midst of a hardcore round of sex, thrusting hard into a random stranger he'd met in a bar, and he'd closed his eyes as he'd neared orgasm only to hear himself cry out Nick's name as he'd come. The twink had pointed it out while they were lying in bed later, dryly asking him if he were hung up on someone. After that, he'd found himself uninterested in the next mindless encounter and the next and the next. None of them were the one person he wanted them to be. It pissed him off. Royally. His anger at himself for being so weak had kept him moving for another couple of months, but the run-in with Matt and the knowledge of the monster he'd created slammed home just how badly he'd screwed up.

Thayne had no idea how long he sat there, a million and one thoughts chasing each other around and around. He waged a war with himself over what to do. The thought of how much of a coward he would be if he ran again won out. He wasn't a coward. Far from it. He couldn't allow anyone, least of all Nick, to believe he was. The only thing he could do right then was to take it one day at a time. Resolved, he stood up and looked at the clock. He started when he saw he'd been sitting on the floor for over three hours. Dusk hung heavy in the sky, and the house was almost dark.

If not for his keen wolf sight, he might have tripped over a table as he moved to turn on the lamp. The soft glow cast shadows over the room, and he noticed several photos in frames on the wall near the couch. He walked closer and found they were of Nick with other men and women. One was of Nick and Seth, but the others were men he'd never seen before. His wolf huffed in jealousy and prowled restlessly beneath the surface. In one picture Nick stood with an attractive dark-haired man, their arms around one another, an office building in the background. An obvious affection shone in their eyes toward one another, and Thayne curled his lip up in a light snarl. How many men had been in and still were in Nick's life?

The other pictures were group shots mostly, and he saw several were of a younger Nick, late teens to early twenties, perhaps. Nick had a huge grin on his face while holding up a diploma of some sort. Thayne had never gone to college. In fact, he'd graduated high school by the skin of his teeth. The only thing he'd ever been good at was working with his hands. His Uncle Mitch had taught him skills in woodworking, and more than once over the years, Thayne had put that to use in his travels. He'd also gotten pretty good at tending bar, waiting tables, and even spent some time as a deckhand on a couple of boats. But seeing the success and drive that Nick had made him feel insecure, lacking. How the hell had the ancestors decided to pair the two of them up? They were nothing alike. They had nothing in common.

Thayne sighed and shoved the feelings of inadequacy away. He had never claimed to be anything more than what he was. If Nick were disappointed, too bad. His stomach rumbled, distracting him from the pictures and his thoughts. He remembered Nick saying something about food in the fridge, and he decided to grab something to eat before exploring his new home. Entering the hallway, he followed it until he found the kitchen and stopped dead, shaking his head. Stainless steel appliances and beautiful hardwood cabinets, a huge island counter with pots and pans hanging over it on a rack, and a small nook near the window with a table and chairs matching the cabinets cemented the knowledge of how much money his mate actually had. It made him uncomfortable and he fidgeted a few moments in the doorway.

Laughing at himself, he stepped inside, flicked on the light, walked to the fridge, and opened the door. It was stocked to the max. Fresh vegetables, milk, eggs, everything you could possibly want. A large glass baking dish sat on the middle shelf with a note on top of the foil, and Thayne pulled it out. The note was in feminine handwriting with instructions on how to cook it. He closed the door, set the dish on the counter, and removed the foil. His mouth watered immediately. The smell of fresh sauce, melted cheese, and spices wafted through the air. His stomach gurgled again, reminding him that he hadn't eaten in almost two days. He turned on the oven to let it preheat. The realization that this had been meant for Nick made him feel even guiltier that he'd run the man out of his own home. He'd done nothing but fuck up since the day he'd met Nick, yet Nick had done everything to help him. Even given up his home.

Thayne tightened his grip on the spatula he'd grabbed out of the drawer next to the stove and took a deep breath. He needed to make a plan, something he had never been too good at. He'd always done things off the cuff, without a thought. Spur of the moment, really. But now… he had to actually think out what he wanted to do. He knew he was being selfish to stay, yet the idea of leaving left a sour taste in his mouth. He still didn't want to have a mate. Did he? *Oh gods*. He'd always been so sure of everything. A mate tied you down. They made you crazy with jealousy and emotion. They stole your very identity and left you without knowing who you are. Didn't they? But Kasey and Seth… they seemed so happy and nothing had changed for either of them. Kasey was still sheriff and would still be Alpha. Seth still worked as a veterinarian for the town and the pack. Neither of them held each other back from their dreams. Was that really what being mates could be like? All he could remember was the darkness that ate away at Paul, the way his best friend's father looked at the very end when his wife finally gave up the fight and passed away.

The beep of the oven indicating the preheat had finished disturbed him from his thoughts. He put the glass dish on the middle rack inside the stove, closing the door after. He set the timer and started washing up the container, enjoying the calming and familiar chore. It made him smile in memory of a particular dive he'd worked in. Though the place had been rundown and obviously needed a serious overhaul, he'd loved working there. The cook and owner had been a former marine who'd bought the diner once he'd left the service twenty years before. Nothing beat the food either. Every truck driver for miles around would stop on their way through the area just to have a double-stacked burger with fries and a piece of the diner's famous blueberry pie. Thayne had met some great people and even thought about staying for a while, except the owner had a heart attack and passed away. The marine's son inherited it and shut it down, selling the land and building to some developers. Everyone mourned the loss of a great man and the home-style diner.

After that, Thayne hadn't remained in one town or state long enough to grow attachments. He'd figured it wasn't worth it. Until he'd met Matt, he'd always been about where to jaunt off to next. *And look how that turned out,* he thought bitterly, tossing the sponge into the sink and slamming the container into the drying rack. Matt was not going to become the doctor he'd wanted to. No one would ever be able to come to love the kindness Thayne had been so enamored with. How many people had Matt hurt since the monster inside of him had taken over? How much blood was on Thayne's hands already, and would there be more?

No one had spotted Matt again after the attack on Bryan Crowsfeet. Bryan would survive, thankfully. Matt could possibly have learned how to hide himself, but the pack had been on high alert after the first incident and would have spotted him immediately. Where had Matt disappeared to? Had the Created One run off when Nick claimed him? Thayne no longer felt as if he had to keep looking over his shoulder now that they were miles from the Senaka pack territory, and they'd left by air instead of ground. Matt wouldn't be able to follow him. The bond between them was broken.

He wiped his hands on a towel nearby before he returned to the fridge for a drink. Two cases of beer sat on the bottom shelf, and he thanked whatever beautiful person had stocked Nick's kitchen. From the note on the front door, the lasagna, and the fact that a lot of the vegetables and fruits were fresh instead of on their last legs, he'd gathered someone had come in during the morning. He snagged two beers and shut the door with one hip. He set a bottle down on the counter and twisted the other one open, taking a large swill the second he could. The sharp tang caressed his taste buds, and he sighed in pleasure, leaning his back against the cold metal of the refrigerator.

He finally took a few moments to appreciate the beauty of the shiny carved-wood cabinets around him. They were exquisitely designed from what he could tell. No notches in the wood or cracks along the grain. Whoever had done it knew what they were doing. He ran his free hand along the molding on the drawer nearest to him. If he was stuck here, maybe he could start a woodworking business or something. His hand stilled as he realized he'd had his first thought of permanence in a long time. The only constant he'd had in his day-to-day life were his truck, his clothes, and his love of the next warm body willing to allow him a few hours of forgetfulness. His truck was back in Senaka. He'd asked Kasey to find a way to get it to him. His clothes were in his parents' house. His mother had told him she would ship them to him. And there were no warm willing bodies around... except he didn't want just anyone. His breath caught as he halted his train of thought. *Damn it*. What the hell was he thinking?

The oven timer dinging stole him from the wayward track his mind had started down. He drained the beer in a few swallows and set the empty bottle on the counter next to the full one before grabbing a couple of pot holders out of a drawer near the stove. The smell of sauce and cheese flooded the kitchen and his senses the moment he opened the oven. His mouth salivated, and his stomach cramped with hunger pains. He was almost tempted to eat it right out of the dish, but figured it wouldn't be right since Nick would most likely want some of it when he came to the house. *If* he came to the house. Thayne shoved aside his thoughts of Nick and opened a few overhead cabinets until he located the plates. He took one out, cut a very large piece of the lasagna, and placed it on his plate.

It took another couple of seconds to find the forks. He chose to sit at the small nook in the corner of the kitchen and dug in, cooling the food off with a few breaths and then shoving the bite into his mouth. The quiet in the house disturbed him more than he cared to admit. In his time on the road, he'd either been in a noisy club or some seedy motel where there were always fights or sex in another room, or cars driving by. Nick's house was nestled in a small community where the closest neighbor had to be a good several hundred yards away, maybe more. There were no sounds except the scraping of the silverware on the plate or his chewing. Gods, he'd never seen how lonely his life actually was until then. Or maybe it was because he'd never slowed down long enough to look at the way he lived.

Thayne berated himself. When the hell had he gotten so melancholy and down on himself? What the fuck had this whole bonding thing done to him? He'd always been certain that he was living his life the way he wanted to: free and unfettered. Now he found himself questioning everything about his life and his future! The constant yo-yo of his own emotions and thoughts were giving him a headache. A drum thumped behind his temples, and he shoveled in the rest of the meal on his plate, barely tasting it now. Once he'd finished, he covered the dish of lasagna, put it in the fridge, placed his dishes in the sink, and grabbed two more beers. His second bottle sat empty on the small table. He needed a break from the merry-go-round of shit in his brain.

By the time the self-doubt about his life had been drowned out, he'd finished off the two cases of beer and rooted out a bottle of fine whiskey, one of the most expensive, smoothest brands he'd ever had the absolute pleasure to enjoy. It took a lot to get a shifter drunk. Their metabolism was extremely fast, causing a lot of the alcohol to burn off so quick they either had to consume a ton of beer or extreme amounts of hard liquor. When he reached the bottom of the bottle, he was feeling pretty good. Warmth flowed through his veins, and his entire body felt like it was floating. He managed to stand but stumbled and hit the wall, knocking a picture off. Swearing, he picked it up and found Nick's green eyes staring up at him.

"Why did you have to come to Senaka?" he snarled, his

fingers tightening on the photograph. "Why couldn't you have been just another human who needed to get off?"

He flung the empty bottle at the fireplace, smirking when it crashed into the grate and shattered into a million pieces. He looked back at the photo of the person, the wolf, who'd been haunting him for months.

"You were just supposed to be another easy lay!" he shouted at it, smashing his fist into the picture.

The glass front cracked, sending fine lines across the face of Nick and the other man in the picture with him. Thayne stared blankly at the pattern it made for a moment. He dropped the frame on the ground and stumbled down the hallway to the nearest bedroom. Beige carpeting and a dark set of sheets were the only things that registered as Thayne slumped down face-first onto the soft mattress. He sighed at the cool sheets on his heated skin.

"You weren't supposed to be my mate," he muttered just before passing out.

A BANGING noise woke Thayne, and he groaned, pulling a pillow over his head in agony. His brain felt a hundred times bigger than his skull, and the light from the window stabbed into his eyes like daggers. Who the hell was making such a racket? The banging hadn't stopped, and he was pretty certain the sound wasn't in his head. Snarling in frustration, he threw the pillow across the room and dragged himself out of the bed.

"I'm coming," he barked fiercely while staggering down the hallway, grabbing at the wall to steady himself.

Whoever the hell was at the door so damn early in the morning had better have a damn good excuse! Thayne glanced at the clock on the cable box in the living room and blinked twice in surprise. Early? Holy shit, how long had he been sleeping? The clock read almost one in the afternoon.

"Nick! I know you're in there. I can hear you! Open the damn door already!" a voice shouted through the door.

Thayne lifted a brow and managed the rest of the walk to the front door. He wrenched it open, glowering at the man standing there. A good-looking guy in his mid to late twenties stood on the front step. Thayne towered over the stranger by a good six inches and outweighed him in muscles by probably fifty pounds. Blond hair feathered around delicate features. Twinkling hazel eyes widened in surprise.

"Oh…. Sorry, bro. Uh…. Is Nick here?"

"You're asking now?" Thayne snapped. "Who the hell are you?"

The stranger stepped back slightly, holding his hands up in a simple gesture. "I'm Carter. Carter Wilkes. Nick's my cousin. Is he here?"

"Obviously not," Thayne replied dryly, slumping against the doorjamb. "He's at his office I think."

"Um…." Carter hesitated.

Thayne glowered at him again, and Carter swallowed audibly. "What?"

"Who are you?"

"No one." Thayne promptly shut the door in Carter's face.

He turned and went back to the bedroom he'd woken up in. He needed to take a piss, and he'd have to see if Nick had any clothing he could borrow because he needed a shower bad. They weren't exactly the same size, but he supposed Nick had to at least have some sweatpants and a T-shirt that would fit. Stopping in the middle of the bedroom, he realized it had to be Nick's. Somehow he'd ended up crashing in the same bed Nick slept in. Damn his wolf.

He made a beeline for the bathroom, tearing open his jeans in a rush. His bladder wouldn't hold it much longer. A long sigh of relief left him as the stream hit the water. It took a few seconds for his surroundings to sink in. *Jesus!* The bathroom was even bigger than the bedroom! He caught sight of a Jacuzzi tub in the mirror and a huge shower stall that took up half of one wall, at least ten feet across. You could easily fit eight to ten people in there. He finished taking a leak and decided to do the shower thing rather than the Jacuzzi, but he'd sure as hell use the tub at some point in the very near future.

The shower handles were under the double heads jutting out from the wall. Thayne turned on the jets to heat up the water and returned to the bedroom where he went over to the second door in the room, which he assumed was the closet. He opened the doors and found a huge walk-in with several racks of business suits and assorted casual things like jeans. A couple of dressers lined one wall. Snorting, he took one of the T-shirts, and after opening a few of the drawers, he found several pairs of sweatpants and shorts. He took one of the pants and closed the drawer. *The man sure has a ton of clothes*, he mused while closing the closet and tossing the clothing on the bed nearby.

The bathroom had begun to fog up by the time he got back, and steam clouded the edges of the mirrors. He stripped off his shirt and jeans. Sometime in the night, he must have kicked off his boots. He didn't really remember too much, actually. When he turned toward the shower, he had a flash of Nick beneath the sprays, water cascading over his body, glistening in the overhead lights. Thayne ground his teeth together in agitation at the reaction of his own flesh. He wrenched open the shower door, stepped in, and practically slammed it closed.

A sound of pleasure escaped him when the hot water splashed against his skin. It felt like forever since he'd taken a hot shower and been able to take the time to enjoy it. He grabbed the bar of soap on a nearby shelf and started lathering his chest, only to be hit with the scent that clung to Nick's skin. His cock hardened even further, and Thayne growled at his reaction. He closed his eyes and attempted to ignore the way the smell sent lust burning straight to his groin, his balls growing heavy with the need for release. Before he could stop them, images of the night with Nick in the alley behind the bar in Senaka flashed through his mind: the broken sound of Nick begging for him to fuck him, his lips wrapped around Nick's hard length, and his own cock plunging in and out of Nick's hot, willing hole. Thayne snarled and wrapped a slick hand around his dick, squeezing the base and shaft, trying to stem his lust. The squeezing turned into tugging and then full-on masturbation. A hiss broke free when his thumb slid over the sensitive head, and he found he couldn't stop as he stroked himself to the memory of Nick bent over against the brick wall of the bar.

Thayne leaned one arm on the shower tile and rested his forehead on it, his eyes closing as he thought back to the moment he'd slid deep inside the tight, grasping channel. His fingers moved faster and faster up and down his cock while his breathing deepened with pleasure. He remembered the eager thrust of Nick's hips back onto him and the urgent desire in Nick's lusty cries. His memories jumped to the night at Kasey's home and the way Nick had felt inside of him. He'd never known submitting to someone could feel so fucking good. There had only been one other time he'd tried it, and he'd hated it, swore he'd never do it again, but Nick…. Oh gods, the sharp plunges of Nick's hard length into him had touched him in places he couldn't have imagined.

He ground his teeth together, his hand a blur on his shaft. The sound of wet skin sluicing over wet skin echoed off the tiled walls around him, stoking his lust even higher. It reminded him of their hips colliding together each time. He almost hated himself for being so turned on at the thought of Nick dominating him. At that very moment, he would give anything to feel Nick's hard body behind him, to hear Nick's throaty cries and grunts. Gods forgive him, but Thayne wanted to be held down and pounded into the mattress just as he'd done to so many twinks in anonymous bars and motels. He wanted Nick's teeth on his throat and Nick's nails digging into his hips as Nick annihilated him and left him a shuddering and shattered mess again.

Thayne hated himself even more as the idea caused his legs to tremble. He bit his lip and squeezed his eyes closed as he felt the familiar tingle in his sac and the heat racing through his groin. Electricity rippled under his skin as he started to come, a loud cry of Nick's name ripped from deep inside. Unable to keep himself upright, he slid to his knees, his body shaking with each spurt of salty fluid mixing with the water and swirling down the drain. He sat there, gasping, his right hand still wrapped around his cock and his other braced on the floor to keep from going face-first into the tiled wall. His muscles burned from the strain as he struggled to recover.

It was only when he could finally lift his head that he blurted out loud, "What the fuck am I going to do now?"

He'd tried fighting it, running from it, ignoring it, but now the knowledge that none of the lengths he'd gone to had changed anything sent sheer panic rushing straight to his belly. He wanted Nick, his mate. Admitting it to himself caused the panic to grow higher, and he wildly pushed himself to his feet and shut off the water. He blindly shoved open the door, grabbed a towel from the rack near the shower, and stepped out, uncaring that water dripped everywhere as he walked into the bedroom while rubbing briskly at his hair. Wanting Nick... what the hell had happened to him?

The day he'd made the pact with his friend Dakota, the day before Dakota's grandmother had come to take him back to Illinois, it had been raining outside, just like the day Dakota's parents had been buried. Thayne had always scoffed at the movies about how it was always raining at a funeral, but maybe the movies weren't a lie. Dakota believed the ancestors were crying when they'd laid Paul and Loretta Blackfoot to rest in the ground. They'd both been in the tree house behind the Blackfoot home when they'd made their vow between them.

*D*RIZZLE FELL *past the window of the small house, the air damp and earthy. Thayne had always loved the smells stirred up by the rain. Today it made him sad and depressed. He was losing the best friend he'd ever had and would ever have. They would write each other, and of course, his parents said Dakota could visit whenever he wanted, but it wouldn't be the same. They spent practically every waking minute with each other. Now he would have to ride the bus to school alone, go to baseball practice alone, and he wouldn't be able to laugh and joke around with his best friend. Everything was changing.*

For the three days since finding his father, Dakota had spoken very little, and when he had, it was only to Thayne. He'd asked Thayne to meet him at the tree house that afternoon because he wanted to talk to him about something. When Thayne arrived, he'd found Dakota sitting there with the knife on his lap, his eyes red-rimmed. At first Thayne thought Dakota was about to do something stupid.

"What the fuck, D?" he demanded.

Dakota managed a broken half smile. "It's not what you think, Thay."

Only Dakota had ever been able to call him Thay without getting threatened with a beating. Thayne gave Dakota a skeptical look and sank down to the floor, sitting cross-legged. "Then what is it?"

"I want us to make a pact. One we'll never break."

Raising an eyebrow, Thayne tilted his head in curiosity.

"I want us to both swear to each other that we'll never let someone make us as weak as my father was. That we'll always be strong against the world."

"What do you mean?" Thayne asked in surprise.

Dakota looked down at the knife on his leg. "My father wasn't strong enough to live without my mother. I never want us to be so powerless that we can't survive if someone leaves us. The only way we can do that is to refuse to accept our mates if we ever find them or they ever find us."

Thayne started, shocked. Since childhood they'd been told the importance of finding their mate and how rare it was to find them, so if they ever did, they should hold on and never let go. "But—"

"What they tell us is bullshit, Thay!" Dakota shouted, his fingers wrapping around the handle of the knife. "How it's such a precious thing to meet our mates and how they make us stronger! They don't. They make us fragile, breakable. I never want to be that. I never want to take my own life and leave my kids alone! What he did wasn't fair, and I will never do that to anyone."

Tears welled up again in Dakota's eyes, and he dashed them away angrily with the back of his palm, the knife close to his face. Thayne reached out and gently pried the sharp object out of Dakota's fingers. He set it on the ground next to them and pulled Dakota into a hard hug.

"Okay, D. It's okay," he shushed as Dakota started sobbing, truly letting go of some of the pain inside his heart for the first time since watching his parents put in the ground. Thayne ran his fingers through the black hair at the nape of Dakota's neck. He would do anything to take away the pain his friend was going through. After Dakota's cries had calmed down to merely hiccups and shuddering sighs, Thayne said, "I'll make the pact, D."

Dakota sat back and scrubbed at his eyes in frustration. He wiped his nose on the hem of his shirt and picked up the knife, still sniffling and trying to get a hold of himself. He had a solemn look when he began to speak.

"From this day on, we both swear to never claim another or to allow another to claim us as mates," Dakota vowed as he sliced his palm open and held the knife to Thayne, who also made a small cut in the center of his palm. They clasped hands and nodded in solidarity.

"We can never break our pact," Dakota said solemnly. "Never allow another to break us."

Thayne nodded again. "Ever."

HE COULDN'T break the promise he'd made to Dakota. Yet his stomach churned when he thought about letting go of Nick. Thayne snatched the sweatpants off the bed and pulled them on roughly. They were tight because his hips were wider than Nick's and his thighs were also more muscular. The shirt clung to him like a second skin, the dampness still on his body not helping. He needed his own stuff, and fast. He glanced at the clock and found it was almost two in the afternoon now. Maybe he could find a store in town to get some things until his mom sent his belongings through the mail.

Thayne returned to the bathroom, dug out a comb from one of the counter drawers, and ran it through his shoulder-length hair briefly. He needed something to tie it back with, as his usual rubber band seemed to have disappeared. He halted in the bedroom long enough to stuff his feet into his boots and grab his wallet, uncaring of the incongruous picture he made at the moment. The door to Nick's office stood open, and Thayne was pretty certain there had to be something he could use for his hair in the desk.

He pushed the door open and strode to the desk. Apparently he'd been too drunk to remember looking into the room. The walls were a light green with a light brown trim around the windows. A large dark brown leather couch sat against one wall, and a similar dark wood desk faced out toward the room. Three computer monitors and a keyboard rested on top, and a sleek padded black chair was pushed under the desk. The office was so different from the rest of the house, it could only mean Nick had taken the time to choose the decor for the room. Thayne set down his wallet, opened the top drawer, and stopped dead. His mouth parted slightly on a swift intake of breath. His own face stared up at him, a light grin playing on the corner of his lips. Thayne couldn't even remember when the photo was taken, but he recognized the barn in the background as Kasey's. Why did Nick have this? Where had he gotten the picture?

Instead of dwelling on the photo, Thayne picked up a rubber band and slammed the drawer shut. He tied his hair back and picked up his wallet again, leaving the office as he found it. He found the keys Nick had indicated the night before and stomped out of the house. It irked him to have to use Nick's possessions already, but he damned sure wouldn't be beholden to anyone. He'd look for work and pay Nick back as soon as possible. He only had a couple hundred bucks in his bank account, which would be just enough to get him some clothes and deodorant until his things arrived.

He locked the front door, walked over to the garage, and opened it to reveal a gorgeous dark blue F-150 pickup truck inside. Whistling beneath his breath, he clicked the unlock button on the keys and climbed inside the driver's seat. The inside of the truck was even more beautiful: black leather interior, new-car smell, state-of-the-art GPS, and stereo system. Nick definitely liked his toys! Thayne started the truck and watched as the dashboard lit up. *Full tank of gas and an open road,* his mind teased. *Shut up,* he snapped. He'd never stolen anything in his life, and he sure as hell wouldn't start with Nick's truck. Not like he hadn't already done enough to hurt Nick. Adding theft to it would only be the icing on the cake.

He put the truck in reverse and backed out of the garage, hitting the automatic garage door opener to close it behind him once the truck was clear. He stopped at the end of the driveway and stared at the attractive little house. Six months ago he'd never dreamed of being in this situation. He'd always imagined he'd be running in the opposite direction if he ever came across his mate. Only now he found himself wishing he'd never made that pact with Dakota, despite how hard his human side fought against wanting that very thing. Complicated had never been to his taste, and this shit was getting more and more problematic by the day.

1 1

NICK

NICK ARRIVED at the office, exhausted in every way possible. He dragged the two carry-on bags out of the trunk, slung his laptop bag over his shoulder, then wheeled the luggage into the building and straight to the elevator. If he'd had the energy, he would have taken the stairs, since he hated being boxed in, but he wouldn't make it up two flights of steps right then. He tossed a quick wave at the receptionist, who smiled at him and waved back just as the doors closed.

When he entered the waiting area outside of his and Ryan's offices, Annie looked up at him in surprise. "Nick! I didn't expect you back yet."

"I came straight from the house after stopping off to...." Nick didn't finish.

"I see. Well, Ryan is in his office. He said you should come in and see him as soon as you get in. Here are your messages." She handed him several little notes. "I put your letters on your desk. Mr. Gregorias from Shrine Technologies called. He sounded a little upset because you weren't available. I did recommend he e-mail you."

"It's okay, Annie. I'll take care of it. Thank you," Nick said tiredly. He continued into his office and set the bags by his desk before promptly turning around and going out to Ryan's office.

Ryan sat leaning back in his chair, phone to his ear, doodling on a paper. Nick almost cracked a smile at the familiar sight. He sank down onto the seat in front of Ryan's desk and listened without really hearing his friend talking to a client. Nick tilted his head back and closed his eyes. The sound of the phone clacking into its cradle jolted him, and he sat up, rubbing his eyes between thumb and forefinger.

"Sorry," Ryan apologized sympathetically. "I take it the trip didn't go well?"

"I think that's the understatement of the year, Ry."

"You want to talk about it?"

"Not really. Annie said you needed to talk to me?"

Ryan sighed and nodded. "Something happened while you were gone. Cole found his mate."

Nick sat up straighter in his chair, mouth open in surprise. "What? Who? Where?"

"Cole was in town at the hardware store when he caught the scent. From what I understand of the story, the guy took off before Cole could stop him or say more than one word to him."

"Wait… guy?" Nick asked in shock.

Ryan laughed. "Yeah. Surprise, right? To everyone. Including Elijah. Let's just say Senior Ferris is not very happy that Junior Ferris is not going to be carrying on the family line. But Cole said his mate was very skittish, almost as if someone were hunting him. And the even bigger bombshell is that the guy might actually be a human."

"Sweet Jesus," Nick breathed and ran a hand through his hair. The whole situation must have set the pack on their asses. A human and a male for the future Alpha's mate? "Did you guys find him?"

"No. That's the shitty part. The guy is like a ghost. He disappeared so fast that Cole could barely get a scent on him. He followed his mate partway out of town and then lost the trail. The only thing he could find out from the others in town was that the guy came in on a bus from San Francisco and he seemed to be in his early twenties, maybe."

Nick swore and gave a sardonic laugh. "Sounds like Cole has hit the same roadblock I have."

"Don't you mean cockblock?" Ryan joked.

Nick gave him a deadpan stare and flipped him off.

Ryan held up his hands in placation. "Sorry, sorry! I thought it was funny. Anyway, Cole wants us to try and find the guy."

"With what? A Cracker Jack decoder ring?" Nick exclaimed. "There's hardly enough information to go on. He's over twenty, and he came in on a bus? Does whoever said he got off the bus have any clue on which bus it was? There are several bus lines that run through here and several times a day. That's searching for a needle in a haystack, Ry!"

"I know that. Cole knows that. He wants us to try, Nick. Wouldn't you want to try if it were your mate?"

Nick ground to a halt and gave Ryan a sad look. "I don't know anymore."

"Shit. I'm sorry, Nick. I didn't think before I said that." Ryan sighed. "I'm guessing things didn't go so well after you claimed him. I would give anything to change that for you. I really would. Is he at the house?"

"Yeah. He practically revolted at the idea of even owing me anything. God, I knew that this would be hard, but I had no fucking idea how hard it would be." Nick stood and started pacing, running his hands through his hair every once in a while. "I mean, he argues about everything. And we aren't even on the ground five minutes before I get the sense he wants to take off. Like I have a disease or something. And the most screwed up part is that I can't feel him, Ry. I can't sense him like others have told me they can tell what their mates are feeling, see their memories. Seth told me that he could see Kasey's thoughts pretty quickly after the mating. But me…. I can't even tell if Thayne has a hangnail!" Nick was shouting by the time he finished, and his chest heaved with his agitation and confusion.

Ryan got up and came around to him, stopping Nick in his tracks with both hands on his shoulders. "Calm down. The connection between mates only happens when both mates are willing, Nick. You know this. If he isn't willing to open himself to you, then you won't be able to reach him. When he comes to accept you is when the gate will open."

"When?" Nick questioned bitterly. "If."

Ryan pulled him into a tight hug. "When, Nick. When. It is literally impossible for a wolf to reject their mate forever. He will come around."

"He's so adamant," Nick murmured, squeezing Ryan briefly, and then he stepped back. "Enough about him. I need to think of something else. So… who gave Cole the information about the bus?"

"Wheaton Little. He saw Cole's mate get off the bus, so I'm pretty sure he knows which bus line and what time. I already called Wheaton, but he didn't have time to talk. He's going to give me a call back later this afternoon."

"And how are we going to get a hold of the information from the bus line? They aren't going to just hand it to us."

Ryan chuckled and leaned one hip against his desk. "You know I have a lot of friends, Nick. Including one on the force. He's just waiting to get the information from me so he can request the list of passengers."

Nick grunted. Ryan did have a lot of friends in a lot of

places. Plus there were several pack members on the police force, but it would take more than the word of a cop to get the list of passengers from the bus company.

"Elijah wants to call a pack meeting next week to introduce your mate, Nick," Ryan said, disturbing Nick from his thoughts.

"Why?"

Ryan shrugged. "Because there's an unknown wolf in the territory for one, knucklehead. And because he believes if the pack accepts your mate, Thayne may be more willing to stick around. Give you a chance to win him over."

Nick snorted without humor. "Elijah has no idea how stubborn and pigheaded Thayne is. He could stick around for a decade, and we'd still be in the same situation."

"So you're really going through with staying in the apartment and giving him your house?"

"What choice do I have? It's not like I can stay there with him." Nick looked at his hands. He'd unconsciously balled them into fists. "I've never really understood how a wolf can end their life when they lose their mate, but I am beginning to see just how hard it is."

"Are you in love with him?"

"How can I be? I've barely exchanged a handful of words with him, and we barely know one another. I know that my wolf wants him because of the mate bond. But love? I don't know if I could love him, Ry. He's not what I envisioned at all while wondering what my true mate would be like. Besides, even in the human world, love isn't instantaneous."

"You know the rest of the pack isn't going to understand what's happening with you two."

"That's why the rest of the pack isn't going to know," Nick stated in a no-arguments tone. "You and Elijah and Cole are the only ones who know."

Ryan gave him an incredulous look. "What are you going

to do on the night of the full moon when we run together as a pack? Are you planning on going alone? Or skipping it all together? You really don't think that's not going to make them wonder, do you?"

Nick massaged his temples, a headache beginning to pound through his skull. "Our agreement when I went through with the claiming was that we would act as a mated pair when in the presence of our pack."

Skepticism and disbelief raced across Ryan's face. "You realize that's going to put you into close quarters with him. Are you going to be able to handle it?"

"I'm not weak, Ry," Nick snapped. "I'll deal with it. It's only for a couple hours three nights a month and whenever there's pack meetings. I doubt I'll fall apart the instant we're around one another."

Ryan moved away from the desk and returned to Nick's side. He put his hand on Nick's shoulder. "I wasn't saying you were weak, Nick, but even the strongest person can only hold on to so much weight before they crack. You are one of the kindest people I know, and it's one of the reasons we're best friends and business partners. Your heart is so big that sometimes you forget to take care of yourself. I worry you'll continually put his needs before your own and end up running yourself into the ground."

Nick heaved a tired sigh and squeezed Ryan's hand briefly. "I'll be fine. I know my limits."

"Do you? Sometimes I wonder, because these past few months since you came back from Senaka, I've seen you run yourself into exhaustion and end up in the hospital. Even us wolves get sick. We aren't impervious to everything."

"Just leave it alone, Ryan. I can take care of myself." Nick snapped, agitated and frustrated. "I'm going to take my bags up to the apartment and get settled in. Do you think you can handle Mr. Gregorias? I need to get some sleep."

Ryan studied him for a silent moment and then nodded. "I'll give him a call. Smooth things over. You get some rest, and I'll see you in the morning."

"I—"

Ryan interrupted him. "You're dead on your feet, Nick. If you set foot back in the office or I see you on the chat system working, I'm going to tie you to the bed so you're forced to get some sleep. I'll have Annie send up something for you to eat."

Nick huffed but agreed and left Ryan's office. He grabbed his bags from his own and then headed to the elevator again. The apartment was on the third floor at the back of the building. It was quiet and discreet, allowing any of their visitors the comforts of home. The entryway had a small table just inside where he set his keys and then pulled his luggage down the small hallway to the living area. The walls were a calming light blue with beige trim, and a matching couch and love seat surrounded the black glass coffee table in front of the fireplace. A forty-seven inch flat-panel television was mounted on the wall above the mantel. A nicely laid-out kitchen with stainless steel appliances and light beige countertops and cabinets complemented the living area, a bar separating the two.

The best part of the apartment, in Nick's opinion, was the view. Large french doors opened out onto a balcony that overlooked the town and trees surrounding the area. It took his breath away every time he stepped out. He set his luggage and laptop down near the couch and walked to the doors, unlocked them, and threw them open wide. He breathed in deeply and closed his eyes, savoring the fresh air and the slightest hint of salt in the air. His wolf whined inside his head, and Nick sighed, wishing things were different and knowing they couldn't be.

"I'm sorry, bud," he murmured, mentally reaching out to his animal counterpart. "I really am."

His wolf whined again but quieted, settling down yet still restless. Sheer exhaustion washed over Nick, and it took all the strength he had to go back inside.

He left the doors open when he returned to the living area, allowing the soft breeze to drift through the condo. He slumped onto the couch and used his arm to cover his eyes. The next thing he knew, he heard dishes being placed on the glass coffee table and the rustle of plastic bags. The smell of classic Italian spices and sauce wafted through the air, stinging his nose. Nick couldn't discern how long he'd been out, but the sun hung low in the sky when he lowered his arm and sat up.

Annie was bent over, setting up a makeshift dining table in front of him. "Good, you're awake," she chirped and smiled. "I ordered from your favorite Italian place. Lasagna, garlic bread, and a side salad. Ryan said if you don't eat all of it, he's going to force you to take another day off tomorrow."

Nick winced. "I'll eat!"

Laughing, Annie handed him a plate loaded with food. Nick accepted it along with a fork and started eating. Annie patted his arm but didn't linger. She grabbed his small suitcases along with his laptop bag and carried them toward the bedroom.

"I can do that," Nick protested around a mouthful of salad.

"No worries, Nick. I can handle it. You look like you're about to drop. Just eat." She smiled and disappeared into the bedroom, where he could hear drawers being opened and shut.

Nick wondered if she found comfort in taking care of others to avoid the emptiness of not having a mate. Annie wasn't very old—a couple years younger than himself. While she seemed so happy to most people when she talked to them, more than once Nick had caught sight of a melancholy buried in the depths of her eyes. Despite everything he'd told her about how having a mate would only hurt, he knew Annie would find her mate and she'd be eternally happy because she deserved it. He hadn't lost that much of his faith, at least.

She reappeared when more than half the food on his plate was gone. He hadn't even realized just how hungry he was. She gave a satisfied nod at how much he'd eaten when she perched on the love seat nearby.

"Can I ask you something, Nick?"

He shrugged, mouth full.

"Maybe it's none of my business, but I can't help but notice you're going to be staying here for a while."

He debated not answering her, but figured, what harm could it do? She wouldn't be running around gossiping with the rest of the pack. "My mate is staying at my home."

Annie broke into a wide smile. "But that's great! Isn't it?"

Nick gave a sharp bark of laughter, his appetite gone, and he set his almost-empty plate down on the coffee table. "He isn't here by choice, Annie. He's here because he had no other options."

Her happy grin faded, and she gave him a sad look. "I'm sorry, boss."

"It doesn't matter, Annie. I've already accepted the fact that he doesn't want me in his life. Perhaps it's better he doesn't. We can't even hold a five-minute conversation where we aren't arguing or at each other's throat. He's just so fucking proud and defensive. The smallest inane comment sets him off." Nick felt his food fighting to come back up. "I couldn't stay under the same roof as him. So I'll be staying here for a while. At least until the situation plays itself out."

Annie moved to sit next to him and picked up his hand,

squeezing gently in comfort. "Maybe if you two spent some time together and tried to get to know each other, things could work themselves out."

"No," Nick denied. "He's made it abundantly clear that he doesn't want me. I won't slink around him like an abused dog waiting to be kicked again. I can't take any more, Annie."

For the first time in a really long time, Nick found it hard to breathe around the tears clogging his throat. He swallowed hard, trying to force them away. Except the fatigue, pain, and the trauma of the last seventy-two hours finally caught up to him, and they spilled over, causing him to choke. Annie made a sound of surprise and wrapped her arms around him. He turned his head into her neck and allowed the tears to silently soak into her hair and blouse. No other noises escaped him after the first. His shoulders shook, and he felt her small, slender hands rubbing his back. He'd give anything for those hands to be the broad, callused ones belonging to Thayne.

The sun had completely sunk below the horizon when Nick finally managed to gather himself. Embarrassed, he couldn't look at Annie when he pulled away. He'd never shown such weakness in front of anyone except Seth.

"I'm sorry," he murmured.

Annie touched his shoulder lightly. "There's nothing to be sorry about, Nick. Even the toughest tree limbs can break sometimes. You've been through a lot, and you have every right to be upset."

Nick pushed himself up from the couch, clearing his throat, still uncomfortable with having broken down in front of her. "I'll uh… help you clean this up."

"No, no, it's okay, boss. I've got it." Annie waved him off. "I'll take care of it. Why don't you go take a hot shower? Once I've cleaned this up, I'll let myself out, okay?"

He started to protest but relented and set the plate back on the table. "Thanks, Annie."

"No problem, Nick. That's what I'm here for." She beamed at him.

"You aren't here to clean up my messes or deal with my personal crap," Nick scoffed gently. "This is outside the realm of your job description."

Annie picked up the plate and utensils, standing. "I want to do it. I like taking care of you and Ryan. You're both really good to me, and I enjoy being able to make your lives easier."

Nick finally found himself able to meet her gaze. "Your mate is going to be a very lucky man." She blushed and looked away. Nick leaned in and kissed her cheek. "I'll see you tomorrow, Annie."

"Good night, boss."

Taking her advice, Nick went into the bedroom, took a pair of sweats from one of the dresser drawers, and headed into the bathroom. The moment the hot water hit his skin, he felt cleaner than he had in a long time. The tears, though unwanted, had cleared away some of the fog inside of him. He had to get a grip on himself. If he continued to allow the emotions to get the better of him, he would be likely to end up as some of the other wolves he'd known who'd lost their mates. Wasting away or drinking himself to death. He wouldn't allow Thayne to do that to him. Not when Thayne had already taken away so much.

He scrubbed at his skin harshly with a washcloth, trying to remove the remembered sensation of Thayne's touch on him. He knew that was pointless, but he needed to know he'd tried. His skin shone bright red by the time he stopped. Nothing would take away the memories. Hopefully time would dull them, though, make them less vivid. Nick soaped his hair without care, hastening through the process. Once he'd rinsed the shampoo away, he turned off the shower and shook his head, much like a wet wolf, to dispel some of the water. He stepped out, grabbed a towel from under the sink, briskly dried his body, and then tied it around his waist.

Nick padded through the apartment to the kitchen. Annie had left the bedroom and living room light on for him before leaving. He opened the fridge and found it fully stocked with groceries, bottles of water, some beer, and his leftovers. Annie really was one of a kind. He snatched a couple of beers from the six-pack and went to the balcony, where he sat on one of the chairs to savor the night sounds. He sipped at his first beer and brooded over the events of the previous months. Nowhere in the stories told by others did they mention being rejected by their mates. The chemistry and attraction were instantaneous, or so the others told. How did he get so lucky to be one of the unheard of?

Sighing, he swigged down the rest of the beer and went to reach for the other one only to stop abruptly. He froze, his hand inches from the bottle. Fear and sadness bit deep and a flash of a dark-haired boy about fourteen slipped through his mind. Another of a knife and blood. Nick felt his stomach churn, and his head swirled as if he'd drunk several six packs of beer. He gripped the arms of the chair, trying to get a hold of himself. What the hell was going on? A single beer wouldn't do this to him. Anger overwhelmed the fear and sadness, drowning the other emotions in rage. Nick's knuckles turned white and the metal arms dented beneath his fingers. The laughing face of a beautiful blond male appeared in his mind, and Nick's wolf snarled, threatened by the presence of another man. Or maybe something else set his wolf's hackles rising. A sense of affection drifted through the anger, and Nick realized what he was feeling, seeing.

Thayne's barriers were down, the connection between them unblocked and allowing a deluge of emotions and drunken recollections to beat at Nick's senses. Nick wanted to turn it off. He didn't want to see Thayne's memories, see the man who'd been special enough for Thayne to want to be by his side. His throat closed up, and the sensation of being choked overwhelmed him. The image of Thayne wrapped up in the blond's arms sent unfiltered fury skittering along Nick's veins. His vision turned red, and he wanted nothing more than to murder the son of a bitch who dared touch what belonged to him. Nick's wolf scratched at the surface, demanding release, insisting he be freed to find and rend the flesh from the stranger's pretty facade. He held on to his wolf by a mere thread, knowing if he let his inner animal take control, he would end up doing something Nick would regret.

His teeth sharpened as his nails lengthened, his canine side showing itself as he battled to keep a hold of himself. Another image passed through his mind, and Nick's eyes widened as he saw himself pinned against the wall, being savagely taken by Thayne. Satisfaction, not his own but Thayne's, soared through him, and desire. A lustful passion dominated Thayne's memories, forcing Nick's body to respond, and he growled in response as his cock hardened. The scene morphed into the one at Kasey's home. Only this time, Nick could only feel himself taking Thayne, thrusting deep into his body, pegging the one place inside that pushed Thayne to let go. Nick shuddered as his balls tightened, and he panted, closing his eyes and trying to keep a grip on his sanity. Sharp pleasure spiraled through him, and Nick arched his back, crying out as he came, soaking the towel across his lap.

Trembling breaths wheezed from Nick as he attempted to recover his wits. He couldn't believe he'd come just from the memories racing through Thayne's inebriated brain. His fingers were cramping and the semen began to grow cold. He managed to shakily pick up the towel with one hand and clean himself off, swiping at the salty fluid. He discarded the towel on the floor and huffed, unable to comprehend just what had happened. Was the connection between mates really that strong? Or was there just such a buildup of emotions on Thayne's side that Thayne totally let go when drunk? Nick sat there, pushing back the images that kept sweeping through him, and tried to erect his own wall against the devastating impact of each one. Seth and Kasey hadn't warned him about how strong they were or just how much they could affect him. He'd been told mates could hear each other's thoughts and know their memories, but he'd never thought it could be like this.

He grabbed the bottle of beer he'd set down and chugged the remainder in a few swallows. He needed to run, to release some of the energy running through him. He stood and entered the apartment, tossed away his bottle, and grabbed a pair of sweatpants to put on before he exited the front door and took the elevator to the ground floor. The night sky hummed with the noises of the creatures and insects in the trees surrounding the area. In the instant his feet touched the cement outside the back door of the company, Nick shifted, releasing his wolf. He shook his coat eagerly and loped toward the forest, his padded paws silent in the early evening.

Nick picked up the pace as soon as he was in the trees, his golden fur prominent in the darkness and shadows cast from the branches above. He lost himself in the joy of setting his inner beast free and allowed his mind to wander while chasing a few rabbits and scuffling in the dead leaves on the forest floor for mice. His favorite place wasn't far from the building, a beautiful clearing where a soft creek ran into a small pond about as wide as his own home. When he needed time to think away from work, he would go there and laze around, enjoying the peace and serenity while seeking the next idea for whatever project he was on at the time.

He found the clearing by instinct and trotted over to his usual stone bed, a rock jutting slightly out over the water. The surface held the heat of the sun for some time after it had set, and he flopped down, sending a shower of leaves into the water below. His tail swung back and forth along the side of the rock while he mulled over everything he'd seen inside Thayne's head. It made him feel good to know Thayne wasn't as resistant to him as he portrayed. The image of the dark-haired teenager came back and the knowledge that the boy was important to Thayne. Somehow, he didn't find himself jealous, and he found that even more curious than the boy, since he was pretty certain the teenager was someone from Thayne's past. Maybe someday he could find out....

A branch cracking brought Nick's senses on high alert, and he lifted his head, peering into the shadows to identify the source. He raised his nose to the air and scented but couldn't pick up on anything. His hackles rose when another snap came from his right this time. Standing, he howled and attempted to scare off whoever or whatever was out there. Snap. Another branch breaking came from in front of him, the direction of the business. Not one prone to fear, Nick felt a bit of it skitter along his nerves. When a fourth sound came from behind him, Nick knew in his stomach, his instincts screaming, it was time to run. He launched himself off his perch to the bank on his left. His heart skipped a beat inside his chest when he saw bright red eyes shining at him from the darkness. He knew those eyes. He'd only ever seen them once up close. Seth's tormentor and abuser Taggart had eyes like those. Only the Created Ones' turned red while in their wolf form. Born wolves' were yellow in the darkness, like pinpoints of a flashlight in the distance. Nick's lupine eyes could just barely make out the hulking shape hiding there, and it was huge! He'd never seen one of such size before.

He knew if he didn't run now, he was dead. Taggart had been a small danger compared to the one he saw in front of him. Turning on his paws, Nick ran full-out toward the business, away from the horror hiding in the shadows. He pushed himself faster when he heard crashing through the trees behind him, indicating the Created One pursued him. Had his past mistakes brought him to this moment? After all, it was his fault Taggart had become a made wolf and his fault Taggart had found Seth. Maybe it all made sense for him to die at the teeth and claws of a Created. More than once Nick sensed his pursuer right on his tail, and then it was gone. It was toying with him. But why? Like a cat does a mouse, perhaps, just before consuming it?

He almost heaved a sigh of relief when the building came into view. As soon as he broke free from the forest, he realized the Created hadn't followed him. It stopped before it reached the concrete, and Nick swung around in the middle of the parking lot, fur trembling as he panted heavily. The red eyes peered out at him from within the darkness, and Nick slowly backed up, never taking his gaze off those pinpricks of blood in the black void. The moment his tail touched the cool metal of the door, he shifted in an instant and grabbed the handle, almost ripping it off the hinges. A loud roaring howl followed him into the building as he slammed the door shut and locked it, knowing if it wanted in, the door wouldn't stop it. He stared out the window, waiting to see if it would come after him, but it never left the safety of the shadows, the red dots of its eyes bouncing as it restlessly paced back and forth. Nick somehow knew it was stalking him, taunting him. What the hell was going on? Was it Taggart? Had he gotten out of that fire alive and now he'd come after Nick for revenge?

Nick had no idea how long he stood there, watching that hulking form, maybe an hour, perhaps two. The Created One finally stopped pacing and locked eyes with him momentarily, sending a shiver down Nick's spine at the cold death in them. Only when the beast turned and became lost in the trees did relief cause him to slump against the wall and attempt to gather his wits about him. He needed to call Elijah and let him know about the Created One. They would need to hunt him, but as a pack, not one-on-one. He felt ashamed at how frightened he'd been at facing the creature, except he'd known he couldn't take it on alone. Not one of that size, anyway.

When he could finally push away from the wall without his knees wanting to give out, Nick strode to his office, snatched up the phone, and dialed his Alpha's number by heart.

"Hello?" the deep baritone said over the line.

"Elijah, we have a problem."

T HE NEXT day, Nick went to the pack manor for a brief meeting with Elijah and Cole to discuss the incident from the previous evening, as well as the events that had unfolded in Senaka. He gave a stoic recount of everything up to and including Thayne's current presence in his own home. Cole cornered him outside just before he went to leave with Ryan to speak with Wheaton Little and demanded Nick tell him the truth about Thayne. Nick tried to get out of it, but Cole wouldn't let up until he spilled the beans, so to speak.

"I know you better than that, Nick," Cole challenged.

"Yeah, I know you do." Nick sighed. Ryan was still inside the house, having needed to use the bathroom before leaving. He'd shown up at the pack manor so they could drive into

Redwood City together. Nick looked toward the lake to avoid having to meet Cole's eyes.

"Talk to me, Nick," Cole said quietly, resting against the side of the Impala near Nick. "I've seen what the rejection from this Thayne has done to you, and now with him being here, the bond cemented, it can't be easy."

Easy? Would his life ever be easy again? Nick shrugged. "I can't feel him, Cole. Not unless he's drunk, anyway," he said bitterly.

"He's got his walls up," Cole observed.

"That's an understatement, Cole. He's got more than just walls up. He's got the entire goddamn castle, mortars and all." Nick ran a hand through his hair, mussing up the neat style. "Everyone keeps telling me to give him a chance. To let him come to me. But what if he doesn't? No one wants to talk about what happens if he doesn't. They all seem to think that the almighty fucking connection between us is supposed to fix everything."

Cole gave him a shocked look. "Nick! You've always believed in the mating bond. Has everything really changed that for you? Even when we were kids, you couldn't stop talking about who your mate would be, what they would look like, and how you'd know it the moment you met them. You knew even back then your mate would be male and big, almost Alpha big. Isn't he what you thought he would be?"

"He's both of those," Nick said in a flat tone. "Only I never once thought he wouldn't want me."

Nick remembered those innocent moments of his youth. He really had spent a lot of time growing up thinking of his mate, knowing they were out there and waiting for him to find them. Maybe that was why it stung his pride so much. He'd never seen any wolf outright reject their other half. Not even Seth, who'd been petrified of being part of another pair after Taggart.

Nick's cell phone rang, disrupting his internal thoughts. He pulled it out of his pocket and saw his cousin's name on the ID. "Hey, Carter," he bid tiredly.

Cole patted him on the shoulder and hooked his thumb toward the house to show he was going back inside. Nick nodded in acknowledgement.

"Nick!" Carter shouted into the phone, and Nick winced, yanking it away partially. Carter always did have only one volume: loud.

"Something wrong, Carter?"

"I just stopped by your place! Some strange guy, pretty grumpy if you ask me, answered the door. He was really rude!"

Nick winced and ran a hand over his face. "Yeah, that's… uh… he's my mate."

"What!" Carter squealed, causing Nick to yank the phone farther away. "When? How?"

"Recently. Look, Carter, is there something you needed?"

"I just wanted to spend some time with you," Carter said. "And now with you having found your mate…."

That meant either Carter was in trouble again or he'd just broken up with whatever loser he was dating. Nick mentally sighed. "What's going on, Carter?"

"Nothing," Carter hedged, but Nick could tell his cousin wanted nothing more than to spill the beans.

"I know something's wrong, so talk."

Carter launched into a rant about his most recent breakup without hesitation while Ryan joined him at the car, and Nick motioned for Ryan to give him a few minutes. Ryan nodded and walked back to the porch, plunked down on the second step, and leaned back on his elbows. Nick listened for the next twenty minutes while Carter went on and on, an occasional "uh-huh" thrown in for his cousin's benefit. Since he could remember, Carter had always managed to get involved with some of the lowest pieces of dirt. It was like his cousin drew them to him. Maybe Carter's looks, almost fragile and porcelain-like, caught their eye, and they thought he could be easily used, which he normally was. Nick had forced more than his fair share of scumbags out of Carter's life without his cousin ever being the wiser. He'd made a promise to his aunt and uncle that he'd watch over Carter, keep him out of trouble.

When Carter finally wound down, Nick said, "Carter, maybe you should spend some time alone. Go out and have fun. You're only twenty-two, and it's like you're in a rush to date as many people as possible."

"I just want to find my mate, Nick, like you," Carter murmured. "Without dating a lot of people, how can I find them?"

"You don't need to date every single guy you meet in order to find your mate. Are you attending the Summit next month?" Nick asked, ignoring the comment about his own.

"Of course!" Carter replied in excitement. "It sounds like a lot of fun, and maybe I'll meet my intended half there."

Nick bit his tongue. Carter's naiveté about mates reminded him of his own. He'd felt the same up until a few months ago when he'd met Thayne and realized he wouldn't be getting his own happy ending like Seth. Nick warred between attempting to warn Carter and keeping his mouth shut. If he told Carter, it would surely get back to other pack members because Carter couldn't keep a secret to save his life. Yet the idea of allowing his cousin to continue to believe meeting his mate was the end-all, be-all to his own happiness left a sour taste in his mouth.

The choice was taken out of his hands by Carter. "Nick, I got to go, but can we meet for lunch soon? I want to know more about the pack we'll be meeting at the Summit and what the people are like."

"Sure, Carter."

"Great! Thanks, Nick. You really are the best!" Carter disconnected the call.

Nick allowed the hand holding his cell to drop down to his side. For a brief moment, he wished he could go back to feeling the same way Carter did. Despite his own fuck-ups with Seth's safety, Nick had always believed in his heart that he'd meet his mate and they'd have a connection just as he'd seen so many others establish. Somewhere along the path of meeting Thayne, the constant bickering between them, and the most recent rash of events, Nick had lost his faith in happily-ever-afters. He'd be spending his life alone, not even able to connect with another soul just for one night now that he'd met and claimed his true mate. His wolf would never allow him to.

"Ready to go, Nick?" Ryan called from the porch.

Sighing, Nick nodded and opened the driver's side door of his Impala. Ryan joined him, and they were on their way to Redwood City with plenty of daylight to spare.

THAYNE

THE MOMENT Thayne stepped out of the borrowed truck, he felt several pairs of eyes swing his way. The scent of multiple wolves assaulted his nostrils, and he knew they'd picked up on what he was. Emerald Lake Hills didn't really have a "town" with stores and restaurants, Thayne had discovered on his trip. It had taken him about two hours to figure that out as he'd driven all over the area, spotting a pharmacy and a couple of grocery stores but no clothing store. So he'd followed the signs into Redwood City instead. Apparently Nick's pack extended past Emerald Lake Hills with how many wolves he could smell just in the small area around him.

He slammed the door and entered the clothing store, nodding at the clerk who called out a hello. It wasn't like the chain stores he'd gone into during his wanderings on the road. There were a couple of sections of clothing, one for men and another for women, and an even smaller section for kids. Thayne headed toward the men's.

"Anything I can help you find, sir?" the woman at the counter called out.

"No, thank you," Thayne said as he pulled two pairs of jeans in his size off the racks and a couple of T-shirts from another, both black. He snagged a package of black brief underwear nearby and a set of black socks. Without even waiting or asking for a dressing room, he headed to the back, entered, and closed the door with a sharp snap. He changed quickly, pulling on a pair of briefs, one of the jeans, and a shirt, ripping the tags off savagely.

"Everything okay in there, sir?" the woman asked through the slats.

Thayne opened the door and stepped out. "Fine. Ring me up please," he said, passing her the tags and the remainder of the clothing.

She scurried to do as he asked. It cost him almost a hundred bucks for the clothing, and he swore under his breath as he handed her his debit card. His funds would just about be cut in half with the purchase.

She beamed at him as she handed him back his card and the receipt. "Thank you, sir! You have a nice day now!"

Grimacing, he took them from her and picked up his bags, stuffing Nick's clothes in with his new ones. He'd never been overly fond of cheerful people. There was no way on earth someone could be happy all the time. He exited the store and tossed the bag into the truck on the floor of the passenger side. At least he felt somewhat normal in his own clothes. Now he needed to find a job. He was stuck there until he could build up enough money to take off, especially since his funds were nearly depleted now. He looked around at the different stores nearby. There weren't many he'd prefer to work at. He spied a hardware store and figured he'd try there first.

Redwood City seemed pretty populated compared to Emerald Lake Hills, Thayne mused as he strode down the street. Maybe that's why Nick's pack chose to live there instead of here. Reaching the hardware shop, he opened the door and stepped into the cool interior, letting his eyes adjust to the dimmer light after the bright sun. When he could finally see, he stopped in his tracks, uncertain if he should turn around and leave.

Nick stood at the counter with the dark-haired shifter Thayne had seen in Nick's memories and thoughts. Nick looked amazing. Faded blue jeans hugged every inch of his toned legs and firm rear end while an emerald green T-shirt clung to his upper chest. Although, it appeared Nick had lost some weight since the first night they'd met. Thayne could clearly see the ridges of Nick's ribcage. He frowned and wondered if maybe he remembered enough to make that call. Until now, Nick hadn't worn anything around Thayne except button-down business shirts, which hid any evidence of his true physique. With the T-shirt, Thayne could see everything, including a tattoo circling Nick's bicep where the sleeve had ridden up enough to make it visible. Tiny wolf paw prints trekked across the skin there. He remembered seeing a similar one on Seth during the two days he'd been in Senaka before Nick's arrival. His curiosity about the tattoo was forgotten as the conversation continued.

"The young man seemed afraid, Ryan. I don't really feel comfortable giving you any other information," the older man behind the counter hedged, glancing away from the two of them and fidgeting.

Nick set his hand on the man's arm. "Wheaton, you know we'd never do anything to hurt him. We just want to find him. For Cole."

Wheaton hesitated at that name, and Thayne wondered who Cole was to cause such a reaction. He sniffed at the air but only picked up Nick and the man named Ryan as being shifters. Thayne waited right along with them to see if the guy would give up the information.

Finally, breaths later, Wheaton told them what he knew. "He got off the bus that travels between here and San Francisco around three in the afternoon. Blond hair, brown or hazel eyes, about Nick's height, and he had a backpack with him. That's all I know."

Nick squeezed Wheaton's hand and patted the back of it. "Thanks, Wheat."

Wheaton grunted and then said, "Don't go scaring the man any more than he already is. I may be human, but even I could smell the fear on him."

Thayne's eyebrows went up. So Wheaton knew about shifters.

"We're just trying to find out where he's gone," Ryan soothed. "You know very well if anything ever happened to Carla, you'd be just as desperate to find her."

Wheaton huffed and glared at them. "I love my Carla, so of course, but it's one thing being mated to a shifter who's just a part of the pack and quite another being mated to the soon-to-be Alpha."

The pieces clicked into place for Thayne. Cole's mate had apparently come through town and then took off before Cole could claim him. *Good for him,* Thayne congratulated mentally. Nick and Ryan thanked Wheaton again, and Thayne considered ducking behind a nearby shelf but figured what the hell. He garnered a little bit of satisfaction when he saw Nick's footsteps stumble a fraction at the sight of him.

"Hello, Nick," Thayne greeted.

Ryan's expression darkened, and Thayne sensed the anger in Nick's friend. Thayne wondered what Nick had told the man. Obviously a lot, if the fury building in Ryan's gaze were any indication.

Nick gripped Ryan's shoulder. "Ryan, stop."

"You're lucky Nick is my best friend, because if he wasn't,

I'd tear you to shreds for what you've been up to, asshole," Ryan spat.

"Ryan!" Nick exclaimed sharply.

"If there's going to be any fighting, kindly take yourselves out of my store!" Wheaton called to them.

Nick gave Wheaton an apologetic look. "There's not going to be, Wheat. Sorry for the noise."

Thayne knew Ryan had a point, but he couldn't help smirking at the threat. Ryan was nowhere near as muscular as he was and most likely didn't have the years of bar fighting and boxing under his belt that Thayne did. Traveling as he did and needing money led to picking up a few skills.

The rage in Ryan's gaze deepened at his smile. "You think it's funny, asswipe? To hurt him, nearly destroy him, and then expect him to help you!"

Nick stepped between them, faced Ryan, and grabbed both of Ryan's biceps. "Stop it, Ry. Now."

Destroy? What the hell did Ryan mean? "What the fuck is he talking about?" Thayne demanded of Nick.

Ryan snorted in disgust. Nick glared at Ryan, who looked at him and said, "If you don't tell him, Nick, I will."

"It's none of his business—or yours, for that matter, Ryan!" Nick shouted.

"None of his business?" Ryan asked incredulously. "You ended up in the hospital because of him, and you don't think he should have to answer for that?"

Thayne stumbled backward slightly, his shoulders tagging a shelf and knocking several items off. He'd hurt Nick that much? A wolf didn't get sick or injure easily. They recovered quickly from most wounds, so for a true wolf to be ill enough to need the assistance of human medicine was pretty serious.

He vaguely registered when Ryan left the store and Nick started picking up what he'd knocked over.

When Nick stood straight again, Thayne grabbed at Nick's upper arms, his breathing uneven. "Why didn't you tell me?"

Nick glared at him, batting his hands away. "Why should I have? You wouldn't have cared even if I had told you."

Thayne felt as though he'd been slapped and he jerked as if struck. Yet he knew Nick's words were of his own making. He'd tried so hard to convince Nick that he didn't want anything to do with him, so why should Nick think he'd care? The knowledge of how badly he'd wounded Nick burned in the pit of his stomach like a ball of acid.

"I'm sorry," he murmured.

"For what?" Nick asked.

More than once, Thayne tried to open his mouth to explain his apology, and he couldn't find the words.

Nick scoffed at Thayne and walked toward the entrance of the store. Thayne didn't try to stop him, but Nick halted in the doorway. "You should wait until Elijah introduces you to the pack before wandering around too much. The others won't take kindly to you in the area until they know who you are."

Thayne swallowed hard and nodded. He needed to process what he'd just discovered about Nick and the way it made his heart ache so fierce. Nick left, and Thayne held himself back from racing after him. *Damn*, if this was how he felt after only two days in Nick's presence, how the hell would a month or two leave him? He gathered the pieces of his consciousness and walked to the counter, waiting for the man named Wheaton to look his way.

Wheaton glared at him when he finished with the customer at his register. "Is there something I can help you with, son?"

"Looking for a job."

"None here." Wheaton brushed him off and went back to making some notations in a ledger.

Perhaps the run-in with Ryan and Nick hadn't helped his chances. "Thanks anyway, old man," Thayne said and left the store.

He climbed into the borrowed truck and traveled a bit down the road, stopping at a couple of places where they all said the same thing. Most of them were owned by wolves, which meant his chances were slim to none at finding a job until they knew who he was. Then he spotted a diner, Jo's Place, and figured he'd try there and maybe get a late lunch. He pulled into the parking lot and into a space.

The diner reminded him of the marine's place a few years ago, except this one was cleaner and looked nicer. White brick walls with a navy-blue roof and matching awnings over the windows. Thayne saw a motorcycle in the first parking spot with a license plate that merely said Jo. *Maybe the guy running the business will be human this time*, he thought eagerly, climbing out of the truck.

A bell over the door tinkled as he entered the building, and he saw five heads swivel his way instantly. Two men in a booth near the back bathrooms stared at him suspiciously, danger in the depths of their gazes. Another man and woman sat in a booth next to the front windows while a third man perched on a stool at the counter. Thayne could pick up the scent of wolf from the man at the counter and the two men in the back, but the couple was human.

The smell of fries and hamburgers cooking on the grill masked the scent of the woman standing over the stove. A second woman, human, came bustling out front holding two plates that she brought to the couple near the window.

"Have a seat, baby doll, and I'll be right with you," she called on her way back into the kitchen.

Thayne chose to sit at the counter on the stool closest to

the front door just in case the others decided him a threat. Being raised in Senaka and traveling through the two or three other wolf territories he'd come across in his wanderings, he knew enough to know not to interfere with the locals and to watch his back. A pack didn't like strangers in their area. It made them edgy and unpredictable, especially if they didn't know if the unknown wolf was a Created One or not. He'd been raised to believe true wolves could only be Native American, and any he'd encountered who weren't from a tribe couldn't be anything other than Created. Those were ones he'd actively avoided while on the move. Now, since Kasey mated with Seth, he knew most likely he'd run into nontribal packs like Nick's before. Maybe if he'd stuck around places more than a few nights, he might have discovered sooner what his father and Kasey had only a few months ago. Although what he would have done with that information, he wasn't sure. Even if he had found out, he knew he wouldn't have done anything with it. It wasn't in his nature to care about those things, and he shook his head to clear it, needing all of his wits about him. He kept his senses on high while he waited for the waitress to come back.

She returned a minute later, sidling up to the counter in front of him, grinning a wide smile. "What can I get ya, sugar?"

"I was looking to talk with Jo?" He glanced at her nametag. "Regina."

The friendly look cooled a little. "What business you have with Jo?"

Thayne knew the woman was being protective and beat back the urge to snap at her. He turned on the charm and lifted one corner of his mouth in a half smirk, leaning in a little closer. "Just hoping he has a need for a cook or dishwasher in the kitchen."

Regina burst out laughing. Thayne wrinkled his brow.

"Hey, Jo!" she screamed toward the kitchen. "You got a visitor!"

The door swung open, and Thayne saw the woman cook. He winced when he realized Jo was a she, not a he. A pair of dark eyes pinned him in place, stripping him bare, as she walked toward him. Jo wasn't a slender woman by any means, but her body wasn't made up of fat. Pure muscle rippled beneath the surface of her tanned skin. Long lashes gave her eyes an exotic, Egyptian appearance and matched well with the dark-as-pitch hair pulled back from her face in a high ponytail. The food no longer covered her scent, and Thayne picked up human mixed with shifter. Maybe she belonged to a shifter in the area.

"Who are you?" she demanded without preamble.

"New to town and looking for a job."

"What makes you think there's one here for you?"

Thayne shrugged. "Hoping. Got a lot of experience. Spent a year working in a small place just like this in Tennessee. I can cook, wash dishes, anything you need around the place."

Jo looked him up and down, judging him. "How do I know I can trust you?"

"How can anyone be trusted?" Thayne tossed back. "I've never stolen in my life. Always worked for my money and food."

She didn't say anything for a few moments. He wondered if he would have to keep looking or most likely wait until Nick's Alpha had introduced him to the pack. The thought grated. He didn't want to have to continue to rely on Nick for everything.

Just as he was about to get up and leave, she said, "I'll give you a trial run. Come back tomorrow morning at six, but know this—I don't take kindly to liars or thieves. If you even try to steal so much as a salt shaker, your ass is ground up in my meat grinder. Got it?"

Thayne nodded and stood, holding out his hand. "Name's Thayne and thanks. I like my ass right where it is, so you don't have to worry about it."

Jo laughed and took his hand, shaking it firmly. "I've got some heavy hauling to do over the next couple of months, so don't thank me yet, Thayne. Sit down again. You look like you could eat something. You can try my meatloaf. It's the special today."

He sank back onto the stool and watched as she returned to the kitchen. Regina returned and took his drink order for water and a cup of coffee. Most of his hangover had dissipated, and he felt relatively normal again. His first sip of the coffee brought forth a moan, and he closed his eyes, breathing in the heady scent. Some of the best coffee he'd ever tasted. He opened his eyes and took another drink.

"Good to the last drop," Regina piped in as she set the plate of meatloaf, mashed potatoes, and corn in front of him. "Jo says you're going to be working here."

"Guess so," he said, picking up his fork and digging in. The meatloaf practically melted on his tongue, and the mashed potatoes were like fluffy clouds. He hadn't eaten such good, home-cooked food since his mom's. It reminded him of Nick. Now that he thought about it, he hadn't seen Nick eat once. Not in Senaka and not on the plane. The only thing Nick had during that time had been alcohol, whiskey for the most part. When was the last time Nick had eaten? Is that why his mate had almost ended up in the hospital?

His hand froze with the fork halfway to his mouth as he realized he'd thought of Nick as his mate. He tightened his grip on the utensil and lowered it back down to the plate, his appetite fled. The strands of their binding were growing denser, thicker, and Thayne knew he was growing closer and closer to capitulating. The longer they were apart, the more his wolf urged him to find Nick and snatch him up, never letting go. Thayne shoved back from the counter, the stool scraping across the floor, and he mindlessly tossed some cash down near his plate. He needed some air. If he didn't get some now, he'd pass out.

Stumbling out of the diner, he headed for the alleyway instead of his truck. He leaned his back against the side of the building and bent at the waist a bit, his hands braced on his knees. He breathed in as steady as he could, trying to get his emotions under control. His blood raced through his veins, pounding along his eardrums. His skin vibrated with how hard he fought to control himself. The need to shift dug deep, ready to happen if he let it. The wolf wanted to take over, to forget his human side and go claim its mate.

A shadow fell over him, and when he looked up, he found the two shifters from the booth in the back corner of the diner standing over him. Thayne managed to stand to his full height, ready to defend himself if necessary.

"Strangers aren't welcome here," the blond shifter snarled, malice in his eyes.

The second shifter circled to Thayne's left, and Thayne pressed closer to the building, keeping them both within sight. "I don't want any trouble."

"Then you should leave."

"Can't."

Blondie growled and moved closer. Thayne tensed and waited. He didn't want to cause problems before Nick's Alpha could present him to the pack. "Outsiders are supposed to announce their presence to the pack's Alpha. Who are you?"

Thayne hesitated. Should he tell them?

His hesitation lasted a second too long, and the two advanced on him, ready to fight. Just as they went to grab for him, a powerful female voice called out, "James, Vincent! Enough!"

The two shifters immediately backed down and turned toward the woman, dropping to one knee and bowing their heads in supplication. Thayne felt the power behind that voice and looked to the end of the alley. A beautiful redheaded female shifter stood there, her arms crossed and her lips pursed. The pure energy flowing from her could belong to no one other than an Alpha or the Alpha's mate, and Thayne knew the Alpha in the territory was a man named Elijah. He tipped his head forward in a sign of respect and waited for her to speak.

She moved closer to them and stopped an arm's length from him. "That is no way to treat a guest in our area, boys," she reprimanded the two kneeling shifters. "Now leave us."

"But, Sara—"

"I said leave us."

The two of them rose but faltered, uncertain if they should obey her and leave her with a strange wolf in their territory or stay and risk her wrath.

"Now!" she thundered.

"Yes, Sara."

Thayne remained silent, watching as the two shifters exited the alley. He still had not made eye contact with the woman.

"Elijah told me of your arrival. Although, I am surprised he did not request that you remain indoors until the pack meeting."

Thayne looked up at her now, surprised. She knew who he was? "Ma'am?"

She impatiently waved her hand at him. "None of that 'ma'am' stuff. Makes me feel old. Call me Sara."

He tipped his head in acknowledgement of her request but waited to hear what she wanted and how she knew who he was.

Her dark green eyes scanned down his body and back up

to his face, appreciation gleaming in them. Thayne could see fine lines around her eyes and mouth that spoke of her being older than she looked. Auburn hair framed her delicate features. She was pretty tall for a woman, her gaze level with his nose.

"I can definitely see what has had Nicky in such a state for the last six months," she drawled lazily. "I'm surprised he didn't keep you in the house until after the pack meeting. Just as a precaution, of course."

Nicky? But the mention of Nick forcing him to stay in the house caught his attention more. "No one *keeps* me from doing anything," Thayne snapped.

"Touchy." She smirked. "I was merely saying that it would have been better for you and him to have remained out of sight until after everyone knows who you are. Less friction among the other wolves."

"Maybe I don't really give a shit."

She raised one delicate eyebrow at his response. "I can see we're going to have our hands full with you. Now why don't you tell me what brought you to town?"

Thayne weighed whether to tell her or not, but figured he'd already been disrespectful enough toward the Alpha's mate. He'd been in town less than twenty-four hours, and he'd already managed to piss off Nick yet again and end up in an altercation with some pack members.

"A job and clothes."

"You didn't bring any clothing with you?" she asked curiously.

"No, ma—Sara."

She hummed in satisfaction when he caught himself and switched to her name. "You know, Elijah has some stuff in the attic at the house that may fit you. From his young days, of course. Why don't you come with me and then you can stay for dinner? We'll call Nicky and make it a foursome, hmm?"

He protested, "I don't think—"

"Good, let's go!" She cut him off and smiled happily. She grabbed his arm, tugging him out of the alley toward a sleek-looking, black two-door coupe. In less than a minute, they were on the road and heading back to Emerald Lake Hills.

Thayne figured Nick would have another reason to be pissed off at him now. He couldn't deny the bite of anticipation at being able to see Nick, though. He'd never understood the meaning of "butterflies in your stomach"… until now. A fluttering sensation spread through his belly, and he couldn't quite suppress the tiny smile creeping across his lips. God, he needed to get out of there before this got worse! His wolf practically rolled over and presented his belly in supplication at the idea of seeing Nick.

"So, Thayne, tell me about your pack," Sara prodded. "A lot of our pack members are still yet unmated and are excited about the upcoming Summit."

"What do you want to know?" Thayne asked, figuring she'd learned a lot about the Senaka wolf pack from his father and Kasey, or at least Nick.

Sara gave a tinkling laugh and winked at him. "I'm not fishing for intel. I can see that's what you're thinking. James and Vincent back there, they are both unmated as of yet, and there are several women under my care that haven't met their true mates either. I was just interested in knowing how many unmated wolves will be attending the Summit." The teasing look faded away to be replaced by a serious one. "I love the wolves in our pack, Thayne. And having been mated to Elijah for over thirty years, I understand the bond between mates is unparalleled, something to be treasured and treated with the utmost care. We can love a human or a shifter who is not the other half of our soul, but that love is a mere shadow in comparison to the connection forged between true mates. I want the wolves in my pack to know such a bond, to feel the power behind it, and truly know the happiness it can bring. You must understand that now, being mated with Nicky, I mean."

Thayne snorted. "Happiness? What about the way it can shatter you? Or how it can strip you of your freedom and the will to live?"

Sara glanced at him in shock. "Is that really how you see it, Thayne? How you see the bond between yourself and Nicky?"

Thayne's stubborn silence filled the air between them. His lack of response apparently igniting Sara's fury.

"No wonder Nick has been working himself to the bone lately." Her dark green eyes flashed with anger as she wrenched the wheel to the right, pulling the car over but leaving the engine idling. She turned in the seat and glared at him, her bright red lips pressed into a thin line of disgust. "The bond between true mates is more powerful than you can understand. Do you even know what you've done to him? You've condemned him to a life of loneliness and pain because you refuse to accept him. When Elijah told me how you didn't want to be mated, I just took it for nerves or your need to protect him from the Created One that caused all this fuss. But now I see you're just a stubborn, selfish fool who doesn't have a thought for anyone except himself."

She lifted a corner of one lip in a snarl. "You're lucky I don't just reach across this car and rip your throat open. If I thought it would lessen Nick's pain, I wouldn't hesitate, only I know it won't help the situation. But you need to make a choice, or I'll make it for you. Either you learn to accept the bond with Nick or you get the hell out of here. I will not have such a jackass as part of my pack. You have until the

Summit to make things right or get the hell out of my territory. Understand?"

A month? He wouldn't have much time to build up some money to leave, but the idea of leaving didn't really have such appeal as it would have a week ago. He stared in silence at the fiery woman seated beside him. How could he possibly accomplish either task in a month? He couldn't exactly blame Nick if he never forgave him. After everything Thayne had put him through, it was a wonder Nick had even kept Ryan from beating the crap out of him in the hardware store.

"I-I don't know."

"You don't know if you understand?" she demanded.

Thayne looked away from her and stared out the window at the mass of trees beside them. "I don't know if I can accept being a mate, having one. I've always known I didn't want one. A connection that can annihilate you makes you weak."

"Weak? The bond between mates is something which makes you stronger, makes you whole inside. It brings the pieces of your soul together as one."

"Then why don't I feel that now?" Thayne challenged.

"Because, sweetie, you haven't accepted the bond. You aren't truly bound to Nick until you open yourself up to him and allow him into your being. And knowing you haven't is worrisome. It means the bond between you and the Created One isn't really broken. It can still sense you, know how to find you. Elijah needs to know. To warn the others. We may have a problem on our hands already." She put the car in gear and pulled back out onto the road, speeding up.

"How can you possibly know that?" Thayne protested, focusing on the first part about Matt still being able to find him rather than the implication Matt already had. He refused to believe Matt could already be in Emerald Lake Hills. They'd flown hundreds of miles from Senaka a mere twenty-four to forty-eight hours ago, leaving no trail for the creature to follow.

A sad smile crossed Sara's face. "My sister fell in love with a human years ago, and she changed him, thinking their love would keep him from becoming a monster. She was wrong. But she couldn't bring herself to kill him or to allow anyone else to either. Eventually, she met her true mate, another human. She didn't want to accept him because she was afraid of a repeat of the past, but as a wolf, she had the duty to protect her true mate from harm. The Created One attacked her mate one night, leaving him with terrible scars across his face and half his body. It was truly a miracle he even survived.

"The attack was enough to convince her to claim her mate in order to protect him by severing the bond. Only the bond didn't truly break between her and the Created One because she didn't accept her mate into her heart. The human she'd loved before held it in his hands. Only she didn't understand the Created One's human side no longer existed. He didn't see or feel the same way. It was merely animal instinct for him to pursue her, to hunt her."

Sara paused and her hands tightened on the wheel. "The Created One attacked while they were sleeping, killing him first and eventually her. I... I found the bodies. He'd torn her to shreds and ripped her mate's heart from his chest, crushing it."

"I'm sorry," Thayne murmured.

"Eventually we tracked down the creature and killed it, avenging my sister and her mate, but it didn't bring them back. There's no peace in revenge. And if the beast is still tracking you, Nick is very much in danger."

Sara's words chilled the blood in his veins. Thayne knew if anything happened to Nick, it would be his fault. The urge to find Nick, to protect him, almost overwhelmed him. He dug his nails into his thighs, struggling to gather his thoughts and gain control of his emotions. Now, after everything, he'd put Nick into danger.

"Do you have a cell phone?" he asked through gritted teeth.

A black object appeared in front of him, and he picked it up but stared at it, realizing he had no clue what Nick's number was. "Speed dial number three, sweetie," Sara muttered.

Thayne grunted and hit the three and the call button. He listened to it ringing and wondered what the hell he would tell Nick if or when he answered. What the hell *could* he say?

13

NICK

NICK FOLLOWED Ryan into their office building just as his cell rang. He dug it out of his pocket and glanced at the caller ID. Sara. He debated ignoring it, not really in the mood to talk after their run-in with Thayne, but knew she wouldn't give up.

With a sigh, he answered, "Hey, Sara."

"Nick?"

A shiver at that all-too-familiar voice trickled along his skin, and Nick swallowed hard, fighting back the instant arousal at the raspy baritone. "Thayne? Why are you on Sara's phone? Did something happen?"

At first he thought Thayne had been cut off or hung up when his questions were met with silence, but he could hear the sound of an engine in the background. "Thayne?"

"I—"

"Spit it out already!" came from a female voice Nick knew without a doubt belonged to Sara.

"What's going on, Thayne?" Nick prodded gently.

"You're in danger."

Nick started, his mind immediately flashing to the

previous night when he'd encountered the Created One. "What?"

Thayne didn't get a chance to reply. Sara must have snatched the phone from him, because she spoke next. "Nicky, I think we should discuss this face-to-face. Why don't you come on over to the house? We're on our way there now."

How the hell had Thayne ended up with Sara in the first place? "I'll be there."

Nick disconnected the call and headed into Ryan's office. He outlined the conversation, and Ryan immediately stood to accompany him to Elijah and Sara's home. Nick attempted to dissuade Ryan from coming, but Ryan refused to let him go alone.

"I'm not going to let you face whatever this is on your own, Nick. Especially since that bastard is involved. Again!"

"I'll be fine, Ryan!"

"Forget it. I'm going whether you like it or not. So let's get out of here."

Nick sighed and relented. "All right, but don't go at him again like you did earlier, okay? He may be a jerk, but he's still my mate."

"He deserved it, and you know it, but I won't," Ryan promised.

They let Annie know where they were going. The ride was made mostly in silence. Nick spent the majority of it lost in his thoughts, trying to figure out what they could possibly have to tell him. Maybe they knew the Created One from the other night was Taggart and that's why they didn't want to tell him over the phone. What else could it be that they wouldn't want to just spit it out?

Before Nick felt ready, they were pulling up in front of the Alpha's house, a huge two-story white clapboard home with a well-kept lawn and beautiful wraparound porch. The house sat on the outskirts of one of the lakes where their town got its namesake. Nick had always loved the Alpha's place and always felt like it was his second home. For the first time ever, he hesitated going inside, sitting in the driver's seat and staring at the house broodingly.

"We're not going to find out what's going on by sitting here," Ryan said dryly.

"I know. I just need a minute."

Ryan didn't prod him to get out of the car again. A couple of minutes passed before Nick opened the door and exited the Impala, slamming the door behind him. He took a deep breath and strode up the walkway to the porch. They entered the house without knocking. Elijah and Sara had always treated their pack like family, allowing them to consider their home their own. Each room had been painstakingly designed and decorated by Sara when they'd had the house rebuilt a few years back, with light-colored walls and carpets throughout every room and slightly darker furniture as accents. Photos of pack members, their families, and the events in their lives decorated the walls, tables, and mantels in each room. Sara had a knack for photography and used it to her benefit to capture the moments she cherished the most. Nick appeared in more than one, being almost like an adopted son in a way. He'd spent the majority of his growing-up years with Cole, and after Nick had been sent to protect Seth, whenever he'd come home to visit the pack and give Elijah an update on his task.

Nick heard voices from the kitchen and turned toward them, stopping in the door when he spotted Elijah, Sara, and Thayne all seated at the table, talking. Thayne's eyes zeroed in on him the instant he appeared in the doorframe. Nick had to do a double take at the worry shimmering in the dark depths. Either something really bad must have brought about such a look, or he'd fallen asleep on his desk and was in the middle of a dream.

"Elijah. Sara," Nick greeted, moving to the table to shake Elijah's hand and hug Sara.

Once both he and Ryan had taken a seat, Nick across from Thayne, Elijah glanced at Thayne, who Nick could see swallowed hard. Thayne dropped his gaze to where his hands rested on the oak wood dining table.

"Tell him," Elijah said gently.

Not a small man by any means, Elijah towered over most men at six foot six and weighed about two hundred and fifty pounds. He had not an ounce of extra fat on his body. The only indications of his age were the deep lines in his face and the gray edging in at his temples and dusting the top of his hair. If asked, no one would guess Elijah was almost seventy-five years old. The strength he exuded would give pause to anyone thinking to challenge him. Nick had seen Elijah take down many wolves in his time as Alpha, wolves who'd foolishly believed they could take what belonged to him.

Nick returned his attention to Thayne, who still hadn't spoken. "Will someone please tell us what is going on?" he finally demanded.

Thayne didn't look up as he spoke. "The binding didn't work."

"What do you mean, it didn't work?" Nick asked, brow furrowing.

"The link between me and the Created One isn't gone. It can still track me."

Nick's stomach clenched as his thoughts flashed to the creature from the night before. "But I thought if we completed the claiming, the tie was severed?"

Thayne remained silent until Nick gave up and turned to Elijah. "Elijah?"

Sara interjected. "The bond isn't complete, Nick. There's

more to it than just claiming your mate through the bite and sexual coupling. It takes a binding of the souls, the acceptance of your mate into your heart. And neither one of you have done so."

Shock held Nick in place, and he stared at Sara in horror. After everything, the claiming had been for nothing. He'd given up his home for nothing. He'd allowed Thayne to hurt him over and over... for nothing.

"I-I need a minute," he stuttered, stood, and rushed out onto the deck overlooking the lake at the back of the house.

He leaned against the railing and dragged in several deep breaths, trying to calm his nerves and come to terms with Sara's bombshell. He almost didn't hear the boots on the wooden planks of the deck. He tensed when the deeply tanned muscular forearms belonging to Thayne came to rest on the railing near his hands.

"You okay?"

Nick bit back a sharp bark of laughter, afraid if he started, he would never stop. "I'm fine," he replied tersely.

"You don't seem fine."

"What do you want me to say, Thayne? You want me to tell you I'm angry? Or that I feel so fucking stupid for giving up so much only to find out it was all for absolutely nothing?" Nick balled his hands into fists on the smooth wood. "Or maybe you want me to say I don't blame you for the shitty situation we're in?" Nick sensed Thayne flinch next to him. He felt awful at the fleeting satisfaction that shot through him, but he forced his guilt away. "The only option we have left now is to hunt it down and kill it."

"How do we even know it will follow me here?" Thayne protested. "We had to have lost it by flying here! I've always driven before now!"

"I know it followed you because I saw it."

"You what?" Thayne demanded, rearing away from the rail.

Nick turned to look at Thayne. "I saw him. Last night. In the woods behind my office. He chased me."

"Why didn't you say anything?" Thayne snapped.

"Because I thought it was something, someone, else! I thought the bond between you and the Created One had been broken! How could I have possibly known the beast had followed us here in less than a day?" Nick shouted.

Thayne opened and closed his mouth several times before his shoulders slumped in defeat. He rubbed at his eyes with thumb and forefinger on one hand. "You're right. I'm sorry. I just wish you had told me."

"When exactly did I have the chance? Besides, it's not like we're best friends or anything. You don't want me in your life, and I'm beginning to see how much I don't want you in mine." Nick immediately regretted his words and gave Thayne a helpless look. "I'm sorry. I didn't mean that."

"Yes, you did," Thayne mumbled, shifting his eyes to the lake. "And I can't blame you for it. I haven't exactly given you much reason to want me around."

Nick fought the urge to wrap his arms around Thayne. The beaten dog expression Thayne wore almost broke his heart. He moved closer to Thayne and laid his hand on Thayne's forearm. "I am sorry."

He saw Thayne's gaze zero in on where Nick's paler hand rested against his darker tanned skin. He went to remove it when Thayne reached up and set his slightly larger palm on top of it. Nick started almost imperceptibly, his body tingling at the contact. He swallowed hard but didn't attempt to pull away until Thayne's thumb brushed over his wrist and the fluttering pulse beating at the surface. Nick cleared his throat and gently extricated himself, putting a few inches between them. He couldn't allow himself to give in to the tiny flame of hope in his heart that Thayne would come to accept him, them. It would only hurt even more when Thayne left.

"We should… ah… go back inside," Nick murmured.

Thayne leaned into the railing again instead of choosing to return to the house. "Can we wait just a little longer to face reality?"

Nick hesitated but gave a small nod and settled back to looking out over the lake. Thayne had surprised him more than once in the space of a few minutes, and his head spun to almost a dizzying point.

"Your pack has a beautiful territory," Thayne commented, interrupting Nick's confusing thoughts.

Nick quirked one corner of his mouth. "Until the last couple of years, I haven't spent much time here. With Seth and what happened to him, I've been away a lot. But quite a bit less since Seth found your brother."

"What exactly did happen to him?" Thayne asked curiously, turning his body a touch toward Nick.

Nick fidgeted. He'd never judged Thayne for his mistake and the Created One that now pursued them, but he couldn't help fearing Thayne would judge him for his mistake. "I screwed up. I was sent to protect him, make sure he could live his life, and instead I put him in danger."

"How?"

"During a brief encounter a few years back with a human, the human became infatuated with me and managed to discover what I am. In his pursuit of me, he fell in with a band of rogue wolves who changed him. Because of me." Nick waited for the explosion, except Thayne didn't say anything, and it encouraged Nick to keep going. "After his conversion, he stalked me further and soon discovered Seth and what Seth could do, so he kidnapped him when I was away on a business trip. I didn't find out until a week later, and by then it was too late. He held Seth captive for months, torturing him, raping him. He even allowed the others he'd created to do the same."

Bitterness and anger at himself rang out clearly in his voice as he continued. "When I finally found Seth, he was nothing but a shell. It took over a year to get him back to a vague impression of who he once was, and another year to get him to accept that it wasn't his fault. He'd wanted so badly to have a mate, someone he could connect to after his parents died, and he'd believed everything the bastard told him because of his need. It's my fault because I wasn't honest with him. If I'd told him the truth of who I was, who he was, none of it would have happened. He'd have been safe and whole. But I was too afraid I'd lose him. I needed him just as much as he needed me."

"I'm sure he doesn't blame you," Thayne said quietly.

"Maybe not, but I blame me."

Thayne turned around and pressed his back to the balustrade, shoving his hands into his jean pockets. "I may not have spent much time around Seth, but I am fairly confident that he wouldn't want you to blame yourself. He doesn't seem the type to hold a grudge, and he certainly cares about you."

Nick stared down toward the water shifting in the light breeze. "How can I possibly forgive myself after everything he went through because of me?"

"By accepting the part you played in it and letting it go." Thayne shrugged.

Thayne's words made it sound so simple. Yet it didn't feel as if it could be so easy.

"What happened to him?"

"What?" Nick asked, confused.

"The Created One. When you rescued Seth from him. What happened to him?"

Nick didn't really have a definite answer to Thayne's question. "We aren't entirely sure. We think he died in the fire that broke out in the warehouse, but we never saw his body."

Thayne grunted. "You thought he was the one from last night."

It wasn't a question. Nick nodded. "Yes. I did think the creature was him. Until I realized just how big it was. Meaner. I've faced a few Created Ones in my life, but this one was different. I've never felt such raw power. I've never feared them before."

"You believe now that it was the one bound to me?"

Nick considered Thayne's words. "Even if it were, how could he possibly have grown so large and so powerful in such a short amount of time?" When Thayne didn't answer, Nick looked over at him. The expression on Thayne's face spoke volumes. "You know it's gotten stronger, don't you? That's why you asked for help."

"The night before I went back home, I pulled over to shift. I hadn't let my wolf out for a while and needed to release some of the energy built up. He found me in the woods. Pursued me. I barely managed to make it back to my truck and get out of there. I'd never seen a Created One so big or vicious."

Nick waited for Thayne to continue.

Thayne curled his hands into fists. "I knew I couldn't handle him on my own. Not when he found me no matter where I went. Not when I couldn't find it in myself to kill him when I knew who he was before I'd fucked up."

Nick sensed there was more to the story between Thayne and whoever the Created One had been before turning. It caused an uncomfortable feeling of jealousy to burn in his lower belly. He wanted to find the Created One and rip its head off for being able to do the one thing he couldn't.

Thayne had cared, still cared, very deeply for the human beneath the monster. Pain stabbed his heart, but he couldn't concentrate on it. He would have to wait until later to go off and lick his wounds in private.

"I didn't mean for any of this to happen," Thayne said helplessly. He lifted his gaze to Nick, a haunted look deep in his eyes. "He wanted to become a doctor. To save lives. I took his life from him. How can I possibly end the life he has now?"

Without giving himself time to think, Nick moved closer to Thayne and placed his hand on Thayne's shoulder. "If his desire was to help others, do you really believe he would want to continue the life he has now when he could, and most likely has, killed someone?"

Thayne hesitantly brought his hand up to Nick's, touching the back of his hand. "No. I know he wouldn't."

Nick squeezed Thayne's shoulder in comfort. "Then we need to find him. Before he can hurt anyone else." Sadness enveloped Thayne, and Nick found himself fighting tears for him. The emotions rolling off Thayne, combined with his own, overwhelmed Nick, and he swallowed hard, forcing himself to turn them off. He carefully extricated his hand from Thayne's. "We should go back inside now."

Thayne wordlessly agreed, and they walked to the door, Nick in the lead. Elijah and Sara were at the table alone.

"Where's Ryan?" Nick asked, frowning.

"A call came in, and he stepped outside," Sara explained, her hawk-like eyes studying him intently.

Nick worked at keeping his expression neutral. Sara had already weaseled the entire story about Thayne out of him a few months ago. She didn't need to know just how much it hurt being so close to Thayne and not being able to have him wholly.

Once the two of them were seated, Nick said, "We're pretty sure the Created One from last night was Thayne's."

Elijah sighed and agreed. "I started to suspect that once I heard the bond between Thayne and the creature hadn't been severed as we'd thought. What are your thoughts on how we should handle this new information?"

Thayne spoke first. "There's no other choice. We have to kill it."

Nick watched Thayne closely, but the stoicism remained the same, unfaltering.

"Or you could stop being such a dense jackass and accept Nick," Sara said dryly.

"Sara!" Nick interjected sharply.

She gave him an innocent look.

"We could set a trap," Elijah replied. "Use Thayne as bait."

Nick vehemently shook his head. "No. I won't allow that to happen."

"It's my choice," Thayne said. "And it's a good idea, because I know he'll find me. He's found me every time I have stopped for the last six months."

"I refuse to let you be put into harm's way to catch him!" Nick barked. "You could get hurt." He hadn't realized how his words sounded until he'd said them and saw the surprise in Thayne's dark eyes. He resisted the urge to fidget under the intense stare.

"Nick is right," Sara said. "We can't use Thayne as bait."

Thayne started to protest again, but Nick pinned him in place with a hard look. "I have never asked you for anything since this whole thing started, but I am asking you not to put yourself in danger." Nick felt Sara watching him knowingly and worked at ignoring it. No matter what had happened between them, he still couldn't bear the idea of anything happening to Thayne.

"Fine," Thayne muttered, slumping in his chair a little.

"Thank you," Nick said gratefully.

If he'd been paying closer attention to Sara, he might have realized what her next intention was. Sara leaned forward into the table a bit and said, "I think until this Created One is caught and put down, neither of you should be alone. Ryan mentioned you were staying at the apartment over the offices, Nicky. It's a much better idea if you returned home and stayed together. Just for safety, of course."

Nick gave her a dirty look and intended on rejecting the idea, but Elijah spoke first. "I think that's a very good idea, Sara. It'll be safer for you both not to be alone. We have no idea what the creature is capable of."

Thayne glanced at Nick, waiting for his outburst most likely. Nick bit his tongue until he could respond without emotion. His wolf gave an eager whine at the thought of spending time in Thayne's presence while his human side cringed at the idea of creating more memories with a man who would be gone as soon as he could get into his truck and take off. Memories that would haunt him through the cold nights and endless days. Right now, all he wanted to do was run and never stop, because the idea of subjecting himself to more pain in the future made him wonder if he were a glutton for punishment.

Sara's hand on his startled him, and he looked at her to find a sympathetic gleam in her eyes. "Nick?"

He cleared his throat and managed a shaky smile. "It makes sense."

Sara smiled and squeezed his hand encouragingly. "Wonderful! I won't worry myself into an early grave if I know you're not alone."

Nick heard a noise in the doorway and turned to find Ryan standing there, an angry expression on his face. Ryan spun on his heel and stalked off. "Excuse me," Nick said and stood, rushing out after Ryan. "Ryan!" Ryan didn't stop. He walked to the front door, his back ramrod straight. "Ryan, damn it!" Nick snapped. "Stop!"

Ryan halted at the door, his hand on the knob. "How can you possibly even think about being around him, Nick?" Ryan asked in a low voice.

Nick sighed and ran both hands over his face in a tired gesture. "Because I really don't have a choice, Ry. I couldn't leave him to face the Created One alone. He's still my mate despite everything that's happened."

Ryan dropped his hand from the handle and shifted around to look at him. "You and I have been friends for a long time, Nick. I've tried to be there and support you for the last six months, but I can't stand by anymore and watch him hurt you again and again. I know...." He let the end of the sentence hang for a several breaths.

"You know what?" Nick prodded quietly.

"I know that he's your mate, but I wish you could have loved me!" Ryan shouted and then backed into the front door, horrified at his words.

Nick's eyes widened, and he stared in shock at Ryan. Never in the time they'd known one another had he ever guessed how Ryan felt. "Ry... I-I'm sorry," Nick said helplessly. He didn't know what else to say.

Ryan covered his face with his hands and gave a shuddering breath. "I've watched you work yourself into the ground since meeting him. Collapsing from exhaustion. I've been there each time the phone rang and you hoped it was him, only to see the disappointment on your face when it wasn't. And now... now that he needs you, he's here. He's taking everything from you and giving nothing in return." He lowered his hands and gave Nick a sad look. "And you're letting him. There really is no hope for us. I've known since you came back and you haven't been the same. Then when you finally admitted what happened in Senaka, any chance I had was gone. You keep allowing him to hurt you, and it kills me to see it."

Nick stared silently at Ryan. How had he never seen it before? He'd been blinded by his desire to protect and be there for Seth. "Ryan, I'm so sorry. I had no idea."

Ryan gave a bitter laugh. "How could you possibly know? You were either never around because of Seth or too busy with bedding the next person who opened their legs to notice."

Nick ignored the jab. He knew Ryan only spoke out of pain. "Why didn't you tell me?"

"Why should I have? So I could humiliate myself or embarrass you? I kept hoping and hoping you'd notice and tell me you felt the same way." Ryan's gaze flitted away from Nick and he whispered, "I-I need some time, Nick. After we put the Created One down, I need some time away from this, from you."

"What are you saying?" Nick asked in bewilderment.

"I'm going to spend some time looking into setting up the second office we talked about in Washington. I need the distance. To gain some perspective. My cousin Kyle said he'd help out at the office here for a while."

"You've already spoken to him about this?" Nick demanded. "Without talking to me first?"

"You haven't exactly been around much, Nick! When you have been, it's like you're not here. Your mind is always somewhere else."

Nick couldn't believe Ryan held him responsible for not knowing he was in love with him. He stepped back a couple of feet to give them some space and breathed in deep. "You know that I love you, Ryan, but as one of my best friends. I'm sorry you feel as if I was doing any of this on purpose. I wasn't. But I am still your partner and deserve to be kept informed of decisions like this. I understand your need for some time away, so take a vacation for a few weeks. Go visit your family or take a trip to Spain like you've always wanted to. Opening the new office without me just because you need to get away is not good business sense, and I won't sign off on it."

Ryan didn't respond immediately. Nick wondered if he would. Ryan's shoulders slumped just before he said, "You're right. I'm sorry. I'm just angry and upset. I wouldn't do any of it without you. I've just got to have some time to come to terms with this."

Nick nodded in understanding. "Take as much time as you need, Ry. I wish I could tell you things could change, but they can't. Now that I've met him, claimed him, there will never be another. No matter what happens between him and me."

Ryan grimaced. "I'm truly sorry, Nick. Spending your life without the ability to move on and find someone else is worse than being in love with someone who doesn't love you back."

"Thanks for pointing out the obvious," Nick said dryly, knowing Ryan didn't mean anything malicious in his comment.

The grimace turned to a grin. "Anytime."

Nick rolled his eyes in exasperation. Neither of them ever could stay mad at each other for long. Maybe it was one of the reasons they rarely fought.

"I think I will take the vacation," Ryan murmured seconds later.

"Where will you go?"

"Maybe to see my parents or go stay with my cousin Shane in Michigan for a while."

"Will you keep in touch?"

"Of course. We still have a business to run. Besides, I'm

not going anywhere yet. Not until this beast is caught and you're no longer in danger."

Nick glanced away from Ryan. "It could take a while."

"Doesn't matter. My feelings weren't your fault. I know you never encouraged me or even looked at me in the same way. I won't abandon you when you need me."

He gave Ryan a grateful look. "You really are a good friend, Ry."

Ryan approached him and gave him a tight hug, slapping him on the back. "I know!" he exclaimed jokingly.

"Will you come back into the dining room please?" Nick asked.

"Yeah."

As they returned to the dining room, Nick wondered if there was anything Thayne hadn't dredged up in his life. For the first time since it happened, Nick truly wondered if he wouldn't have just been better off never having gone to the bar that night in Senaka. If he hadn't met Thayne, he never would have been on the longest roller coaster ride of his life. A ride he wouldn't be leaving anytime soon.

When he and Ryan entered the room, Thayne's eyes were on him instantly, a sharp look in their depths and his mouth in a flat, grim line. Nick knew Thayne had to have heard most of the conversation between him and Ryan. Somehow he couldn't find the energy to care as he dropped onto the chair across from Thayne.

14

THAYNE

T HE ENTIRE time Nick was in the front hallway with Ryan, Thayne felt every emotion Nick ran through and heard every word exchanged, more than one of which had caused him pain. The worst of those statements being Ryan's regard of Nick's collapse from exhaustion and how Thayne was doing nothing except using Nick. He'd been torn between jumping up and ripping Ryan in half for admitting his love for Nick or turning toward the door to disappear from Nick's life before he hurt Nick any further. How had he missed that since their mating? He'd sensed many things from Nick, but nothing that spoke of the pain Ryan implied Nick felt. Or maybe Nick really wasn't as wounded as Ryan thought? The memory of being able to see the outline of Nick's ribcage flashed through Thayne's mind. The man hadn't been that skinny in Senaka. He was sure of it.

Nick wouldn't look at him when they returned to the dining room. He had to know Thayne had heard everything they'd said.

"Everything settled, then?" Sara prodded.

Ryan nodded while Nick remained silent.

"Wonderful!" Sara exclaimed. "Now then, let's see if we can't put our heads together and come up with a plan. I think it would be best if this is resolved before the Summit next month."

Elijah agreed. "We definitely need to take care of the Created One before the majority of our pack leaves the area to attend the Summit. I will call the pack together tomorrow evening to introduce them to Thayne and alert them to the creature's presence here. Cole, Howard, and Wilson should be informed tonight."

"Cole is Elijah's son," Nick explained at Thayne's blank look. "Howard and Wilson are Elijah's Betas."

"What if we find another way to lure it into an enclosure?" Ryan asked, tapping lightly at the tabletop.

"Using what?" Elijah asked.

Ryan shrugged. "Well, we know once the inner beast has entirely taken over the human side of a Created One, they no longer crave human food. They begin to hunt only meat. What if we use an animal or something?"

Nick refuted the idea. "No. It won't work."

"How can you be sure?" Sara asked in curiosity.

"Because in the woods last night, I saw an intelligence in its eyes. It knew what it was doing."

Thayne saw the tension in Nick's shoulders. He barely stopped himself from reaching out and picking up Nick's hand. "What do you think it was doing, then?" Thayne asked.

"When it pursued me through the woods, more than once I got the sense it was teasing me, taunting me. There were several times it caught up to me to where I could feel his breath on my tail, but then it would be gone again. Once I reached the parking lot, the creature stopped following me. It paced along the tree line but wouldn't come out of the shadows."

Elijah made a pensive noise. "Interesting. I've never heard

of such a thing before. Created Ones are not known for having patience or thoughts beyond devouring flesh once the beast has fully taken over. We may be dealing with something new here. But I think we should attempt Ryan's idea. You said you saw it in the forest behind your business, right?"

Nick grunted. "Yes. There's an old mineshaft there, from the gold rush days in the eighteen hundreds. It's been closed off for quite some time, but perhaps we could lure him in there somehow and trap him?"

"How do we lure him?" Thayne asked. "You don't want to use me as bait. So what do you suggest?"

"Fresh meat," Ryan interjected.

Thayne snorted. "You really think that'll work?"

"It's worth a try," Ryan snapped.

Elijah sat back in his chair. "Ryan's right. We have to start somewhere. If the scent of blood doesn't draw it in, we can put together several groups and begin patrolling the area, looking for signs of its den. Maybe we can catch it by surprise. I would prefer we have the advantage by controlling where we fight it."

"How do you know it won't be staying at a motel? He can still take on human form." Thayne pointed out.

"We don't," Elijah answered. "But we can also have some of our own checking for single male occupants at the motels in the area if the mineshaft doesn't work. Tomorrow evening we'll have the pack meeting and afterward gather those who will be involved to discuss the best options to put the plan into action. Now I would suggest you all go home and get some rest. We aren't going to solve this tonight."

Thayne ignored the zing of anticipation that slipped through his belly. He surreptitiously glanced at Nick to see his reaction. Anxiety sparked in the emerald-green eyes staring at him, and Thayne swallowed hard. Was being around him really so bad? Shit, why did he care so much?

"What about tomorrow?" Thayne suddenly asked.

Nick frowned. "What do you mean?"

"We can't just sit around the house. I have to work."

Nick's eyebrows went up. "Work?"

"I got a job at the diner in Redwood. Jo's Place." Thayne watched as Nick's mouth flattened into a thin line. *What the hell?*

"I see."

"Is that a problem?" Thayne challenged, his hackles rising.

Shaking his head, Nick replied, "No. It's perfectly fine. As for tomorrow, I am sure we do not need to remain glued to one another's hip. I'll be at work with Ryan and the others in the office, so I doubt the creature will try anything there. As for the diner, there's people in and out all day long, so it's probably safe to say you'll be good in public."

Thayne wondered at the anger that had crossed Nick's features for a split second. Why would Nick be so mad he'd gotten a job? Would he rather he sat around the house doing nothing all day?

"I—"

Sara interrupted him. "Good. It's all settled, then. Thayne, be careful tomorrow at the diner. Until the others know who you are, there may be some friction."

"I'll be fine," Thayne said.

Ryan stood, looking at his watch. "I have to check into something about Cole's mate before heading back to the office, but I'll see you in the morning, Nick."

"I have to go back to the condo to pick up my things," Nick said, standing also.

Thayne grimaced. "The truck is back at the diner."

Nick gave a short nod. "You'll have to ride with me. I'll drop you off at the diner in the morning, and you can pick it up then. I need to stop at the office to get my laptop and the clothes I brought with me. After, we'll head back to the house."

Ryan and Nick both hugged Elijah and kissed Sara on the cheek before leaving. Thayne tipped his head at Elijah and Sara in respect, but Sara didn't accept the small sign. She threw herself into his arms and embraced him tightly.

"Stop being so stubborn," she snapped at him as she leaned back to look at him. "I can see you fighting yourself, your instincts, about Nicky. Whatever happened to make you hate the bond so much is in the past and is the rarity rather than the norm. Give him and yourself a chance to be happy." She let him go, handed him a bag with some of the clothes she'd found in the attic for him, and moved back to Elijah's side. "Have a good night, Thay!"

Thayne blanched at the nickname she'd given him. He gave her a wan smile and turned, leaving the house quickly to find Nick and Ryan waiting by the black Impala.

"Ryan's car is at the office," Nick explained at Thayne's questioning look.

Ryan gave him a hard stare but didn't say anything, instead opening the door and climbing into the backseat. Thayne settled his long form into the passenger seat next to Nick, who started the engine and backed the car out of the driveway. The ride to Nick's office was tense, and Thayne sensed Ryan's gaze on him more than once. A headache began to knot at the base of his neck and travel up to his temples. His wolf remained on high alert the entire trip, snarling whenever Ryan even twitched in the backseat. Thayne kept tight control of his wolf's instincts to turn around and rip out Ryan's throat for even thinking he had a chance in hell at being with Nick. Thoughts that sent him into a further tailspin of distress internally.

He almost dove out of the car the moment Nick pulled into a parking space outside of a three-story office building the color of desert sand. Thayne rubbed at the base of his nape, trying to ease the tension in his muscles. Ryan bid Nick good-bye, glared at Thayne, and walked to a nondescript white sedan nearby. Thayne followed Nick to the front door and stopped just inside to look around. The entryway had marbled floors with a large receptionist desk patterned with faux white stones and light stormy-blue walls. Nick waved at a pretty blonde woman behind the desk and strode to an elevator. Thayne's eyes were instantly drawn to the muscular rear end flexing with each step. His jeans suddenly felt extremely uncomfortable.

Nick looked back at him, one delicate eyebrow arched in question. "You coming?"

Thayne cleared his throat nervously, his palms sweating, and trailed Nick to the elevator. "Nice place," he murmured.

"Thank you."

Two-word sentences. It was going to be a long night at this rate. The door opened, and Thayne gestured for Nick to precede him inside. Nick hit the button for the third floor, and the doors slid closed. It didn't take long to reach the top floor.

Thayne followed Nick down a small corridor. He was so caught up in his thoughts he didn't realize Nick had stopped and bumped into him. "Sorry," Thayne muttered, his skin tingling at the contact.

Nick grunted but didn't reply.

The inside of the apartment made all of the places Thayne had stayed during his travels look like a cardboard box under the overpass of a major highway. Thayne stared around him at the fancy leather couches, marble countertops, and rich, dark wood furniture. He shifted in discomfort.

Nick headed straight toward a room at the back of the apartment, leaving Thayne alone. If Thayne felt out of place in Nick's world before, this just cemented the feeling. He was pizza and beer while Nick was wine and gourmet meals. The ancestors had really decided to fuck with him by making him the mate of a man the complete opposite of himself. Nick had money and grace. Thayne was uncouth, had no manners, and seriously didn't care what anyone else thought. *Except Nick*, the stubborn little voice in his head whispered. Thayne reprimanded himself mentally. He really needed to get the hell out of Nick's life before he ruined the good one Nick had.

"Would you grab the laptop bag next to the couch, please?" Nick called out from the bedroom, disrupting Thayne's inner monologue.

"Uh... sure." Thayne spotted the black leather bag Nick had carried on the plane from Senaka, snatched it up, and took it to where Nick was. He halted in the doorway when he saw Nick bent over near the bed, unplugging a power cord. The jeans were tight across Nick's backside and Thayne stifled a groan at his body's instant response.

"I... uh...."

Nick straightened and held out his hand without looking at Thayne. "Thank you."

The blatant distance Nick displayed toward him angered him. Thayne waited until Nick looked at him to hand him the bag. He set the strap in Nick's outstretched hand, allowing his fingers to drift across Nick's palm.

"We're obviously stuck together until this thing with Ma... the Created One is over, but I would appreciate it if you wouldn't just ignore me," Thayne said.

Nick raised both eyebrows at Thayne this time, dropping the laptop bag on the bed. "I would think that's how you want it to be, considering you're so anxious to get the hell out of here and away from me."

"What the hell are you talking about?" Thayne demanded, stepping closer to Nick. He'd sensed something wrong since

Sara and Elijah's. They'd reached a relatively shaky truce out on the back deck, but something changed before they'd left to come here.

"You couldn't even wait to get a job so you could have the cash to leave," Nick accused coldly.

Thayne breathed in deep, trying hard to hold his temper in check. "Did it ever occur to you that I don't like owing anything to anyone? I'm not going to sit around your house and be taken care of like a fucking pet!"

Nick sneered at him and moved until they were almost chest to chest, his hands tightened into fists at his side. "Why should I believe you? You've never wanted this." He gestured to himself. "You've made it abundantly clear the only thing you want from me is rescuing from the fucking creature you created!"

Thayne shouted, unthinkingly, in return, "Maybe that isn't all I want anymore!"

Nick's mouth opened and shut several times before he responded, a sharp, humorless smile on his face. "You expect me to believe you want this to be more than just needing my help? When did that change? Or maybe it's because you can't go find the next willing body to roll around in the hay with and I'm the only one available!"

At first Thayne allowed Nick's words to hurt him. They struck him hard. He stared at Nick, watching the emotions racing across his lightly tanned features, a five o'clock shadow dusting his face. A tight fist wrapped around Thayne's heart and squeezed. Anger followed on the heels of the pain, and Thayne reacted. He grabbed Nick, one arm sliding around the narrow waist, and yanked him close. Thayne slammed his lips down on Nick's, thrusting his tongue inside Nick when Nick tried to protest. Thayne didn't let up despite the half-assed struggle Nick made before capitulating. A groan rattled in Thayne's throat when Nick's tongue slid out to caress his. He tightened his embrace around Nick's waist, his other hand sliding into Nick's hair to hold Nick steady as he plundered the depths of his mouth.

He knew he'd broken Nick's request to never touch him without permission and Nick would be furious when the kiss ended, but he'd allowed his pain and anger to guide his actions. Thayne wanted nothing more than to throw Nick down on the bed beside them and bury himself in the heated body against his, but Nick would never forgive him for taking advantage. He found himself wanting to prove to Nick that he was worthy to be his mate, and his wolf whined in agreement, wagging its tail in excitement. He'd never been very good at verbally expressing his feelings or thoughts, really, even with his brother. Thayne softened the kiss, slowed the pace while loosening his hold on Nick's waist. He wanted to show Nick this was more than just a reaction to their argument. He moved the hand holding Nick's head in place to the side of Nick's neck and gentled his touch, stroking along the smooth skin.

Nick sighed into their kiss, and Thayne's pulse quickened. He tentatively stroked his tongue over Nick's, enjoying the slick feel of wet skin over wet skin. Taking a chance, Thayne slipped his hand beneath the hem of Nick's shirt and lightly caressed the warm flesh exposed at the waist of Nick's jeans. It delighted Thayne when he felt Nick's palms slide under his shirt and across his back. This… this he knew how to handle. Sex was uncomplicated, simple. They didn't need words to tell their intent or to show how they felt. Just touches and kisses, sighs of pleasure and lust. Thayne knew how to communicate through sex.

Thayne broke their kiss and brushed his lips over Nick's stubbled jawline. Nick didn't attempt to stop him as he moved farther along to Nick's ear, where he skated the tip of his tongue over the lobe and neatly curved cartilage. A shudder rippled through Nick's lean length, and satisfaction nipped at Thayne. When Thayne pressed a kiss to the skin behind Nick's ear, Nick gripped him tighter, and a small sound, almost a whine, came from Nick's throat. Apparently, Nick had a hot spot there! Thayne filed the tidbit away for later and followed the kiss with a heated lick of his tongue over the same spot. Nick arched against him, and this time a true whine escaped Nick. Thayne growled lustily at the noise and gently raked his teeth over Nick's throat.

"Thayne!" Nick cried out, his nails digging into Thayne's back.

Thayne shoved his thigh between Nick's, pressing into the hard cock straining to be free. He wanted to make Nick feel good, to replace the memories of the unwanted touches with new ones. Rocking his leg, he ground into Nick and tightened the arm around Nick's waist again, holding him steady for the ride. Nick undulated his hips in need while Thayne captured Nick's mouth once more in a deep kiss. Everything else became background noise: the danger of the Created One, the uncertainty of their future, the promise Thayne had already begun to wonder if he would be able to keep or if he really even wanted to anymore. Nothing else mattered right then except Nick in his arms and keeping him there as long as possible.

Every touch of Nick's hands on his body, every sigh, and every quiver wracking Nick's frame encouraged Thayne. It gave him hope that the damage wasn't irreparable, and that hope gave him pause because he shouldn't want to feel hope for a future. Forcing those thoughts away, he concentrated on Nick. He could hardly differentiate between Nick's pleasure at his touch and his own at Nick's response to him. Thayne continued to rock Nick along his thigh, urging him closer to the edge and the greatest desire for release. Nick whimpered into Thayne's mouth, and Thayne couldn't help the satisfied rumble that ripped from his throat.

He returned to Nick's ear and murmured in a gravelly voice, "Let go, baby, let go and fly."

If Thayne were an arrogant man, he'd swear just his voice pushed Nick over the cliff and into a hot, shattering orgasm. Nick arched his back, almost bending halfway over Thayne's arm still wrapped around his waist, and gripped at Thayne's broad shoulders, desperately seeking an anchor in the storm. Thayne could feel the jets of creamy liquid soaking through Nick's jeans and into his own. The tangy scent of come saturated the air and stung Thayne's nose, igniting his own passions further. He struggled to ignore the aching cock between his thighs, choosing to bury his face in Nick's throat and hold on until Nick's release came to an end. He just hoped Nick wouldn't be upset with him.

As the passion between them cooled, Thayne sensed Nick's withdrawal, and sadness enveloped him. He couldn't blame Nick for it, though. Not after everything he'd done to insist he didn't want a mate. Nick loosened his fingers and carefully pushed against Thayne's shoulders. Thayne didn't know what else to do except let him free. He saw a large patch of wetness on his jeans and looked up at Nick to see a matching one on the front of Nick's.

"I...."

Nick brushed past Thayne dismissively, snagging a different pair of jeans from his suitcase on the bed as he went. Thayne watched helplessly as Nick closed himself off again just like he closed the door to the bathroom behind him.

Sinking down on the edge of the mattress, Thayne dropped his head into his hands and berated himself for thinking a single frottage session would possibly make Nick forget all of the awful things he'd done.

He looked up when he heard the door open again and Nick came back into the room. "Nick, I—"

"That shouldn't have happened." Nick cut him off coldly, stuffing the dirty jeans into his suitcase. "Please wait in the other room while I finish."

Thayne opened and closed his mouth several times, trying to think of the right thing to say. Nothing came out. He stood and walked toward the bedroom door, stopping at Nick's side for a single breath before continuing to the living space. Thayne snarled at himself mentally and resisted the urge to punch the nearest wall. He'd broken his fair share of fingers in the past, plus he didn't want to damage Nick's place. Sighing, he went to stand by the french doors overlooking a balcony and waited. The sun hung low in the sky, a big ball of fire sinking into the horizon steadily. He could just barely see a few of the lights in the parking lot below click on one after the other.

He heard Nick enter the room behind him and turned. Nick wouldn't look at him, and Thayne ground his teeth together. The whole reason for his angry reaction had been the cool detachment Nick treated him with, and it reminded him why he'd grabbed Nick in the first place.

"Nick," he snapped.

Emerald-green eyes zeroed in on his. Thayne's breath caught at the spark of pain in them, and he crossed the room to Nick. He slid his arms around Nick and pulled him into a gentle, undemanding hug. Nick held himself stiff at first, the two suitcases in his hands, but eventually the desire for comfort won out, and each suitcase hit the ground with a thump. Satisfaction roared through Thayne when he felt Nick's arms tentatively wrap over his back. It was a simple hug, without lust or passion. Thayne closed his eyes and savored the moment. Nick didn't struggle to be released or push him away, and it increased the hope inside his heart that maybe his stupidity wasn't undoable.

The sun had disappeared completely, and they were surrounded by darkness when Thayne finally found it in him to pull back from Nick. He cupped Nick's face in his hands and tilted Nick's head up, encouraging him to look at him. Nick resisted halfheartedly but gave in and raised his eyes to Thayne's. Thayne brushed his thumbs over the high ridge of Nick's cheekbones in a light caress, marveling at the sheer difference in his tanned skin against the soft white of Nick's. He did something he'd never done to anyone, not even Matt. Instead of kissing Nick's lips, Thayne placed an undemanding kiss on each of Nick's cheeks and then stepped away, trailing his hand down Nick's arm as he did so.

Nick studied him in the dim light cast by the rising moon until Thayne shifted in discomfort, and Nick murmured, "We should go."

"Yeah," Thayne returned.

Thayne followed Nick from the apartment down to the elevator. No words were exchanged as they descended to the first floor. Most of the lights in the building were off and the parking lot nearly empty when they exited the front door. Nick's Impala and one other vehicle sat there, forlorn in the darkness.

"Ryan's still here," Nick said inanely and glanced back at the building, hesitating. "I thought he left."

Biting back jealousy at the obvious worry on Nick's face, Thayne asked, "Do you want to go check on him?"

Shaking his head, Nick pulled out his keys and locked the building. "No. He'll be okay. I don't think he really wants to be around me right now."

Thayne remembered the conversation he'd overheard earlier in the day and figured he'd stay out of it. They walked to

Nick's Impala and were on the road in minutes. Thayne couldn't help but steal several looks at Nick, wondering what was going on inside Nick's head. He didn't really know how to "turn on" the ability to read Nick's thoughts. Everything he'd picked up since their mating had been accidental. It frustrated him to not really know how Nick felt right then. Closing his eyes, Thayne tried to open his mind to Nick's, letting his own guard down in the process. Emotional distress swamped him, and Thayne couldn't stop the small noise he made. Apparently Nick was well versed in hiding his emotions behind a façade of indifference.

"What the hell?" Nick demanded. "Get out of my fucking head!"

Opening his eyes, Thayne turned in his seat toward Nick. "I'm sorry. I was just—"

"We may be mates, but that doesn't give you the right to invade my privacy!" Nick snarled, hands tightening on the steering wheel. "Not when you can't seem to figure out just what it is you want!"

Thayne remained silent, searching for a way to explain why he'd been trying to "read" Nick. "One minute you're hot, and the next you're cold. You say you don't want a mate, and then you...." Nick trailed off, the lapse implying the recent embrace inside the apartment.

Thayne didn't really know how to answer Nick. He knew since they'd met he'd played the tag-and-run game. He ran a hand through his hair and sighed. He owed Nick something. Didn't he? Except he wasn't sure if he could give Nick what he wanted.

"All this time I've wondered if I had done things differently that night in Senaka, maybe it wouldn't have turned out this way," Nick said quietly when Thayne didn't answer right away. "But I finally realized it's just because you don't want me in your life. Nothing could or will change that."

Breath catching in his throat at the solemn defeat evident

in Nick's voice, Thayne protested, "That's not true!"

"Isn't it? You certainly haven't done anything to convince me otherwise."

"No!" Thayne exclaimed in desperation. "I-I just don't know how to do this."

"Do what?"

Thayne waved his hand between them and looked out the window at the road ahead. "This. You. Us. I've never allowed myself to care about anyone before, except my family."

Nick glanced at him. "Not even the man you changed?"

Shifting in his seat a bit at the question, Thayne murmured, "I started to, but I knew it wouldn't last."

"Why?"

"Because I didn't belong in his world," Thayne replied simply.

Nick didn't respond immediately. His next question set Thayne's mind on a whirlwind of remembrance. "Why have you been so afraid to let someone in?"

The memory of Dakota's father on the couch with a gun in his hand and blood splattered across the back of the couch and wall behind it flashed in front of him. Thayne's hands tightened into fists on his lap. More images of Dakota's father as he'd gone through the loss of his mate played through his mind like a minimovie: the weight loss, the exhaustion, and the pure agony he'd experienced before and after she died. He'd been witness to almost all of it, constantly with Dakota through the months she suffered. Thayne had seen Dakota's pain as he'd lost his mother, but it didn't even begin to rival what his father felt. A bereavement so deep he couldn't bear to live with it longer than a matter of a few hours. How could he possibly admit to Nick the fear he carried inside of himself about going through that very same thing?

"I'm not afraid," Thayne lied.

Nick glared at him. "You want me to believe you when you say you want to be in my life, but you don't want to tell me the truth?"

"I'm telling you the truth!"

Snorting, Nick turned into his housing development. "Yeah, right. I haven't been around you long, but I know you're lying!"

Before Thayne could say anything more, something hit the side of the car hard enough to send it into a crashing roll. Glass exploded from the windshield and side windows, cascading through the car and along the ground. Thayne tried to cover his face but felt several shards scratch his cheek and forehead. The screech of metal impacting the pavement and crushing echoed inside his ears. The Impala flipped several times before coming to a rest, upside down, on the empty acre of grass just past the sign announcing the name of the community.

Thayne had hit his head hard at some point while the car was still in motion, and hung there, suspended by the seat belt, stunned. He could smell gas and hear the crinkle of glass still falling out of the busted-out windows.

"Nick?" he gasped out in question when he could breathe.

Nick didn't respond.

Thayne blinked to clear his vision and looked over to see Nick also hanging by his seat belt with his eyes closed and blood dripping from a bad gash on his forehead and soaking into his blond hair, staining it red.

"Nick!" Thayne shouted in panic and reached for his buckle, landing with a thud on the roof. "Nick," he called again, crawling out of his window and rushing around to Nick's side.

He grabbed the handle and tried to open the door, but it stuck from being crushed during impact. Dropping to his knees, Thayne could hear Nick's heartbeat, but his breathing was thready at best. Nick's skin was paler than normal, causing the blood to stand out starkly against his forehead. Thayne didn't know whether to pull Nick out of the car or to call an ambulance first. The choice was taken away from him when he picked up the smell of smoke and knew something was or would be on fire. He reached in and undid the buckle on Nick's belt, softening his fall as best he could. Thayne tried to be as gentle as possible while pulling Nick through the window. As soon as Nick was clear, Thayne picked him up in his arms and carried him far enough away that if the car exploded they wouldn't be in harm's way.

He set Nick on the ground carefully and started searching Nick's pockets for a cell phone. What the hell had happened? What had hit them? Thayne located the phone in Nick's front jean pocket and pulled it out to dial 9-1-1. The operator answered, and Thayne gave brief details while scanning the area for whatever had hit the Impala on the passenger side. He didn't see another car, and he was fairly certain no animal could have caused them to flip like they had. Unless… no, it wasn't possible. The Created One would have to have immense strength to be able to knock the car off the road and not be injured itself!

"Please, hurry!" he barked into the phone.

"The ambulance is on its way, sir," the operator soothed.

Nick still hadn't regained consciousness, and Thayne was starting to worry even more as Nick's breathing got shallower with every passing minute. Thayne's wolf whined in fear at losing Nick, and Thayne ground his teeth together.

"Don't you fucking die on me. Not now. Not when you made me care, you son of a bitch!"

He stripped off his T-shirt and pressed it to the still-bleeding gash on Nick's forehead. The minutes ticked by in agonizing slowness. Not only did he have to keep an eye on Nick, but he had to stay alert in case it had been the Created

One and it came back for them. Maybe it had been hurt and that's why it didn't try to attack again? Nick's skin grew paler and paler, increasing Thayne's panic that he'd witness Nick dying while he sat there and did nothing. He could die before Thayne had the chance to tell Nick the truth about the pact or that he wanted to give them a chance. A big step for himself. Only he needed to take care of something first, and then he could be free to try to be the mate Nick always wanted.

Thayne held Nick's hand and prayed to his ancestors to return Nick to him safe and alive. "Please," he murmured. "Please don't let him die. I know I've been a bastard, but I can't lose him."

He heard the siren of the ambulance first, and he almost passed out in relief when he could finally see the lights of not only the ambulance, but also a couple of police cars. He swore beneath his breath. What the hell could he tell them? He couldn't exactly say they'd been run off the road by a monster. They'd think he'd hit his head. Well… technically he had, but he wasn't crazy.

The ambulance pulled to a stop in front of them, and the EMTs rushed out of the vehicle. They basically shoved Thayne out of the way, forcing him to suppress the urge to snarl and lunge at them for pushing him away from Nick's side. He knew they were there to help Nick.

"Sir? We need to ask you a few questions about the accident," a young male police officer said as the EMTs carefully lifted Nick onto a gurney and began to load him into the ambulance.

"I need to go with him," Thayne insisted, his eyes never leaving Nick even as they put him in the back of the vehicle.

"Sir, we need to get the details of the accident from you," the cop tried again.

Thayne took his eyes off of Nick long enough to give the

officer an icy-cold glare. Something in his expression made the guy back up a step. "I need to go with him to the hospital. I can answer your questions later."

The policeman swallowed and tipped his head. "Sure, mister. We can handle the report at the hospital."

Thayne strode to the ambulance and climbed inside just as the driver went to shut the doors while the second EMT began working on Nick. "I'm going with him."

The EMT placed an oxygen mask over Nick's nose and mouth and took his blood pressure and heart rate on the way to the hospital. Thayne remained as close to Nick as possible, only moving when the EMT needed to get to Nick. Words of punctured lung, broken ribs, and possible internal bleeding froze Thayne's blood in his veins, and he started begging his ancestors. *Please, I'll do anything. Just don't take him away from me. Please don't let him die!*

"Sir, were you injured?" the medical technician attending to Nick asked.

Having been focused entirely on Nick, it took a moment for Thayne to realize the EMT spoke to him. "No," Thayne replied. "The blood—the blood is his." He tripped on his words, knowing the red staining his clothing and skin belonged to his mate.

"Are you certain? You may not even realize you've been injured." The EMT moved to check him, but Thayne waved him away, refusing.

"I'm fine. Please, just help him," Thayne pleaded.

"We're doing everything we can, sir," the man placated him. "I'd like to have you checked out at the hospital, just in case."

"Fine," Thayne grunted, clasping Nick's hand tighter.

By the time they reached the hospital, Thayne's temples were throbbing with a headache because of his teeth clenched so tightly. He jumped out of the vehicle and stood to the side, waiting helplessly as they unloaded the gurney, and raced along with them into the ER.

A nurse stopped him from following past the nurses' station. "Sir, are you a family member?"

If one more person called him sir, he was likely to snap. "No."

"I'm sorry, but you're going to have to wait out here." She pointed him toward the waiting room. "As soon as we have any information, we'll let you know," she said firmly when he tried to protest.

He wanted to tell her to go to hell and push past her, rules be damned, except he didn't want to take the chance that they would have security or the police remove him from the building altogether. So he stalked to the place she'd pointed and immediately proceeded to pace the waiting room like a caged lion.

Thayne didn't remember a time he'd ever felt so afraid in his life. What if Nick died? Even shifters can die from serious injuries, despite their advanced healing. He needed to be with Nick! Frustration and impotence built to an unbearable level, so by the time the police arrived at the hospital to get his statement, he quaked with suppressed rage and fear. In his worry for Nick, he hadn't noticed the scent of a wolf on one of the cops at the site of the accident. This time the smell stung his nose seconds before the man stepped into the waiting room. Thayne spun around and snarled at him, eyes flashing between human and lupine.

The shifter held his hands up in a nonthreatening gesture. "I'm just here to inform you Elijah and Sara are on the way here."

He gave the unknown wolf a suspicious look. How the hell did he know Thayne would have a clue who Elijah and Sara were?

"I recognized Nick as soon as we got to the scene and

called Elijah on the way here," the shifter explained and offered his hand to Thayne. "I'm Mikhail Bryce."

Briefly shaking Mikhail's hand, Thayne resumed pacing again in silence.

"Not much for talking, are you?" Mikhail asked dryly. Thayne stopped and glared at him. Mikhail gestured at a nearby seat. "Sit. It's going to be a while before we hear anything."

He ignored the directive and resumed his endless cycle of walking to one side of the room and then back again. His mind focused on keeping himself in one piece emotionally. The hollow feeling inside of his chest was the number one reason he'd avoided attachments. He didn't want to feel as if a black hole were threatening to suck him in at any moment, or the awful sense of powerlessness. If he hadn't allowed himself to become so distracted by the conversation with Nick in the car, maybe the accident could have been avoided. Maybe he would have been able to sense the creature and have Nick stop the Impala.

A hand on his shoulder startled him, and he halted. Mikhail gave a small squeeze and pushed him toward a chair. "Wearing yourself out isn't going to help Nick. He needs you there when they bring him out of surgery. Now, why don't you have a seat? I'll grab you a cup of coffee. Sara and Elijah should be here soon."

"I can't sit," Thayne muttered, running his hands through his hair. "If I hadn't let myself become so agitated, this never would have happened." Hell, if he'd never allowed Nick to claim him, this never would have happened. Gods, not only had he hurt Nick in countless ways, but now Nick's life was in danger. If Nick died, he'd never forgive himself.

"If the creature is as powerful as Elijah thinks it is—and seeing the damage it caused to Nick's Impala, it looks as if it's pretty damn powerful—then there's really nothing you could have done to stop what happened. Nick's a strong man, and he will pull through this. Just have a little faith," Mikhail encouraged him.

Thayne felt the cell phone he'd unceremoniously shoved into his pocket vibrate. At first he ignored it, but the person was persistent. He yanked the phone out of his pocket and saw Seth's name on the caller ID. He knew Seth would blame him just as he blamed himself, but Seth had the ability to heal others. Why hadn't he thought of that in the first place!

Jabbing the button, Thayne barked, "Seth," into the receiver.

"Thayne?" Seth sounded confused. "Why are you answering Nick's cell?"

He swallowed hard and quickly outlined what had happened.

Seth didn't even hesitate. "I'm on my way. I'll be there on the first flight out of Casper!"

Thayne prayed that if the doctors couldn't save Nick, Seth would arrive in time to heal him.

15

NICK

NICK SMILED as he watched his wolf playing in the wide-open field, the tall grasses blowing gently in the breeze coming down from the mountains to the east. He stood in the center of the clearing, looking at the trees surrounding him. He'd always loved nature—the smell of the dirt on the forest floor, the tickling sensation of the grass brushing over his fur, even more so when running with others from his pack. There was nothing as sensual as the full moon high overhead or the scent of mated pairs coupling drifting on the cool summer air. Nick had always been envious of those wolves. Every full moon, he prayed hard to find his true mate, to run with him and become one with him under the soft glow above. Now the thought caused him pain, and he frowned.

His wolf let out a sudden snarl, and Nick jerked himself back to reality. Black fur standing on end, Nick's wolf growled deeper, chest rumbling with the ferocity of the sound. Nick peered toward the shadows of the trees his wolf stared at. Two red dots shone out at him, and Nick stumbled back several steps, his heart beating frantically against his ribcage like a bird cornered by a predator. Everywhere he turned, the red eyes were there, taunting him.

"What are you?" Nick shouted. "What do you want?"

There was no answer, just the endless red. Nick's chest suddenly constricted with mind-numbing pain, and he cried out, wrapping his arms around himself. The pain grew steadily worse, bringing him to his knees. A deep baritone voice washed over him, and he tried to move toward the source only to find himself unable to budge.

"Shhh. Relax, baby. You're safe."

Nick tried emphatically to alert the owner of the voice to his distress and danger. He wasn't safe. He glanced at the trees again, and the red dots were gone. As he frantically searched the darkness for the threat, he felt a hot breath on his neck, and the slick wetness of saliva dripping onto his nape.

"Leave me alone!" he pleaded.

The sensation of a strong hand wrapping around his wrist brought surprising comfort despite the menace hunting him. "Open your eyes, Nick. Come on, baby. I know you can do it," the voice murmured once more.

Suddenly, he found himself falling, the ground sucked out from beneath him. He tried to scream, only his voice had been stolen away like the forest floor. He frantically tried to hold on to the hand gripping his wrist as light rushed up to meet him.

"No!" he cried out as he opened his eyes and struggled to sit up, held in place by the strength of someone.

"Nick! Stop! You're going to hurt yourself further."

Nick blinked frantically, clearing the fog from his mind, and realized the person restraining him was Thayne. The steady beep of a nearby monitor brought about the knowledge that he lay in a hospital bed.

"Thayne?" he whispered unsteadily.

Thayne sighed and carefully released his death-hold on Nick's shoulders. Thayne sat perched on the edge of the bed.

Nick looked around them to see sunlight filtering through the blinds and a room full of flowers. "What happened?" he queried uncertainly, searching his memory for the reason he was in the hospital.

"We were in a car accident," Thayne said in a flat tone. "You were hurt."

The events of the drive home came flooding back. Someone or something had sideswiped them. Nick immediately searched for bandages on Thayne, worried. "Were you injured?" he asked when he didn't spot any visual evidence of Thayne being hurt.

"No," Thayne replied.

Nick gave him a skeptical look. "Did you see a doctor to know for sure?"

"The EMTs insisted and wouldn't let me see you until I was checked over," Thayne muttered, a miffed tone ringing through.

Nick almost smiled, knowing his mate didn't like being forced to do anything he didn't want to. "How long have I been here?" Nick asked.

Seth's voice came from the doorway. "Two days."

Nick's gaze swung toward the source and stared in shock. "Seth? What are you doing here?"

Seth glared at him and stalked to the bed. Thayne stood and moved away to stand by the window. "What do you mean, what am I doing here? I came because you're my best friend and you needed me!"

Nick tried once more to sit up, only to grasp that his chest was wrapped in bandages when he felt resistance. He frowned. "Why am I mummified?"

Seth took Thayne's original seat. "Your ribs were broken during the crash, and one of them punctured your left lung.

The doctor said it was a miracle you survived. If it weren't for you being a shifter, you would have died. I came as soon as I could."

"You healed me?" Nick asked, worried for his friend.

Seth shot him an incredulous look. "Of course, you dolt, at least as much as I could without causing too much suspicion. I wasn't going to let you die."

"But it's dangerous for you to use your abilities, especially in a place where a human could discover what you can do," Nick protested.

"It was worth the risk," Kasey said as he entered the room and came to a stop at Seth's side, his arm instinctively slipping around Seth's shoulders. "Besides, your Alpha has a lot of contacts and a lot of sway here. No one will suspect anything more than a miracle having happened."

"Seth's safety isn't worth my life!" he exclaimed.

"Bullshit," Seth barked. "Your life is just as valuable as mine is."

Kasey held up his hand when Nick tried to argue further. "While I agree that Seth's life matters the most to me, your life is important, too, Cartwright. Now shut up and let him hover. We've been suffering through the god-awful excuse for coffee around this place since we got here and the pathetic cuisine they call food. He deserves the right to worry about you."

Nick snapped his mouth shut with an audible click and gave Kasey and Seth an apologetic look. "I'm sorry. Thank you for saving my life."

Seth waved his hand at Nick. "Not me. I only helped speed up the process. Thayne saved your life. If he hadn't acted as quickly as he had and called for an ambulance, you wouldn't be here right now."

Nick had almost forgotten Thayne remained in the room. Thayne hadn't spoken a word since revealing the crash. He shifted his gaze to Thayne's broad back. "Thayne?" He saw Thayne's shoulders tense and sensed Thayne expected rejection from him. "Thank you."

The tension visibly eased from Thayne as he turned toward Nick. Shock barreled through Nick when he saw the dark circles beneath Thayne's eyes and the haggard look of a man who obviously hadn't slept. His worry before about Thayne being injured hadn't allowed him to really take in Thayne's appearance otherwise. He found it difficult to reconcile the distressed man before him with the one who'd been so adamant about not caring for him. Maybe his immediate assumption about Thayne's distraught state was only wishful thinking, though. Did Thayne really care so much about him after everything? Had Jeremiah been right and Thayne had begun to accept the mating bond between them? His belief in the connection between mates had been tarnished since the night he'd met Thayne, and he couldn't quite bring himself to believe Thayne had done a complete one-eighty.

Thayne visibly swallowed and moved to his side. Nick couldn't stop the hitch of his breath when Thayne slumped down on the chair beside the bed and picked up his hand. Nick glanced at Seth in surprise. Seth gave him one of his "we'll talk later" looks and patted Nick's hand.

"I think now that you're awake, Kasey and I are going to go grab some much-needed shut-eye."

Nick started to protest, but Kasey agreed and took Seth's hand. "Good idea, pup."

Seth sighed and rolled his eyes. "Despite the many hours of threatening death by dismemberment, he still refuses to stop calling me that ridiculous name."

Nick chuckled lightly, regretting it immediately when his ribs protested and sweat beaded on his forehead. He groaned and took shallow breaths. Thayne's hand squeezed his in comfort, raising Nick's confusion even higher.

Seth patted Nick's thigh. "After they let you out of here, I'll take care of the rest. Didn't want to raise too much suspicion with how bad a shape you were in when you got here."

"Thanks, Seth," Nick gasped.

Seth smiled and stood.

Thayne frowned at him. "Maybe I should get the nurse to give you some more morphine if you're in that much pain."

The idea of returning to the haze of sleep and the haunting red dots caused Nick to vehemently shake his head. "No! I-I mean, I'm fine. I think I've slept enough for two days."

"You still need to rest." Thayne grunted.

"I can rest later." Nick tried more than once to extricate his hand from Thayne's without making it too obvious. "What happened to my car?" Thayne winced, and Nick almost cried. His grandfather's Impala. "Where is it?"

"The cop who came to take my statement said it would be towed to the nearest junkyard. I told them you would decide what you wanted done with it once you'd seen the damage."

"How bad is it?" Nick asked. Thayne hesitated. "Come on, Thayne. How bad was the damage?"

"The impact by the Created One was so hard it caused the car to roll several times. There was a lot of body damage from what I can remember, and the windows were pretty much gone. I don't know about the rest of the car."

Nick had lost a lot in the last six months since meeting Thayne. He hadn't let the loss of his house, claiming a mate who didn't want him, or the sting of Thayne's rejection affect him beyond sleepless nights and the dull ache he carried in his chest. The knowledge that the one tie he had remaining to his grandfather was most likely gone brought every feeling he'd kept buried straight to the surface. Tears burned his eyes as emotion clogged his throat.

"It's just a car, Nick," Thayne soothed, stroking Nick's arm.

"It's not just a car," Nick choked. "It belonged to my grandfather, and it's all I have left of him."

Thayne moved to perch on the edge of the bed, lifting Nick's hand onto his thigh. "He was important to you?"

Nick rubbed at his eyes to force back the sting of tears and nodded. "He raised me. My parents died when I was a kid. He took me in and cared for me, helped me watch after Seth, and never once made me feel like a burden. He passed away while I was in college, leaving me the Impala. He loved that car." A small smile flitted across Nick's lips. "We spent every Sunday working on it, changing filters or whatever else he could come up with that needed some kind of repair. I remember the smell of the grease and how he would run his hands over the fender as if it were the most beautiful thing he'd ever laid eyes on."

"I'm so sorry, Nick," Thayne murmured.

Shrugging, Nick winced as the motion caused his ribs to twinge once more. "It's not as though I haven't already lost everything else. The only thing I have left is my company."

"That's not true," Thayne protested. "You have Seth and Kasey and…."

Nick raised an eyebrow as Thayne trailed off. "And?"

Thayne didn't answer him.

"And what, Thayne?" Nick repeated.

"And me," Thayne whispered, looking away from him.

Nick raised an eyebrow. "Again with this? I don't have you. I've never had you. All I've ever been to you is a means to an end, Thayne."

"No!" Thayne jerked his gaze back to Nick.

"Bullshit. If it weren't for that damned Created One, I

wouldn't even have heard from you at all!" Nick glared at Thayne. "Don't try to lie to me because I'm not fucking stupid."

Thayne glared right back. "You have no idea what I would have done, damn it! And neither do I. Maybe you're right. Maybe I wouldn't have contacted you if it weren't for the Created One, but I'm here now, and maybe *I* was the stupid one."

"Meaning what?" Nick probed.

The question stalled Thayne for a split second before he blurted out, "Maybe my feelings have changed and I want to give this a shot."

Nick's breath hitched, this time not from the pain in his ribs but the skip in his heartbeat as hope wrapped a hand tightly around his heart and squeezed. Thayne looked away from him again, embarrassment written on his face. Nick wanted so badly to give in and just believe Thayne was telling the truth, but the past several months, especially the last few days, made him wary of accepting Thayne's words at face value.

"How do I know you won't change your mind again tomorrow? Or the next day?" Nick murmured.

Thayne returned his gaze to Nick's. "How does anyone know that, Nick? What if you change your mind? Everyone lives with the same fear in the back of their mind that the person they're with will fall out of love with them and leave. Even if it's only subconsciously. They still try, though, and try again when their fears are realized. No one can know the future."

Nick had never thought Thayne verbal enough to speak so openly. Nothing he'd seen up until then had given him any other impression, so the outright emotional honesty gave him pause as he studied Thayne. A small white scar he'd never noticed before curved in a slight half-moon at the corner of Thayne's mouth. Without thinking, he raised his hand to touch it. Thayne caught his wrist just as his finger grazed the mark, giving Nick a questioning look at the soft stroke.

"There's a scar there," Nick said inanely.

It took a great trauma to leave a scar on a wolf, since their healing abilities were well advanced over a human's. Nick's own scar over his eyebrow had been caused during Seth's rescue from Taggart. A window had shattered, spraying them with glass. He'd been lucky to retain the sight in his eye.

"A bar fight," Thayne explained in a low voice, not having let go of Nick's wrist.

Nick's wolf whined and urged him to accept the words Thayne offered. He couldn't be sure he could trust his wolf to think beyond the need to be with its mate. Maybe if he had time to accept the idea and learn to trust Thayne, but he couldn't just forget the harsh rejection or the blatant disregard Thayne had treated him with since their first encounter. He gently extricated his wrist and brought it down to his lap.

"You want me to accept you've suddenly had a change of heart these last couple of days as if it were so easy to forget everything that's happened."

"I've never tried anything except a couple nights in bed with anyone. I don't know how to do something beyond that. I…." Thayne left the sentence hanging there.

"You…?" Nick queried, his mouth dry with nervousness.

Before Thayne could answer, the hospital room door swung open. Both of them looked toward the intrusion to find Ryan standing there. Nick saw a flash of anger flicker in Ryan's gaze for a moment when his friend spied Thayne sitting on the side of the bed.

"Nick," Ryan said as he walked to the side closest to the door, outright ignoring Thayne.

Nick mentally sighed. Not only had Ryan interrupted

whatever Thayne had been about to tell him, but Ryan was angry again. Ryan knew they weren't mates and knew mates couldn't deny their other half once they'd found them. Nick felt awful for unknowingly hurting Ryan, but he couldn't return Ryan's feelings. Especially since finding Thayne all those months ago.

"Ryan," Nick greeted.

"Sara called and said you were finally awake. Is there anything I can do?" Ryan asked, reaching out to touch Nick's shoulder.

"I'm fine, Ry. I'll be healed in a few days. I'll be even better once they let me out of here."

Ryan grinned. "You always did hate being inactive."

Nick smiled back at him. "It's from the years of traveling. You know it's hard for me to stay in one place for too long."

"That's why you always do the presentations to our clients. I can't stand being on planes, confined to that small space and knowing I can't get out." Ryan visibly shuddered. "You've never had any issues with flying. Always made me think you should have been born a bird."

Thayne abruptly stood from the bed and gruffly said, "I'm going to grab something from the vending machine. You want anything?"

Nick shook his head, wondering what had set Thayne off as he watched Thayne's broad back and muscular rear end leaving the room. His wolf whimpered and weakly wagged its tail, wanting to follow Thayne. He couldn't control the longing look on his face, and Ryan snarled in disgust.

"You can't really be falling for him, Nick!" Ryan exploded the moment Thayne had disappeared.

Nick wondered if Ryan's words held any truth. Had he already fallen for Thayne? Despite fate tying them together, true mates' emotions did not come immediately into the equation. It took time for feelings to develop, some shorter than others, as was the case with Seth and Kasey, but it wasn't instant devotion.

"I don't know what I'm doing, Ryan. Things aren't so black and white anymore!" Nick grunted.

Ryan sneered and started pacing. "He's treated you like shit since the moment you met, and yet here you are, panting after him like a school girl in heat, conveniently forgetting everything he's done."

Nick frowned at Ryan. "That's not fair, Ry, and you know it. This isn't what I anticipated when I found my mate. I may not have expected instant love, but I sure as hell wasn't prepared for the outright hostility. Things have started to change, though, since we've bonded, and he isn't on the run anymore. I'm not naive enough to believe it's all sunshine and rainbows from here on out. I do, however, think I owe it to the sanctity of the mating bond to give it a chance if he's willing as well."

"You know, Nick, the poet Rilke said a person isn't who they are during the last conversation you had with them, they're who they've been throughout your entire relationship," Ryan pointed out, halting his pacing next to the bed and staring at Nick.

The words certainly couldn't be truer, and it caused Nick's uncertainty to surface once more that Thayne's declaration of wanting to try was nothing except a way to get him back into bed until he grew bored or the Created One was dealt with. He tamped the fear down ferociously. People can change, if the right situation were presented to them.

"Ryan, I know you care about me and you want to protect me, but you can't. This is my choice. For whatever reason, the gods chose to connect us together, he's my mate, and I can't turn my back on the slightest chance at having him in my life."

Nick felt his heart beat faster as he realized just how

true his words were. Despite everything they'd been through, he wanted Thayne in his life, no matter how he had to have him. Kasey hadn't given up on Seth, and he couldn't give up on Thayne. Not until he knew if there was absolutely no hope left. His wolf wagged his tail in eagerness at his acceptance of the hand he'd been given. Nick was certain his inner beast would have licked him to death if he could have.

"I don't know if I can stand by and watch him hurt you again, Nick."

"What are you saying?" Nick asked in shock.

"I'm saying that I can't be there to clean up the mess he leaves behind this time. The last two days have been hell for me. Knowing you were lying here in the hospital because of him and not being able to do anything about it killed me. I can't stand by and watch as he destroys you!"

Nick couldn't believe what Ryan was telling him. They'd been friends for a long time, and the idea of not being able to pick up the phone and talk to Ryan about anything other than business hurt.

"Are you saying if I choose to forgive Thayne and remain with him, we can no longer be friends? What about our company?"

"We can be business partners without being friends," Ryan replied flatly. "I can't do this anymore, Nick. Maybe I'm being selfish as hell, but I just can't handle this right now. Good luck, Nick, because I think you're going to need it where he's concerned."

Before Nick could even call out, Ryan stormed out of the room, the door slamming behind him. Nick sat there flabbergasted, unable to believe Ryan had broken off their eight-year friendship because he'd found his mate and couldn't return the feelings Ryan felt for Nick. The reality of just how much he'd lost and would risk losing by accepting Thayne's request to begin anew settled heavily on his shoulders. Could he risk the only things he had left?

"Nick?"

Forcing his distress back, Nick looked up from his lap to see Thayne standing in the doorway, a hesitant expression on his face. He'd seen many emotions on Thayne, but never one where it seemed as if he waited for Nick to kick him.

Nick cleared his throat and motioned Thayne inside. "Did you get something to eat?"

Thayne shook his head as he moved to Nick's side. "Not really hungry."

Nick frowned. "When's the last time you ate?"

"Ah…." Thayne couldn't seem to remember.

"You need to eat," Nick admonished gently.

Thayne shrugged one broad shoulder. "I'll eat once we're back home."

Nick wondered if Thayne realized he'd used the word home. He ignored the secret thrill it gave him to hear Thayne call the house by that word. "Have they said when I can go? I am not overly fond of hospitals."

"They said tomorrow if there are no complications." Thayne hooked the leg of the nearby chair, tugged it closer, and settled his long form into it. Nick had a feeling Thayne wasn't going to leave anytime soon, and it confused him even more. Thayne's actions certainly didn't match those of the man Nick thought him to be before now.

"Tell me about your business," Thayne said.

"What do you want to know?" Nick asked.

"What do you do? How'd you get into it? Anything you want to tell me."

Nick started talking about how being on the move all the time with Seth had left him no time for a job that required him to be in one place for long, so he'd gotten into coding and developing. Over the years, he'd taken online courses and studied whatever books he could, as well as learning hands-on by trial and error. It was easy to do at night while Seth was most likely sleeping and Nick didn't need to watch over him. Eight years ago, he'd met Ryan and they'd become fast friends, since Ryan also attended school for computer development. It didn't take them long to come up with the idea of going into business together.

"What about you?" Nick asked after he'd finished talking about the company.

"What about me?" Thayne grunted.

"In your traveling, you must have had to have a job. Otherwise how'd you support yourself?"

"I did a lot of odd jobs. Mostly manual labor, bouncer, kitchen dishwasher. Did some boxing a few times to earn some money on the side."

Nick remembered the job Thayne had gotten at Jo's. "What happened with your job at the diner?"

"Elijah straightened it out with Jo. I don't start until next week."

"I see." Nick couldn't shake the feeling of how the job would give Thayne the opportunity to leave him. He'd felt the same thing before at the main house when he'd first found out about it. Once Thayne had money in his pocket, there would be nothing to keep him in Emerald Lake Hills with Nick. Only he knew he couldn't keep Thayne relying on him and only him. If there was one thing he knew for certain about Thayne, it was that he didn't like being beholden to anyone.

"You said the same thing at Elijah and Sara's place. You don't want me to have a job?" Thayne asked, sitting forward in the chair.

Nick looked away, ashamed at his thoughts. He couldn't exactly tell him the truth.

"Nick?"

"I...."

He felt Thayne's hand on his, and he turned his head, staring down at the contrast of their skin. "You really think I'm going to use the job as a way to leave, don't you?" Thayne murmured, curling his fingers around Nick's hand, the tips resting against Nick's palm. Nick darted his gaze up to Thayne, who gave him a sad smile. "I can't say I blame you. I haven't given you any reason to believe I want to stick around. All I can say is I'm not going to leave, Nick. I promise."

"You promise?" Nick whispered, skeptical of the phrase coming from Thayne.

Thayne seemed to understand his unspoken question and lifted Nick's hand to his mouth and pressed a light kiss to his knuckles. "I promise."

SUCH A small phrase established an uneasy truce, and over the next couple of days, Nick saw a side of Thayne he hadn't even imagined existed. Once they'd returned to the house, Seth healed the remaining injuries, leaving Nick without pain and giving him the freedom to get to know Thayne even more. There were still walls in place in Thayne's mind, leaving Nick shut out of the memories he wanted more than anything to understand, but Nick knew if he were patient enough, the walls would crumble, granting him everything he'd ever wanted. The sexual tension grew by leaps and bounds as they became closer, but Thayne never pushed him for more. Nick slept in his own bed while Thayne slept on the couch in the living room.

There was still the Created One to deal with, and their plan to draw it out would take place mere days after Nick's release from the hospital. Elijah wanted to have the pack meeting and inform everyone of what was happening in their territory before the plan was set in motion. Thayne tried to argue about Nick being involved in killing the monster, but Nick had taken care of himself and Seth since they were kids, and he sure as hell wouldn't stand on the sidelines while everyone else risked their lives to take down the creature. He also wouldn't sit by the window like a housewife anxiously waiting to hear news of her husband's return from war. Needless to say, his insistence on going frustrated Thayne, and Thayne took it out on one of Nick's walls.

"Anyone ever tell you that you have anger-management issues?" Nick drawled as he eyed the damage from a stool at the island in the kitchen. "You're going to fix that, by the way."

Thayne gave a frustrated grunt and paced restlessly, running his hands through his hair in irritation and leaving it mussed, as if from a freshly ravished session in the bedroom. Nick cleared his throat, picked up the ham sandwich he'd prepared, and took a bite, chewing calculatingly while anticipating Thayne's next words.

"This is my mess, Nick, and I don't want you to be the one who has to clean it up. Again."

Nick swallowed the bite before saying, "I'm not going to sit by while everyone else risks their lives. I'm in line to be one of Cole's Betas when he becomes Alpha, which means I will be in the line of fire more often than not, and you're going to have to get used to it."

"Not if I kidnap you and take you somewhere far away," Thayne muttered darkly.

Nick laughed. He'd learned in the last seventy-two hours how Thayne hid so much of his emotions behind anger or an expressionless facade. Thayne cared very deeply about things, yet seemed to be afraid to show those feelings. He couldn't stop himself from constantly wondering what made

Thayne so fearful of letting anyone in or letting them see the real person beneath the hard exterior.

"I doubt kidnapping is one of your many talents learned on the road, Thayne."

Thayne stopped moving and stared at him for a long stretch of silence until finally Nick shifted in his seat in discomfort.

"What?" Nick asked.

"That's the first time I've heard you laugh," Thayne said.

He didn't really know what to say to the almost-awed note in Thayne's voice. He dropped his gaze to the crumbs on his plate. "I… ah… usually laugh a lot."

"Not when I've been around you, but I guess I haven't really given you much to laugh about," Thayne replied in a bitter tone.

Nick sighed, slipped off the stool, and walked around the island to where Thayne stood. He placed his palms on Thayne's forearms, squeezing in comfort. "You know, we'll never get past this if you keep beating yourself up over everything that's happened. I've let it go, Thayne. Things happened, but we're here now and we're together."

"I don't know how you can be so quick to forgive me," Thayne murmured.

"Maybe I haven't entirely," Nick admitted, "but I have started to see past the mask you put in place for everyone. I don't know what's made you so scared of showing yourself to anyone, most of all your mate. It'll take some time for me to come to trust you completely, but you are my mate and I have to take that chance. One day, I hope you come to trust me enough to tell me why you hate the idea of having a mate." As he expected, Thayne didn't jump to answer his curiosity. Nick stifled a sigh and dropped his hands from Thayne's arms. "Eat. We have to be at Elijah's in an hour."

Nick returned to his seat and picked up his sandwich,

barely tasting the remaining half. He knew he couldn't expect Thayne to open up so quickly, even with how much time they had spent together over the last couple of days. While Seth had been to the house to heal Nick, he'd revealed how Thayne had never left his side while he'd been unconscious in the hospital. Seth had been surprised at how worried and upset Thayne had been those two days. He'd never expected Thayne to make such an abrupt U-turn in their relationship. Even Kasey had expressed his own astonishment, as he'd never seen his brother care about more than the next time he could be on the move.

All of it made Nick feel more confident in Thayne's professed desire to give their mating bond a chance, but Nick still couldn't shake the feeling of how tenuous their relationship was and how the tiniest thing could send Thayne running again. Would Thayne actually stick around once the beast was destroyed? Stress twisted his gut as Nick watched Thayne demolish his sandwiches. He wasn't sure he would survive if Thayne rejected him again. He'd barely hung on to himself last time.

Glancing at the clock, he saw it was almost time to leave. "We should go," he said, standing and placing his plate in the sink.

Thayne grunted in agreement.

They didn't speak as they left the house, Nick locking the door behind them. Nick tried not to think about his grandfather's Impala, which sat demolished in a junkyard somewhere. He was dying to go see the damage and if it could be repaired, but Elijah had ordered them to remain in Nick's home until after the meeting. The Alpha had assigned his own Betas, Howard and Wilson, to watch over them while they waited to meet with the pack and carry out their plan to take down the Created One. Nick knew them well and had brought them food and drinks, chatting with them for a few minutes about anything they'd seen while patrolling. Elijah had brought them into the fold and given them the heads-up on who Thayne was and why they were standing guard.

Nick waved at them as he and Thayne climbed into the truck Kasey had brought back over from the diner. Their protective detail followed in a dark sedan as they drove toward the pack manor. Nick wondered how the rest of their pack would accept the danger Thayne's arrival had brought with him.

16

THAYNE

THAYNE COULDN'T sit still as he and Nick waited for Elijah to call them out onto the deck. He wandered aimlessly around Elijah's living room, taking in the multitude of pictures lining the walls and fireplace. He spotted Nick in several of them, including one with Ryan. It pained him to know his arrival had cost Nick their friendship. He'd already taken so much from Nick, and the losses just seemed to keep coming. Was he selfish to stick around if his presence continued to cause Nick pain?

"Thayne?" Nick prodded behind him.

He turned and spied Nick standing near the doorway, obviously given the signal to go out in front of the pack. A slight sense of panic caused his stomach to clench, and he debated running out the door and as far away as possible. Some of what he felt must have shown on his face because Nick approached him and took hold of his hand, entwining their fingers together. Nick didn't speak, just waited for him to gather his courage. The warmth of Nick's palm against his own seeped into Thayne, traveling up his arm and into his chest.

Thayne squeezed Nick's hand and gave a lopsided grin. "I'm being childish, aren't I?"

Nick gave him a surprised look. "Why would you think that?"

"For not wanting to go out there."

"I'll share a little secret with you," Nick said, wrinkling his nose at him. "I hate public speaking. My palms sweat and my heart races. Sometimes I hyperventilate, and most of the time I want to throw up. It isn't a pretty sight."

Thayne raised a skeptical eyebrow. Nick seemed as cool as a cucumber. His hand was soft and dry, and Thayne could hear the steady, slow beat of Nick's heart. "You aren't doing any of those things right now."

A tender smile slid over Nick's lips. "Because I know we're going out there together."

Thayne's own heart skipped a beat at Nick's words. Words that sent a spiral of emotion rushing through his body, and the way Nick's lips curved upward caused his knees to weaken. Things he'd never experienced with anyone, not even with Matt. Thayne ignored the wolf waiting for them near the door and leaned down the few inches separating him and Nick to press a light kiss on the corner of Nick's mouth. He squeezed Nick's hand again and gestured for Nick to precede him from the room.

Nick led the way through the kitchen to the same deck they'd been out on the day of the accident. Thayne sensed every single pair of eyes on him the moment they stepped through the doorway. He forced away his urge to flee and tried to give a nonthreatening appearance. There were so many! They outnumbered his pack. There were a variety of people, nothing like his own, where they were all Cheyenne.

Elijah smiled and beckoned them forward. "Come, Nick. Let us introduce your new mate, Thayne, and welcome him to the pack!"

To Thayne's surprise, the entire group began to applaud as both he and Nick came forward.

Sara smirked at him and leaned in to murmur, "You shouldn't look so shocked, Thayne. Every wolf here knows finding your mate is a thing to celebrate, even if you don't believe the same."

Thayne attempted to focus as Elijah gave the formal introduction. His mind whirled with how things weren't what he'd thought they would be. He'd thought everyone in Nick's pack would be angry because he'd brought a Created One with him, but instead they opened their arms and embraced his arrival, happy for Nick... and for him. He'd really expected them to want to exile him from their pack just as his family's had.

Nick leaned into his side and gently nudged him in the ribs. Thayne started and looked over at Nick in question. "Smile," Nick whispered and winked at him.

He gave another lopsided grin at Nick, and it naturally migrated onto the group looking up at them. Elijah continued speaking to his pack and told them to be aware of their surroundings, to never let their guard down, not until they were sure the Created One was gone. They were working on a plan to trap and destroy the creature, and they would need help doing so. Several men spoke up, offering their help or to provide assistance however they could. Elijah thanked them and told them to see him after the meeting.

"Now, in celebration of Nick finding his mate, Sara and I thought it a wonderful idea to have a barbecue today as an ending to our meeting. Howard, if you would be so kind as to light up the grill."

The crowd cheered and began to disperse, most going to help set up the nearby tables Thayne hadn't noticed until then or bring out trays of food and drinks. Others formed a group around Elijah to discuss what they could do to help take down the beast. Thayne felt winded at how everyone had rushed to help. While his pack was tightly knit and took care of each other, they were nothing like this one, open and accepting. In fact, most of the time, the Senaka pack reacted suspiciously of anyone new to their town and pack. It made him wonder why Nick's had been so ready to discard Kasey's mate, Seth. If they were so perfect and cared for one another this much, why would they throw Seth and his parents out like that?

"You look shell-shocked," Nick mused, resting against the railing.

"I guess I am. It doesn't make any sense how they can just welcome me here, knowing what I brought with me."

Nick turned toward him, setting his elbows on the wood balustrade. "Elijah and Sara are the kind of people who care about their pack. We are suspicious of strangers in our territory, don't believe we aren't, but you aren't a stranger, Thayne. You're one of us."

"I guess I can't really relate what I see here today with knowing Seth's past. Kasey told me what happened to Seth and how he wasn't allowed to stay here because of what he is. If they're as caring as they seem, then why did they send Seth away?"

Nick pushed away from the railing in surprise. "Is that what you think? That they sent Seth away?"

"Didn't they? Why didn't they try to protect him more than just sending one person to look after him?"

A wounded look crossed Nick's features, and Thayne immediately felt guilty. "Seth wasn't sent away, Thayne. His parents took him away. They were afraid for his safety. Elijah and Sara did try to talk them out of it, but Seth's parents wouldn't stay." Nick glanced at their Alpha. "Elijah sent me because it was about more than just protection. He knew Seth would need a friend, someone he could rely on and talk to. I think I did pretty damned well at protecting him until Taggart got hold of him during one of my business trips. By the time Seth was an adult, it never occurred to me to believe he would still be so vulnerable." He returned his gaze to Thayne, this time a self-deprecating emotion in his eyes. "You have no idea how many times I've asked myself why they sent me, and only me, to watch over Seth. I've blamed myself more than you can know for what Seth went through."

"Nick, I—"

Nick held up his hand to stop him. "No one knows what is going to happen in life. One single choice can lead to so many different paths. If I hadn't decided to take the trip to Japan, Seth wouldn't have been left vulnerable to Taggart. Instead of going to the bar that night in Senaka, I could have chosen to remain at the house with Kasey and Seth, and we never would have met. Maybe things happen for a reason or they're just twisted designs of fate playing games with us. Sometimes we make decisions that may not have been the best ones, but we make them anyway. Elijah could have commanded Seth's parents to stay with the pack, but he knew as a father himself he would do anything he could to protect his son. He couldn't deny Seth's parents the same rights he would demand for his own."

Ashamed, Thayne tore his gaze from Nick and stared down at the natural patterns in the wooden deck floorboards. "I'm sorry. I didn't mean to imply you weren't the right choice to protect Seth."

"Maybe I wasn't, but it's too late to change it. Whatever reasons you have for being so afraid to open up are yours, Thayne. I just want you to know I'm here no matter what. You don't have to lash out every time you're feeling cornered or overwhelmed. I'm not going to push you for more than you're ready to give."

Thayne couldn't have felt any smaller than he did right then. Nick had already punched holes in so many of his defenses, and yet here he was again, swinging a sledgehammer against another wall he'd built around himself. How the hell could Nick know exactly what was going on inside his head? He'd been so strict with keeping his guard up around Nick, but Nick had figured it out as though there were nothing except thin glass between them.

"How do you do it?"

"Do what?" Nick frowned.

"How do you see me when I try so hard not to let you?"

Nick tilted his head to the side. "You really don't understand what being mates means, do you? No matter the distance between us, we are one soul. I see you because you are the other half of me. It's taken me longer than I care to admit to see past the barriers you've put up to the world around you, but now that I have, I understand so much more than I did six months ago."

Before Thayne could answer, Elijah called Nick's name, interrupting their conversation.

"Enough serious talk for the day, you two!" Sara shouted from behind Elijah. "Time to eat and have some fun. Get over here."

Thayne gnashed his teeth in frustration. This was the first conversation they'd had about being mates that didn't end in an argument or Nick getting hurt. He didn't want to drink and make nice. He wanted to snatch Nick up and head for the nearest empty room away from everyone else. Nick stopped him from giving in to his impulse by grabbing his wrist and tugging him toward the picnic tables.

For the next several hours, Thayne was introduced to more wolves and human mates than he thought possible. He met the two who'd attacked him in the alley again, and they apologized profusely, causing Nick to give him one of those "we're going to talk about this" looks. Thayne had always taken care of his own problems, and being roughed up by wolves or humans in an unknown territory wasn't an unlikely occurrence in his travels over the last few years. He hadn't felt it necessary to divulge the incident to Nick, but somehow, he knew Nick wouldn't just accept his "it's been handled" brush-off.

Nick was tackled unexpectedly near the picnic tables by the young blond man who'd come pounding on the front door Thayne's second day in Emerald Lake Hills. Thayne tried to remember the kid's name.

"Carter!" Nick admonished, trying to get the guy to let him go.

Thayne hid a smile behind a cough.

Carter noticed him standing there and released Nick, putting his hands on his hips. "You should be more polite to visitors. Especially since we're family now."

Raising his eyebrows, Thayne asked, "Family?"

"Nick's cousin, remember?" Carter huffed. "You were really rude the other day."

"Sorry," Thayne said with a shrug.

Carter rolled his eyes and dropped his hands from his waist. "Nick, when are we going to have lunch together like you promised? You said you'd tell me about the pack we're meeting next month."

Thayne tensed at the mention of his own family. Nick surprised him by sliding his arm through Thayne's and squeezing in comfort. "It'll have to be next week, Carter. After the situation Elijah explained before is dealt with."

Carter pouted. "All right, I guess." He brightened immediately. "Hey, remember the guy I was telling you about the other day?"

Nick sighed. "Yeah, I remember."

"We're back together." Carter beamed.

Thayne sensed Nick's frustration with his cousin and wondered what was going on but didn't ask. Instead he stopped listening to Carter's rambling and looked around them, watching the other Emerald Lake Hills pack members.

It seemed as though an hour had passed by the time Carter ran off to whoever else he was dying to speak to. Nick smiled ruefully at Thayne. "Sorry. He's a bit much to handle sometimes. I promised his parents I'd look after him."

"He seems hyper," Thayne said.

Nick chuckled. "That's an understatement. Let's go grab a seat. I'm not really hungry since we ate before we left the house, but we can't leave just yet."

Thayne nodded and followed along behind Nick, who found an empty spot at one of the tables. He snagged a couple of beers from one of the coolers and set one down in front of Nick before taking his own seat. They weren't alone for long. Many of the wolves stopped by to welcome Thayne and chat with Nick.

Sara joined them at one point, plunking herself down across from them. She smiled and looked around at her pack. There were about a dozen cubs playing and yelling at one another.

"Ever thought about having kids, Thayne?" she asked, her tone baring innocence but her eyes showing the deviant gleam in them that Thayne had begun to expect.

Nick choked on the sip of beer he'd taken. "Sara!" he spluttered.

Thayne hadn't thought about having kids before because he'd never thought he'd have the chance. He hadn't wanted to have a mate and having one usually came first. He wondered what it would be like to see a mirror image of Nick running around—dirty blond hair, bright green eyes, and a smile that could melt anyone's heart, especially his father's. For some reason the idea appealed to him more than he'd thought possible.

He shrugged. "Maybe one day."

Nick swiveled his head toward him so fast, it would have been flung off his shoulders if it weren't attached.

Thayne thanked his tanned complexion when he felt heat suffuse his cheeks. "What?" he muttered defensively.

"Nothing," Nick murmured and resumed watching the children playing, taking another sip of his beer.

Thayne shifted in his seat at the knowing look on Sara's face. He knew his answer had surprised Nick, since Nick knew his distaste for mates and the permanence they signified. Having a child would make it even harder to just take off and leave. He started as he realized it had been more than a few days since he'd actually felt the urge to pack up his stuff and move on. The idea of being away from Nick left an acrid taste in his mouth now. Were these emotions his own, or were they his wolf's brought out by the bonding? For the last week, even longer if he'd admit it to himself, he'd been on an emotional roller coaster ride, one he found took unexpected dips and loops he didn't even begin to know how to approach.

"So tell me about your pack in Senaka, Thayne," Sara prodded, interrupting his whirling thoughts.

"They aren't my pack anymore," he replied stiffly. His chest ached at knowing he could never return to his birth home. He'd paid a high price for his mistake.

Sara gave him an empathetic look and reached out to pat his hand resting on the table. "I'm sorry, sweetie. I didn't mean to bring up bad memories. I was just being my usual curious self. We'll be meeting them next month during the Summit. The good news is that it's on neutral territory, so you'll be able to attend and spend time with your parents."

Nick pressed his thigh along Thayne's, offering comfort.

"Has there been any progress on Cole finding his mate?" Nick asked, changing the subject.

Sara nodded. "Ryan's contact on the police force came through with the details from the bus line. The young man was registered under the name of David Freeman, but Cole thinks he was traveling under an assumed name with how frightened he seemed to be."

"Does that mean he won't be able to find him again?"

"Cole is fairly certain his mate will continue to use David Freeman's identity, so he may be able to find another hit on the ID soon."

"Where is Cole?" Nick queried, searching for his friend.

Sara shrugged. "He left early this morning and hasn't come back yet. I figure he's trying to track down young David."

Thayne knew Nick hadn't missed Ryan's absence, and he noticed the deliberate avoidance of asking after Ryan, but he'd caught Nick glancing around more than once in the hopes Ryan would show. On one side of the coin, he felt bad for Nick because he knew how much Nick cared about Ryan, but on the other side, Thayne couldn't quite suppress his jealousy at knowing another man was in love with Nick. He forced away his wolf's and, if he were honest with himself, his human side's need to crowd Nick and show his dominance. He really needed some time to himself to gain some perspective over the emotions conflicting inside of him. The last fifteen years didn't just disappear or suddenly morph into wanting a mate. Both parts of him were in constant battle over which one would win. Did he walk away when the creature was destroyed, or did he remain with Nick and hope he never had to experience what Dakota's father had gone through?

"I think we should head home and get some rest." Nick interrupted his thoughts, standing abruptly. "Tomorrow night is going to be stressful and dangerous enough without us being tired."

Thayne found it curious at the sudden urge Nick had to leave, but he stood and followed along as Nick thanked Elijah and Sara and bid others good-bye. They were in the truck and on the way back to Nick's not long after. He'd been happy to get away. He just didn't understand why Nick had been eager to leave so quickly.

"Are you okay?" he asked, looking over at Nick in the driver's seat.

"I'm fine," Nick replied.

"You sure? We left out of there as if your tail were on fire." Nick's hands tightened on the steering wheel in response, and Thayne knew Nick wasn't fine. "Nick?"

"It's nothing. I just needed some space from everyone. Felt as if I were suffocating," Nick muttered.

Had his own emotions welled over to Nick?

"He couldn't even be bothered to come to the pack meeting," Nick said in a bitter voice. "Eight years of friendship, five in business together, and he throws it away because of something so stupid. As if finding my mate were a personal slight on him! I mean, who the hell does he think he is?"

Thayne now understood Nick's need for space. He didn't exactly know what to say to give Nick comfort, as he had never really been one to understand relationships. He struggled to find something to soothe Nick.

"He doesn't understand. Until he finds his own, he'll never understand!" Nick shouted, slamming his fist against the steering wheel.

"Hey," Thayne said quietly, reaching out to grab Nick's hand when he went to punch the wheel again. "Stop. Hurting yourself won't change the situation, Nick."

Nick flexed his hand in Thayne's grip, stretching his fingers out to ease the strain. Satisfaction trickled through

Thayne when Nick didn't immediately take his hand back. "I always thought I would lose Seth because I had lied to him and it was my fault Taggart came after him. But to lose Ryan because of something I can't control is just…."

"I met a lot of people over the last ten years," Thayne said, "and the one thing I learned is to never expect anything from people. We think we know someone, and then in a split second, they turn into someone we never knew. I think Ryan is just upset right now, and he doesn't know how else to handle it. Anger makes us into foolish people. I should know." The last part he admitted with a wry twist of his lip. "I got into quite a few fights because of anger."

The words he hadn't thought he'd had in him tumbled out so easily, surprising him. He sensed Nick's distress fading away as they got closer to Nick's house. He rubbed his thumb along the inside of Nick's wrist in a light caress, absorbing some of the raw emotion racing through Nick.

When Nick pulled into the driveway, he extracted his wrist from Thayne's grasp and turned in his seat enough to look at him head-on. "Thank you."

"For what?"

Nick gave a soft smile. "You have no idea what you just did, do you?"

He furrowed his brow at Nick in confusion. What did he do?

"One of the strengths between mated wolves is the ability to share the burden of any pain or trauma inflicted on their other half. I could feel you here"—Nick touched his chest —"and your desire to remove the hurt I carry over Ryan."

"If I had such an ability, why didn't I use it in the hospital? Or at the accident?" Thayne rasped.

"Because you were still resistant to the bond. It wasn't until now that you've allowed part of those walls you keep so tightly around you to crack. The connection between us is growing stronger the longer we're around one another."

Panic surged over his human side while his inner beast gave a joyful howl. "I… I need some time alone," he murmured.

The happiness on Nick's face died away, replaced by a shuttered expression. "Of course. I have work to do anyway."

They exited the truck, and Nick tossed an acknowledging wave at Howard and Wilson parked at the curb before walking to the front of the house. Thayne waited impatiently as Nick unlocked the door, then entered it ahead of him. He knew he'd hurt Nick just then, but he needed time to gather his thoughts and to come to terms with Nick's revelation. He'd been on his own for so long, not relying on anyone except himself, and the old fear, of being vulnerable enough with someone to lose who he was, raised its ugly head. The color of red flashed in front of his eyes while the memory of Paul Blackfoot's sightless eyes chased right on its heels. The pure anguish on Paul's face in death had been etched in his mind for over a decade, and it terrified him.

Nick didn't say anything as he walked to the back of the house. Thayne watched, wondering if his heart would be able to take Nick leaving him for good now that he'd come to know and love him. The word sent an icy chill tearing through his body at rapid speed. He dropped to his knees right there in the entryway, his chest so tight it seemed it would explode. When had his subconscious given in and accepted Nick so wholly?

He felt almost dizzy from the endless ride he seemed to be on. He needed a stiff drink! Standing, he trudged into the kitchen and started digging through the cabinets, searching for any type of liquor. It took him opening several doors and digging through the walk-in pantry to find a bottle of Scotch hidden behind some jars of spaghetti sauce. He gave a small sound of triumph and returned to the kitchen to snatch a glass snifter out of a cabinet near the sink.

The alcohol burned smoothly on its way down and spread warmth through his limbs. Leaning one hip against the island counter, he stared into the glass and brooded over the self-revelations he'd made. Could he free himself enough to give Nick everything he deserved? As soon as the Created One had been dealt with, he needed to seek out Dakota and talk to him, explain to him that he could no longer keep their pact. Hell, he'd already broken it, really. The moment he'd agreed to let Nick claim him, he'd broken it. He just hadn't allowed himself to accept the truth.

Even though it was still early, the sun just beginning to lower in the afternoon sky, Thayne's skin itched with the need to shift and run. He hadn't done so since the night of their claiming. His teeth elongated, and his eyes flashed between lupine and human several times. The urge began to grow the longer he thought about it and the longer he pushed it off. Finally, he couldn't bear any further, slammed the glass down on the counter, and took two strides to the door leading from the kitchen out to the backyard. He wrenched the door open, and the moment he stepped through the threshold, he shifted.

His wolf gave a joyful howl at being released, free to expel the energy built up inside. He started toward the line of trees at the back of Nick's property only to freeze at Nick's voice.

"Thayne!"

Thayne glanced back to see Nick standing in the doorway, a frown on his face. He whined and glanced longingly at the trees. He heard Nick approach, and his tail wagged in eagerness at Nick's nearness.

Nick sank down to a crouch next to him, placing a hand on the scruff of his neck. "I understand the need to run, Thayne, but you can't go alone. Not with the Created One out there. Let me close up the house, and I'll go with you, okay?" Another whine rattled in Thayne's throat, and Nick smiled, ruffling the fur along Thayne's back. "I won't be long. Please don't leave without me."

Plunking himself down on his haunches, Thayne huffed impatiently, to which Nick laughed and stood, rushing to the house to go inside and lock the front door as well as the kitchen entrance behind him. Thayne's coat practically vibrated with excitement while waiting. He was on his feet the moment Nick started back toward him, trotting ahead of Nick until they reached the forest entrance. Nick shifted just inside the shade of the branches, and Thayne halted in his tracks, staring at Nick and the beautiful golden fur covering his sleek form. He'd only ever seen Nick in his wolf form once before, and he'd been too angry to really concentrate on the magnificence of Nick's true shape. Nick's fur was a gorgeous deep golden color with a fine dusting of darker color along the tips, giving it an almost color-changing effect.

Nick stared back at him, his muzzle gaping in a happy, panting grin. *"Are we going to run or not?"*

Thayne jerked in shock. Only his father had ever been able to speak to him mentally. It was another new experience to hear Nick's whiskey-rough voice echoing in his head. Instead of responding, Thayne bolted through the trees. Nick followed close on his paws, keeping up with him easily. Thayne didn't have any idea where he was going and allowed his wolf to guide him. The cool depths of the forest soothed his soul much more than the drink he'd taken at Nick's. He'd forgotten just how much he loved to run, carefree and instinctive. His wanderings on the road didn't leave much room for shifting when he merely moved from motel to motel or bar to bar. With the creature on his trail, he'd spent even less time as a wolf than ever.

The restless emotions sweeping through his body earlier began to fade, and he soaked in the essences of nature: the scent of damp leaves and grass, the soft sounds of other animals foraging for food, the companionship of another wolf running with him. His wolf gave a sharp howl, letting out the sorrows of the last several months and the overload of emotions inside of him. Nick gave an answering howl, causing a shiver of pure joy to run along his spine.

He didn't know how long they ran or how far, but eventually they came to a clearing and he finally stopped, crashing onto a pile of leaves and huffing in ecstasy.

Nick slid to a halt near him and sat, staring at him. *"How long has it been since you've allowed your wolf release?"*

"I shifted at Kasey's," Thayne replied.

Nick roughly shook his head. *"I mean truly allowed your wolf the freedom he needs? I could barely keep up with how much energy you've had pent up. I know you couldn't have been letting him out regularly."*

Thayne pushed himself up into a sitting position, his body still heaving with heavy breaths. *"It's hard to shift when you're in towns or cities, and even more so when you're close to other wolf territory. With the Created One, it made it even harder to find the chance."*

"You can't go so long without releasing your wolf, Thayne. It's dangerous. For everyone, not just you. You know that."

An irritated noise rumbled in Thayne's chest. He knew keeping his wolf locked up for long stretches of time could cause him to lose control as it got closer to the full moon. If a wolf went too long without changing, they could potentially shift wherever they were if the right emotion were powerful enough to push them over the edge. Most humans went about their lives blissfully ignorant of the dangers of the world beneath their own. Every wolf would be at risk if the human population were to ever find out the truth. Thayne knew he could keep a leash on his wolf, so to speak. He'd done so for so long that it was second nature.

"I've managed just fine."

"You shifted in the backyard because you couldn't 'manage' it, Thayne. Any one of my neighbors could have seen you! Not all of the residents in Emerald Lake Hills are wolf. Thankfully, most of them are at work during the day, but you need to be more careful."

Snapping his fangs together in irritation, Thayne glared at Nick. *"I'm fine, Nick. You're right. I shouldn't have shifted in your backyard. Back in Senaka, everyone on the reservation was either wolf or knew of their existence and we didn't need to worry. I won't make the same mistake again."*

Nick sighed. *"I'm not trying to sound like a nagging parent, Thayne. I'm just asking you to be careful because I care about you."*

Thayne's annoyance died away, and he instinctually slunk over to Nick, pressing close to him. He nuzzled at Nick's throat and swiped his tongue over the side of Nick's muzzle. Nick responded by leaning in to the affectionate gestures in acceptance. There was no sexual intention behind the motions, merely a need to comfort and reassure one another. Neither rushed to pull away or to head back to Nick's.

It was only when dusk had settled over the forest that Nick reluctantly freed himself. *"We should head back. I don't think it's safe for us out here until the Created One is gone."*

Thayne didn't want to remember why they were there or remember the chain of events leading up to tomorrow night. If anyone were hurt or killed, it would be another death on his soul. He wanted to lock Nick up in a room with no windows or doors until the beast had been put down, but he knew Nick would never forgive him, and he'd barely earned the forgiveness he'd felt in Nick moments ago.

Nick led the way back home while Thayne silently followed behind. His thoughts raced between the impending danger and the discoveries he'd made that day. Darkness had fallen by the time they reached the edge of the tree line near the house. Both of them shifted and headed to the house. Nick dug out a key hidden in a planter near the kitchen door and let them in.

"Take the bed tonight, Thayne," Nick murmured as he flipped on the light.

"I can't kick you out of your bed again!" Thayne protested.

"I'm not going to sleep much tonight anyway. I'll more than likely be working in my office most of the night so I can take the couch in there."

Thayne frowned. "You need to rest."

"I doubt I'll be able to sleep knowing what tomorrow brings," Nick said with a shrug. "Just take the bed. If I get tired, the couch in my office is really comfortable. I've slept there more than once."

Nick started to leave when Thayne stopped him. "Nick, I...."

Turning in the doorway to look at Thayne, Nick replied, "Get some rest, Thayne. We can worry about everything else once the Created One is destroyed."

Thayne didn't say anything more, merely watched as Nick left him alone in the kitchen. He'd wanted to offer to share the bed but had been afraid of Nick's rejection. Sighing, he left the kitchen, turning off the light on his way out. The door to Nick's office was partially open as he walked past to the bedroom, and he could see Nick already at the computer.

For the first time in his life, Thayne felt lonely. The silence in the bedroom crowded in on him. He stripped his clothing off, leaving his briefs on, and climbed between the sheets. A shiver slid through him at the coolness of the bedding whispering across his body. Nick's scent clung to every inch of the bed, and his body reacted instinctively.

Thayne groaned and rolled onto his side to bury his face in the pillows, only to regret it when the perfume of Nick's skin engulfed him further. His cock didn't stop leaking in lust until he finally fell into a fitful sleep, ravaged by dreams of losing Nick and being lost forever in a sea of darkness.

17

NICK

NICK SPENT the night immersed in one of his many projects. He consciously avoided thinking of the hard, delectable body wrapped up in his bed mere feet away from where he sat. More than once he had to fight the urge to go down the hall and peek into the bedroom to watch Thayne sleep. He knew if he did he wouldn't be able to resist the urge to get closer and eventually end up joining Thayne in the king-size bed.

He saw Ryan logged into the instant messenger service they used to chat, and it took all of his willpower not to message his friend. He already missed him, and it hadn't been but two days since they'd argued with one another in the hospital. Annie had called him to find out what was going on since Ryan wouldn't give her any answers. Nick gave her a brief explanation and told her there might be some adjusting with how things were handled between them at the office. She'd been upset about the whole thing, but he'd reassured her that she didn't have to worry about losing her job. Nick smiled in remembrance at her instant response of calling him a butthead for thinking she was more worried about her job than their almost decade-long friendship falling apart.

The run with Thayne had burned off quite a bit of the excess energy in him, although it had only made his doubt about their situation deeper. Nick knew Thayne hadn't meant to hurt him by not really knowing how to react to their bond getting stronger, yet he couldn't stop the ache it caused in his heart. Would Thayne ever truly be able to accept their mating? After tomorrow night, Nick would know Thayne was serious, because if everything went as planned, the Created One would be destroyed and Thayne wouldn't have a need to stick around for the long haul anymore. His jaw clenched at the thought of Thayne leaving him now that he'd come to love him.

Nick's fingers froze on the keys. He loved Thayne. No ifs, ands, or buts about it. Thayne had a softer side he kept buried beneath a tough facade, letting no one in. During his time in the hospital and the brief hours at home before Seth healed him, Thayne had taken care of him in the way any mate would care for their own. Nick had seen into Thayne's heart and knew if they only were granted the time, Thayne could come to love him. But would he have the time he needed to gain Thayne's trust and his love once the creature was no longer in the way?

He sat back in his seat and opened the drawer to his right. He reached in and picked up the photo he'd swiped from Kasey's home. Thayne stood there, his arm wrapped around Kasey's shoulders and a huge grin on his face. He looked so happy and carefree in the picture. Something Nick had never seen on the other man in the entire time he'd been around Thayne. Would he ever see the same smile directed at him or see Thayne happy to be in his life?

Grinding his teeth, Nick replaced the picture in the drawer and forced his attention back to his work. He lost himself in the soothing monotony of coding, allowing the numbers and parameters to take over. Around two in the morning, he sent off the test file to Ryan via e-mail with a brief message. Standing, he stretched with a soft moan. A huge yawn broke out, and Nick rubbed at his burning eyes. He managed to stumble to the couch, slump down on the soft plush leather, and passed out in a half-sitting, half-lying position.

He didn't know how long he slept, but the sound of the shower running woke him. He groaned as his neck protested the strange position he'd slept in for the last few hours. Rubbing at his nape, Nick got up and struggled to the bathroom across from his office, needing to relieve himself urgently. After emptying his bladder, he brushed his teeth and ran a comb through his disheveled hair. He really needed a shave, but his razors and shaving gel were in the master bathroom. The shower had gone off by the time he made his way to the kitchen to make coffee.

There were only hours left until they had to meet everyone else at Elijah's. Eight wolves were involved in the plan: Ryan, Nick, Thayne, Elijah, Howard, Wilson, Wilson's son Joe, and Sara's nephew George. Kasey had wanted to help, but Elijah refused, needing him to keep Seth safe in case they needed his help. Nick hoped the eight of them would be enough to take the beast down. If the creature had done that much damage to the Impala, how strong was it? The thought reminded him that he needed to go down to the junkyard and see if the Impala were in fact salvageable.

Nick filled two travel mugs with coffee and walked outside. He waved the mugs at the men sitting in the car in front of his house. Howard eagerly nodded and opened the car door, getting out to almost snatch the drink from him. Nick laughed and handed the other one to Wilson, who had also gotten out of the car, coming around the front to lean against the vehicle.

"Good morning," Wilson rumbled.

"Thanks for taking the time away from your families to be here for us," Nick said.

Howard moaned, in absolute heaven at his first sip of coffee. Wilson rolled his eyes at his partner. "No worries there, Nick. Maggie's in Tennessee visiting a friend from high school, and Gina's off at college for the semester, so the house is pretty much empty."

"Would you two like some breakfast?" Nick asked. Howard gave another enthusiastic nod to his offer, and Nick grinned. "Why don't you both come inside? I'll make us some eggs, bacon, and toast. It's the least I can do with you two spending the night watching out for us." Nick led the way into the house and gestured for them to sit at the counter while he started pulling eggs and bacon from the refrigerator. Thayne entered the kitchen just as he set the frying pan on the stove. "Are you hungry?" Nick asked him.

Thayne grunted and walked around the island to the coffeemaker. He added about a cup of sugar and three dairy creamers to his coffee, to which Nick gave him a raised eyebrow. "What?" Thayne demanded defensively.

"Nothing," Nick replied with a small laugh. "Eggs and bacon?"

"Sure. Need help?"

They worked side by side in relative ease despite the upcoming events sitting in the corner of the room like a huge elephant. Nick scrambled the eggs and cooked the bacon while Thayne made the toast and set out butter and plates with silverware. It wasn't long before the four of them were eating and talking. Wilson told stories about his time as Elijah's Beta, including several hilarious ones about scrapes he'd pulled Cole out of. Nick found himself relaxing in the jovial atmosphere, the first time in a long time he'd truly been content enough to let go of the stress and tension inside.

After breakfast, Nick invited the two Betas to remain, ignoring the inner voice calling him a coward for not wanting to spend time alone with Thayne. He was afraid of what he'd do since his self-discovery the evening before. His humiliation and anguish would increase tenfold if he blurted out his love for Thayne only to have Thayne leave him in the dust the second the Created One was dead.

The time to leave came faster than any of them wanted. Nick and Thayne followed the other two toward the pack manor in a strained silence. During the drive, Nick saw Thayne nervously tapping his fingers on his upper thigh and wondered if Thayne worried more about the danger they were in or about how he'd feel when they destroyed the creature. The man beneath the monster's fur had meant a lot to Thayne at one time. Acknowledging the truth caused Nick's heart to clench with pain. Somehow the turned human had gotten beneath the mask Thayne wore and been given the one thing Nick craved more than anything: Thayne's heart.

There were already several cars in the drive when they arrived, and Nick pulled the truck in behind Ryan's. He turned the engine off but didn't immediately exit the vehicle.

Thayne looked at him in question. "Nick?"

Nick couldn't deny he felt afraid. There were so many possible outcomes to the night ahead, and his skin almost quivered with nerves. "Why did you let him in?"

"What?" Thayne frowned in confusion.

"The Created One. Why did you let him in? You cared about him enough to show him a part of yourself you keep hidden from everyone else." Thayne didn't respond right away, and Nick gave a bitter twist of his lips. "You don't have to answer that. Let's just go inside."

He'd just placed his hand on the door handle when Thayne spoke. "I've never found it easy to let anyone in before."

Nick froze and waited for Thayne to continue.

"Matt made it easy. He wasn't a wolf or my mate. We connected in a way I hadn't with the others I'd meet and pick up at whatever bar or club I happened to find in the town I chose to stop in. He was smart and funny. He wanted to save the world.

"From the day we're old enough to comprehend, we're told of our mates and how they're the other half of who we are. We'll know them when we meet them, and it'll be an instant connection unlike anything you could ever understand until it happens. What they don't tell you is how your true mate becomes your world, your life, and how vulnerable it makes us. As a kid, I witnessed my best friend's father fall apart as his mate, a human, slowly passed away because of cancer. His father faded with her, becoming a shell of who he was."

Thayne stared out at the front of the house, his face stoic and unemotional. "I met Dakota when we were still crawling around on all fours. His father, like my own, was strong and fierce, brave to a fault, and I never thought of him as weak. But as I watched him lose his mate, I saw that strength disappear. I saw the once larger-than-life man wither until he'd lost so much weight his skin hung on his bones. The day Dakota's mother died, his father went home from the hospital and shot himself."

Nick sucked in a breath of dismay. The only outward indication of any emotion in Thayne was his hands clenched on top of his thighs.

"Dakota and I found his father on the living room couch, a gun in hand, and his blood all over the couch and wall behind it. I swore from that day on I would never allow myself to become so dependent on another as to lose who I am."

"I'm so sorry, Thayne," Nick murmured, turning in his seat to fully look at Thayne. "But that isn't what being a mate is about. What happened to your friend's father is not the norm for a mated wolf. Yes, there are times when a wolf will let the darkness consume them, crumbling under the weight of their loss, but it can happen to anyone. Not just wolves. Humans take their life every day because of losing a loved one or even just a depression so deep in their souls it can't be erased. He wasn't as strong as you may have believed him to be. You were a child, and as children, we see the adults in our lives as unbreakable and infallible. We only learn as we grow up they're mortal just like us."

"No," Thayne denied roughly.

Nick reached out and set his hand on top of Thayne's. "We make our own choices, Thayne. He chose to end his pain in a selfish way, leaving behind your friend and uncaring who found him or how it may affect the person who found him. That isn't strength, Thayne. It's weakness, and most likely one he carried inside him before then. You have to see that."

Thayne curled his lip in a snarl. "What do you know? You weren't there!"

Nick struggled to remind himself Thayne was only reacting out of instinct. "You're right. I wasn't there, but you were and only you can remember what happened back then. I have witnessed many wolves lose their mates, and the ones who couldn't bear the weight of their loss were the ones who gave their power to their pain. You aren't one of those people, Thayne."

"How can you say that? You barely know me," Thayne whispered.

"When you aren't working at keeping your guard up, it

slips," Nick admitted. "The wall you've built around yourself came down enough for me to see inside of you while you took care of me after the accident. I saw the good in your heart that you struggle so hard to lock away from everyone. You're strong and kind and amazingly gentle when you open up to the people around you."

Thayne vehemently shook his head. "The one time I let someone in, I hurt them. I took away their life and left them a monster."

Nick squeezed Thayne's hand. "You couldn't have known what would happen. There are accidents every day where people hurt other people and they didn't intend to. The only thing you can do is work through it, accept it, and move on."

"How is it right for me to move on when his life ended because of me? And tonight it will end permanently!"

"Maybe it isn't right," Nick replied, "and it is a hard reality to face, but are you going to stop living your life because of a mistake you made in the heat of the moment? Shouldn't I feel the same about Taggart? What makes my previous situation any different? After all, Seth was hurt immeasurably because of my lapse in judgment. I've learned to accept my role in what happened and have worked at putting it behind me. You can too. You just have to forgive yourself first."

Thayne made a frustrated gesture with the hand not held by Nick. "There's no way I can forgive myself. I've done a lot of stupid things in my life, but murdering someone tops them all."

Nick made a small noise of dismay. "You didn't murder him, Thayne."

"No? What else do you call it when you steal someone's life?" Pure pain and anguish resonated in Thayne's voice. Nick saw Thayne blink heavily and knew Thayne was fighting his emotions. Had Thayne allowed himself to cry at all since discovering the life-changing mistake?

Without giving himself a second to rethink his choice, Nick reached up and forced Thayne to look at him. He leaned forward and pressed his lips to Thayne's in a gentle kiss. Several breaths passed before Thayne responded. The kiss remained soft and comforting, no passion involved except the feelings Nick could sense still roaring through Thayne. Thayne cupped the side of Nick's neck, deepening the kiss a little farther. Nick tasted salt and knew the dam holding Thayne's sorrow inside had broken. Nick slid closer on the bench seat and wrapped his arms around Thayne, breaking the kiss and pulling Thayne tighter against him. Thayne crushed Nick to him, nearly wringing the breath from Nick, but he wouldn't have given up those moments for anything, even if it meant suffocating to death.

Thayne buried his face in the crook of Nick's neck. Nick could feel the heat of Thayne's tears. He ran his hand through Thayne's hair in a comforting gesture as silent sobs shook the broad shoulders. Nick didn't speak, unwilling to break the first real connection between them. The walls holding him at bay came crashing down, and Nick sucked in a deep breath as memories of a gorgeous young man flooded into his mind. He knew without a doubt the man he saw was who the Created One used to be. Pain nipped at the fringes of his consciousness, but he refused to let it in. He didn't expect Thayne to have been a monk before they'd met, just as he hadn't been, and he couldn't blame Thayne for caring so deeply about another person. Flashes of a bright smile and shining blue eyes bombarded his senses. Nick suppressed the urge to growl in fierce jealousy. He wanted nothing more than to leap into Thayne's mind and remove any trace of the man who'd held, and perhaps still did, a part of Thayne's heart.

Time passed slowly for them. It didn't matter that the others waited in the house or that in a few hours they would be facing great danger. What mattered was Nick comforting Thayne and offering him a release Thayne had needed for a long time now. Nick hoped with enough time Thayne could overcome the memories of his childhood and let go of the abject terror he held at being vulnerable to another. He could only imagine the horror of finding his best friend's father having taken his own life, and the scars seeing such a thing could leave behind on an impressionable young teenager. Then to finally let someone in, only to end up hurting them. Nick didn't know how Thayne had stood for so long under the weight of everything without cracking. He had to swallow back the words he wanted more than anything to say. Right then, Thayne didn't need anything but support.

Nick had no idea how long they sat there, but Thayne finally quieted down and lay against him, drained. He toyed with a long lock of the dark hair beneath his fingers while waiting for Thayne to gather himself. The walls came back up first, signaling Thayne's return to normal, and Nick couldn't help but be sad at how far away Thayne withdrew. Even after everything, Thayne still hadn't accepted the bond between them. He slowly freed himself from Thayne and moved back to his side of the truck.

"You okay?" he asked.

Thayne nodded, unwilling to look at Nick, keeping his face turned toward the passenger window and scrubbing at the tear tracks still on his cheeks. "We should go inside," Thayne said quietly.

Agreeing with Thayne, Nick exited the truck, slamming the door behind him. Thayne followed suit, and they were both silent during the short walk to the front of the manor. Howard and Wilson had politely waited at the far end of the porch and tailed them into the house. A sense of solemnity clung to the air. Even Sara, normally smiling and teasing, had a somber mask on when they joined the others in the dining area. Ryan sat away from the group and didn't even glance up as Nick and Thayne entered the room. Nick ignored the hurt he felt at the slight. Maybe over time Ryan could come to accept that he hadn't really done anything wrong. Until then, he needed to give Ryan space, so he remained at Thayne's side while everyone began deliberating over who would do what.

Elijah spoke first. "Last night we discovered where the creature has been staying. There's a clearing with a cave a few miles east of here. During a patrol through the forest, one team stumbled on it and found evidence of the beast's presence. We will need to decide on a plan of approach and attack."

"I'll take down Ma—the Created One," Thayne said without emotion.

"No," Nick protested immediately. "If the creature is as powerful as we think, there is no way just you can take him down."

Elijah agreed. "Nick is right. I also do not feel you are the right wolf to do this, Thayne. You still see and think of the Created One as the person he once was. He's not, and we need to ensure we make this as quick and clean as possible. Your hesitation could cause the others to end up hurt. George and Ryan will take care of the beast's destruction. The others will assist in bringing it to the clearing and, if necessary, help in killing it."

"This is my problem. I need to be the one to make it right." Thayne gave a snarl, and Nick gripped Thayne's arm, hard. Thayne had just defied their Alpha.

A feral look came into Elijah's eyes, and Thayne's wolf cowered in fear. Nick could feel the two halves of his mate warring one another. Thayne's wolf wanted to kneel down in subjugation while the human half wanted to take control and do as he wished.

"I will not say it again, Thayne. I will not take the chance of any one of my wolves being injured or worse. Including you. Is that understood?"

Thayne took a moment to answer, but gave a jerky nod of his head in agreement.

Nick stifled a sigh of relief and released his grip on Thayne's arm.

The rest of the scant hours prior to heading into the forest were spent with the group going over the area where the Created One had made its home. They looked for possible escape routes should something go wrong. Nervous energy exuded from each wolf, increasing the harsh taste to the air around them. Nick couldn't wait until the beast was gone. *Even though it could mean Thayne leaves,* his inner voice taunted him.

Yes. Even if Thayne didn't remain with him afterward, at least Nick would know Thayne was safe.

"How are you doing, Nicky?" Sara murmured beside him. Nick attempted to give her a reassuring smile, but the knowing look in her eyes told him he didn't fool her. She reached out and ran her hand across his cheek in a brief caress. "Everything will work out, sweetie. Thayne isn't going to run after this is over."

Nick jerked in surprise. How had Sara known what he was thinking? "How can you be so sure?" he whispered.

The others hadn't noticed their private conversation and continued going over the map Elijah had produced. Sara smiled softly and glanced over at the man in question. "Because despite all the bluster and the anger he wears around him as a shield, he loves you. He may not even know it yet, but I see it in the way he looks at you."

A humorless smirk twisted Nick's lips. "I doubt it, Sara. At every turn he pulls farther and farther away from me. Just when I think he may finally be coming to accept the bond, he withdraws even more."

Sara gave a small shake of her head. "I don't know what has happened in his past, and it's not really my business, but the only way he knows how to protect himself is to keep his walls in place. He's burying his emotions behind those walls because he doesn't want anyone to see the sheer vulnerability he carries."

Nick looked at Thayne, crowded around the map with the others, and saw the deep concentration on Thayne's face. Was Sara right? He'd seen bits and pieces of Thayne over the time they'd been together, showing a truth in Sara's assumptions. He knew Thayne's heart was bruised and had never really healed over the years, but he didn't know if anyone as wounded as Thayne would ever truly come to trust someone and open himself to further pain.

Thayne sensed his stare and looked up at him, a serious gleam buried in his dark eyes. He held Nick's gaze for a moment and then returned to studying the map. Nick felt the minutes ticking by, one second at a time closer to potentially losing the man he loved, the only one he would ever love. Sara's words only served to frighten him further. If Thayne did love him, would the realization scare him off even faster?

Elijah finally broke up the little group. "I think it would be best if we drove as close to the area as possible to conserve our energy. We should leave in a few minutes."

The sun had started to sink below the horizon as they exited the pack manor and piled into two cars. Nick ended up seated between Thayne and Ryan. It almost made him laugh uncontrollably, hysterically. Hostility emanated from Ryan, and Thayne only made the overwhelming scent increase by pulling Nick close to his side. Nick raised an eyebrow at Thayne, who refused to acknowledge the proprietary action. Nick rolled his eyes and settled against Thayne for the short, twenty-minute ride.

Dusk had blanketed the area by the time they arrived, and Nick shivered, except it wasn't from the light chill in the air. An ominous trickle slid down his spine. Something about the night seemed so familiar.

"You all right?" Ryan queried, breaking the silence between them for the first time.

Nick nodded and rubbed at his upper arms, trying to ward off the strange sense of being there once before. "I'm fine. Just want this over with."

Ryan grunted. "Nick, I—"

Elijah interrupted whatever Ryan had been about to say. "Remember to stick together. Do not deviate from the plan. Got it?"

Everyone gave a silent agreement, and several flashes of light later, they were all in wolf form. Thayne's wolf was big, almost towering over the others by a good couple of inches and by far more muscular. If Nick didn't know any better, he'd believe Thayne was meant to be an Alpha. With Kasey being the older brother, Nick had just assumed Thayne wouldn't have been born with the traits to become one. Elijah was the only one who matched Thayne in stature as a wolf. Seeing Thayne beside Elijah caused Nick to realize why the Created One had grown so strong and huge. An Alpha's mate matched them in strength and cunning. If Thayne's bloodlines decreed him as a potential Alpha, it made sense for the creature to have inherited the same characteristics Thayne possessed. Nick wondered if Elijah had already recognized what Thayne was.

Elijah sent Howard and Wilson ahead of the group to scout the beast's territory, waiting for the word from them of the Created One's position. The remainder of their group milled around restlessly, anxious for the night to be over.

None of them liked the idea of just sitting there and waiting. Their wolf sides were nervous and ready to end the threat to their pack and their territory.

Once they received word from Howard that the Created One was indeed in its cave, everyone looked to their Alpha for direction. Elijah went first and each wolf followed, running as close together as possible. Trees flashed by at a fast pace. Nick could hear the scurry of small prey scuttling through the leaves, frightened by the scent of over half a dozen wolves racing through their home. Thayne remained close to his side, tempering his stride to match Nick's. Knowing what he knew now, Nick realized Thayne could have easily outrun him last night, but hadn't.

The group split off into pairs, heading for the previously designated spots on the map. Nick remained alongside Thayne, and the moment they approached the edge of the tree line, Nick froze. He'd seen this place before. In fact, he could have sworn he'd been here before too. The smell of death and decay clung to the area like snow. He searched in vain for why the almost perfectly circular area seemed familiar or why the place sent his blood racing in pure terror. He didn't scare easily and had faced his fair share of Created Ones, yet this felt different. Something wasn't right. He could practically feel the hair along his body vibrating with alarm and tried to figure out what caused his uneasiness. Shifting from paw to paw, Nick intently scanned the area, trying to catch sight of the creature. His wolf instincts screamed for him to run, for all of them to run, but Nick dug his nails into the ground and held on.

What's wrong, Nick? Thayne's voice rang loud and clear in Nick's head, startling him.

Nick swung his gaze toward Thayne. *Don't you smell it? Can't you taste it in the air?*

Thayne lifted his head and sniffed, trying to understand

what Nick referred to. He looked back at Nick. *I don't smell anything.*

Suddenly a loud, vicious howl ripped through the night. Nick stiffened, a fine sweat breaking out all over his lupine form. The sound sent a shiver down his spine. Another howl came from opposite their position in the trees and then a loud yelp of pain. The Created One had found one of them! Nick heard a second shriek of agony before it abruptly cut off. Then Nick saw them—the red dots moving through the darkness. His nightmare in the hospital! He'd forgotten about it. He resisted the urge to cower, to turn around and tuck his tail between his legs to run.

Do you see them? Nick asked.

See what?

The eyes. There. Nick couldn't look away. If he looked away, they could disappear again. The beast could be on him at any time. To his abject horror, the red dots turned toward them and started approaching the clearing until a human form stepped from the shadows into the half-moon light. Nick could see blood covering the lower jaw of the creature and whined, knowing someone had been hurt, if not killed. The Created One's body had become twisted, muscular yet bulging at odd angles.

The beast gave a snarling smile, fangs glistening in the white glow. "Thayne," it sang out almost playfully. "Thaaayyynnnneee."

Nick shuddered and glanced at Thayne to see a horrified expression at the sight of his previous lover standing in the clearing. Empathy flooded Nick. He knew the regret and self-hatred Thayne held had just increased tenfold. When shifted into their human form, Created Ones looked just like the rest of them usually. The only differences tended to be a wildness in their eyes, and their actions became more feral, more dangerous. This was an entirely new breed of beast.

"Thayne!" it roared when Thayne didn't immediately come out into the clearing. "Come to me, or your friends will be the ones to die while you watch!"

Thayne took a step forward, and Nick dashed in front of Thayne, shaking his muzzle in negation of Thayne listening to the monster. *I have to, Nick. If I don't, he could hurt someone else.*

He will hurt someone else! You! I can't lose you, Thayne. Not now. Not when I.... Nick whimpered, shoving his body hard into Thayne's to try to stop him from approaching the Created One.

Thayne nuzzled Nick's throat momentarily. *I'm sorry, Nick.*

Before Nick could anticipate Thayne's actions, Thayne darted around him and entered the clearing, shifting as soon as he did. "Matt!"

Smirking, the red in the creature's eyes deepened. When it spoke this time, there was so much hatred buried in the gravelly voice, it sent dread curling into Nick's belly. "You did this to me, Thayne. You stole my life and left me to suffer."

"No!" Thayne denied. "I didn't know what I'd done until it was too late! You have to believe me!"

The smirk died away, and the beast shook its head in a harsh movement. "Don't lie to me, Thayne. You've been screwing that other whore wolf of yours while I've been left to endure pain beyond anything you've ever felt night after night!"

"I'm sorry, Matt. I truly am. What happened in New Orleans shouldn't have happened. If I had known...."

What sounded like a humorless laugh fell from the creature's mouth. "You say this, yet you found out and did nothing! You ran every time I got near. You told me you loved me, yet it meant nothing to you!"

Nick's heart clenched at hearing the truth, one he'd tried so hard to ignore. He'd known Thayne had cared for the human Matt had once been, but to hear it out loud brought reality crashing in along with the agony of losing Thayne. He couldn't concentrate on that right now, though. He'd deal with the pain after they'd ended the Created One's life.

"I cared about you, Matt, but I couldn't stay with you because it would have been selfish. You wanted to do so much with your life, to save lives. I couldn't take that dream away from you. When I realized what had happened to you, what I had done to you, I didn't know what to do. I knew I had ruined your life, and the only thing I knew how to do was run. So I ran, and I didn't stop."

"You came here tonight to kill me," the Created One said flatly. "Is that how you have finally learned to deal with me? How you will repay me for stealing my future and ending my life?"

Nick couldn't stand there any longer and do nothing. He trotted into the clearing, returning to his human form in a split second. "He couldn't kill you. He cared too much about you to do it."

Those blood-red eyes zeroed in on him, and the smirk returned. "Yet you came here with him to do it for him? How sweet." Without looking away from Nick, the monster continued. "I will make you pay, Thayne. You stole my life, and now I will take yours."

Moving faster than anyone thought possible, even Elijah, the creature shifted and launched itself at Nick. The others rushed into the clearing to help, but it was too late.

Nick grunted as the Created One hit him square in the chest and slammed him to the ground several yards from where he'd stood close to Thayne. Agony ripped through him as the creature's claws dug into his flesh, tearing and shredding the skin. It was aiming for Nick's heart, and Nick found himself too stunned to fight back, his head having hit the ground hard during the fall. He heard Thayne scream his name and the thud of wolves crashing into the body on top of him, but they seemed as if gnats to the giant, slavering beast. Is this how he would die? Before he had a chance to tell Thayne he loved him? Black dots danced along the edge of Nick's vision, and he struggled to remain conscious.

Thayne, Nick whispered over their link.

Nick, please hold on. Don't leave me alone. I need you.

A smile flitted across Nick's blood-covered face, his own life essence spraying from his wounds and soaking into his hair. Thayne had finally admitted he needed him just as much as Nick needed him.

I-I'm sorry, Thayne. I wanted to help you. I wanted to be the one person you could trust more than anyone to know I would never abandon you.

You are, Nick! It's why you can't die on me. I... I love you, Nick. I want, need, you in my life. Please don't let go.

Something changed the moment those words took hold. Nick gasped aloud as a warm rush flooded through his being. The Created One lifted its head and howled, fairly crushing Nick's ribs beneath its paws. The others took the beast's momentary lapse in attack and struck hard. The weight on Nick's chest disappeared, and Nick could hear the angry snarls and shrieks of pain from his packmates. Suddenly Thayne was there in human form, lifting his bleeding, nearly broken body into his arms. His blood immediately saturated the clothing Thayne wore, but Thayne didn't seem to care.

Nick gave a weak smile, unable to move from the pain tearing through his lean form. "You said it first."

Thayne lifted him closer, anguish streaked across his tanned features. "I did. I love you, Nick. I won't ever stop loving you."

The Created One unleashed another loud, furious howl

as Thayne repeated the words Nick had waited so long to hear. Nick struggled to remain conscious but couldn't fight it any longer, the darkness sucking him down into the depths of its embrace, and he let go, carrying the knowledge of Thayne's love with him into the black.

18

THAYNE

THAYNE'S HEART stopped as he watched the attack on Nick almost as if in slow motion. He couldn't do anything except cry out Nick's name when Nick fell. Now he held him in his arms, his blood soaking into his clothing, only able to witness as Nick was taken from him. He threw his head back and issued a howl so loud, so forlorn, even the fighting stopped momentarily. Thayne held his mate tighter, rocking Nick gently. The pain in his heart was so great, there were no tears for him to shed. He'd destroyed not only Matt, but now Nick was gone too. He finally understood exactly what Dakota's father had gone through when he'd lost his mate and why he'd been unable to live without her.

Despair settled over him like a cloak. He stroked Nick's hair, uncaring of the stickiness of the blood. How had everything gone so wrong? Thayne gave a choked, tearless sob. It felt as if his soul was being shredded into a million pieces all at once. He remembered Nick's smile, the way he'd give one of those looks whenever Thayne frustrated or exasperated him, and the sparkling green of Nick's eyes whenever he laughed. Those had been stripped from him as carelessly as he'd tossed Nick aside. Maybe he deserved to have everything taken from him and be left in a never-ending sea of loss. He'd messed up so many times in his life, but rejecting Nick and allowing this to happen to him after Nick had given him so many second chances was the worst mistake of his life.

The Created One shifted back to his human form, having freed himself from the other pack members, and laughed harshly at Thayne's torment, red eyes shining with malice. Thayne stared at the creature that was once Matt. What had happened to the radiant, kind, and gentle man he'd met in New Orleans? The one who wanted to become a doctor to help children and heal them? Had becoming a made wolf actually turned him into such a monster, hard and cold?

"Why?" Thayne said hoarsely.

"Because you deserve to watch him die for what you did to me!" Matt roared. "I wanted to be a doctor, to help save lives. Now all I can do is take them!"

Elijah started toward Matt, and Thayne shook his head. "No, Elijah."

Elijah halted as Thayne placed a gentle kiss to the top of Nick's head, carefully lowered Nick to the ground, and stood. He felt numb, empty inside, but he wouldn't allow Nick's death to go unavenged. His teeth gnashed together in rage.

"You want me to suffer, Matt? It's my turn! Now kill me!" he screamed, bashing his fists against his pecs in a "bring it" gesture.

Matt shifted, and Thayne followed suit, rushing at the huge beast. He was no longer afraid. Flashes of Nick's blood spilling over from the gaping wounds on his chest and the echoes of Nick's cries of pain fueled his wrath. Thayne snarled and flitted around the Created, nipping at its heels on each pass. The creature grew angrier as Thayne remained out of reach, and wrenched around to intercept him on the next pass. Thayne danced backward, farther into the clearing. Matt pursued him, stalking slowly. Thayne remembered seeing a ravine nearby on the map. If he could get Matt to chase him, maybe he could force the bastard over the edge of the cliff. Even if he had to go with him!

He continued the taunting actions, calculatingly moving back toward the other side, away from Nick. His heart cracked a little more with each step farther from his mate, but he persisted. He had to do this. For Nick. For the man who'd captivated him from the beginning and shown him a glimpse of redemption. Snarling, Thayne slashed at Matt and turned, bolting into the trees. He gave a grunt of satisfaction when he heard the beast following him. If he remembered right, the ravine wasn't far, perhaps a half mile from the cave.

Thayne's mind flashed back to the last time he'd been able to run as a wolf. Last night, with Nick. He dug his claws deeper into his sanity, refusing to release it just yet. After he'd killed Matt, who'd taken Nick from him, he would allow the desolation to reap his heart and soul. Thayne pushed his paws faster, urging his ancestors to help him avenge Nick's death.

He burst through the cropping of trees lining the ravine, barely managing to stop himself from going over the edge. He prayed the Created One's anger would prevent it from foreseeing the cliff until it was too late. He remained there, turned to face the beast, but his prayers were denied when the creature didn't come through the trees right behind him. Instead, it came out to his left, surprising him. Matt must have known about the ravine from the beginning. Thayne squared off against the monster and snarled, drool dripping from his teeth. His own rage fueled his desire to end its life. He couldn't fail. He had to do this, for Nick and for Matt.

Thayne watched the beast, trying to anticipate its movements. When it took a step toward him, Thayne surprised it by taking one forward. Its red eyes narrowed at Thayne's unexpected boldness. A smirk lined Thayne's muzzle, and he tensed his muscles, waiting for the creature to make its next move. The Created One's anger overruled any common sense, and Thayne watched as the monster prepared to launch itself at him. Claws digging into the ground and muscles flexing were the first indication as it sprang toward him.

Thayne didn't move fast enough and yelped when Matt hit his left side, one claw slicing a deep wound down his flank. Thayne ignored the bleeding gash and quickly spun, head-butting the other wolf in the side and shoving him toward the canyon. Matt swung around, clamping his jaw down on the meaty area where Thayne's shoulder connected to his neck, and Thayne howled in agony, beating his paws against Matt's belly. He tried to rake his nails into the soft skin, but he couldn't get enough traction. Matt wrenched him side to side, fangs shredding the tender flesh. Thayne brought his hind legs up higher and slammed them into the Created One's chest, digging at its ribcage and successfully tearing the skin open. The Created One only held on tighter, increasing the pressure of his jaws. Numbness set in where the Created One tore at his shoulder, and refusing to give in to the pain, Thayne clawed harder at Matt's chest.

Satisfaction soared through Thayne when he felt his nails hit bone and Matt faltered slightly. Thayne took the chance and rolled them toward the ravine. He would take the bastard with him if he had to! Matt didn't realize Thayne's intentions until it was too late. They both went over the edge in a tangle of limbs. Thayne closed his eyes and waited for the impact, never letting up on his attempts to tear out Matt's heart. They landed with an echoing thud at the bottom of the ravine. Expecting to be knocked out the moment they hit the floor of the canyon, it surprised Thayne when he heard the echo of their impact and his own ragged breathing. He shook his head to clear it, trying to understand what had happened. Thayne tensed when he realized he lay on top of the Created One.

Somehow during the fall, they'd twisted, and Matt lay beneath him, still as death. He stumbled away from the Created One, his body screaming in pain from the gash in his side and the gaping wound in his shoulder. He shifted and grabbed at the wall, forcing himself to remain standing in case Matt awakened and he needed to be ready to fight. There were no sounds or movements from the creature to signal it was still alive. Thayne glanced away when a bright flash of light filled the ravine, and when he looked back, Matt lay in his human form. The change allowed Thayne to see a broken limb from a fallen tree buried in Matt's back. If it had been any longer, the branch would have gone through Thayne as well, something Thayne would have welcomed to end the agony of losing Nick.

It was over. Matt was dead… or dying. Thayne noticed Matt was still breathing. The enormity of everything hit him, and he stumbled to Matt's side. Matt opened his eyes as Thayne dropped to his knees beside him. The red was gone, and all he could see was the beautiful blue he'd fallen for all those months ago in New Orleans.

"Matt," Thayne choked.

Blood trickled from the corners of Matt's mouth as he gave Thayne a relieved smile. "Th-thank you."

"I'm so sorry, Matt. I really am."

Matt coughed, wheezing. "I couldn't stop it."

He ran a shaky hand through Matt's dark locks. "I understand, Matt. I never meant to hurt you."

Matt reached up to touch Thayne's cheek. "I forgive you,"

he whispered as the light faded from the cerulean-blue eyes for the last time, his hand falling limply to the ground.

Thayne could do nothing but watch and attempt to stop the tide of anguish threatening to consume him. Everything seemed to be crashing down around him. He wished he could trade places with Matt, because he didn't know how he could survive the grief crushing his chest, threatening to implode his heart. Thayne threw his head back and screamed, his hands balled into fists on his thighs. Is this how Dakota's father had felt after his mate had died? Is this how all of those mates who'd wasted away to nothing suffered? He wanted nothing more than to end his life, to join Nick in their afterlife and see that gorgeous smile once more. He wished he'd never met Nick because then Nick would still be alive. If only he hadn't gone home to Senaka six months ago. He should have bolted the moment he knew Nick agreed to help him instead of greedily latching on to the life raft Nick tossed his way.

Thayne.

The fog cleared a little at the commanding voice of his Alpha, and Thayne scrubbed at his tear-streaked face. He hadn't even realized he was crying. *He's dead.*

Elijah didn't respond immediately and then answered, *I'm sorry, Thayne, but you need to come back.*

I-I can't leave him here like this.

Someone will retrieve his body. Nick needs you now.

Thayne jerked at hearing Nick's name echo in his head. *How can he need me? He's dead because of me,* he replied bitterly.

No, he's not, Thayne. Nick's alive. Ryan's taken him to meet Seth.

Hope bloomed in Thayne at knowing Nick could still yet live, but the knowledge of his own hand in Nick's condition weighted the emotion. *I shouldn't be around him, Elijah. Not when it's my fault he's hurt.*

It will hurt him worse if you run again, Thayne. If you aren't there by his side when he wakes up, it'll be more painful than anything he's already been through. Before you came back into his life, he stopped smiling and enjoying life. He worked himself until he dropped from exhaustion. I saw an immediate difference when you returned with him from Senaka. His smile came back, and I could see the change in him with you by his side. He needs you now more than ever. Don't leave him again.

He'd messed up so many times and so many ways, yet Elijah was giving him the one thing he wanted more than anything. But he didn't deserve it. He dragged himself to his feet, staggering when his wounds protested. What did he have to offer to Nick? Homeless, jobless, penniless, and too stubborn to admit how he felt until pushed. Yet the memory of Nick's utter joy at his words of love came rushing back, and he crashed to his knees once more. He'd felt the pure exultation racing through Nick when he'd finally given his heart to the mate fated to be his by whatever gods deemed him good enough to be tied to Nick forever.

Thayne's chest hurt at the overload of emotions. He wanted so badly to give in to the selfish side of him screaming for him to rush back to Nick and grab at the chance for happiness Nick offered. What if he continued to do nothing except bring harm to Nick?

Stop overthinking it, Elijah said gently. *Take it one day at a time. Give yourself the chance to let go of your past, and give Nick the one thing he's wanted since he could remember.*

I....

Where are you? I will send Howard and Wilson to retrieve the Created One's body, and we can take you to Nick.

Thayne warred with himself, but he finally gave in to the part of himself clamoring for him to grab on and never let go, praying he wasn't making another mistake. He told Elijah about the ravine north of the cave and how to get there. He glanced around the narrow canyon for a way to get out. The sides were steep, but he could see small jutting rocks at varying levels up the sides and wondered if he could make it with his own injuries. *You have to,* his wolf spirit whispered. *Your mate, our mate, is waiting for you. Hurry!*

He stood again, managed to stumble to the wall, and grabbed hold of the first set of rocks. They were slippery, damp from mildew and weather exposure, and it took him several tries to get to the next set. Each movement sent agony racing through him, but he gritted his teeth and persisted. Nick had suffered far worse than what he experienced now. If being by his side would make Nick happy, he would be there no matter what he had to do or how he did it.

"I promise I'll be with you soon, Nick," he swore.

Sweat poured down his body, his muscles quivered in exhaustion, and his wounds had started bleeding more profusely by the time he reached the top. His hand was on the edge when he felt his foot start to slip. *No!* He had to keep his promise. He scrambled to get a better grip, but he couldn't get any traction. A hand clamped around his wrist just as he thought he'd been about to fall, and he was pulled up onto even ground once more. Thayne lay there, gasping for breath, his eyes shut.

"You've got balls of steel, man," Wilson rumbled to his left.

Thayne opened his eyes to find Wilson peering over the edge of the cliff while Howard crouched near him. "Nick?" Thayne rasped.

"With Seth."

"I need to go," Thayne managed, fighting to sit up.

Howard gripped Thayne's shoulder. "You need to rest for a few minutes. You're bleeding, badly."

"I have to be there when he wakes up."

Howard smiled. "You will be. He's going to be out of it for

a while. Let me at least take a look at your wounds and see how bad they are."

"No, I need to go to him!" Thayne snarled.

Howard snarled right back. "You won't be doing him any good if you die from blood loss, Thayne. Now shut up and let me take a look."

Thayne grumbled but acquiesced and settled back long enough for Howard to look at the gash on his side and the one on his shoulder. Howard gave a grunt, tugged his shirt over his head, and pressed it tight to the bite on Thayne's shoulder and neck. Thayne hissed in pain at the pressure and glared at Howard.

"He got you good, Thayne. The climb from the bottom of the ravine didn't really help the situation. We need to get the bleeding to stop." Howard looked at Wilson, still staring into the canyon. "Yo, Wil. Need to take him back to Elijah. See if you can find a way down."

Wilson nodded in silent understanding, shifted, and set off along the line of the ravine. Howard hefted Thayne to his feet, slinging Thayne's arm over his shoulders.

"I can walk," Thayne snapped.

Raising an eyebrow at his argument, Howard stepped away from Thayne, hands up. Thayne took a step and collapsed to his knees. "You were saying?" Howard replied dryly as he helped Thayne stand once more.

Thayne ground his teeth together at the smugness in Howard's tone, but this time accepted the assistance. It took longer to get back to the clearing than Thayne would have liked, and Howard handed him over to Elijah the moment they reached it.

"Wilson is trying to find a way to get down to the Created One. Keep pressure on the wound on his shoulder, or he could have some serious complications very soon."

Elijah nodded in understanding. "Be careful. We'll see you back at the manor."

Howard gave a small smirk at Thayne. "Take care, balls of steel, and take care of that mate of yours."

Thayne gave a strained smile in return, his pain finally catching up to him now that the adrenaline in his body was gone. "You too, dickhead."

Howard hooted with laughter and clapped Thayne on his uninjured shoulder, uncaring how it jarred Thayne and caused him to hiss in pain. "You're going to do just fine in this pack, Thayne. Just fine. Now go see to your mate." Howard shifted and raced back into the woods, letting out a howl to signal his return to Wilson.

Thayne leaned heavily on Elijah. "He's an irritating prick."

Elijah chuckled, and with Wilson's son, Joe's, help, they started off toward the SUV. "He's definitely got a way of getting under someone's skin."

After that, they made the trip to the car in silence, and it took the last bit of strength Thayne had to remain awake on his way to Nick. More than once he felt himself start to nod off and lifted his head, forcing his eyes open. They didn't return to the manor as Thayne expected. Instead, they arrived at Nick's business within a few minutes. Or maybe it seemed only minutes.

"Why are we here?" he gasped.

"It's closer than the house," Elijah explained as he turned off the engine and climbed out to open Thayne's door, catching him when Thayne almost fell from the SUV. "Ryan brought Nick here and had Kasey and Seth meet him." Joe and Elijah practically dragged him into the building, his legs unable to support him at all.

Ryan stood just inside the front door, waiting for them. "He's upstairs in the apartment."

"Is he okay?" Thayne demanded, breathless and weak.

Ryan glared at him without offering any word on Nick's condition. The little patience Thayne possessed fizzled out, and he roared in a deep voice, "Is he okay?"

Taken aback at the force and power in Thayne's tone, Ryan's eyes opened wide and he nodded. "Seth has been working on him nonstop for the last thirty minutes. Kasey said he's out of the woods but still in a lot of pain."

Thayne sighed in relief and promptly passed out.

LIGHT FILTERED through his eyelids first, and then the sensation of lying in a soft, comfortable bed hit him. Cool sheets rested against his heated skin, and he sighed in pleasure. It took several moments for the events of hours ago to come rushing back, and Thayne jackknifed straight up, looking around anxiously for Nick. The panic lessened the moment his gaze landed on Nick lying asleep in the bed beside him, and died completely when he saw the easy fall and rise of Nick's chest. He took a deep breath and let it out, leaning over to study the lean, lightly tanned form. Seth had done an amazing job. There were still patches of pink marring Nick's skin, but his injuries were healed. Thayne blinked back tears of relief and reached out to trace along the edge of one of the still-reddish areas.

Nick's skin quivered beneath his touch, and Thayne glanced up to see Nick's eyes flutter open. Bright green emeralds focused on him, confusion in their depths. "Thayne?" Nick rasped. Thayne couldn't hold back a smile at hearing his name once again in the whiskey-roughened voice. Nick frowned and sat up, causing Thayne to remove his hand from Nick's chest. "What happened?"

"You don't remember?" Thayne asked.

Nick furrowed his brow as he searched his memory for the events that had unfolded the evening before. Thayne watched in silence and saw Nick's eyes widen the second he remembered. Nick brought his hands up to inspect his torso for injuries.

"Seth healed you," Thayne offered when he saw Nick's shock.

"Is he okay?" Nick asked.

"I don't know exactly," Thayne mumbled. "I, uh… sort of passed out."

Nick began looking for injuries in an instant. He yanked the sheets back in desperate need to verify Thayne's condition. Seth must have had them remove his clothing, for he sat in nothing except for the briefs he'd worn the night before. The gash in his side was gone, and only red splotches remained where his shoulder had been torn open.

Thayne grabbed at Nick's hands, bringing them up to rest over his heart. "I'm fine, Nick. The injuries weren't that serious," he lied. Some of the tension in Nick's shoulders eased for a moment, only to go rigid once more. Thayne looked at him in concern. "What's wrong?"

"Did you mean it?" Nick whispered, unable or maybe unwilling to meet Thayne's gaze.

Thayne knew immediately what Nick was referring to, and he smiled, tugging Nick across his lap and into his arms. He ran his palm down the center of Nick's back along his spine in a comforting caress. "I meant every word," he said softly. "I love you, Nicholas Cartwright. I'm sorry it took me so long to get here and for the pain I caused you along the way."

Nick threw his arms around Thayne's shoulders, and he buried his face against Thayne's throat.

Thayne felt tremors trickle through Nick and held him tighter, stroking the golden-blond locks. "I love you, Nick," he whispered again.

Warm wetness dampened his skin, and Nick clung even

harder to him. Thayne's heart clenched, and he swore he'd spend every waking minute possible reassuring Nick for the rest of their lives. He was well and truly bound to Nick. Not even the pact he'd made with Dakota could change that. After the dust had settled, he would see his old friend and break the promise they'd made to one another all those years ago. Because there was no way in hell he'd give Nick up now.

"You never said it back, you know?" Thayne prodded gently.

He sensed Nick's grin on his throat, and Nick managed to sit back enough to look at him, a mischievous gleam in the depths of his eyes. "Who says I'm in love with you?"

Thayne growled with fake menace and in a flash had Nick pinned underneath his larger frame. "Are you saying you aren't?"

Nick rolled his eyes and huffed. "Why would I be in love with such a stubborn, pig-headed wolf?"

"I'm stubborn and pig-headed, am I?" Thayne raised an eyebrow.

"Yeah, you are, and a royal pain in the ass," Nick teased.

Smirking, Thayne leaned down until they were nose to nose. "I do believe, Mr. Cartwright, that's a bit like the pot calling the kettle black, isn't it?"

Nick started to protest, but Thayne cut him off by angling his head a little to the left and covering Nick's mouth with his own. Whatever Nick had been about to say was lost in the deep kiss. Thayne groaned at the sweet taste of Nick and slid his tongue along Nick's, coaxing Nick to come out and play. Nick responded, bringing his arms up around Thayne and burying his hands in the cascade of dark hair.

When Thayne felt Nick's erection dig into his thigh, Thayne made a guttural sound and ground his equally hard cock against Nick's hip. He wanted nothing more than to flip Nick over and bury himself so far inside him neither of them could tell where one began and the other ended. Only he had no idea how severe Nick's injuries had been or if Seth had been able to heal them all. He didn't want to risk injuring Nick any further and reluctantly broke the kiss, rolling to his back next to Nick. He almost gave in to his need when Nick tried to prevent him from being the sane one, following him.

"Nick, stop," he gasped.

"Why?" Nick asked, almost whining.

"Because I don't want to hurt you."

"You won't hurt me," Nick insisted, trying to reinitiate the kiss.

Thayne grasped Nick's shoulders and held him at arm's length. "Stop," he said in a gentle tone. "For my sake, please."

Nick sighed but gave in, flopping onto his back beside Thayne. "Fine," he said petulantly.

Thayne chuckled. "Don't worry, babe. When we have the clean bill of health from Seth, I'm going to nail you to the mattress and not let you leave until the house comes crashing down around us."

"Promise?" Nick asked, tilting his head to look over at Thayne, a smile flitting around the corners of his gorgeous mouth.

"With my life," Thayne said lasciviously.

Nick laughed and sat up again, running a hand through his tousled hair. Thayne followed suit and sat cross-legged on the bed. Nick's expression turned serious. "Did anyone else get hurt?"

"I don't know," Thayne replied honestly. "When it was over, my only thought was getting to you."

Nick flushed and grinned, but it died out fast. "And the Created One?"

Thayne tensed and said stiffly, "Dead."

Sadness covered Nick's features as he placed his hand on Thayne's shoulder. "I'm so sorry, Thayne."

Shifting his gaze from Nick, Thayne tipped his head in acknowledgement of the empathy. He would never forget the look in Matt's eyes when the light faded from them forever. The memory of what he'd done would haunt him for the rest of his life.

"Matt, the human Matt, cared about you, Thayne," Nick murmured. "He wouldn't have been so connected to you as a created wolf if it weren't for those emotions."

"How do you know?" Thayne muttered.

Nick reached out and forced Thayne to look at him again. "You forget, I also made a mistake, which Seth paid the price for. If Taggart had cared about me as a human, then he would have come after me, not Seth. Matt deeply cared for you, and it became part of who he was as a wolf. The part of Matt that loved you wouldn't want you to spend your life with regret in your heart."

Thayne searched Nick's eyes for guile or deceit and found none. He leaned his forehead on Nick's shoulder, closing his eyes. "There's something I need to take care of."

"What?"

"I need to go see Dakota."

"Oh?"

Thayne heard the note of uncertainty in Nick's voice and knew only one way he could reassure his mate he wasn't going anywhere. "Will you go with me?"

"Of course!" Nick agreed.

Hiding a smirk at the sudden happiness resonating from Nick, Thayne lifted his head and glanced around the room. He recognized it as the same room from the other day where he'd gotten Nick off during a frottage session. The smirk turned into a full-fledged grin at the reminder of Nick's passionate cries and the red blush staining his cheeks as he'd come.

"What are you thinking about?" Nick queried as he slid off the bed.

Thayne raked his gaze down Nick's body, taking note of the light dusting of blond hairs down Nick's legs and the lean muscles flexing under the skin. "Just remembering the last time we were here."

Right then, Thayne learned something new about his mate. The man's entire body turned red when he blushed. Nick snatched the sheet from the bed and wrapped it around himself with a huff of indignation before stomping off into the bathroom. Thayne's laughter followed Nick the entire way.

He heard the shower turn on and slid off the bed, snatching up his bloody and torn jeans to pull them on. His stomach rumbled, and he wondered if there was any food in the kitchen. After opening the door, he walked down the short hallway and stopped. Kasey and Seth were sitting at the bar separating the kitchen from the living area.

Kasey smiled at him and pointed to the coffeemaker. "Heard you both get up. How are you feeling this morning?"

Seth turned around on the stool he was perched on, and Thayne saw how exhausted Seth looked. He frowned as he approached them. "You okay?"

Seth nodded. "I'll be fine. Healing Nick took a lot out of me."

"You shouldn't have healed me, then!" Thayne protested.

Giving Thayne a look of exasperation, Seth replied, "I don't think I could have left my best friend's mate bleeding to death on the bed next to him. I'm fine. Just tired."

"Are Nick's injuries gone completely?" Thayne asked after a moment. He went around the counter to fill a mug of black coffee.

"I wouldn't recommend running a triathlon or doing backflips, but yes. There may be some residual aftereffects,"

Seth admitted. "I have never healed injuries of that magnitude before. My suggestion is for him to rest a few days and take it easy."

Thayne would've been lying if he claimed he wasn't disappointed at having to wait even longer to indulge in Nick's body, but he wouldn't endanger Nick's life any further. "I'll make sure of it."

"Make sure of what?" Nick asked from behind him.

The three of them turned to see Nick standing in the doorway in a fresh T-shirt and jeans, a towel draped around his neck. Thayne swallowed hard at how good Nick looked with hair dripping and bare feet.

He stood up and cleared his throat. "I'm going to grab a shower while Seth explains."

He rushed past Nick and into the bedroom, shutting the door behind him. It took all of his willpower to keep his mind blank as he hurried through his own shower. He'd have to dress in his dirty, torn clothing from the night before, but it was doubtful Nick had clothes here that would fit him. When he exited the bathroom, a towel wrapped loosely around his waist, Nick sat on the edge of the bed, and Thayne had to bite back a groan. Especially when Nick's gaze turned into that of a hungry wolf, ravishing every inch of Thayne's bare skin. Thayne spun around to hide his body's reaction, but Nick wouldn't let him escape. Suddenly Nick's arms were around his waist and pulling Thayne back against him.

"We can't," Thayne ground out.

"Why not?" Nick whispered heatedly, kissing at the nape of Thayne's neck and along his shoulders.

"Because you are supposed to be resting for a few days, not having sex with me," Thayne moaned.

Nick had untied the towel before Thayne realized, and

Thayne almost howled when Nick wrapped one long-fingered hand around his hard-as-nails cock.

"Stop," Thayne said weakly.

"You don't want me to," Nick replied with confidence, stroking him in a calculating up-and-down motion.

"No, I don't, but we can't do this." Thayne sighed and grabbed at Nick's wrist.

Nick resisted at first but eventually gave in and released his leaking shaft. "You owe me," Nick pouted.

Thayne gave a feeble chuckle. "Yeah, I know."

Stepping away, Nick pointed at the bed. "There are some clothes that should fit you. Kasey said you guys are about the same size and brought some of his here this morning."

Snatching up the towel, Thayne covered himself again and walked to pick up the clothes. "I think I'll get dressed in the bathroom," he mumbled.

This time it was Nick's laughter echoing on the walls of the bedroom and Thayne fighting a blush.

19

NICK

AFTER THE tantalizing moments in the bedroom, things moved at a lightning pace. They ended up at the pack manor to speak with Elijah about the events they'd missed because of their injuries. Nick winced when he heard about George's death. Sara was beside herself with grief over her nephew, and Nick immediately picked up on Thayne's overwhelming guilt. Would there ever be a time when Thayne could forgive himself?

Kasey and Seth eventually left to go back to Senaka, and Thayne arranged a beautiful, quiet funeral for his ex-lover. Nick still fought his jealousy over knowing Thayne had loved someone other than him, but he reminded himself Thayne was his now. Everything else was in the past.

Nick ran into Ryan at the pack manor, and apparently almost dying negated Ryan's anger. They hugged, and Ryan apologized, although he didn't lose the hostility toward Thayne. Nick knew it would take time for Ryan to truly warm up to Thayne, and perhaps finding his own mate would speed the situation along. The upcoming Summit would be a great thing for many wolves amongst theirs and the Senaka pack.

No matter how many times Nick tried to seduce Thayne over the course of the next few days, Thayne stubbornly refused to give in. He'd done everything possible short of yanking Thayne's pants down and blowing him wherever they were. Thayne seemed so sure he'd injure Nick again and insisted on waiting the amount of time Seth suggested before he'd even think of touching Nick. It frustrated him to no end, and he wanted to tie Thayne up while he slept and just have his way with Thayne. The idea was tempting, but he didn't want to ruin the still-tentative truce between them.

Now that they were no longer in danger, Nick was able to make the trip to see his grandfather's Impala. It nearly broke his heart when he saw the damage to it. The entire passenger side was buckled in from the impact. All of the windows were blown out, and the roof was partially ripped open. The owner of the junkyard gave him a rundown of what it would take to fix the car, but Nick didn't have the heart to just let the Impala go. The car was the only connection he still had to his grandfather. He instructed the owner to have it towed to a body shop close to the junkyard. He prayed his friend at the garage would be able to restore it back to its former glory.

The morning of the third day following his near-death experience, Nick woke to find Thayne sitting at the foot of the bed, fully dressed and ready to go somewhere.

He sat up, straightening out his hair. "Thayne?"

"I have to see him."

Him being Dakota, Nick realized and nodded. "I'll only be a few minutes."

He dressed quickly, forgoing the shower, and exited to find Thayne no longer in the room. Panicking a bit, he rushed down the hall, peering into his study and the living room. Had Thayne left him again despite asking him to go? Nick's heart beat hard at his ribcage as he headed to the last room in the house, the kitchen. His stomach nearly dropped into his feet when he didn't find Thayne there either. He'd left him. Nick stood there in the doorway, his legs almost unable to support him. Depression and desolation shrouded him. How could Thayne leave him now? After everything? Maybe that's why he'd insisted so hard on not having sex with him. Maybe the words of love had been a lie while he lay dying.

"You don't have your shoes on yet," Thayne said from behind him.

Nick swung around in shock. "Yo-you didn't leave me," he gasped.

"What?" Thayne asked in surprise. "Of course not. I packed a bag for both of us, since we'll most likely have to stay somewhere a couple nights. Did you really think I'd leave you?"

Shame and embarrassment caused Nick to turn his head away. He really had thought Thayne would leave him behind. "I couldn't find you," he mumbled.

Nick heard Thayne approach, and then he was jerked against Thayne's chest. "I'm done running, Nick. I know it will take time for you to trust me not to bolt at the first sign of trouble, but I'm here and I'm not going anywhere."

Feeling foolish at his reaction, Nick kept his face buried in Thayne's shoulder. He'd never been a needy person. In fact, he'd always considered himself to be fiercely independent, since his grandfather had raised him to be and he'd been on his own since his early college years.

"I'm sorry," he managed.

"Don't be," Thayne admonished. "I'm the one who should be sorry. If it weren't for my stubborn refusal to accept you as my mate, you wouldn't be so uncertain of me."

Nick leaned back enough to see Thayne's face. "I think we should wipe the slate clean. From now on, no more assumptions or ideas based on our past. We'll start fresh."

Thayne smiled. "I'd like that."

Nick returned his smile. "Okay, let me get my shoes on, grab my wallet and keys, and we'll get out of here."

Dropping a quick kiss on Nick's mouth, Thayne released him.

Nick returned to his bedroom, stuffed his feet into a pair of sneakers, and snatched up his wallet and keys from the nightstand. Thayne waited for him by the front door when he came back out.

Within minutes they were on the road, this time with Thayne at the wheel, and Nick took the opportunity to ask, "Thayne?"

"Hmm?" Thayne grunted.

"Your friend... Dakota. Why do you want to see him so badly?"

When Thayne didn't answer right away, Nick wondered if maybe he'd overstepped his boundaries, but Thayne's next words surprised him. "I have to break my promise to him, and I can't do it over the phone."

Nick frowned. "Your promise?"

"When we found... when Dakota's father took his life, Dakota and his sister were being sent to live with relatives off the reservation in Senaka. Finding his father like that made him withdraw from everyone around him except me. It changed him like it changed me. We made a blood pact to never accept our mates and to live our lives without allowing anyone to make us weak. I need to tell him I can't keep our oath any longer."

Nick's breath caught in his throat at the meaning behind Thayne's words. "Thayne...."

"It was a long time ago," Thayne offered flatly.

"Where does he live now?"

"Oregon."

"Wouldn't it be faster to fly there?" Nick asked.

"I need the time to think," Thayne said.

Nick took his statement as a request for silence and shut up, turning his head to watch out the window as they headed north. They were on Interstate 5 within less than an hour. Nick dozed off at some point, and it wasn't until he felt the truck turn off that he came awake. Blinking open his eyes, he found them parked at one of those rest-stop places with food and gas.

"Where are we?" he asked, yawning.

"Just at the Oregon state border."

Holy shit! He'd slept a long time. "Damn, I'm sorry!"

Thayne waved away his apology. "You needed the rest. We should have eaten before leaving home, but I was so anxious to get on the road, I forgot I'm used to going for long periods of time without stopping and you aren't."

Nick noted Thayne's use of the word home but didn't acknowledge it. "I'm fine. I wasn't really hungry this morning anyway. Although, I am starving now."

He gave Thayne a chagrined look when his stomach made a loud grumble. Thayne grinned. "Why don't you head inside and find something to eat, and I'll gas up."

"Do you have enough money for gas?" Nick asked, frowning.

"Don't worry about it. I'm fine."

Nick knew Thayne was a proud person and didn't want to accept handouts, but Thayne still hadn't started his job at the diner and couldn't have a whole lot of resources at the moment. He dug a credit card out of his wallet and stepped out of the truck. Before Thayne could protest, Nick had swiped his card, punched in the necessary info, and started toward the building. He smiled when he heard Thayne grumbling as he walked away. Thayne would learn he didn't give up so easily.

Thayne handed him the receipt for the gas when he joined him for lunch. "I can pay my own way," Thayne grunted.

"I know you can," Nick said innocently. "But it is my truck. I figure it's my responsibility to fill the tank."

Thayne scowled. "The trip to Oregon was my choice. I should have to pay for it."

Nick waved his hand at Thayne's word. "We'll split it. You pick it up on the way back, okay?"

The offer seemed to appease Thayne, and they both settled down to eat. In less than an hour, they were back on the road and driving toward wherever Dakota lived. Nick spent the second half of the trip asking about Thayne's friend while hiding the fact that he was probing for more information about Thayne's childhood. Several tidbits were things he filed for later. He fully intended on giving Thayne the chance to see his horse again, since Thayne couldn't return to Senaka. It also fascinated him to learn about the many places Thayne had visited over the years of roaming he'd done.

"You spent time in a lot of places," Nick mused.

"I never really found anywhere I wanted to call home," Thayne replied. "Until now."

Warmth bloomed in Nick's chest, and he had to turn his head to look out the passenger window to cover the huge grin on his face. "So, Dakota owns a ranch, huh?"

"Yeah. He raises cattle and trains horses. When his parents passed away, his grandmother took him and his sister in. She'd lived on a ranch her entire life and knew a lot about horses. She taught him everything she knew and brought in others to teach him the things she didn't. Last I heard, his training skills are the most coveted in the horse industry."

"I'm glad his life turned out so well with everything that happened to him, to both of you, when you were kids. I know it's difficult enough losing one parent, but for both to be taken at once is almost unbearable." Nick closed his eyes in dismay when he remembered Thayne had also lost both his parents in a way. He couldn't see them anywhere except at the Summit or if his parents chose to visit them in California. "I'm sorry, Thayne. I'm such an idiot."

He felt Thayne touch his hand. "It's okay, Nick. Everything that caused me to be unable to see my parents or visit them is my own fault. I knew pack laws, and I should have been more careful to prevent what happened."

Nick turned his hand palm up and entwined his fingers with Thayne's. He opened his eyes and looked at Thayne to find him with a calm expression. It surprised him, but he couldn't deny his happiness at seeing Thayne coming to accept what he could.

"You're amazing, you know?" Nick said.

Thayne gave him an incredulous look. "What are you talking about?"

"You don't even see it either."

"I'm not amazing!" Thayne protested.

"Yes, you are. Amazing, brilliant, beautiful, and underneath the hard shell you show to the world, soft."

"Take that back!" Thayne demanded in horror. "I'm not soft!"

Nick laughed. "You are soft, Thayne. Doesn't matter how hard you fight the truth. You are like a great big marshmallow inside."

Thayne glared at him. "Don't make me pull this truck over and force you to take it back."

"Pfft. You couldn't if you tried."

Nick gasped when Thayne jerked the wheel to the side, sending the truck skidding off onto the grass lining the highway. Thayne put the truck in park and turned in the seat toward him. Nick held no fear of Thayne and waited with an expectant expression. When Thayne slid over on the bench seat, he had to check a tiny bit of uncertainty of what Thayne intended, but what Thayne did next was unexpected. Thayne reached up with both hands and attacked… his ribcage. Nick struggled, laughing and attempting to grab Thayne's relentless fingers. He'd never seen this playful side of Thayne, and he couldn't deny how happy it made him to see it. The love he already held for Thayne deepened even further. He knew without a doubt Thayne would be okay, given enough time. The scars Thayne carried inside would heal and eventually fade away.

"Okay! Okay!" Nick cried for mercy. "I give, I give!"

Thayne stopped, his fingers poised to attack again if Nick wasn't truly sincere. "You admit I'm not a, what word did you use… marshmallow?"

Nick bit his tongue and nodded his head. Something in his face must have given away that he was lying. The same gleam entered Thayne's eyes, and he dove for Nick's ribs again. Nick successfully snagged Thayne's hands this time, stopping him before he could continue his unyielding tickling.

"You aren't soft," Nick said in a quiet manner. "You're strong, but you do care about others, even if you won't let anyone know it."

Thayne eyed him for a moment and sat back behind the wheel. "I'll accept that."

Grinning, Nick reached over and poked Thayne in the side lightly. "We should get going. It's going to be dark soon."

"It'll be better if we stay at a motel overnight," Thayne muttered as he pulled back out onto the road. "I don't want to show up on Dakota's doorstep in the dark."

"Okay." Nick knew Thayne was nervous about his friend's

reception to Thayne's news about having found and claimed his mate. Yet he couldn't help his own excitement at spending the night completely alone in a motel room with Thayne who'd stubbornly refused to let him ravish every inch of his body. He wondered if maybe Thayne would finally give in tonight and let him have his way with him.

The remainder of the trip was spent with Nick talking about his grandfather and the many would-be suitors of Seth's he'd scared off over the years. Nick still remembered the guy at the pizza place who'd had a bet going on when he'd get into Seth's pants. He'd lost that bet before it even got started.

By the time they reached the town close to Dakota's ranch, it was already almost nine at night, and Nick sensed Thayne's anxiety increase.

He reached out and grabbed Thayne's hand. "Relax, babe. Everything is going to be okay. Let's find somewhere to crash for the night, and we'll get some rest."

Thayne nodded, and they found a small motel close to the opposite end of town. Nick rented the room against Thayne's protests once again. With a lascivious grin, he told Thayne he would take it out in trade later on. Thayne growled at him and huffed, but stopped rejecting Nick's help. The motel room was the typical flowered-wallpaper scheme you see in most places, with green carpeting and salmon-pink walls. Nick couldn't help but shake his head. He'd been in many hotels and motels across the world, and the majority of them went with the most unappealing decorum he'd ever seen. The only region he'd been to where the rooms were different was Asia. He thoroughly enjoyed the change in scenery there.

Nick tossed his bag down on the floor near the bed and stretched, yawning. "I forgot how traveling by car can be so exhausting even doing nothing except sitting there."

"You always travel by plane?" Thayne asked, setting his own bag on the small table in the room.

Shrugging, Nick replied, "Most of the places I travel in the US are hours or days to travel by car. It's more efficient and time-saving to go by airplane than ground."

"What places have you been to?" Thayne asked curiously.

Nick sank on the edge of the bed, leaning back on his palms. "Japan, China, Australia, Germany, Italy, France, Canada, and just about every state in the US except Maine, Idaho, and Nebraska."

"Wow," Thayne said, propping a hip against the dresser. "That's pretty impressive. You must have business in a lot of places."

"Well, not everything is done on-site, but Seth's family also moved a lot and we would follow him, so there were a lot of places we ended up where I haven't been back since leaving."

Nick glanced at the clock. "We should grab something to eat and hit the sack."

Thayne nodded. "I'll go back down the road to that burger joint we saw. What do you want?"

"Just a couple of burgers and a soda would be good. But I really should be the one to go," Nick said with a frown. "After all, you've been doing all the driving."

"I'm used to it. Besides, it's my turn to pay for something," Thayne replied dryly.

Nick rolled his eyes. "Okay, if you insist."

"I do," Thayne rumbled and left.

Giving a small chuckle, Nick flopped back entirely onto the bed and stared at the water-stained ceiling. Thayne was certainly something else. Life would never get boring.

The next thing he knew, Thayne shook him awake and pointed at the table. "Food, Nick."

Nick blinked several times to clear the sleep from his eyes. "That was fast."

"I've been gone thirty minutes. You fell asleep." Thayne pulled out one of the chairs and sat, shoving the other away from the table with his boot. "Sit, eat. Then you can go back to sleep."

By the time he'd polished off the two burgers, fries, and soda Thayne had brought back for him, he could barely keep his eyes open. He heard Thayne laugh as he almost landed face-first on the table at one point.

"Wuss," Thayne teased and stood, helping Nick to his feet. Thayne stripped Nick's shirt over his head and undid his jeans. He pushed Nick down to the edge of the bed and squatted to pull off his loafers.

Nick put one hand on Thayne's shoulder to steady himself. "I'm not a wuss." Nick sighed.

"You are." Thayne smirked up at him while grabbing the hem of Nick's jeans and tugging them off.

Nick slid his fingers through Thayne's hair, yanking out the rubber band his mate had used to tie it back. "I'm not usually."

Thayne frowned then. "You're still healing from the other night. Even with Seth's help, your body had a lot of trauma. Sleep. I'll join you in a little while."

"No. I need you, Thayne. Please," Nick murmured. "Don't leave me alone again tonight."

"Nick," Thayne sighed.

"Please," Nick whispered.

"You can barely keep your eyes open!"

Nick wrapped both arms around Thayne's neck and planted a kiss on Thayne's upturned mouth. "Sex is like caffeine. I'll be wide awake in no time. Now make love to me, Thayne. I don't want to go another night without you."

He could see Thayne warring internally with himself and

knew he had him right where he wanted him. Without giving him the chance to rationalize refusing his request, Nick kissed Thayne again. He slid off the bed, forcing Thayne onto his ass, and straddled Thayne's waist.

"You're..."—he pressed his tongue along the seal of Thayne's lips—"so..."—demanding entrance into the warm depths—"stubborn," he breathed just before dipping inside and cutting off any further protests from Thayne.

Thayne groaned, and Nick felt Thayne's hands grip his bottom, squeezing and rocking him against the obviously hard cock straining at the front of his jeans. Nick slipped his hands beneath Thayne's shirt and explored the crevices and valleys of Thayne's body. Muscles rippled under his touch, flexing with each move of Thayne's hips. He hadn't really had the time to learn Thayne's form either night they'd coupled. This would be the first time he'd have the chance to discover what drove Thayne wild. The tiredness he'd felt only moments ago was gone and in its place was the absolute need to feel Thayne inside of him, the driving urge to taste and caress the long length of his body.

Nick broke their passionate kiss and sat up, still straddling Thayne. He could see all reason gone from Thayne, and smirked. The stiff length biting into the crease of his ass spoke of the desire racing through Thayne. He shoved the white shirt Thayne wore higher up, bunching it under his arms. He drank in the sight of the deeply chiseled chest, tight abdomen, and well-defined pectoral muscles. Dark rose-colored nipples dusted the center of each pec, beaded and at the ready for his mouth. Nick tugged at the shirt, indicating Thayne should slide it off. With some awkward maneuvering, Thayne managed to shed the offending fabric, leaving him completely bare-chested.

Nick leaned down to nip at Thayne's collarbone, laving the tiny wound with his tongue. A shudder ran through

Thayne's long form, and satisfaction broke over Nick. He wanted to make Thayne feel good, to make him remember every single second of this night. He wanted Thayne to forget every other man he'd ever been with, including the man he'd once loved.

He ran his fingers over Thayne's nipples, tracing the puckered flesh. Thayne moaned aloud, and Nick tweaked the right nipple, forcing another groan from Thayne. Perhaps it was genetics of Native Americans or maybe just Thayne, but there wasn't a stray bit of hair on any inch of his chest. It was smooth and warm under Nick's hands. He lightly scratched his fingernails along the ridges of Thayne's ribs while slipping farther down Thayne's body, far enough to latch on to the left nipple with his mouth. Thayne cried out and clutched at Nick's biceps. Nick swirled his tongue around the small point, raking his teeth over it between licks.

"Nick, I—oh, fuck," Thayne panted, thrusting his still-clothed cock against Nick's belly.

Nick stroked his hand from the curve of Thayne's pec down to the small trail leading into Thayne's jeans. His fingers nimbly made short work of the button and zipper, the backs of them pressing along the underside of Thayne's prick. Pure heat seared into Nick's skin from the straining length even through the fabric.

"Mmm, so beautiful," Nick murmured when he set Thayne free.

A drop of clear precum welled from the slit and trickled down the hard, bulging shaft. Nick watched until he couldn't hold out any longer. Using only the end of his tongue, he lapped at the salty liquid, tracing the same path it had taken. Thayne's cock jumped at the slick touch, and Nick went to the base and back up again. His taste buds sang with joy at the earthy taste of Thayne's skin. He wrapped his lips around the flared tip and sucked slowly, languidly. The outside world didn't exist. Nothing except the pure pleasure of Thayne's shaft in his mouth registered.

Nick brought Thayne to the brink over and over, letting the tasty prick bob free in the cool air of the room whenever Thayne got too close to coming. In between sucking Thayne's cock, Nick would show equal attention to the tight, round orbs, drenching them with saliva. Thayne's entire body was quivering by the time Nick stopped teasing him and pulled away. Pure animal lust burned in the depths of Thayne's gaze when Nick stood and removed the last article of clothing he wore, his briefs. He snatched up his bag and yanked out the tube of Vaseline he'd purchased at the rest stop while Thayne gassed up the car.

Thayne let out a low guttural sound when he saw the container. Nick tossed the Vaseline on the bed, crawled after it, and lay on his back, spreading his legs. He beckoned Thayne to join him. In a flash, Thayne was on him, rubbing their cocks together as he kissed Nick breathless. Nick scratched his nails down Thayne's back and felt Thayne purr against him.

"Thayne," Nick gasped.

Thayne didn't waste much time. He prepped Nick's hole with first one, then two fingers until he could slide three in without resistance. Hooking them, he thrust the ends along Nick's prostate, stimulating him until Nick cried out Thayne's name, arching his back from the mattress. Thayne yanked his fingers free, ripping another small mewl from Nick, and slathered his stiff shaft with lube. He guided the dripping tip to Nick's entrance, pressed in, and pushed forward until his balls rested at Nick's ass.

Nick hooked his legs around Thayne's waist and tried to pull Thayne even deeper into him. "Thayne," Nick moaned.

The feel of Thayne inside of him after so long brought Nick right to the edge, and he had to force himself not to come. Thayne pulled out and pushed back in, thrusting slow and steady. Their breathing grew heavier as their passion flamed higher, and Thayne moved faster and harder. Nick buried his face against Thayne's sweaty shoulder, holding on for dear life out of fear of flying apart and never being whole again. He wanted to erase the last seven months. He wanted this to be the only memory he held dear to his heart. The harsh rejection in the alley after their first coupling and the emotionless claiming were parts of a past he didn't want to relive. He wanted to remember this as the first time they'd held one another, the first time they made love to one another.

"So close," Thayne grunted near Nick's ear.

"Come, my mate," Nick whispered. "Come inside me. Mark me as yours."

As Thayne tipped over the edge, he sank his teeth into the tender section of Nick's shoulder, causing Nick to cry out in exquisite pain and pleasure. Nick felt every pulse as Thayne emptied inside of him. He relished the sensation of Thayne's fangs in his flesh, claiming him as his own, finally. Shattering into a million pieces, Nick tightened his limbs around Thayne as he came, his essence spraying both their chests and bellies.

They collapsed into a quivering, sweaty mass on the bed as their passion ebbed. Nick panted for breath, his eyes closed in ecstasy after being deprived of Thayne's touch since they'd declared their love for one another. He sensed Thayne rise up enough to look down at him, still buried inside of him. Thayne brushed a strand of hair back from his cheek as Nick opened his eyes to look up at him.

"Wow."

Chuckling, Thayne dropped a kiss on Nick's forehead and slid free of his body with a small groan. Nick shivered as Thayne's seed trickled from his well-loved hole. "You can say that again," Thayne responded, flopping onto his back beside Nick.

"Wow." Nick snuggled up to Thayne's side and curled into him. "Never go so long again."

"Agreed."

Thayne pulled Nick closer, his fingertips brushing over the tattoo on Nick's arm. Nick shivered when Thayne began to trace the paw prints, skin whispering over skin. "When did you get this?" Thayne asked.

Nick yawned. "A few years ago."

"I saw the same one on Seth," Thayne muttered.

Nick let out a tired laugh, hearing the jealousy in Thayne's voice. "Seth is like my brother. Never been anything more. It was a way to show our bond as friends and connect us no matter where we are in the world."

Thayne grumbled but didn't say anything else. Nick burrowed closer to Thayne and briefly tightened the arm he had slung across Thayne's midsection in a half-hug. "You're the only one I see, Thayne. No one else," Nick murmured.

Nick's eyelids drooped as he tried to stay awake until he was certain Thayne felt confident the tattoo meant nothing more than a symbol of friendship.

A bigger yawn broke out, and Thayne laughed, nuzzling at Nick's temple. "Go to sleep, baby. I'll still be here in the morning."

"Love you," Nick whispered as he drifted off. He just barely heard Thayne say it back.

THAYNE

IT TOOK a long time for Thayne to fall asleep, and he listened to Nick's soft breathing in the quiet of the motel room. Nick muttered in his sleep, but never let go of Thayne. He knew they had a long way to go before Nick fully trusted he wouldn't leave. Only time would show Nick he was in it for the long haul.

Would Dakota be happy for him? Even though they hadn't seen each other in five years, they still spoke on the phone once or twice a month, and they considered themselves to be best friends, but Thayne worried his acceptance of Nick would break the decades-long friendship. Although he wouldn't give Nick up ever again. He'd finally come to understand what he'd been told for over twenty years. Mates were precious. They were the other half of you, the good half, and without them, you could never feel whole. In the years he'd roamed across the country and the many bodies he'd lost himself in, he'd never truly been complete. He'd always been looking for something. He'd found the piece that was missing—Nick. Nick felt like home. No matter what happened tomorrow with Dakota, he would never leave Nick alone again.

Despite driving for hours and falling asleep way after Nick, Thayne woke first to sunlight filtering between the shabby curtains over the window. He blinked and glanced over at the clock on the nightstand. It was seven. Nick gave a gentle snore and hugged him tighter, sensing Thayne's stirring. Thayne smiled softly and gave a light caress down Nick's bare arm, his fingers lingering over the paw print tattoo circling his bicep. The jealousy at knowing Nick shared a special bond with someone else simmered in the back of his mind, but Seth being mated to Kasey muted the strength of it. Nick looked good in the morning with the just-loved tousled blond hair and sleep-softened expression.

"Baby, I think we should get up," Thayne murmured, brushing a strand of hair back from Nick's cheek.

"Mmmm, nooo," Nick whined, burrowing in closer to Thayne. "It's too early."

Thayne laughed. "I've already figured out you aren't a morning person, baby. If you get up, I'll go get us some coffee."

Nick perked up a tiny bit but still refused to budge, holding on stubbornly.

Thayne smiled. "We still have about a half hour to forty-five minute drive to Dakota's ranch, Nick. Let's get dressed and grab something to eat. You can sleep in the car if you're still tired."

Nick sighed and reluctantly released Thayne, sitting up with a sexy pout on his face. Thayne suppressed a groan and fought off the desire to tumble Nick back to the bed and have his way with him. He forced himself off the bed and into the bathroom to relieve himself.

"I'm going to grab a shower, Nick," Thayne called out as he turned on the water to let it heat up.

"I'll join you," Nick said from behind him.

Thayne immediately refuted Nick's offer. "We'll never get out of here if you do."

Nick gave a wicked grin, his emerald-green eyes sparkling lustfully. "We'll save water and time if we shower together, though."

"I don't think so." Thayne pointed at the door. "Go. I'm not going to take long."

Another disappointed look crossed Nick's face. "Okay, but you owe me a week in bed after we get home."

"Agreed. Now go," Thayne ordered, no heat in his voice, just amusement.

Nick grumbled as he went back into the room. Thayne hurried through his shower, just rinsing off his body with soap. When he finished, Nick took his turn while Thayne dressed and packed up the few items they'd taken out of the bag last night, including the tube of Vaseline. Thayne's body responded to the reminder of being inside Nick last night, and he adjusted his cock in his jeans, demanding his body remain under his control. Nick had been so tight and hot around him, like a furnace in winter. Thayne had forgotten just how good Nick felt all those months ago in Senaka. Even before finding out who Nick was, he'd sensed something different about him. He'd experienced so much more pleasure with Nick than the many random twinks he'd fucked during his travels. But he'd refused to believe it to be more than a willing body to get off with. Now… gods, he wanted to remain buried in Nick every single second of every single day.

"Did you get my coffee yet?" Nick sounded muffled, and Thayne swung around to see Nick drying his hair with one of the towels. Another towel sat low on Nick's hips.

Thayne licked his lips at the sight. "Uh… Not yet. We can grab it on the way out of town, okay?"

Nick sighed and dropped the towel around his shoulders. "Okay."

Thayne kept his back turned as Nick dressed, staring out of the gap in the curtains to avoid getting further aroused by his mate. Once Nick was fully clothed, Thayne picked up both their bags and ushered Nick through the door. They checked out and were on the road after a quick stop in a McDonald's on the way out of town. Thayne barely managed to keep the truck on the road when he heard Nick's ecstatic moan at the first sip of coffee.

"You're going to be the death of me," Thayne muttered under his breath.

"What was that?" Nick asked innocently.

"Nothing. Was just wondering if Dakota hired any more hands on."

"Ah." But there was a depth of smugness in Nick's tone, and Thayne knew he hadn't fooled Nick one bit.

The closer they got to Dakota's, the tenser Thayne got. His hands had a death grip on the wheel by the time the fence with the Circle D brand came into view.

Nick reached out and touched the back of his hand. "Relax, Thayne. If he's as good a friend as you've told me, then you have nothing to worry about."

Thayne worked at relaxing his hold on the steering wheel and turned the truck onto the long drive up to the house. His gaze zeroed in immediately on Dakota perched on horseback in the corral. Dakota looked their way when he heard the tires crunching on the gravel. A grin spread over Dakota's face when he recognized Thayne behind the wheel, and Thayne couldn't help but return the smile. His friend dismounted and handed the reins off to a cowpoke. He left the corral and waited at the top of the drive for Thayne.

Turning off the engine, Thayne exited the vehicle and

approached Dakota. They exchanged a backslapping hug, then Dakota stepped back.

"How the hell have you been, Thay?" Dakota crowed.

"Good. You?"

"Great! The ranch is doing well. Got about three hundred head of cattle right now and more horse-training business than I know what to do with. I still want you to come work for me here." Dakota glanced past Thayne to the truck. "Who's this?"

Thayne turned to see Nick standing near the truck, waiting for them to finish their greetings. "Dakota, this is Nick Cartwright. Nick, Dakota Blackfoot."

Nick came forward and stretched out a hand. "Nice to meet you."

Dakota nodded, accepted the hand, and shook it briefly. "Nice to meet you as well. So what brings the two of you to my neck of the woods?"

Thayne swallowed hard. "I… uh… had something I needed to talk to you about."

"Why don't I leave you two alone for a little bit?" Nick offered and strode toward the paddock Dakota had just left.

"What's going on, Thay?" Dakota asked with a frown.

"Can we sit down somewhere?" Thayne asked, stalling.

"Sure. Let's go inside."

Dakota led the way into the house, and Thayne followed behind, glancing back once to look at Nick, who was talking to the cowboy who'd taken the reins of the horse. The door swung closed behind Thayne, and he blinked, adjusting his eyes to the darker interior of the house. He'd been there a few times after Dakota had moved in with his grandmother, so he knew the layout and easily navigated to the kitchen. What he saw in the kitchen caused him to come to an abrupt halt.

A young woman—a very pregnant young woman—stood

at the stove cooking eggs. Her brown hair and blue eyes reminded him of Dakota's mother. She smiled when she saw him. "Hi! It's so good to finally meet you! Dakota's told me so much about you that I feel like I already know you. I'm Laurel."

Thayne opened and closed his mouth several times.

Dakota laughed and clapped Thayne on the shoulder. "Sit. We can talk."

Taking a seat, Thayne tried to reason why there was a pregnant woman in Dakota's kitchen. He could tell she wasn't wolf, but she had Dakota's scent all over her. Who was she?

Dakota waited until after she'd brought over two cups of coffee to them before speaking. "She's my mate."

Thayne's gaze flew to Dakota in shock. *He'd claimed his mate?* "What?"

Sighing, Dakota explained. "We met about eight months ago. She came here to have one of her family's horses trained by me."

"I don't understand. What about the pact?"

Laurel turned off the oven range and said, "I'll leave you two to talk." She gave Dakota a quick kiss and left.

Thayne was flabbergasted. He truly hadn't expected to find Dakota mated when they'd gotten there. "Why didn't you tell me?"

"How could I?" Dakota asked. "How could I admit to the friend I'd made a pact with over ten years ago to never claim our mates that I'd found mine and I bonded with her? I didn't know how to tell you. I can't say I didn't fight it every step of the way. She was bound and determined. She had no idea I'm a shifter, but she knew what she wanted and didn't give up. It took almost losing her for me to realize just how foolish we were as kids."

"All this time," Thayne murmured.

Dakota took a sip of his coffee and set the mug down on the table. "I know what happened to my parents left us both despising the idea of claiming our true mates. Even though it was my parents, we both lived through the tragedy. For a long time, I couldn't let go of my fear, and with living on the ranch, I never expected to meet her. I was ready to live my life alone here. When she came... I tried to send her away. I refused to train her family's horses. She persisted until I caved."

Thayne could barely process the idea. "I came here to tell you something."

"You found your mate too," Dakota said simply.

"Yes."

"The man who came with you today."

"Yes."

Dakota smiled. "I'm glad."

"I was so sure you'd be furious with me. That you'd think I'd betrayed you."

"I never should have asked you to promise such a thing all those years ago, Thayne. It was stupid and childish. It also was wrong of me, because my father's weakness wasn't from losing his mate. His weakness had always been there, we just never saw it. Grandmother told me before she died. I guess she thought if I knew about Dad's depression, I would accept my mate. I've tried so many times to tell you over the phone these last few months, but I didn't know how. More than once I thought of inviting you here to tell you, and I backed out," Dakota admitted.

A bark of laughter surfaced and another until Thayne was laughing so hard he couldn't stop. Years they'd spent holding true to a pact both had broken without telling the other.

When he'd managed to quiet down, Dakota asked, "How long?"

Thayne slowly went through the details of the long,

arduous seven months from finding out about Nick to the moment they found themselves in.

Dakota sat and listened without a word, never judging. "You should have called me and told me," Dakota grunted. "I could have helped you."

"I didn't want to get you involved," Thayne replied.

"We're best friends, Thay. I am here for you whenever you need me, doesn't matter what the situation is," Dakota admonished. "I'm truly sorry about your family."

He shrugged, and a small smile played at the corners of his mouth. "I have a new home, and I'll be able to see my family whenever there's a Summit."

"Summit?" Dakota queried.

Thayne explained about the Summit and how the two packs would meet every six months on neutral ground. "It'll help a lot of the pack members find their true mates."

"That's good to hear." Dakota paused for a moment and then asked, "Are you happy, Thayne?"

He didn't hesitate. "Yes. You?"

"Definitely." Dakota smiled. "Now, take me outside and introduce me to your mate."

If he'd heard those words seven months ago, Thayne would have been horrified and bolted in the opposite direction as far as his paws could take him, but now he was eager to introduce Dakota and Nick to one another.

Nick sat on the corral fence, watching one of the cowboys walk a horse around the edges of the paddock, when they exited the house. Thayne saw Nick look their way, and he waved at Nick, beckoning him over. Nick swung his legs around to the other side of the fence, hopped down, and headed toward them.

"Everything okay?" Nick asked over their mental link, and Thayne smiled. The obvious concern in Nick's voice caused Thayne's heart to swell with love.

"More than okay, my mate. I'll explain later."

Their connection grew stronger each day, intensifying with every moment they were together. At first, Thayne had been uncomfortable with letting Nick see his memories, ashamed of the multitude of men he'd bedded, but eventually Nick forced his way through that wall. His reaction humbled Thayne, offering nothing except acceptance and love instead of judgment and censure. He couldn't believe how blinded he'd been by his past and how wrong he'd been about the mating bond. Every day the joy of being bound to Nick edged out more and more of the darkness from that day almost fourteen years ago.

"He's a good-looking guy, Thayne. You're a lucky man," Dakota said.

Thayne couldn't agree more. He really was lucky. He didn't know how Nick had found it in his heart to forgive him, but he had, and Thayne couldn't be more grateful. The idea of not having Nick in his life left a hollow feeling in his chest. He'd spend the rest of his days showing Nick just how much he loved him.

Nick came straight to his side and slid his arm around Thayne's waist. "Hi."

Dakota grinned and held out his hand again, yanking Nick into a bear hug when Nick accepted the gesture. Thayne saw the surprise on Nick's face when Dakota released him, and he grabbed Nick's hand, pulling him back to his side. "Are you two going to stick around for a while?" Dakota asked.

Thayne looked at Nick, and Nick shrugged. "Whatever you want to do, babe. I don't have to be back at work for a few days. Ryan refused to let me in the door for at least a week."

"I have to be back the day after tomorrow, but I think we

could stay the night. I'd like to get to know Laurel," Thayne said.

"Sure! I know she's been dying to get to know you. I thought for sure she'd call you herself soon if I didn't," Dakota admitted.

Nick laughed. "Sounds like a woman after my own heart."

Thayne huffed. "Your heart belongs to me."

"Of course it does," Nick soothed.

Dakota chuckled. "I'm glad to see your mate is going to keep you on your toes, Thay. You need someone who can go head-to-head with you."

Thayne grumbled but smiled.

By the time the two of them were ready to hit the road the next day, there was no doubt in Thayne's mind Dakota had found a mate who complemented him well. Not only beautiful, Laurel held her own with Dakota, and Thayne could see the deep love shared between the two of them. She'd helped heal Dakota's heart and soul of the hurt he'd carried since the day his parents died.

Thayne thanked her when they left and hugged her tight. "Take care of him for me, Laur."

She smiled and returned the hug. "You better come visit more often than every five years, or I'm going to come down there and drag you up here, kicking and screaming."

Thayne laughed and released her. He gave Dakota a hearty hug as well. "Good to see you again, Dak."

"Let's make a new pact," Dakota said near his ear. "Promise to take care of our true mates and never let them ever believe we regret having them in our lives."

"Definitely a promise I intend to keep," Thayne swore as he stepped back and walked over to join Nick at the truck. "See ya soon, Dak."

Thayne climbed onto the driver's seat and started the engine. Laurel and Dakota stood near the porch, waving at them, as Thayne reversed and turned around to head home. *Home....* He glanced at Nick, who leaned out the window to return the waves. Home was wherever Nick was. It didn't matter if it were in Senaka or Emerald Lake Hills. All that was important sat in the seat next to him, and for the first time in his life, he looked forward to whatever the future would bring for the two of them.

"Ready to go home?" Thayne asked Nick.

Nick settled into the passenger seat and smiled. "Maybe after we stop at that motel again," he replied suggestively.

Thayne threw his head back and laughed. "Insatiable, aren't you?"

"Only when it comes to you," Nick said in a quiet tone.

Those words sent a zing of lust through Thayne, and he pushed the truck a little faster. He thanked the ancestors for giving him another chance with Nick. He would have lost out on the greatest thing to ever happen to him, and he'd have spent the rest of his life regretting it.

"I think we can arrange a pit stop," Thayne said teasingly.

Nick slid over on the bench seat, dropped his hand casually into Thayne's lap, and massaged him through his jeans. "It's going to be an interesting ride... home."

"Mmm, I really hope so," Thayne growled, wrapping an arm around Nick and pulling him tight to his side.

They did make it back to Emerald Lake Hills... eventually.

Interested in catching up with the original True Mates book that started it all? Chasing Seth is available in Kindle and Kindle Unlimited!

Can he let himself believe in true mates after his past has left more than one scar on him?

Also available on Kindle and Kindle Unlimited, Spell of the Werewolf!

The next moonrise might be his last when a werewolf with a death wish crosses paths with a hybrid hunter who wants him dead.

A NOTE FROM J.R.

Thank you for reading Forgiving Thayne. If you enjoyed it, I would truly appreciate if you could let your friends know so they can also enjoy the relationship between Nick and Thayne.

If you leave a review for Forgiving Thayne on the site in which you purchased the book, Goodreads or your own blog, I would love to read it. Please email the link to jrloveless@gmail.com

ABOUT THE AUTHOR

J.R. Loveless began her adventure in writing at the young age of twelve. Her foray into creating her own worlds and telling her characters' life stories was triggered by her own love of reading. She currently resides in South Florida with her dog and two cats, and by day works as a manager for a financial lending institute.

Her journey into gay romance began in 2005 when she began posting her original fiction on a forum for feedback and readers' pleasure. In 2010, a good friend urged her to submit to a publishing company, and the day she received the acceptance and contract was the best day of her life. Since then, she has been noted to be one of the most purchased audio books after Fifty Shades of Grey on Audiobook.com and received best gay romantic fiction for Touch Me Gently in the 2011 TLA Gaybies.

J.R. adores her fans and loves hearing from them.

Never miss out on an update or sale by by subscribing to J.R.'s Website. As a thank you, you'll receive a free short novelette called White Rain about two friends who become lovers!

J.R.'s Blog

J.R.'s Facebook Reader Group

facebook.com/authorjrloveless
twitter.com/J.R.%E2%80%99s%20Twitter
instagram.com/jrloveless
amazon.com/author/jrloveless
bookbub.com/profile/j-r-loveless
goodreads.com/jrloveless